The Painted Lady

by

Avery Sterling

The Painted Lady

Cover Art by *Rae Monet, Inc.*

The Wild Rose Press, Inc.
PO Box 708
Adams Basin, NY 14410-0708
Visit us at www.thewildrosepress.com

Publishing History
First Edition, 2024
Trade Paperback ISBN 978-1-5092-5405-7
Digital ISBN 978-1-5092-5406-4

Published in the United States of America

Chapter One

1796, New Orleans

Night had fallen on New Orleans when the brigantine drifted into the harbor. Delaney Harper rested her hands on the railing and observed the city growing closer. The hour was late, and the moon was barely visible behind thick clouds. Yet the moonlight wasn't necessary to see her new home. The taverns were full, and brightly lit streets were filled with people. Pubs and hotels were bustling with excitement. She listened to laughter and the faint sounds of music as the ship docked.

"Lively, is it not, Delaney?"

She was unable to tear away her gaze but smiled at the familiar voice. "It is."

Remi sauntered up to the railing and rested his burly arms. Together, they watched a group of young men reveling on the docks and shoving playfully at one another, until one of them fell into the water. She clasped her hand over her mouth, stifling a gasp, while the young man's friends and surrounding spectators, roared. Even Remi chuckled.

"This is the city I've come to live in?" She shook her head.

"They're enjoying the new year until Carnaval. Get used to it, Delaney," Remi replied. "You've seen nothing. You'll witness festivities like never before in Nouvelle Orleans."

He watched the other men pull their friend out of the water and snorted.

Delaney had witnessed Carnaval before but was never allowed to participate. During her last three years, she'd traveled to many countries, studying art under Fredrick Lacroix, a former member of *l'Académie des Beaux Arts*. Venice had been one city in the long list of places she visited, studying paintings and murals among some of Europe's most impressive architectures. She recalled the Carnaval celebrations in Venice were quite grand. She wished she could've been allowed to attend. Then, she'd been under the supervision of her mentor. Now, she was woman, nearly twenty-and-one. One corner of her mouth lifted slightly. "I will enjoy that immensely."

"As long as the authorities don't break up any of the festivities," Remi said, scratching his rough jaw. "They try to suppress the season for its debauchery."

The captain announced their arrival, and Remi offered his elbow. She curled her gloved fingers on his arm and followed several passengers onto the gangplank.

"Is it comforting to be home?" she asked, taking note of the glimmer in his usually glum expression.

"*Oui*," he said as he guided her down the long gangplank leading to the dock. "Although I must say it's been an experience, traveling these last years. Particularly while in the company of a young, golden-haired beauty such as you, *mam'selle*."

She smiled, flashing him a playful look. "How many people thought we were lovers, Remi?"

He laughed at her bold comment. "Too many.

Although it's a compliment to think I could catch the eye of such a lady. Yet I must give myself credit"—he lifted his nose and straightened his coat with a quick snap—"it's believable. My aging process has been so handsome and distinguished."

She observed her warden's aged but comely features, supposing he was quite a catch in his day.

"*Touché.*" She added laughingly, "You're a refined gentleman—and so modest."

He let out a guttural sound. "I can appreciate my own qualities as much as I appreciate the qualities of others."

They skirted around a crowd that had gathered and appeared to be welcoming the travelers. As she passed, she eyed what looked like some sort of gifts they were offering.

"What are they giving them?" she asked him.

"They're passing out trinkets, charms, bonbons. Anything, really," he commented as he guided her to a nearby hackney awaiting customers.

She looked over her shoulder and noticed some of the passengers wandering off with the crowd and heading to the nearest tavern.

"What an interesting place my mother decided to live in," she commented.

He didn't respond, only paid the driver and ordered him to take them to l'hôtel d'Amédée.

"We're not going to my mother's home?" she asked. "I've waited so long to see where she lived."

"We will," he said. "But it's late. I think it best we go tomorrow. Our trunks are being delivered there now. And don't worry about your paint box. I've already given strict instructions to handle it with the utmost care."

"You know me too well, Remi."

Once she had climbed into the carriage, it immediately jolted into motion, and she stared out the window, curiously watching all the people in the streets. So many of them wore masks and colorful costumes. A bittersweet smile tugged at her lips. Since she was a child, she'd imagined what it would be like to come home and finally meet her mother, Bernice Harper. She'd imagined seeing her in person and embracing her for the first time. She used to picture the two of them having tea, attending the theater, and other social gatherings with their peers. That wouldn't come to pass now.

The carriage rolled to a stop at a large, street-front inn, and no longer did the smell of the docks curl her nose. But the sounds of festivities still echoed through the streets. The air was cleaner, and now she was gazing through floor-to-ceiling windows that gave her a peek of the magnificent chandeliers lighting the inside. A boy waited at the front of the building, and when they climbed out of the carriage, he quickly assisted Delaney. They were headed for the door when Delaney's attention was stolen away.

"Delaney?" Remi asked, halting when she released her hold in his elbow and wandered back to the street. "Delaney," he repeated. When she didn't respond—focused on the happenings on the street—he called out, "Very well, I'm checking in."

She waved her hand and told him she'd be along. She was drawn to a commotion starting at the far the end of the street. For a moment, she couldn't tell if it was a brawl or a celebration. She took a few steps closer, then noted a circle of brightly dressed men causing a scene.

All of them were wearing masks, some extravagant, some simple. To her astonishment, some of them were dressed in women's attire! As she moved closer, she could see it was more revelry. She became fascinated by the scene, having never witnessed such audaciousness. They shouted something, started laughing, then tossed a young man onto their shoulders. The young man was dressed in a white gown. The commotion had generated so much attention that men and women were coming out of their homes, the inns, and businesses.

"Will, dear boy, is taking his vows tomorrow," someone announced, their voice echoing off the line of tall buildings. "Please, ladies, offer him kisses!"

Her eyes sparkled with merriment as the spectators began cheering the young man on, offering him congratulations and tossing him charms. Many of the observers left their places on the sidelines and joined the procession. They were met with offers of drink and welcoming embraces.

"Come now, ladies, wish his freedom farewell. Give him his last kisses!"

Women from the balconies blew him kisses. Those who stood on the street reached up and kissed him. Some were chaste and some brazen.

Then the parade started moving up the street, collecting more people, and more kisses. Suddenly, a couple of youths ran past, nearly knocking into her. They charged the parade and threw what she assumed was flour, making a dusty cloud over everyone. She thought the prank would anger the revelers, but they only tossed the boys charms and treats before they ran off. Music and singing commenced as they continued slowly up the street, carrying the young man above their heads.

So enthralled was she by the surreal scene, she'd considered herself only an onlooker until someone shouted to her. She was broken from her trance and looked curiously at them.

"Oh, if any lady will test your loyalty, it will be this one!" one of the men in the procession shouted.

She could smell the spirits wafting from the group. Not to mention they could barely stand. They put the husband-to-be down—and not too gracefully. He stumbled slightly, then lifted his white skirts and slowly staggered toward her.

"Kiss, kiss, kiss!" The procession began chanting and clapping.

"*Mam'selle*, please, give me one kiss," slurred the young man in the gown, whose face was smeared with rouge. He gave an awkwardly careful bow.

The smell of strong drink and tobacco was jarring, but she remained impassive, concealing her cringe as he puckered his lips and leaned in. A mess though he was, admittedly, he had a naturally charming smile and a flirtatious mannerism that was undeniable. Silently, she wished his bride luck, for she could assume his future wife's hands would be full. She cupped his flushed face and planted him a decent kiss. As she suspected, he tasted of whiskey and tobacco. It was all in good fun, and regardless, she couldn't deny a proper farewell from bachelorhood.

"I wish you happiness." She smiled.

He mumbled his appreciation, gaping at her openly for an extended moment before he was yanked back and heckled about his obligations come the morning. He raised his arm high in victory and was applauded. Then he was hoisted above the crowd once again and taken to the next woman on the street.

What kind of place is this? she mused.

The parade continued up the street. She remembered that Remi was checking them in and was no doubt waiting for her. Still laughing at the spectacle she'd just witnessed, she turned and headed for the inn, only taking two steps toward the door when someone caught her elbow. She spun back around and the sudden shift in direction nearly made her lose her balance. She was steadied by a man in a black mask, lightly dusted with flour. Beneath the scant shields were golden-green eyes laced with mischief.

"*Mam'selle*, may I?" the man asked with a thick, French flavor.

She blinked at him. "May you what?"

He flashed a wicked grin before he sank to capture her lips in his.

Stunned by the intensity of his unexpected kiss, her lungs locked as she tasted sweet wine. The smooth movements of his lips melded with hers and it was dizzying, even if it was only for a moment.

When he pulled away, she took a second to breathe. He flashed another bright smile, and the mask did little to veil the handsome face beneath. She felt her cheeks flush.

"A-Are you also getting married, *monsieur*?"

"No, *mam'selle*," he said. "But I could not resist."

His forthright reply sent her heart racing. She returned his playful smile with her own.

"Then you have stolen your kiss, and have no justification," she said.

His eyes held hers and she couldn't pull them away. "Indeed, I am a thief."

The next moment, a group of men started pulling him away, taunting him.

"This night isn't yours, Alderic," one of the men chuckled.

Alderic. She mulled over the name of the masked stranger who'd just kissed her. He was ignoring his friends' pleas to leave. He remained still, holding her gaze prisoner.

"Your name, please, *mam'selle*," he insisted. He shrugged off his friends as they continued tugging on his fine shirt and silk waistcoat. "I shall not forget such a beautiful face and promise to look for you come morning."

Years of being groomed by a strict authority who mercilessly instilled forbearance and fortitude served her well in that moment. Exteriorly, she was a cool, statuesque display. Inside was a demonstration of shambles. Her heart was hammering in her ears and her feet were anchored to the street as she offered a small smirk. Shaking her head, she replied, "I don't think it wise, *monsieur*."

"Come now, Alderic," another one of his friends said as he wedged himself between them. "They're going to toss poor Wil in the water."

Alderic didn't seem to be paying attention to the man between them.

"Your name," Alderic repeated. "*S'il te plaît*."

Delaney was tempted, that was certain. The bold stranger had enticed her, she had to admit. But something told her a man like that left a trail of hearts in his wake…and she didn't want to be one of them.

Two more men grabbed him, and Alderic finally nodded, determining that she wouldn't oblige him. He gave her one last warm smile, conceded, and finally allowed his friends to drag him away.

She felt the impact of his presence lessen as the distance between them grew. She was about to return to the inn when he tossed her something from across the street. She caught the object, and having seen her make the lucky catch, he returned to the procession.

She inspected what she assumed was another carnaval trinket. It was a coin with a mask on one side, and a ship on the other.

"Alderic," she whispered to herself, watching the tall stranger's retreating back until he slowly disappeared into the crowd.

Chapter Two

When Delaney woke early the following morning, she anticipated the day to come. She'd had an introduction to the city worth remembering. And now she'd finally see her mother's house.

She frowned. The only relationship she had with her mother was built from exchanged letters and likenesses. She'd spent her life communicating from a distance, conveying ideas and stories with a woman she barely knew. Bernice Harper eventually became more of a fairytale figure, and Delaney filled in all blanks with imaginary details. She didn't know what it was like to hold her mother, to smell her hair, or kiss her cheek. Now she never would. After finishing school, she'd been granted the opportunity to spend two years traveling through Europe, observing historic architecture and paintings. Her mother funded her expedition and sent Remi along for her protection. She'd viewed—and learned from—some of the world's most priceless pieces of art. She never imagined it would cost her the opportunity to meet her mother.

Delaney finished her toilette and donned a yellow gown with a silk ribbon tied along the high waist. She then chose a sage ribbon to match her eyes and laced it through her flaxen hair. She couldn't keep the sadness from her eyes when she received word that her mother had passed. She was overwhelmed with regret and longing.

There was a knock on the door, and Remi peeked inside her room. "Are you almost ready?"

"Yes, I'm coming," she said as she grabbed her fringed shawl and gloves. She took his outstretched hand, and they proceeded down the stairs of l'hôtel d'Amédée.

She now had the chance to experience New Orleans in the bright light of day and was curious to see what the growing city had to offer. Remi explained that New Orleans had been founded by the French but had been taken over by the Spanish many years ago. As they strolled aimlessly, she noted that the architecture was predominantly Spanish. Its structures were pale-colored stucco, topped with flat-tiled roofs, and ornately decorated with ironwork. There were arched passageways and very little space—if any—between buildings. The language and food were greatly influenced by its integrated citizens.

She was intrigued by all of it. They spent the morning walking through the streets after they broke their fast. Then they lounged by the river, her eyes fixed on a barge slowly drifting downstream.

"Delaney, there's something we must talk about," Remi said.

The hesitation in his voice caught her attention, and she tore her gaze from the river and turned to Remi. He shifted his stance, then paced. Watching his profile as he fixed his gaze ahead, she waited patiently to hear what he was struggling to get out. When she had first met Remi, she found her warden to be kind of a bear. A grumpy, bossy grouse. But over time, she came to appreciate him. He was amusing… in his own way. And he truly cared about her welfare. To her, he was the closest she had to a parent in the flesh.

"What's wrong?" she asked. He didn't meet her gaze, only stared at the vast openness of the river, and she urged gently, "Well, come on, say it."

"Your mother…" he began, then remained silent another moment. "She was not the woman you imagined her to be."

"What do you mean?"

He finally turned to her, reached out, and gruffly took her hand in his. He gave her a pat and frowned. "I want you to understand that your mother wanted the best for you," he said. "The absolute best. She made sure you wanted for nothing."

Her brow creased as she observed the pain in his eyes when he spoke about her. "I've always been exceedingly grateful for my education and luxuries," she said.

"You have to understand, though, that there was one thing your mother never wanted for you."

"What was that?"

"To be like her."

She was taken back by his statement and stiffened. "Why would she think like that?"

Remi stepped away from her and drove his meaty hand through his graying hair.

"Your mother was always such a healthy woman, and still quite young. Her death was so unexpected. She never truly figured out how to handle the situation when you finally became a woman…"

"Remi," she interjected firmly. "Stop speaking in riddles."

He wiped down his face with his hand and let out a

frustrated sigh. "Your mother paid for your education, your clothing, your art tour—*everything*—by selling…services."

"She was in sales? What kind of services?"

He shoved his balled fists in his pockets. "Services of a more…intimate nature. For the pleasures of others."

She continued to stare at him. Her mind was blank. She had no idea what Remi was talking about, nor why he was struggling to spell it out. An uncomfortable silence lingered between them, and she watched his expression turn from troubled to a sense of guilt. Slowly, the realization of what he wouldn't say outright began to seep in. And with it, her chest sank, and she imagined she must look quite ashen.

"A-Are you saying my mother…w-was a prostitute?" she asked, barely able to choke out the word.

His aged eyes hardened, and she noted how he'd jumped to her mother's defense. "Your mother was a visionary," he said, and she felt the edge of steel in his words. But she remained still, emotionless. The only reaction she could muster was a slack in her jaw. She couldn't mouth a single word. She just gaped at him, and upon seeing her reaction, he continued rather shakily. "After being disowned by her own family, she was reduced to walking the streets. She encountered the many dangers of that profession. As soon as she was able, she pulled herself from the gutters and opened the first successful brothel in the city. She wanted to offer a comfortable place where women could work their trade and feel safer. This, of course, attracted a much higher class of individuals, who were drawn to a lavish environment where they could still slake their needs but in separation from their social settings."

She found her voice. Finally. "How delicately you put it, Remi." It was all she had, but it was something. It was enough to encourage him to continue talking, giving her more information…more time to fathom all he'd just thrust at her.

"By using her wits and assets, she become one of New Orleans' leading madams," Remi countered. "Your mother was a beauty, but make no mistake, she wasn't delicate. She was the fiercest creature I've ever had the honor of knowing."

The silence between them ticked by at an agonizingly slow rate. "Sh-She was a madam."

"*Oui*, and at one time, she owned the most well-known establishment in the Quarter," he acknowledged.

"Past tense, Remi?"

"I heard she was struggling the last two years while I was gone. Please, understand that Birdie loved you so much she never wanted to meet you. She thought you'd hate her, or…be ashamed of her."

"Birdie?"

He closed his eyes briefly. "*Oui*, Birdie. That's what everyone called her."

Delaney began chewing nervously on her lower lip, a terrible habit she'd never outgrown. So many questions were surfacing.

"I-I don't want to hear this." She stammered for words. Her voice began to rise frantically. "Could you not have told me before this? Let me decide if I even wanted to come to New Orleans, considering the facts? After all, it was her wish to keep me from all this. Why would you bring me here?"

His gaze dropped to the tip of his boot. "I've argued with myself for some time. I'll be honest. I wasn't sure what to do." Then his eyes shot to her. "But in the end, I had to make the decision based on who I know you to be. She never had that privilege. Perhaps her fears were unwarranted?"

"Maybe they were," she snapped. The words spit out, and she swiftly caught herself. She took a deep breath. Once she'd regained her composure, she asked, "Why did you think it was necessary that I come here, blindly?"

"Your mother's house and her business. It belongs to you now."

Her eyes rounded, but this time she was able to hold back her initial tart reply. "You mean her house of ill-repute? I own that now? What do you expect *me* to do with it?"

He held up his hands and used his usual, calm tone. "Not *it*, Delaney. *Them*."

"Who's them?"

"Her birds."

She shook her head and gaped at Remi. A shooting pain caused her to briefly hold her temples as she sighed. "Her…what?"

A small smile tugged on his lips, and for a moment he looked as though he'd left her, mentally returned to another time. "One time, as word of her popularity rose, a crowd of people visited her at the peak hour of business. They shamed everyone inside and wanted to storm through her doors, expose all her clients. They equated her and all her 'fallen frails' to that of a sewage system for public morality."

"What did she do?"

Remi shook his head. "She told them 'fallen frails' build wings and learn to fly. She said her birds soared above the stench of self-righteousness, no matter how high the horses. She declared that not one of them would pass her doors. As if the moment couldn't be more perfect, the sky opened and dumped its fill on the mob. Birdie used that opportune moment to turn her back on them and walk inside. It was perfect, and they never passed her doors. From that day on, her ladies were called her birds. Her birds relied on her for pay and protection. By now, I suspect the place is going mad without leadership."

She shoved away from Remi as she felt her resolve crumbling and her temper rising.

"Surely, you're not suggesting I run a whorehouse, Remi!"

Remi reached for her, but she pulled away from him.

"It's a lot to take in, I know that, *ma chérie*. I'm not saying you should take over the house. I'm saying whether you like it or not, it's your responsibility. Until you decide what to do with it, those women are lost."

She scoffed. "That's absurd. They're grown women! They don't need some slip of a girl overseeing their…encounters. For heaven's sake, Remi! I've never even known a man—what can I help them with?"

He tilted his chin. "Now you're giving yourself no credit. Knowledge of men isn't what they need from their madam. What they need is a savvy, intelligent woman to lead them and protect them."

She threw her hands up and turned away from him, unable to endure the desperate look on his face another moment.

"All I ask, Delaney, is that you take the time to see the place and understand the position of these women. Come to the house with an open mind and take as much time as you need to come up with a solution. There are options—you needn't take the responsibility. But you must make a decision, nonetheless. The Bird House is yours."

Her gaze sought refuge in the simple boat shrinking in the distance as she muttered, "The Bird House." The realization of his words sank in as the name of her mother's business slipped passed her lips. She felt cheated, duped. Tricked by the one person she'd learned to trust those past years. Remi was the only person she'd grown close to, after being raised in boarding schools. Now he was throwing this revelation at her! "Remi, how was it that my mother came to send you to watch over me?"

He eyed her cautiously. It was probably a relief to finally tell her everything that had been haunting him since her mother's death, but he'd deceived Delaney and risked losing her trust.

"I protected your mother for many years," he said. "Your mother was quite desirable, so I was entrusted with her safety."

"Then why did she give you up?"

"She knew I would keep you safe. She valued your life more than her own."

The silence returned. For a long time, Delaney stared at the shifting hues of the river, her eyes drinking in every detail of its beauty. One thought drifted to another. Then ideas bombarded her brain, bewildering her, and she shut down completely. What was she to do now? Where was she to go?

Cradling her aching temples in her hands, she let out a frustrated sigh. "All right, Remi. Let me see this place, first. I imagine it's the only thing to do at this point."

His expression lifted. "We'll take this one step at a time," he said.

Chapter Three

Alderic discovered Jack Chanfray lounging on his sofa, his head resting on a pretty chit's lap while she rubbed his temples.

When he strode in, Jack's eyes opened and widened slightly upon his presence. "Beaumont!"

Alderic slowed his pace and sauntered farther into the grand parlor, his cane swinging loosely in one hand, his fine hat in the other.

Jack's butler, an aged, slender man, rushed up behind him. "My apologies, *monsieur*, he refused to wait," the butler said, rather breathlessly.

Jack slowly sat up, and chuckled. "He often does."

Alderic didn't break eye contact with Jack. "You know why I am here."

Jack's lips curled at Alderic. He got off his sofa and dismissed the lovely chit. She dutifully exited the room, offering Alderic a small smile and a passing wink. "It's early. Would you care for some coffee?" Jack asked.

"I do not intend on being here long enough," Alderic said curtly.

Jack nodded. The butler, too, was dismissed, and when they were alone, Jack said, "You're angry, Beaumont—"

"Your cellar is stocked now, because of my shipment last night," he interrupted. "Imagine my disappointment to discover that my men delivered as promised, yet your payment was withheld. You are fortunate to be breathing."

"I'm a trusted customer," Jack said. "I wished to speak to you."

"I do not make house calls, Chanfray. What do you want?"

Jack offered him a seat, and he refused. He was also offered a drink from a fine set of crystal decanters, which he also refused. "As you mentioned, it is rather early in the day," he said.

Jack poured himself a drink and strolled back to the sofa. He sat down and grinned. "Well, I've yet to go to bed."

Alderic wasn't in the mood for Jack Chanfray's games. It was early, and after a long night of celebration, he too hadn't slept. When the sun came up, he'd cleansed and changed, so he could return to l'hôtel d'Amédée in hopes of finding the woman he'd met last night. After a hefty sum paid to the front desk clerk, he learned only her name. Delaney. And that she'd checked in with a man. Was that man her lover? Her husband? He wanted to know. When he discovered the man's name used in the ledger was clearly fake—as he was certain the prime minister of England hadn't come to Nouvelle Orleans for carnaval—he realized he'd reached an end to his inquiry. To further his disappointment, he'd discovered they'd already left the establishment. Then, as if his morning hadn't been frustrating enough, his men came to him and told him Chanfray had received his order, yet demanded Alderic come to collect the payment.

"Why did you wish to see me, Jack?" he demanded.

Jack inhaled and rested his arm on the dramatic central arch of his sofa. Crossing his legs, he mulled another moment. Alderic was growing increasingly impatient by the second.

"I have a shipment of my own that I wish to be transported up the river. To a friend of mine. Your partner, Tarquin, refused my offer."

The mention of his partner and best friend, Nye Tarquin, put Alderic on guard. He took a warrior's stance at the direction the conversation was taking. He and Nye knew Jack Chanfray had another business, and suspected it was a much darker side to the façade he stood in now—which was just a house of sex and gambling. Jack provided workers for other bordellos and gambling houses offering much more sinister services.

"Of course Nye Tarquin would refuse you," he said. "We do not transport that sort of cargo."

Jack frowned, his eyes shifted to his glass as he said, "A rather docile man, Nye has become of late." Then Jack's focus and tone lifted, and he continued with an airy whisk. "Risky, I'd say, for a man such as he, to take on a wife and...what did they have...a son?" His stare challenged Alderic's as he took the conversation further. "Puts men like us at a disadvantage, for we create a weakness for ourselves, don't you think?"

A smirk crept onto Alderic's face, a mere veil for the darkened mood welling rapidly within. He kept his tone light and carefree, though his eyes were anything but, as he replied, "Precarious verbiage, Jack. Nye is content in his new life, but hardly docile. He would be most concerned to hear the mention of his family passing your lips. I would tread lightly. If word of it were to reach him, you would have a crew of cutthroats surrounding these grounds."

Silence lingered a long moment, until Jack released

a hearty laugh. It carried no merriment. He swirled the contents of his glass before he said, "I've no wish to trigger a confrontation. It's bad for business. Which is why I lured you here. I want to convince you to reconsider moving my cargo upriver."

"I told you, I do not partake in the transport and sale of human cargo."

"But you are the machine that keeps moving the flow of goods from the Quarter all the way up the river."

Alderic was growing bored and let out a long breath. "I wish for my payment. Find someone else."

Jack straightened, swiftly set down his snifter, and stood up. "I haven't been able to find a reliable transporter for over a year! Before that, I had someone, Beaumont. Benjamin Tarquin," he replied sternly, then daringly pointed at him. "And you killed him!"

Alderic wasn't perturbed by Jack's stark accusation. It was no secret that he'd killed Ben. It was also no surprise that the bastard would take on such a task.

"I suspect your newfound success and growing influence has caused you to forget just whom you are dealing with," Alderic said, taking a step toward Jack. "Allow me to humble you. The Quarter is my home and I run the river. I have no obligations, and no *interest* in striking a deal with you. Continuing your attempts reeks of desperation. Your problems are not mine, and I have no need for the blood and despair that would come with the money I would make off your shipment. And, lest you forget… Nye and his wife and child are my family. Any threat made toward them, I take as a direct threat toward myself." His mouth twisted into a grin before he continued. "And I am not so content. In fact, I can be utterly callous."

Jack's face reddened, but he remained still, chewing on the inside of his cheek as the severity of the words penetrated. "Beaumont—"

Alderic had heard enough. He turned on his heel and headed for the door.

"But your payment?" Jack called.

His steps didn't falter as he replied over his shoulder. "I will send someone to collect, and you *will* pay. With a ten-percent increase for my time and my toleration of your annoyance."

Chapter Four

Delaney stood in the street and stared up at the house that didn't exhibit New Orleans' popular Spanish flare. Remi explained that it had survived the fires that decimated most of the original structures built by the early French citizens. Its tall windows had black shutters, and the steep roof over its front entrance was supported by thin columns. The property filled the corner just outside the Quarter, and she could see several gambling houses and dens dotting the lane. The street was quiet, being so early in the day.

But filth scattered the modest lawn in front of the house. She compared the building and its qualities to others on the street. She couldn't deny her mother's house lacked the luster of its neighbors.

"I thought you said her establishment was prestigious," Delaney commented.

"I've been gone," he reminded her. "I received word that her business was struggling. Another establishment opened and began taking a lot of her high-paying customers. I offered to return and help her regain her status, but she insisted I continue my efforts as your guardian."

Delaney's eyes caught the red-lettered sign advertising *The Bird House*. She lifted her yellow skirts and strode toward the house. She could always appreciate beautiful architecture, and she couldn't deny the potential in her mother's house. The front entrance was elegant, nicely covered, and spacious. Trimwork and eaves were elegantly etched, though the paint was faded and peeling. As she was inspecting the exterior, the front small-paned door flew open, and someone stumbled out. She started at all the blood staining his face. Seconds later, a brute of a man with broad shoulders marched through the doorway and onto the porch. The brute kicked the injured man down the steps. She swiftly jumped back before he tumbled into her. The man groaned, the smell of rum emanating from him. He far surpassed simple inebriation.

"Don't come back," the brute barked. The sheer force in his voice frightened her. Even though he wasn't directing his wrath at her, the rage in his round dark eyes was enough to make her want to shrink away. The doorway flooded with women just then. They were pointing and shouting obscenities at the drunkard, who was attempting to drag himself upright. Delaney was mortified by his bloodied face.

So dire was the scene, yet hearing laughter burst out was even more jarring. "Still abusing the customers, Rafe?" Remi chortled.

Delaney's jaw went slack as the man on the top step looked at Remi, then hooted. "You finally came home, Remi!"

Remi was actually friends with the man. She hurriedly stepped aside as the brute cleared the steps, and she gaped as they embraced one another.

Meanwhile, the drunkard managed to pick himself up and slowly hobble away. The man Remi had called Rafe glared at the drunkard's back and snarled.

"What did that poor fool do?" Remi asked.

"He roughed Fannie up pretty good. He wanted extra services he didn't pay for."

"So, business as usual." Remi shook his head.

Their casual demeanor was incomprehensible, considering their conversation was centered on a woman being assaulted. She stepped forward. "This sort of thing is usual?" Delaney asked.

Rafe and Remi halted their conversation, and she noted the change in Rafe's expression as he stared at her. His humor halted, and his squared, shadowy jaw went slack.

"My God, Birdie has returned from the dead," he said with wonderment.

He's teasing, Delaney thought. But then she noted the women at the doorway were also gawking at her. Almost on cue, they began praying and spitting on the ground. Now she wanted to laugh, but refrained. Instead, she raised a brow at Remi.

Remi cleared his throat. "Rafe, meet Birdie's only child, Delaney Harper."

His dark eyes assessed her in one sweep, then he shook his head. "I don't believe it! Birdie had a child?" he asked, his tone lifted with disbelief. "And she's...*English*?"

"She's been away at school. That's why I've been gone. Birdie sent me to watch over her. Delaney was a student of the arts and had secured an apprenticeship. She's been touring Europe."

The women were causing a ruckus within the doorway, and Rafe shouted at them. Then he softened his tone and took Delaney's hand, kissing it. "What an honor, *mam'selle*. Please, let's go inside."

"*Oui*, there's much to discuss," Remi added.

Delaney couldn't push down the sense of dread that filled her when they headed for the entrance, where a group of rowdy women waited expectantly. Their eyes pierced through her, and some almost seemed to be mocking her.

"Move aside, you nosey hens," Rafe growled as he entered the house, Remi and Delaney right behind him.

"Remi, darling, 'ow 'ave ye been?" one woman with wild red hair asked, tipping her low neckline toward him.

"It's good to see you, Gertie." Remi grinned. "You look well."

"Come find out how well this afternoon." She smiled. "You've been gone so long!"

One woman stepped up to Delaney and laughed. "So, a child like you gonna save us?"

Delaney didn't reply. She was too distracted by the young woman's raw beauty.

"What kind of dress is that?" asked another woman with a chuckle, and Delaney glanced down at her high-waisted muslin gown.

"Delaney's wearing the latest fashion, Marla," Remi said. "Get out of your old rag. Did Birdie not inform you of the latest fashions?"

"Birdie wasn't much help with anything by the time she died, Remi," the woman he'd called Marla said, crossing her arms over her chest.

The curt comment about her mother caused a pang to shoot through Delaney. What had happened to her mother, that she'd grown so ill she offered no guidance for those in her care? Within seconds, Delaney was pulled into a study where her slippered steps were cushioned by a plush carpet that took up most of the floor. She spotted a large mahogany desk in front of a small-paned window. To her left was a massive portrait of her mother. She halted with her gaze fixed on the painting, mesmerized by the beauty lounging on a red sofa. Her long pale hair cascaded over one shoulder, her lowcut black dress draped around her with one leg exposed, propped on the sofa. She noted the artist had an amazing talent for lighting, having draped the dress with such detail, the colors accurately affected by the lamp painted behind her in the portrait.

"Meet your mother," Remi said, coming to stand beside her. "Birdie was a beauty, was she not?"

"Yes, she was," she said, entranced by the seductive painting. The only likenesses her mother had sent her were prim and proper. Now she was seeing a side of her mother she'd never been privy to. Her true nature. Her eyes captured her. They looked powerful, even in the image. Her posture, even though seemingly relaxed, told Delaney how and why she'd made her success.

"Delaney, are you going to take over The Bird House?" Rafe asked, drawing her away from the portrait. "Do you have any idea how to run a bordello?"

Remi held up his hand. "Rafe, we're not sure what is going to happen here. Delaney has only just learned about all this."

Rafe's brow creased and his face pinched. "Are you saying that you're not…"

"No, she is not, Rafe," Remi stressed. "You'll do well to remember that Delaney has spent her entire life in school, and as an artist's apprentice."

Rafe let out a boisterous laugh. "Are you joshing me, Remi? What's she even doing here then?"

"The Bird House belongs to her now, and she must have time to assess the situation and reach a decision about its fate."

"She'd do better to just sell the place to Chanfray, over on Basin Street," Rafe said.

Remi cocked his head. "Chanfray opened a house?"

"He did a couple of years ago. It's quite a deal, took most of Birdie's elite customers. But he's shown interest in this property, since it's closer to the…finer side of the Quarter."

Remi rubbed his jaw. "That's an option."

"What option?" she asked, peeling her attention from her mother's portrait.

"Jack Chanfray owns some of the gambling houses," Rafe supplied. "You might be able to convince him to buy you out. The girls would be happy to work for him. Some of them went to him a few months ago, hoping for work."

"Did he take any of them?" Remi asked.

Rafe shook his head. "He declined."

Delaney looked confused. "Why?"

"Some of the latest girls Birdie took in were…not quite sophisticated enough to entertain the higher class," Rafe explained.

"So if he didn't want them a few months ago, what makes you think he'll take them now?" Delaney asked. They both shrugged, and she furthered her inquiry. "What would happen if he purchased the property, but still didn't want them because they're not…refined enough?"

"He'd toss them out, I suppose." Rafe shrugged.

"They're grown women, Delaney," Remi said, deliberately using her words from earlier that morning. "At least you'd be free of the responsibility. Or are you considering the alternative?"

"She can't take on a such a task," Rafe scoffed.

"That's nonsense," Remi said.

Rafe tossed a careless hand her way, replying with an exasperated sigh. "She looks like an angel! She doesn't understand the first thing about what these women do."

"She's innocent, not daft, Rafe," Remi argued.

Rafe shook his head, chuckling. "Come now—"

"You do realize I'm standing right here," she interjected.

Remi and Rafe glared at one another.

"Rafe, I don't know you. Don't presume to know me," she said. "And if I need anything from you, I expect you'll be ready to accommodate."

Rafe straightened his spine, his eyes widening a bit at her hard tone. "*Oui, mam'selle.*"

She steadied her hands and inhaled sharply. "I want all of my mother's ledgers and notes. Anything she's written down, journals, whatever. Lay them out on the desk. I'll return momentarily."

Remi stepped forward. "Where are you going?"

Delaney headed for the door and stopped to glance over her shoulder. "I want to see the place, obviously."

"Let me go with you," Remi said.

She held up her hand and stopped him midstride. "*Non, merci.*"

Chapter Five

Delaney left her mother's study. *Her* study now, she supposed. She observed the entrance, which was decorated in the Rocaille style with elaborate gold mirrors and trimmed paintings. Elegantly carved furniture, such as side tables and chairs, were set against walls of robin's-egg blue. The main staircase was centered and split in two directions at the second floor. Above her head was an enormous crystal chandelier.

She went to the front parlor and discovered much the same. Gaudy furniture with plush carpets and overstuffed sofas and settees touting wild upholstery. In the far corner was a dressing screen, the only plainly decorated piece in the entire room. It was the only thing she thought needed decoration. The folding screen was a perfect canvas waiting to be transformed into a garden, adorned with wild greens and small wildflowers. She then noted all the dull polish on the dark wood furniture. She ran her finger along, and it was covered with dust. She masked her revolted expression as she inhaled the scents of unwashed bodies and foul perfume.

"Are ye the new madam?"

Delaney started and spun around, spotting a young woman with a hard stare. The woman looking at her expectantly appeared nearly the same age, but with almond eyes and rich brown hair.

Delaney couldn't miss the terrible swelling on the

corner of her mouth. "You must be Fannie. Are you all right?" she asked, eyeing the bruise.

The woman lifted her nose at her and frowned. "I'm fine."

"You were struck. Do you have other bruises that should be checked over?"

The young woman crossed her arms over her chest. "I wasn't struck. I tripped and fell into the doorknob."

Rafe had told Remi that the drunkard had struck a woman named Fannie. And she believed him. What she found curious was the girl's denial of it.

"But you are Fannie?"

"Aye." The woman smiled, then winced and quickly covered her bruise.

Delaney shook her head at the audacity of the drunkard who helped himself to one of the ladies, didn't want to pay, and then dared to strike out. What kind of world had she stepped into?

"Miss," Fannie said, and stepped farther into the room. "The girls was sayin' you're Madam Birdie's daughter."

"I am."

The girl's eyes swept over her, and she gave a slight smile. "You're so refined. Like she was. You certainly look like 'er."

"Was there something you wanted to ask me?"

Fannie tucked a fallen curl behind her ear and her eyes dropped to the red carpet at their feet. "Jane is ill. Birdie knew of such things…and I thought you—"

"I don't know much about illness or medicine," Delaney interrupted.

"Oh, but we've tried fixin' her up, but nothing's working."

"What kind of illness is she suffering from?"

"A rash—she's been real sick," Fannie said.

"What kind of ra—never you mind, show me to her," she said. She couldn't ignore a sick woman.

"It's quicker to use the back stairs." Fannie rushed from the parlor.

Delaney was brought through another parlor—it looked much like the front parlor—the kitchen, and then up a narrow staircase leading to a long corridor.

When Delaney entered the room, the smell of it was repulsive and the stuffy, stale air nearly gagged her. The drapes were drawn throughout the dimly lit room, and Marla was standing over the sick girl.

Delaney recognized the swarthy woman from that morning—her flawlessness was undeniable. Delaney involuntarily tapped her own hair and smoothed out her gown.

"Marla, I brought the new missus," Fannie said.

Marla squared her shoulders, saying, "You don't want to be here, madam." She lifted her chin before she waved her hand dismissively at Delaney and shifted her focus back on Jane.

Delaney marched to the window. "I can't imagine anyone would. Even Jane." She threw open the drapes and opened the window. "It's stifling in here."

A soft breeze instantly swept through the room.

She went to the bed where Jane was curled up under her covers. She was another young beauty with ebony curls fanning out on the pillow. Rafe said these girls were turned away from another establishment. Did this man Jack Chanfray not see these women's potential? Each was uniquely beautiful.

"Let me see your rash," Delaney said, and Jane lifted

her deep-set eyes at her.

"Madam, you don't want to touch 'er," Marla warned. "You may catch it."

"Let me see it," Delaney said firmly.

Jane slowly pulled back her covers. She slid up her gown and revealed a rash that spread from her thighs to her stomach.

"*Monsieur* Rupert had a rash a couple of weeks ago. I figured it was only a matter of time," Jane said.

Delaney shook her head and looked at Jane with wide eyes. "You knew the man was sick and you still offered him services?"

Fannie chimed in. "We need all the funds we can get."

"And so you risk illness? You realize some die from these rashes," Delaney replied harshly. She couldn't believe the women were willing to sleep with sick men! "Did my mother permit this?"

They looked from one to the other. Then Marla said, "Birdie would send for a physician if there was something she couldn't treat. But we can't afford one now."

Delaney raised a brow. "You can't afford sick women who can't work, either. Isn't that correct?"

Silence.

Delaney noticed a bundle of herbs at Jane's bedside and smelled them. "Garlic is more helpful if you ingest it. Steep red clover or coneflowers in water and make her drink it several times a day. Keep the windows open and get fresh air in here. Jane, get out of that bed and wash yourself."

She glanced at the plate next to her bed. It consisted of a biscuit and plain broth. "I'll speak with cook," she said.

Fannie wrung her hands. "The cook left us a couple of weeks ago."

Delaney sighed and went for the door. "Who made the broth and biscuits?"

"Billy," she replied.

"Who's Billy? How many girls are here?"

"Aren't you madam?" Marla smirked. "Shouldn't you know?"

Delaney ignored Marla's sharp retort. She wasn't sure she could bear being in Jane's room another moment. "Fannie, come with me."

She marched down to the kitchen and saw dishes piled nearly to the ceiling and the floor unwashed and layered with grime.

"Is there something you want?" Fannie asked, following Delaney's glances at the dirty kitchen.

Delaney pinched the bridge of her nose as a pain shot through her head. "No, Fannie," she sighed. "Just help Marla with Jane. She needs a tonic and anything citrus."

"What's citrus?"

Delaney sighed and left the question unanswered. She stomped her way back to the office and when she flung open the study door, she discovered Remi and Rafe relaxing at the desk, drinking and chatting. She planted her hands on her waist and announced—rather loudly, "I can't imagine my mother being the shrewd businesswoman you described, then having this house in complete disarray and buried in filth."

Remi swallowed the contents in his glass, his eyes widening slightly.

"Birdie has been gone for a few months and this is

now a house without leadership. And from what Rafe has told me, she'd been growing tired, reclusive even. I believe things have not been right here for quite some time."

Delaney stood at the center of the room, her finger pointing to the ceiling. "There's a sick girl upstairs and there aren't even funds for a doctor." She was met by silence. She crossed her arms over her chest as she peered at Rafe. "Who's been dealing with the money these past months?"

Rafe put down his empty glass. "Me, but I'm just the muscle, not a businessman. My talents are limited to making sure the house is paid and the girls are not mistreated."

"Accepting men with disease is the worst sort of mistreatment," Delaney said.

Rafe tossed up his hand. "That's up to the girls, Delaney. I'm not at liberty to check men for disease. If they tell me to toss them out, I will without question."

Remi stood up from behind the desk. "Why does this concern you, Delaney? Are you planning on taking the position as madam?"

She flexed her jaw and bit back a reply she was just itching to let slip past her lips.

"Don't wield your influence by manipulating my concerns, Remi," she said instead. "You asked me to look at all this with consideration, and I'm doing so. And I'm finding out—by the second—why the house lost its status. Because I have compassion, I can't ignore a sick woman. This place reeks, it lacks luster, and it's quite run down."

"Her records are all right here. Perhaps you should look at them," Remi suggested.

"I plan to. I can't very well strike a deal with Jack Chanfray if I don't even know what I'm selling him."

"You think you want to sell it, then?" Remi asked.

Delaney picked up the ledgers and began searching through them. "I don't know how to run a brothel, Remi. And I don't *want* to know how!" She cleared her throat while she regained her lost composure and silently stared at the elegant scratching in the ledger.

Rafe slowly straightened from his chair. "Then let's leave you alone to review the records."

Remi agreed. He stopped at her trunks stacked by the office door. "I'll have your things brought to your chamber—"

"No, thank you, Remi," she said, her eyes still blankly staring at the ledgers. "Leave my things where they are."

Remi paused, and she could feel his eyes on her, but she didn't look up. Not until both Remi and Rafe left the room, and quietly closed the door behind them.

Chapter Six

The next morning, Delaney put on her claret gown and pinned on her hat. She slid the small black veil down until it curled under her chin. She took Remi's directions to the cemetery and set out first thing.

She stopped at the market and purchased a small bunch of flowers before proceeding to the cemetery. She found her mother's tomb with several other names etched in stone and propped up the humble bouquet.

She lightly touched the letters that spelled out *Bernice Harper* and tears stung the backs of her eyes. She wanted to cry for all the memories she'd never make with her. Questions she'd never have answered. Delaney lowered her head and frowned. She wanted to spend that time thinking about her mother, but she kept wondering why she'd been put in such a predicament. She'd spent the entire night reading through ledgers and adding up expenses. Delaney wanted to figure out how she could be free of the brothel. She should be crying over the loss of her mother, but she couldn't stop crying over her own situation. "I'll come back another time, Mother," Delaney said, wiping away the tears that were soaking her thick veil.

She left the cemetery, lost in her thoughts. She needed to be rid of the brothel. It wasn't her responsibility, and she had no idea how to run it. She knew nothing about men and women, nor how they entertained each other intimately. She didn't know why women gave something so personal, so special, to just anyone for a price. Perhaps that was why she was so unqualified to be their madam. She found a nearby bench and sat down, resting her elbows on her knees. She buried her face in her gloved hands and let out a long, tired breath. She was exhausting herself with a myriad of emotions—fear, anger, and shame were only a few. She sat there a long time replaying her options in her head, over and over, until she thought she'd drive herself mad.

Finally, she pushed off the bench and found her way to Basin Street. She walked along the back side of the Quarter until she came upon Jack Chanfray's establishment. She stared at a mansion that took up a good portion of the street. It was attached to a gambling house he no doubt owned also. The impressive building was trimmed with black, and matching shutters adorned every window.

She was shaking as she climbed the stone steps leading to the double doors where a brass lion knocker peered back at her. She fixed her veil, assuring it remained under her chin, before she grabbed the knocker and rapped on the door. Within a few moments, the door opened, and a butler stood staring down at her from his long, hooked nose. A set of lidded eyes rested upon her and waited silently. The words stuck in her throat as she watched his frown deepen by the second.

"M-May I speak with *Monsieur* Chanfray?"

"State your business, *mam'selle. Monsieur* doesn't usually see anyone at this hour."

"It concerns Bernice Harper and the Bird House," she stated, finally gathering a wisp of confidence.

He sniffed and stepped aside so she could enter the

foyer.

"Wait here," he said. "I'll see if he has time to speak with you."

"*Je vous remercie*," she said.

"*Je vous en prie*," he replied.

She took off her gloves and went speechless as she observed marble floors so glossy she feared walking on them and marring their perfection. The foyer was inspired by Roman and Greek architecture, with columns that touched ornately decorated ceilings. There was a mural above her head of Athena casting out Aphrodite from the Garden of Virtue. She sighed inwardly. *What a wonderful depiction.*

"Please wait here," the butler said, as he motioned her to a soft settee below a painting strongly emulating Titian's *Venus of Urbino*.

She began fiddling with the fringe of her shawl as she waited for Chanfray.

When the butler returned, he said, "*Monsieur* will see you."

She was promptly shown to the front parlor and froze. She thought she was imagining things, but reality was quite sobering. On the settee was a couple in a rather compromising position.

"Marielle, Gus, relocate," the butler stated.

Delaney anchored her gaze to the floor, knowing her face was burning with embarrassment at what she'd witnessed. She had to remind herself that even though the manor was stately, it was still a brothel. This was where gentlemen came to satisfy their lust within the bounds of an environment they related to, standards they expected, for it was the price they paid. This was what her mother's establishment was supposed to be. But it was Chanfray who had contributed to the Bird House's decline.

As she calculated the priceless pieces in the parlor and took into account the exotic beauty of one of Chanfray's girls, she could see why her mother began to struggle.

"*Mademoiselle, comment puis-je vous aider?*"

A lanky gentleman with ebony hair sauntered into the parlor, a wide grin crossing his face. His eyes slid over her while he closed the distance between them, and she quickly checked her veil before holding out her hand. He instantly took it, kissing it. "*Bonjour, Monsieur* Chanfray,*"* she replied. She noted he was holding her hand a little longer than was proper. "I'd like to speak with you about the Bird House."

He looked momentarily taken back as he commented, "You're English." Before she could respond, he walked to a variety of decanters set on a handsome side table. "Please, call me Jack." He poured two snifters and handed her one before they each took a seat.

"I-I, uh, thank you, Jack…for seeing me." She didn't offer an explanation. She was fixed on his smooth movements and charming manner. The simplest gesture was elegant, each step like a languid dance he was performing. Indeed, he was striking. She kept a cool head as he raked his eyes over her, almost suggesting he knew her without her clothing.

"How can I help you?" he said. "Please tell me you saw the low standards offered at Birdie Harper's den and decided to come here, looking for work…or, perhaps, for company?"

He flashed a devilish grin and something new in the

glint of his eyes sparked caution. *Snake*. That broke her from her trance, and she remembered her reason for knocking on his door. Delaney put down her drink. When she spoke, she sounded more like herself instead of an inept, lovesick schoolgirl. "I wish to sell you the Bird House, *monsieur*."

He was silent a moment and stared blankly. Then he let out a belt of laughter. "What do I want with the Bird House?"

"Before you opened, it was the leading brothel in town."

"It's that no longer. Indeed, I hear it only services the local drunkards and miscreants."

Delaney winced. She couldn't deny his claim. He was correct. He had no reason to buy the house. Except...

"The location, *monsieur*," she reminded him. "The property is closer to the finer side of the Quarter and is spacious. It offers much privacy for your most elite clients."

He was quiet a moment, the fine creases on the sides of his mouth deepening slightly as he thought. Then something in his expression changed, and a small, twisted grin curled his face.

"Will you come with the house, *mam'selle*?"

She arched her brows and was thankful the veil concealed her nervous, repeated blinking. After taking a second to still her wringing hands, she said firmly, "No, *monsieur*."

"That's unfortunate. What is your price then?"

Her heart leapt at his question. Her prospects seemed to be brightening. Could it be she'd be rid of the brothel by the end of the day? She reached into her reticule and took out a small parchment she'd written up last night. She calculated what she'd need to cover all expenses owed to the house and to the ladies. She needed a small bit of funds, as well, to reestablished herself. Far from New Orleans.

He took the parchment and looked at her price.

"This isn't reasonable," he said, cocking a brow at her.

"I believe it is," she replied confidently. "We both know the money you'll make at this location."

He folded up the parchment and tossed it aside. She eyed it lying carelessly beside him as he relaxed in his seat. "Absolutely *no*," he said flatly.

"I don't understand," she said. "I've read Madam Birdie's letters. You offered to buy the house from her already. For nearly that same price."

"I did, but that was a year ago. I won't pay such a price now," he scoffed. "No matter what I make on the deal, I still must fix the house, cover the debts Madam accrued, and the harlots there are shoddy, to say the least."

Her chin lifted. Her ears burned. "Is that so?"

"It is," he said, waving his hand dismissively. "Now, who are you, *mam'selle*? I'm truly intrigued. Will you lift your veil?"

Her better judgment warned that Jack Chanfray was the last person she wished to reveal her identity to. In a mocking tone, she replied, "Absolutely *no*."

Her comment sparked something in him, and his eyes darkened. His glare instantly evoked an uneasy feeling, despite his leisured position on the chair. "How is it you've come to handle Madam Harper's affairs?"

"Will you not counter my offer?" she asked,

ignoring his inquiry.

She could tell his mind was scheming up something. It was practically written in his sly smile. "My offer stands nowhere near what you're asking," he said. "If the house were returned to its former glory, then I'd consider, but it isn't. Why should I pay this price when I only need to be patient? The creditors will take the place soon enough, and I'll get it even cheaper."

She smoothed her hands over her skirt. "I see," she said.

He leaned forward and peered through the thick, dark material concealing her features. "But you and I, *mam'selle*…we can strike a deal."

His suggestive tone slithered through her, and she tilted back. "No, I don't believe we can," she said.

"Come now."

He set down his snifter and leaned even closer, until his knees just barely brushed hers. His voice dropped considerably, and thickened. She couldn't help but respond to his allure. It came with such ease and such natural seduction, it was arousing. And her arousal was unnerving.

"You're frightened of me, I can tell," he said, leaning forward until he was only a breath away. "Maybe you're curious about the reaction you're having toward me. Either way, it can be easily remedied." His finger traced over her glove, running along the line of her wrist, between the leather and her bare skin. "Do you know what it's like to have a man undress you, one simple garment at a time? To have him kiss every inch of you, bury himself inside you, making you shake with ecstasy? I can do that, *mam'selle*, I assure you. I'm very skilled."

His voice was melodic backdrop to the pounding in

her ears. Her heart was slamming inside her chest, and she was struggling to maintain a composed front.

"*M-Monsieur*, I came to make an offer on Madam Harper's property. I'm not looking for a lover."

"I can't imagine someone as…innocent, as you appear to be, daring to come here," he said. "It fascinates me. It also makes me think you have a growing curiosity for this world."

"You're mistaken," she quickly replied, meeting his gaze squarely.

"If I may have you," he said. His sweltering eyes drifted from her face and rested boldly on the dip of her gown where her thighs ran parallel. "If I may taste you, I'll be willing to make a deal on the property."

She swallowed hard to remove the blockage suffocating her words. "A deal for me? A person you don't know? That you can't even see?" she asked.

"I'm a gambling man, and my instincts hardly ever fail me. Although I can't see your face," his eyes journeyed back, up the length of her neck, then assessed her shielded features, "I think you might be a worthy investment."

She took a deep breath and stood up, making him quickly lean back to avoid collision.

"Good day, *monsieur.*"

"The responsibility of Birdie's establishment is—no doubt—overwhelming for a delicate flower such as you," he said with smirk. "When the burden becomes too heavy, you know where to find me…and you know what I want."

Chapter Seven

When Delaney stormed out of Chanfray's brothel, her mind was racing. She thought she'd found her way out when she discovered his letters, written only last summer, expressing his desire to buy her mother's business. Her mother had declined vehemently, and now she had an idea why. He was a ruthless cad! Entrancing, but a rake, nonetheless. What was she going to do?

Now she'd have to seek out other options. Someone had to be willing to pay her price for the business. Delaney was fuming. She cursed her mother, then cursed Remi for bringing her there in the first place! Engrossed in her miseries and sorrows, she finally looked up and realized she was lost.

"Blast it," she mumbled as she made a full circle. She was in the middle of a busy district and had no idea which way to go. She took a random turn and returned to her miserable thoughts. She had no answer to her problem. At least not an instant solution. Several minutes later, she assessed her surroundings again and determined she was still lost. She prayed for a hackney as she tore off her hat and veil. It was no wonder she couldn't find her way, trying to stare through the damned black covering.

That was when she discovered a small shop lined with color and a few canvases. Forgotten were all her troubles. She felt like the shop was surrounded by a beam a light and sparkles! A momentary escape from her predicament, and a glimpse of that with which she was familiar. It had appeared when she needed it the most. Delaney rushed inside and was immediately greeted warmly by a young man behind the counter. She offered a wide grin and warm greeting as she began searching through the cluttered shop, an array of random goods provided with no theme or reason. She sought out the paintings and pottery. She was fascinated by the bright hues and scale of colors. It was impressive. She turned to the young man at the counter. She glanced at his stained hands and the paint caked beneath his nails. "Did you paint these?"

The young man's eyes widened, and he shook his head. "No, *mam'selle*, I could only wish to hold such level of skill. My mentor, Lucien LaMar, painted those." She understood the admiration for his mentor—the paintings exhibited great talent. "Do you paint?" he asked.

She hesitated to answer. Did she want to reveal anything about herself to anyone in New Orleans? She was quickly realizing that nothing was what it seemed. She searched the shop, hoping to figure out what was stopping her from replying. As the young man raised his brows expectantly at her, her search ended on a small painted ship encircled on his counter. She was instantly drawn back to the stranger who'd kissed her. Alderic.

"This image is on a coin I've seen," she said. "What is it for?"

The man seemed taken back by her question, and he followed her eyes, then nodded. "Aye, that's—"

"Delaney?"

The sound of her name gripped her, as did the rich

accent within the melodic waves of a sultry voice. She turned just as Alderic entered the shop. Closing the shop door behind him, he swept off his hat, and his thick, sun-exalted hair brushed his brow. His skin was as darkened by the sun as his hair had been lightened by it. She shook off the unnerving realization that the man she'd just thought about was standing before her. Alderic was taller than she recalled. In the light of day—and with the lack of a mask and a dusting of flour—she confirmed he was even more appealing than she'd presumed him to be.

Slowly, she was settling into the reality of the moment. "Y-You know my name."

His smile was broad, exposing white, even teeth. He took a step farther into the shop, and the intensity of the small space amplified. She wondered if only she'd felt it. "I promised I would look for you come morning. But you were gone, and I was left with just your name. I apologize for the informality, I'm afraid your name slipped from my lips before considering propriety."

The mischievous glint in his eye struck her, and she matched it with a small smile. "Are you truly sorry, *monsieur*?"

His laugh was short, but deep and intoxicating.

That was her answer. He wasn't sorry at all for speaking her given name. After all, he did boldly kiss her in the street. Clearly, propriety and decorum didn't take the lead in his actions. Her smile widened, and she shook her head at her strange reaction to him. It seemed New Orleans was swiftly eroding years of her school's staunch lessons of gentility.

"Might I ask what brought you here?" he asked.

She snapped back, again catching her thoughts straying. "W-Where? The shop, o-or New Orleans?" She briefly closed her eyes. Her ears shamed her stammering words and shaky voice.

Alderic, however, tilted his head and braced his stance, his hands loosely holding his hat and cane. "I would like to know the answer to both. And much more," he leaned in slightly and gave another tip at the corners of his lips as he added, "As much as you would like to share with me."

Her mind raced, and all her anticipation was dissipating at an alarming rate. It was replaced by anxiety, fear, and caution. What was she supposed to tell him? She released a shaky breath and shook her head. "I-I'm afraid I must go," she blurted. She skirted around him, and he was barely given the time to move aside before she flew out of the shop and took a random direction down the street. The clicking of her shoes echoed off the cobblestones, but not nearly as loudly as his booted heels behind her.

"*Mam'selle*, please," he called. "Please, stop."

Despite her judgment demanding she continue her path, her steps slowed. Alderic came up beside her, his golden-green eyes slightly widened, no doubt in wonderment at her skittish behavior. She felt like a fool.

When she remained silent, he asked, "What are the chances I would run into you again? Please, if you rush off, I am left with nothing but a prayer that I will stumble upon you later when you are in a more favorable position to speak with me."

His gaze lured her in and captured her will to turn away. She wanted only to oblige him. It was ludicrous! Still, he was standing there, waiting patiently for her answer. Words. Words! "If it's fate's will that we are to be within each other's company, I daresay I will see you again when I'm able to speak with you."

"Why are you unable now is what I do not understand," he said. When she didn't elaborate, he added with a tone much gentler than his gaze in that moment. "You arrived here with a man—is he your lover? Is this why you cannot speak with me?"

Her answer should be a resounding *yes!* That would successfully end everything. He'd go away, and she'd never have to tell him the truth about why she was in New Orleans, why a man—clearly a gentlemen, regardless of his unruly mannerisms—couldn't enjoy her company within a level of respectability. But she chewed her lip on the matter, pondered over her reply...and stalled. She didn't want to lie to him. She had no answer, no solution to her problem now.

She turned on her heel and started back up the road until she heard him say, "You are lost in this city, *mam'selle*, no?"

She spun around. "I'm not, *monsieur*. You don't know where I'm going."

He reclosed the space she'd made and said, "You are heading to the seedier side of town. You will not make it to your destination if you continue this path."

His words explained her predicament on a deeper level than she wanted to admit, and she let out a slow, ragged breath. She toyed with the veil in her hand and fixed her defeated gaze on the knobbly cobblestones lining her path. When he spoke again, his words were soft. Uneasily kind. "You should not be walking alone. Allow me to escort you to your destination?"

Her expression fell, and she wanted so badly to spend a few more moments with him. But he couldn't take her home. She looked up at him and felt every dream of a husband and family she ever envisioned swell within her breast…and shatter to pieces. Her life had been a lie. All the years of schooling, breeding, and expectations of a respectable life were lies. Her mother had offered her all the tools to live within a certain status that she wasn't allowed to participate in, that she wasn't born to have.

"I very much appreciate your concern," she replied. "But I must decline."

His eyes lowered a shade and he nodded, then said, "At least let me show you to a hackney. It will assure me that you get to your destination safely." She felt nothing short of enchanted by every move he made. She'd had her fair share of beaus and courtiers, and she'd been exposed to teachings and readings that were highly inappropriate for a young, unmarried woman. Art demanded that she not be squeamish or faint of heart. If anything, she'd been given opportunities to develop a unique perspective. So, while she might be inexperienced in the ways of love and intimacy, she was in no way ignorant of its essence. She wasn't one to be moved—for long—by just any man's attention or circumstance. But indeed, she'd been bewitched by Alderic, and it was unshakable. He was no more than a stranger, and she had no logical explanation for it.

"My safety is also not your concern," she replied, pushing aside another bout of senseless thoughts altering her focus. "As flattering as it may be that my welfare takes such precedence."

He chuckled and shook his head. "I respect your sense of independence and am intrigued by your obstinate determination to position me at arm's length. But I beg you to allow my assistance, if only to rest my own troubled thoughts." He added with a wink, "I must assure that fate brings you back when you're willing to oblige my intentions."

"And what are your intentions, *monsieur*?"

Her question caught him a moment before he replied, "My intentions—at the moment—are within a wide spectrum, in which I have no idea how it's come to such. Perhaps when I see you again, I'll have them reined in so I may impress you with an intelligent response."

She took the glint in his eyes, and she released a short laugh, fighting her desire to say she didn't need him to do any of that, for she was already completely enthralled. "Then I'll return home safely, so fate may bring us back."

His smile was bright as he offered her his arm. Her fingers in the crook of his elbow, he guided her the opposite way from the direction she had taken. They strolled slowly up the street, silently, for a long time. She appreciated that he didn't press her with questions. He seemed content merely to be walking with her.

As they neared the end of the street, they both spotted a hackney sitting at the corner. Her steps started to slow, and she wasn't sure if she was taking a cue from Alderic, or if it was her own desire to delay. He glanced at her, then back to the hackney.

He finally broke the silence. "You are new here, which puts you at a disadvantage, no? If you need anything, *mam'selle*, you are welcome to go to *Le Café des Deux*. Give them my name, and they will help you with whatever you need."

They approached the hackney, and each step they took seemed to dull the excitement he'd sparked in her. It was replaced with the crushing reality that she might never see him again. "I'll mind the invitation," she muttered.

They reached the driver, who had jumped down from his seat to meet Alderic. Alderic dropped several coins into his palm and the driver's eyes widened almost as much as his toothy grin. "Where to, *monsieur*?"

Alderic met her eyes and leveled his stare. "She will tell you momentarily. My generous payment expresses my confidence that you will get her there safely."

"Aye, of course, *monsieur*," came the quick reply.

Alderic opened the carriage door as the driver climbed back onto his seat and gathered his reins. "I must confess at least one of my intentions, *mam'selle*," he said. "In case life has a different design for us, and we don't meet again."

She didn't want to admit how possible that was. "What do you confess, *monsieur*?"

"I wish to kiss you again, without having to steal it."

She smiled at wickedness in his eyes. "I'm sorry, but you'll be disappointed," she said smoothly, despite her catching breath. "I don't give my kisses lightly."

He released another soft laugh that melted her. "I see. Only to drunkards on their way down the aisle to meet their bride?"

She flashed him a spirited smile. "That was a playful buss, *monsieur*. Not a real kiss."

He cocked a brow at her and leaned in. "I can settle for a playful buss."

She witnessed that mischievous glint in his eyes again, and she was finding it rather amusing. She didn't want to think that it would be the last time she laid eyes on his charming face. "You said you wanted to receive a kiss that you didn't have to steal. You wish that kiss to be a simple buss?"

"When you get in this hackney, there is the chance I may never see you again. It would be better than nothing."

"It's a risk, I'll admit," she countered. "But I believe a real kiss from you, that I consent to, may be worth waiting for," she replied.

She knew she was being bold, but she simply couldn't help herself.

The humor faded from his eyes and his gaze turned ardent, making her heart race. "Then I will make it a point to see you again, if only to meet your expectations."

She smiled. "I hope to do the same."

He shifted his stance, the corner of his mouth turning up as he searched her gaze curiously. "You need not concern yourself in that respect."

The driver cleared his throat—rather obnoxiously— and they were both drawn out of their longstanding farewell.

Her cheeks burned. She'd forgotten the driver was there. She'd forgotten there was anything in the world outside of their encounter in that moment.

"It truly was a pleasure seeing you again, *monsieur*," she said.

"Please, call me Alderic."

She'd twisted her veil so tightly in her hands she feared to see the damage she'd caused to the delicate fabric. "Alderic." She smiled and released the strangled veil to hold out her hand.

He took her hand, though his eyes never left hers. " 'Delaney' is all I have been given. Is this all you wish me to have?"

"*Delaney* is all that you need."

His gaze held hers and he wouldn't release it. He took her hand, kissed it, and appropriately released her. She climbed into the carriage, and he closed the door. His careless smile—which seemed like something he wore habitually and was rather becoming—dissipated. His golden-green eyes darkened slightly, as his voice turned grave. "Delaney—as I cannot find you—I have a ship that frequents the harbor. *La Bella Ascension.* If ever you decide to tempt fate and seek me out."

Her chest locked, as did their eyes. She finally nodded and gave him a winning smile. If ever things changed and she was able to seek him out, she absolutely would.

"I shall never forget that name, Alderic," she replied.

His intensity melted into a brilliant smile, and she knew, that moment, she could stare at Alderic for the rest of her life. But the carriage jolted into motion and tore them apart.

As she proceeded down the road, she gave the driver her destination. With a gripping sense of loss, she watched Alderic shrink in the distance. She was determined now, more than ever, to be rid of the Bird House.

Chapter Eight

When Delaney returned to the Bird House, she was in a sour disposition. She scowled at the house as she marched up the steps, threw open the front door, and stormed into the office. She glared at her mother's portrait before she flopped into the chair behind the desk.

Delaney stared at the ledgers on the desk and shook her head. No matter how many times she looked at them, the numbers didn't add up. The house was failing, and in the end, the women who worked there would be just as homeless as she was. A part of her just wanted to hand the whole thing over to Jack Chanfray and be done with it. When Remi walked in, she sighed, held her temples, and began rubbing the throbbing ache in her skull. "What do you want?"

"Tonight the doors will open. I hope you're prepared for the scene."

She leaned back in the chair and gave him a sharp look. "What scene, men and women romping on the sofas?"

He closed the door behind him and found the chair opposite the desk. "Sometimes."

"I think I'll stay in here."

"You could, I suppose."

Silence hovered a long while. Finally, she blew out a heavy breath. "Do you want a brothel, Remi?"

He let out a laugh and shook his head. "No, *ma*

chérie, I do not. I haven't a head for business."

"Rafe said that Gertie was keeping the girls in line after my mother passed. Maybe she'll take it."

"Gertie only kept the place functioning. And she did a poor job, at that."

Delaney let out an unladylike growl and rested her head on the back of her chair.

"It doesn't matter either way, Delaney."

She opened her eyes but didn't lift her head. It hurt too much.

Remi twiddled his thumbs and stared at her mother's portrait. Delaney followed his attention and guessed her mother couldn't have been much older than she herself when that portrait had been made. "What doesn't matter?" she asked.

"You've seen the numbers. This place will be shut down soon enough. It's only a matter of time. I think we need to tell the girls to start looking for another place. It's only right. They've been waiting for a miracle. They're going to have to find it elsewhere."

Remi got up and left the office, leaving her to stare at her mother's likeness.

She spent the next several hours staring at the walls, the ceiling...and her mother. She stared until her eyes burned. Her trunks were still stacked by the office door, and she sighed. When they'd been delivered, she'd told Remi to leave them as close to the front door as possible. Last night, she'd fallen asleep at the desk, and she had the knot in her neck to prove it.

She walked to her trunks and sat on the floor. Taking out her paintbox and brushes, she opened the case and examined her color pigments. When she was troubled, she painted. It was soothing and cleared her head, or at least gave her some peace—and that was what she needed. She dug out a small flute filled with poppyseed oil, grabbed her board, and began mixing colors. She'd made a deep walnut brown, then pinks—dark and pale— and white. She remembered the blank screen in the parlor and went straight for it.

The parlor was empty when she set her sights on the screen. She eyed it for several minutes before making the first strokes. A sense of serenity washed over her, and she let out a long breath. At least, for the time being, she was able to forget her situation. She filled all three pieces of the screen with intricate detail, the lighting, and the three-dimensional folds.

"That's beautiful!"

She looked over her shoulder as Fannie and another girl swayed up to her.

"What is that?" the other girl asked.

Delaney slowly stood up. "Sakura branches. Cherry blossoms. What is your name?"

The girl squared her shoulders. "Billy. And you're Madam Delaney."

Delaney blinked. "N-no, I'm not the madam—"

Fannie stepped forward. "Are they really that pink?"

"Some are," Delaney said, glancing back at the screen. "I was fortunate to see them on my travels."

"You've seen these?" Fannie asked.

"Uh, when I was in Spain. I saw them in a garden inspired by the Orient, particularly Kyoto."

Now a line of women streamed into the room. They were all pretty enough, all different ages and sizes. Every hair color. A variety, to suit every man's taste, she supposed.

They were all dressed in…well, not much. They

wore corsets, lacy garters, and stockings. They had bright ribbons in their hair, and their faces were colored with rouge.

"What are those flowers?" another girl asked as she strolled over and reached for the screen.

"Please, don't touch it. It's still wet," Delaney said.

"They're cherry blossoms, Penelope," Fannie said. "She saw them for real."

They all stared at Delaney, eyeing her up and down. "You've traveled?" a girl asked.

Delaney didn't know anyone's names, and she felt as though they were ready to pounce.

"A bit, yes," she replied simply.

Gertie weaved her way through the group of women and folded her arms over her chest, pushing her ample charms over the line of her corset. "I heard the women in Kyoto were banned for being too erotic."

Delaney blinked like an owl at the girl's random statement.

"What are you gassin' 'bout, Gertie," Penelope scoffed.

Gertie planted her fists on her sides, her eyes narrowed. "I read stuff," she said.

"She's correct," Delaney said. "The *onna Kabuki,* you're talking about. It was a theatrical form that entertained everyone, from the poorest farmers up to the emperor himself. It was performed strictly by women."

Gertie stepped forward. "They acted out politics, danced, and sang, but they were also for sale. Like us."

Penelope looked to Delaney. "You ever see it?"

Delaney shifted her stance. "Eh, no. The women were banned from participating in the *Kabuki* long ago. But I-I saw an interpretation of it. The performers dressed elaborately, and they painted their faces. But most amazing was their level of skill. Now it's performed by young men."

Billy laughed. "By men?"

"So you're really smart," Penelope chimed in.

"Do you have any ideas for us? How we can get more clients in here?" Gertie frowned. "We need to fill this place if we're going to survive."

"God's tooth, she's blushing. Look at 'er." Fannie laughed.

Delaney's eyes shot from one girl to the next as they commented on her flushing cheeks. "I-I don't have any ideas for you. I'm sorry."

"The men will love ye," Penelope said, chuckling. "Stay 'ere with us. We can make a fortune just off that embarrassed look on your face."

Billy laughed. "Rightly so. You're blushing like a virgin."

There was a series of loud claps. Remi and Rafe barged into the parlor and started shouting. "Come on, take your places, the doors will be opening soon enough."

When Billy walked by, her shining, ebony hair all in place, Delaney stopped her, again mesmerized by her overall beauty—but something wasn't right. A red heart patch on her cheek. Patches were vastly outdated, and Delaney swiftly removed it.

Billy glowered at her. "Why would you do that? I like that patch!"

Delaney was quick to reassure her that she wasn't being malicious. "Can I replace it with something better?"

Billy looked skeptically at Delaney and then at the

paint board in her hand.

"If you don't like it, I'll wash it off immediately," Delaney blurted.

Billy sighed heavily. "Fine, hurry."

Delaney painted a small cherry blossom on her cheek.

When she was finished, Billy went to the mirror and smiled brightly. "Amazing!"

That caught everyone's attention, and Billy was quickly surrounded. Within seconds, they were rushing to Delaney, begging her to paint flowers on them. "On my bosom, paint one right on my bosom!" Fannie exclaimed.

Delaney was instantly overwhelmed by their reaction. Remi broke up the swarm gathering around her. "She hasn't the time, ladies," he barked. "The doors are opening."

There was a wash of sighs, and he shoved Delaney out of the parlor. "Come on," he said. "Let me take you to your chamber. I had your things brought there."

"My room?"

"Your mother's room is yours now."

Remi led her across the main hall and down a corridor on the left side of the staircase. He unlocked the door and stood aside. Delaney walked into the extravagant setting and scanned the lavish decor. Much like the rest of the house, the room was filled with mirrors that reflected the damask-papered walls. The bed centered against the back wall had to be the largest she'd ever seen. Tall posts nearly touched the ceiling, the netting tied to them with silk ribbons. The ceiling was decorated with lavish trim and plaster, sconces lined the walls, and a thick carpet covered the floor.

Remi had set up her canvases in the corner, and she turned to him. "Thank you."

"The room was cleaned, and fresh bedding applied. I implore you to lock the door, Delaney, and do not come out," he said, and handed her the key.

When he left, she locked the door and started inspecting the room. Her fingers slid across the soft fabric of the bedcovers and then the thick drapes that skirted the windows. Pulling them back, she could barely see the small courtyard outside.

She went to her trunks and opened them, taking note of how wrinkled her fine clothing had become. They'd been stuffed in trunks far too long.

Delaney ventured to the massive wardrobe, filled to the brim with gowns of every color and print. Some were quite exotic. She carefully set them aside and began filling the wardrobe with her own clothing. They were fine, expensive pieces her mother had paid for.

Noises on the second floor caught her attention, and she looked at the chandelier slightly swaying from the romping going on upstairs. She tried to block it out. When her eyes returned to her delicate silk gowns, she was given a harsh reality. It had been the romping from all the girls in the house that had paid for those gowns, paid for the expensive education she had received, paid for the lovely paints and art supplies she'd bought.

And how was she going to repay them? She was going to hand the house off to anyone willing to buy it. Guilt sickened her stomach, and she groaned with misery. What would happen to them? Would they be abused or thrown in the streets? She didn't know.

The hours passed, and voices filled the house. Music and laughter drifted everywhere, accompanied by occasional squeals of delight. She undressed and lay down in her mother's bed. *Her bed.* The mattress was the softest she'd ever lain on. Certain she could fall into eternal rest from lying in such comfort, she buried her head in the thick, fluffy pillows. She tried to block out all the mayhem outside her door and above her head. Finally, sleep took over.

Sometime in the early-morning hours, she was jolted from her slumber by a loud crash. She momentarily forgot where she was. Another loud crash shook away the fog in her brain, and she climbed out of bed. There was more crashing and now screaming. Delaney panicked and immediately slipped on her night rail, unlocked her door, and darted into the corridor.

What she witnessed shocked her. A brawl had broken out in the foyer. Rafe and Remi were throwing men one way and then another. Gertie and Fannie were throwing things at the men Rafe and Remi were roughing up. When Gertie lifted a valuable piece of crockery and aimed it, Delaney rushed to her and pulled it from her grasp.

"What are you doing? Trying to make things worse by destroying the place further?" Delaney asked.

"Those imbeciles started it," Fannie replied.

"And the men are handling it," Delaney snapped. "You're making more of a mess!"

Gertie opened her mouth to argue, but after the look she received from Delaney, she closed it instead. Rafe and Remi each got a handle on the drunken men and dragged them out of the house.

"We need to clean this up," Delaney ordered.

The girls gathered together and glared at her. "That's not our job," Gertie said, flipping her hair.

"If they have to shut down the place, you're unable to do your job." Delaney lifted her chin at the haughty group. "Clean it up quickly, and you can go back to work."

Remi strode into the parlor and instantly spotted Delaney. "You need to go back to your room." He shuffled her out of the room, shoving aside drunken men before they could take a keen interest in her.

"Do you have to close the house?" Delaney asked.

"We can't really afford to. So long as the authorities don't shut us down, we're fine."

"When is she available?" one of the men shouted from the parlor.

Delaney and Remi ignored the man.

"Delaney, I don't want another brawl," said Remi. "Please go to your room before they start fighting over you."

She ran to her room and locked the door. Resting against the door, she felt the dull ache return in her head, and she groaned.

"This is madness," she mumbled to herself.

Chapter Nine

Come morning, Delaney woke early, washed, and dressed. She donned a simple blue gown with a white petticoat and tied her hair up in a chignon, pinning back some of the loose curls that stubbornly fell out of the knot.

She was starving. She marched into the kitchen and cringed. It was filthy and smelled of rotten food and grease. Curling her nose, she went to the parlor and found it nearly destroyed. Broken glass was scattered on the floor, and flowers had been thrown carelessly over furniture. Beneath her feet were someone's undergarments. She instantly stepped back and made a disgusted sound.

"I've had enough," she snapped. She was seething when she stormed to the back of the house and threw open a bedroom door, discovering Remi and Rafe passed out in their cots. "Convenient," she said, taking the pillows from beneath their heads. "I've found both of you. Get up!"

Rafe growled, tore the pillow from her grasp, and covered his face with it.

"Get up, Rafe."

Remi sat up slowly and rubbed his eyes. "What's wrong, Delaney?" He suppressed a yawn.

"I need your help."

Rafe peered at her from half-open lids. "Can it wait?

Our last customer left only a couple hours ago."

"No. Get dressed and meet me in the office."

"*Oui*, madam," Remi said with a hint of sarcasm.

Minutes later, the two grumpy men trudged into the office and found the nearest place to rest their heavy bodies. Delaney was at the desk, looking over the ledgers yet again, when they entered. She ignored their grumbling about the hour and sat back in her chair.

"Remi, I've looked over the numbers several times, and though this place is run down, my mother was still quite wealthy."

"What do you mean?"

"I've added up the last three years of monies received and all the expenses. They still don't add up. A lot of money is missing. From what I can see, my mother was an exceptional bookkeeper, and her numbers were never off."

Remi scratched his whiskered chin. "She put money aside for emergencies, but I suspect most of it was for your dowry."

Her jaw went slack, and it took her a second to recover her shock. "I have a dowry?"

Remi said through a wide yawn, "*Oui*. She was hoping you'd find a gentleman while you were away, and then she could give you a handsome dowry."

Delaney fell silent, pondering this new information. Her eyes narrowed on Remi. "She really never wanted me to come here, did she?" Delaney asked.

Remi looked away.

Rafe observed Remi with a lazy stare. He was going to fall asleep any second.

"Delaney, she wanted you to have the life she was supposed to have," Remi said.

"Supposed to have?" Delaney arched a brow.

Remi ran his hand down his face and shifted in his chair. "When your mother was young, her family caught her rolling in the hay with the stable boy. She was already engaged to a wealthy businessman, but she explained that she didn't love him, that her engagement was their decision. She told them that she and the stable boy were in love."

"How did they handle the situation?" she asked.

"They threw her out with nothing more than the clothes on her back. To further her dismay, she discovered the stableboy wasn't as…besotted as she was. She was on the streets for over a year, and she kept hearing about Louisiana. Many people had nothing positive to say, but Birdie saw potential. She saw opportunity. She came here with nothing but the clothes she wore and a few things she could carry. Eventually, she changed her name and opened her business. When she discovered she was pregnant—a risk in her line of work—she kept it a secret as long as possible. She told me she had to go away and explained why. She birthed you, then called in a favor from an English gentleman who'd become quite friendly with her. He arranged to have you sent to London."

"This gentleman, could he have been my father?"

"I know he was paid handsomely for the strings he'd pulled to get you to London and enrolled in the best boarding schools England had to offer. I remember as she watched your ship sail into the distance, she told me she wanted you to travel, become educated, and start whatever life you chose. Even if it was marriage. Hence your dowry."

For several minutes, Delaney sat silently, listening

to the ticking of the clock on the mantel as she filtered through everything she'd just heard. Allowing herself to wallow in the emotions the news had invoked was too overwhelming. She owed her mother for everything she had, and she also owed the women who had worked for her.

A loud snore startled her back into the present, and she chucked a book at Rafe, shaking him awake. "Where is the money?" she asked Remi. "Do you have any idea where she kept it?"

"I was her most trusted employee. Of course she told me where she kept her money," Remi said.

"When were you going to tell me?" Delaney demanded.

Remi shrugged. "We haven't had much time to talk since putting all this on you."

"Show me," she said curtly.

She followed Remi to her room, where he moved aside a painting near her canvases in the corner. Behind it was a hole with a locked box inside. He handed her the key. "This is yours now."

She picked up the box and walked to the bed. She sat down and rested the rather plain chest on her lap. The only adornment was a blue etching of her mother's name across the front. She opened the box and gasped when she discovered it filled to the top with money. "She could've fixed this place with these funds," Delaney said.

"It was meant for you," he clarified.

She imagined how the women in the establishment had been living since her mother's passing. Jane's illness, the filth and wear of the establishment. She closed her eyes briefly and considered all she'd learned since arriving in New Orleans. When she opened her eyes again, she inhaled, and said with all finality, "Now it's going back to the house."

"Delaney, this is for your future."

She snapped the lid shut and stood. She held the chest close to her chest as she said, "Whatever I invest in this house will be repaid when again it becomes the most desired establishment for nighttime entertainment."

Remi crossed his arms and leaned back, arching a brow at her. "I thought you were going to be rid of it. That you were going to just sell it."

"I can't, not in this condition," she said. She skirted around Remi and headed for the door. "If I want to sell it, I have to make it worthy of a good price. That will secure my future, as well as the future of those working here." She reached for the door and paused, resting her hand on the latch as she turned back to Remi. With a small smile, she added, "That includes you, as well."

He rubbed his jaw, leveling her stare with one that seemed almost amused, or disbelieving. "So you're going to become the madam of the Bird House?"

"I suppose I am," she mumbled, before she opened the chamber door and took her box to the office. Her office.

She discovered the office empty. Rafe had most likely dragged his feet back to bed. She sat behind the desk, reopened the money box, and began calculating the value inside. The decision she'd just made weighed heavily, and mentally she began tallying what she had and what the house needed most. She was halted by Remi, who'd followed her to the office. "Are you sure you want to do this, Delaney?"

She took a moment to reflect on the burly man

standing in the center of the room, his legs braced apart and arms crossed over the wide expanse of his chest. His warrior-like image appeared to be only a shell of the uncertainty she so often witnessed in his aged eyes. He'd deceived her in many ways, and she didn't know what to make of it. "Is this not what you wanted, Remi?"

Remi's eyes dropped and anchored on the floor for a long moment. When he met her rather hard stare, he looked defeated. "I think this house needs you. Even if it's only temporary."

****

Delaney announced she was shutting the doors for two weeks.

That caused an uproar, and the girls gathered in the parlor where they bickered about what they couldn't afford and how were they going to live without two weeks' pay. Delaney tried to explain, but she was constantly being drowned out by their sudden ire toward her and her first decision as madam. It took Delaney shattering her wine goblet on the hearth to grab their attention.

"I've heard your grievances, and it will be worked out. Each woman needing compensation for something of importance, see me later in the office and we'll work it out. These two weeks are merely your investment in the success of this house. If done properly, with your cooperation, you'll be making more money than you ever have. But I need your patience and compliance."

Silence hovered now, and Delaney glanced at Remi. Her eyes were pleading. He nodded and gave a small, rare smile. This gave her the reassurance she needed to continue with confidence. She lifted her chin and went on, "There are rules that will be followed," she said.

"Rules?" Gertie said, standing up from the armrest she'd been perched on. "What do you know about running this place?"

"I know things aren't working the way they are," Delaney said firmly. "Do you want to do more than just scratch by? I heard several of you went to Jack Chanfray and he turned you away, calling you gutter whores. He took your customers and left you with drunkards and degenerates."

Gertie couldn't argue, and she sat back down, still glaring. She was one of those girls who went to Chanfray.

"First of all, this place is filthy and outdated, and so are all of you," Delaney began. There was another uproar in response, and she flashed Remi another look. He barked at them to be quiet, a lot louder and more effectively than she could. When the chaos calmed down again, she continued. "Cleanliness is the most important thing. After each customer, you're to clean yourselves and your rooms. That will help in preventing illness. No gentleman wants to smell another man on you." She didn't know where her statement had blurted from, but it made sense to her.

"What do you know about that?" Fannie laughed. "You blushed just from saying it!"

She wasn't wrong. Delaney could feel the burning in her cheeks and knew she'd have to get a handle on her embarrassment. "Fannie, don't question my advice," Delaney said, pushing through the shake in her confidence. "From now on, anyone who questions me may pack their things." She straightened her shoulders and lifted her chin. "You'll learn manners and receive new attire. We'll also update and mend any clothing and corsets that are salvageable. If any man looks ill, has any rash—anything that's questionable—you're to send them away. If they won't go, get Remi or Rafe and they'll remove him. Any fighting amongst you will be dealt with by me. Harshly. You shouldn't be fighting amongst each other. We're all in this together. If you get into any more scuffles with Remi, Rafe, or the customers, you'll be sorry. If you want to scrap, go to the gutters." Everything kind of spilled from her mouth, and she could hardly believe her own words. What had happened to her? She looked around and discovered all the women gaping at her. She reminded herself it was all necessary. How else was she to get away and start a life of her own?

She cleared her throat and said in a softer tone, "On a more personal note, I-I'm asking you to keep my identity a secret. If you tell anyone who I am, I'll leave, and you'll be on your own. You know how well that has worked out, these past few months."

There were hushed whispers as they all looked from one to the other.

Billy shifted on the sofa and flipped her curls as she said, "Eh, I think that may be too late. Word's spread that a young woman from out of town has taken over Birdie's house. I heard it in town this morning."

Delaney cursed quietly. "Gossip spreads faster than Jane's rash."

"If it helps, no one knows your name," Fannie said. "So they don't know your relation…"

"I suppose," Delaney mumbled.

Billy chimed in, "And no one knows what you look like."

Delaney's emotions lifted slightly at that.

"They're gonna know who ye are eventually." Gertie chortled. "They're gonna see your face, and God knows you look like Birdie."

"Hmm. I'll figure that part out later. In the meantime, this house will be filled with people this week as we clean the place up."

She turned to Rafe and Remi. "I've marked the furnishings I wish to be removed. We're stepping into eighteen hundred."

"*Oui*, madam," they said uniformly, and began removing the gaudy mirrors and furnishings.

"Remi, did you find me a cook?"

"I did," he said. "She's in the kitchen right now, cleaning the mess. I had to pay her extra for the first cleaning."

"Splendid. I want healthy meals provided for the staff, with lots of fruit. Refreshments will need to be prepared in the evenings for customers."

"I gave her all your instructions," he replied. "And I sent Jane down to help."

Delaney was relieved that Jane was feeling better and was delightfully surprised at how enthusiastic Jane appeared when she mentioned assisting the cook. Delaney was pleased at how everything was beginning to take shape. She'd be free of it all before she knew it!

****

Ten days later, Delaney sat in the office with her brow planted firmly on the desktop. She let out a long shaky breath. Next to her head, her damp palms stuck to the polished mahogany top as she sat draped in despair.

"I'm broke," she voiced aloud to the lonely office. She repeated her words again in her head. The Bird House's substantial debts had taken a good percentage of her money. The house was under new management, and the first impression was detrimental. She didn't have the funds to lavishly entertain. She had the premise of something of quality, but not the essence. She couldn't afford the essence!

"Delaney, are you well?"

Delaney's head shot up from the desk as Remi strolled in and wiggled his finger toward her brow. "You have a…red mark on your…"

"The essence, Remi!" she cried.

Remi ventured farther into the room and eyed her curiously. "The what?"

She let out a sigh and sat back, her gaze settling on the money box blocking her inkpot. She slid it over and opened the lid, cursing the thin stack of notes inside. "Everyone is depending on me. I made promises and now I don't know if I can fulfill them!"

"This place is transforming nicely, and almost overnight," Remi countered. "You've given more than anyone could've hoped for already."

She shook her head, one corner of her mouth lifting with skepticism. "I don't want to fulfill hope! I want everyone to bask in the house's success. But upon my ambitious timing factor, I'm afraid my sources have been depleted."

"Demanding that everyone drop their current jobs to focus on your tasks alone is expensive. But understandably, you don't want to miss the city's prime time of indulgence. Let me remind you—when the city's more respectable entertainments cease for Lent, a bordello becomes even more appealing."

"Yes, but I want to establish the house's new status immediately upon carnaval," she muttered. "And I want gaming tables."

Remi raised his brows. "You need more than what's in that box for gaming tables, Delaney." He let out a heavy breath and nodded as he added, "And connections even to obtain the permits."

"I must open." She tapped her temple as she continued to sulk.

"Perhaps, upon paying Birdie's debts, you can start a new line of credit?" Remi ventured.

"I've considered that. Unfortunately, those who were willing to grant me credit came with conditions I deemed unacceptable." Delaney curled her nose and let out groan laced with anger and frustration. She took out the last stack of notes and looked them over. Beneath the stack was Alderic's coin. Remembrance itched the corners of her lips.

"What are you smiling at?" Remi asked, leaning forward as he took his seat.

She picked up the coin and observed it in her palm. Sliding the pad of her finger over the ship on the coin, she turned it and inspected the mask on the opposite side. She longed to be rid of her troubles and responsibilities, and find Alderic...

"Delaney?"

She held out the coin. "What is this?"

Remi reached out and took the coin. He walked to the window and held it up to the light. "Where did you get this?"

"Someone gave it to me the night we arrived."

"It's a club coin."

"What's that?"

He left the window. "Whoever gave it to you is part of a gathering of men who gained their wealth after coming from nothing. They support one another, whether it be by services, trade, or other things of that sort."

"Alderic gave it to me. Do you know him?"

Remi's eyes widened. "Alderic…Beaumont?" He chuckled. "The fallen French aristocrat. He has the devil's streak running through him."

She creased her brow. "An aristocrat," she muttered. "Then it can't be his coin, if it means he's supposed to have risen from nothing. Being a gentleman, he didn't build his own fortune."

"Not necessarily." Remi found the nearest chair and lounged in it, resting his leg over the armrest. "The key word is *fallen*. If anyone has risen from the ashes, I'd say it's Beaumont. He was a breath away from the hangman's noose."

"What?"

"Alderic was a corsair, long before the destruction of the French aristocracy."

"How does an aristocrat become a corsair?"

"I don't know, Delaney. Times are strange," Remi sighed. "Why so interested?"

She shrugged, clearing her throat. "I suppose I wanted to steer away from my current dilemma. You seem to know a lot about him," she commented.

"Most people in these parts do." He stood up and handed her back the coin. "He and Captain Nye are legends around here."

"*Legends* is quite a claim," she mused.

Remi scoffed. "But appropriate when it comes to them. Nye Tarquin all but rose from the dead." Her jaw went slack, and she was about to demand details when he abruptly stood and said, "Now, I have to get back to mending the courtyard. I think you'll be surprised the lighting is just what you pictured."

She barely heard anything about the courtyard. "Nye Tarquin?"

He rolled up his sleeves, shooting a quick look at her. "Another time. I'm excited about this project in the gardens. And one could spend days talking about those two."

"I'm thinking it will be an interesting tale, when you have the time, Remi."

Remi cleared his throat. "Absolutely. The only answer I see to your current predicament is right in your hand."

She glanced once more at the coin. "Alderic? How could he help me?"

"He's established a strong network here."

"I-I can't ask him."

"He may be your only option, and one I'd say is trustworthy enough to not take advantage of your situation."

She tilted her head at him. "You know him that well?"

"I know his reputation. He's probably the closest thing you'll get to a decent proposal. And I know you well enough to know that if he's not respectful, you'll give him hell." Flashing her a wink and a smirk, he turned on his heel and left the office.

She played with the coin in her hand, lost in thought. She didn't want to ask Alderic for help. She didn't want him even to know why she was in New Orleans. There had to be another way.

Chapter Ten

Alderic calmly brushed the cuff of his fine coat as the chief law enforcer, Bastia Galliano, read over the documents he'd handed him. Bastia placed down the parchments and signed them. "I'd assumed this was a misunderstanding, Beaumont. Thank you for clearing it all up. I'll have Nye's men released immediately, and I apologize for the inconvenience."

Alderic finished inspecting his cuff, then straightened his waistcoat. He waved a hand carelessly as he said, "Quite all right. Nye sends his regards for your swift clearing of this matter."

Bastia handed one of the documents back to him, and as Alderic went to take it, he tightened his grip on the parchment just slightly and held his stare. "This week seems to be a time of several misunderstandings."

Alderic straightened his stance as the deputy released the parchment. Bastia had his attention. "What do you mean, Bastia?"

"Ledgers are being confiscated, at an alarming rate, on the question of cheating taxes," Bastia said, suddenly appearing nonchalant as he shuffled through some papers on his desk. "A great interest in smuggling seems to be surfacing. Nothing substantial has turned up thus far. However, that's not deterring the search."

Alderic took the law enforcer's grave warning. He was going to be visited by the authorities soon. That didn't sit well with Alderic. For further frustration, he'd just gotten word that one of his suppliers had upped their percentage on his goods. His supplier had said he'd been offered more, and Alderic could either match it or forget about making a deal. Alderic had been furious. Now he discovered that his books were going to be investigated.

"That is unfortunate for you," Alderic said lightly, despite the simmering within him. "How distressing."

"It is, and to further waste even my personal time, I must take my wife to *Le Café des Deux*, before a long afternoon of shopping."

Alderic inhaled sharply—he was now being given a stark warning about his place of business. Most of his dealings were conducted at that coffee shop, and many of his goods were stored in the warehouse above. Still, he remained composed.

"When does this long day of shopping commence?" he asked.

"Tomorrow," the deputy stated, briefly looking up from his desk. "Early."

Alderic nodded and gave a small smirk. "Well, at least you get to spend quality time with your wife."

"Then you have not met my wife," Bastia replied dryly.

Alderic chuckled. "I am fortunate to call the café owner my friend, as everyone knows my passion for coffee brings me to his establishment often enough to provide quite a bond. I will make sure I have him set aside a special brew for you and your lovely wife."

Bastia grinned and held out his hand. Alderic took it, and his expression held a gracious *thank you*. Indeed, Bastia would be compensated well for the information.

Just then, the door opened and Nye's men, Mitch

and Amadi, were escorted inside. Alderic's unfailing composure was quite the opposite within, as he watched Nye's men—his friends—standing there, shackled. He'd received word just that morning from Nye that his barge had been seized, with Mitch and Amadi apprehended. They'd just returned from a delivery upriver and their vessel had been empty, but that didn't stop the authorities from detaining them. It was frivolous and petty, a mere inconvenience. Perhaps even a warning. Now his warehouse was going to be searched.

Bastia had the shackles removed and announced they were free to go. As he, Mitch, and Amadi left the prison, Alderic was boiling inside.

"I'm indebted, Alderic," Mitch said. "It was awful being in that holding cell, even if only for a few hours."

Alderic glanced at Nye's protégé. Mitch was a young lad, his dark curls as wild as his spirit. He'd known Mitch since he was barely out of nappies. He was growing into an admirable young man. Then he looked at Amadi, another good friend and a loyal part of the crew. A man who'd saved his arse a few times. It was he and Amadi who'd carried Nye's bleeding body to the marshes when he was attacked and left to die on the street. The three of them had been through many trials together. Now, he declared within himself that he'd find whoever was targeting them and their business. Even as he considered who it might be, one person came to mind—Jack Chanfray.

****

In two weeks, Delaney settled several accounts, and she was relieved to not have creditors knocking at the door. The Bird House was freshly painted. Flowers and shrubs were weeded and trimmed back in the small courtyard out back. She also added lamps to the small garden there, and furniture for customers wishing to seek fresh air. She decided it was impossible to redecorate the entire inside, but anything too elaborate was sold, and more modern furnishings were added. She didn't adhere strictly to Roman décor, which was the norm now. She blended the Roman flair with a toned-down version of her mother's taste.

She searched the city until she found an abundance of oil, and she collected berries, roots, and stones to mix her paints and create murals on the walls invoking emotions of desire and passion. She focused on curved lines and wild gardens. She also thought it was appropriate to paint birds in different places throughout the house as a tribute to her mother.

Now it was getting close to the reopening, and she needed to make it grand. She'd made the Bird House as sophisticated as possible, worthy of recognition from wealthy gentlemen. When Remi knocked on her chamber door and entered, she was sitting cross-legged in the center of the bed, fiddling with ribbons. He carried a ledger and the notes she'd written down for him. "Do you think anyone will pay these prices?" he asked.

"If they want services, they will," she said, cursing as she tried to thread a needle. "We'll have to be booked till dawn every day for a week just to get back the money spent on the wine collection."

Fannie barged in, nearly knocking over Remi. "I'm not a server, Delaney."

Delaney sighed. She couldn't believe she was going to have the same argument with Fannie that she'd just had with Gertie.

"Fannie, everyone has to serve the drinks until we

can afford a server."

Within moments, her room was filling with girls complaining about one thing and then another.

"She stole my corset!" Gertie shouted, pointing at Billy.

Billy planted her fist on her hip and struck a haughty pose, throwing her black locks over her shoulder. "Your beastly legs stretched out my stockings!"

An argument ensued, and Delaney had to raise her voice to be heard over the festering commotion. "Why is everyone in my chamber?"

They stopped bickering and looked at her, sitting like a child in the middle of her massive bed.

"Are you going to get ready, Delaney?" Gertie asked. "We open in four hours."

Delaney looked at Remi and the barely covered women. They looked expectantly at her.

"Do you think it takes me four hours to get ready?" she asked.

Gertie shrugged. "Well, you put on so much, it must take time."

"What solution have you come up with to conceal your identity?" Rafe asked as he, too, joined the spontaneous house meeting.

"I don't know," Delaney mumbled. "Can't I just stay in the office? I've been so busy, I only had time to come up with this." She held up the mask she'd been sewing the ribbons on.

"The madam must be seen," Remi insisted.

"It's rather full," Fannie said, and she sat at the edge of the bed and inspected the elegant lines of the white silk mask. One side dipped dramatically down the right side of the face. "It should cover almost half of your face.

Let's see it."

Delaney tied the mask behind her head. She looked up, and everyone stared blankly at her.

"We're...not supposed to recognize you?" asked Billy.

Delaney tore the mask off. She wanted to cry. "It's hopeless... I can't very well put a sack over my head!"

Silence hovered as everyone shot glances at one another.

Fannie gave Delaney a wide grin and, trying to sound optimistic, said, "Well, we know what you look like, but for those who don't...maybe it will work. It's not like they'll recognize you on the street."

"No, it's just not distracting enough," said Remi.

"What do you mean?" asked Delaney.

"You're eye-catching, Delaney," said Rafe. "Men will just want to see behind the mask."

"That's true," Gertie said, breaking a rather sudden and awkward silence. "The mask is a small barrier, but it's not going to deter them from trying to make the connection of what ye look like underneath."

"So I need to make my mask more eye-catching than the exposed part of my face?"

"*Oui*, lots of distractions," said Remi.

"A lot of distractions, Delaney," Fannie agreed.

"Oh, let me dye your hair!" exclaimed Billy.

"No!"

"Just a little," Billy said. "During the carnaval last year, my aunt created a colored paste with chalk, using those same pigments you use for your paint. My cousin put streaks in her hair. I have several colors—they're temporary. Your blonde hair will hold color much better than hers did."

"What colors?"

Billy tossed her hand in the air. "Red, blue, purple, and green."

She was truly interested. She was aware that women had been dying their hair for centuries, and using chalk for something less permanent was an interesting idea.

Soon the girls were jumping on her bed, climbing around her, and taking her hair out of its chignon to inspect it.

"*Oui*, we'll put your hair high and streak it with color," Billy said. "It'll be perfect!"

"You're sure it will come out?" asked Delaney.

Billy paused. "Of course it will. It'll just take some scrubbing."

"Our job here is done," Remi announced, and he and Rafe headed for the door with a roll of their eyes.

"When they start decorating, it's time to go before we grow breasts," Rafe mumbled as they exited the room.

"I can paint my mask, make it lavish and colorful," Delaney suggested.

"That's a good idea," said Billy.

"If only I could dye my face," Delaney threw out offhandedly. "A shocking blue would deter their attention."

"Ew, Delaney. No," Gertie said. "We can't be sure the dye would come off your skin."

Delaney sighed. "No, I wasn't being serious... I..." She pulled away from them as a new idea struck her. She rushed to her paintbox, and began mixing pigments and oil on her board.

"We'll get some color ready for your hair," Billy announced.

"All right, I'll be up momentarily." Delaney's room finally cleared out, and she inspected her mask. The way one side dropped to a point reminded her of a butterfly's profile. A small smile tugging on her lips, she began painting butterfly markings on the mask, adding lavish decoration to the other side, over the left eye. She made sure there was a lot of detail and contrasting bright colors. She left it to dry while she went to the wardrobe and took out one of the newest silk gowns.

She dressed and then tested the mask. The paint was still wet. She held it carefully, blowing on it, before she finally went upstairs. All the birds were stuffed in Billy's chamber. Delaney tried to avert her gaze from the leather straps tied to the bedposts, but it was difficult when Fannie was hanging playfully from one.

Billy ushered Delaney to her vanity and brushed out her hair. Before she could prepare herself mentally for what the girl was doing to her hair, Billy began putting purple and red in it. When they finished, it had thick, heavy streaks of pink and lavender.

"You think five streaks are enough?" Billy asked.

"It has to be. The clock is ticking," Delaney replied. Then she tried to imagine how she'd make her hair more flamboyant and extravagant. She had no idea. "Can you do my hair?"

Billy squealed. Penelope and Fannie joined in, and soon everyone started playing with her hair.

"What are you wearing tonight?" Gertie asked.

Delaney glanced down at her pale blue gown. She heard a few sighs. "Is there something wrong with what I'm wearing?"

"No, it's beautiful," Gertie said. She and Billy seemed to have a silent conversation with their eyes. "If you're going to the theater or a tea party."

Delaney buried her face in her hands. She was doing everything wrong, and she was never going to keep her identity a secret.

Billy disappeared, then quickly returned with a black velvet gown.

Delaney looked at the low neckline and then the wide slit going up the front of the gown. Her finger lightly brushed the soft velvet, and she itched to rub the material against her cheek.

"This was your mother's, and it was always my favorite," Billy said. "You're about the same size. You should wear it tonight."

That was her mother's? She could almost imagine it on the woman of the portrait in her office. But on her? Before she could respond, the girls started unlacing her gown. They slipped her into a sheer black petticoat and then into the velvet gown. She looked at herself in the mirror and witnessed her own jaw drop. The neckline was so low and tight she thought her breasts would fall out. The slit revealed her sheer petticoat, which did nothing to veil her short chemise, stockinged legs, and garters.

They rushed her to the mirror and finished dressing her hair, making a point of revealing the streaks of lavender and pink. They draped pearls throughout the curls and dressed her neck and ears with them, as well.

When they were done, it was time to don her mask. They returned to her room, where everyone passed around the mask, complimenting the artwork, before Fannie tied it on Delaney. She put on her long white gloves, turned around, and waited for approval. They all cheered and clapped. Her cheeks grew pink.

"I believe it's time to open the doors," Delaney announced, and shied away from the attention.

"No one will be here for a while yet," Gertie said.

"Why?"

"There's a carnaval gathering a few streets away," she replied.

"But they'll congregate after the procession," Billy supplied. "The parade will come down this street and eventually stop outside the Cabildo. When it's over, the men will be looking for some private fun."

"So you just wait here?" Delaney asked. "That's silly."

"What do you want us to do?" Gertie said. "All the men are gathered along the streets, reveling."

"Once it breaks up, they'll go to Jack's or us," said Fannie.

The mention of Jack Chanfray triggered Delaney's temper. "We don't want them going to Jack's," she snapped. "Get up, all of you! Put on covers, cloaks, shawls, I don't care what—but get out there in the street and bring in the men. Invite them here, instead."

"Are you off your rocker, Delaney?" Gertie asked.

"Blend in with the parade," Delaney countered. "I've seen them. They're more of a messy crowd, trampling down the street. They won't know what's going on. Invite them."

Gertie snorted, planting a hand on her hip. "Do ye want us to make invitations?"

Delaney thought a moment. Gertie had a point, that did sound ridiculous. She needed to sell the intrigue. Some way to grab the men's interest so they'd come here instead of going to Jack's. Drumming her fingers on the vanity as she thought, she touched a loose ribbon on

Billy's vanity. She smiled and took two ribbons. She tied them on Billy's wrists. Then she took another and tied it around Billy's neck.

"Let the men you choose untie your ribbons, and then tell them to bring it back to the Bird House," she announced. "Each one of you, grab some ribbons and only invite gentlemen, men who look refined. Hurry!"

They rushed to their rooms, gathering covers and tying ribbons on each other's wrists and necks. Once they finished, she sent Rafe and Remi with them. She hid her smile as the scantily clad women raced down the street toward the music and lights. Silently she prayed the intrigue would work. When she returned to her room, she caught her reflection in the mirror. She observed her reflection for a long time. Her hair was high and curled, and she was full of color. Her dramatic mask concealed most of her face, but in her opinion it wasn't enough. It was so important for her to hide her identity. But why? She wasn't altogether certain. What was her identity? Who was Delaney Harper? Everything she'd thought herself to be had been proven false. But she decided, in that moment, that she'd determine her own identity, on her own time. The brothel would not.

Dropping her gaze, she sighed and fixed on her brushes, still wet with paint. She picked up the paintbrush covered with ebony paint and inspected herself in the mirror. "I wonder..." She painted a curved line—resembling a vine—along her jaw and curled it up to her cheek. She continued painting the exposed side of her face, adding blues and greens, making vines along the side of her face and down her neck. She inspected her work and then touched it up for more depth. To balance it, she put a few strokes down her low neckline. She dropped the paintbrush and stared at her reflection, holding her breath as she observed her work. She'd nearly hidden her face. She'd made the blank canvas of her skin into a piece of art.

Chapter Eleven

Alderic had had a long day, and his body ached. Clearing out his warehouse overnight was no easy task. He and Nye had decided it was best to relocate the goods from all their storage facilities and move them upriver for a bit. After the last forty-eight hours, he was happy to return to his room at the inn and wash. He was exhausted. His bath had been refreshing; now he wanted a hot meal and sleep.

He was shaving when there was solid pounding on his door, and his hopes were dashed. He looked at the time and let out a growl. He could guess who it was. "Go away," he called, then continued sliding his razor down the side of his cheek.

The knocking persisted. "Beaumont, the procession is forming!" he heard from outside his door.

He ignored Wil's voice, carefully sliding his razor along his jaw. "I'm busy," Alderic said.

"We don't want to miss it!" Wil shouted, and then he began trying the doorknob.

Alderic nicked his skin. Slamming down his razor, he marched to the door and threw it open. "Wil, what the hell—are you a child?"

Wil's eyes were round pools. "I'm unhappy," he whined. "I need revelry."

"Your heartbreak was weeks ago. You were the one daft enough to get caught rolling with some chit when you were supposed to be on your way to the church. It is not my job to lift your spirits."

"So… are you coming then, Cap'n?" Wil blinked owlishly.

Alderic lifted his gaze to the heavens before letting out a frustrated snarl. "Give me a damned minute." He slammed the door before Wil could say another word.

He wiped off his smooth face, then donned a creamy silk waistcoat and dark breeches. As he tied his cravat, he heard more of his crew gathering outside his door. He swore one day he was going to get a place of his own and never tell them where it was! He opened the door and caught their looks of anticipation. "Can you not do anything without me?" he asked, raising a brow as he stepped out of his room.

Wil scratched his dull brown locks and glanced at the gathering of men. "We can, but it's not nearly as entertaining."

The crew simultaneously agreed. Alderic shook his head, slid on his fine black coat, and shut the door. They stopped at the nearest tavern and drank heartily until the procession made its way to their street. When they heard the distant gaiety of the revelers, everyone in the tavern exited the building and stood along the street. The last time he was part of a procession was weeks ago. The night he'd seen Delaney. The night he'd resentfully watched her kiss Wil. She'd been standing on the street, watching their spectacle. When they'd gotten to her, she'd played along well. Her pouting mouth had been too inviting. Indeed, he hadn't seen such a beauty since he'd met Sarafina. His best friend's love. He wasn't about to lose his chance with such a remarkable beauty, so he'd boldly kissed her. When he'd discovered her again in the shop, he'd wanted so badly to whisk her somewhere and make love to her. Somewhere…where? He shook his head. Most of his days were spent on his ship. He rented a room at the local inn when he wanted a place that wasn't confined and constantly in motion. A space to stretch out. He was a bachelor and a captain, always networking, always putting in long hours to build his fortune. And he had a fortune, but he didn't have a stable life. Now that he'd found the first woman to make him question his devil-may-care lifestyle, he had no way of finding her. He only had her given name, and that didn't help much. No one in town seemed to know who he was even talking about.

Screeching horns and shouting tore him from his thoughts. "Come, join us!" the people in procession shouted to the onlookers as they tossed out bonbons and other bits of charm. Many of them were playing instruments and singing. A lot of them were falling-over drunk. Alderic and his crew joined the procession, and the parade expanded with each street they toured.

He'd spent many years in New Orleans. He had made it his home when he was but a young noble escaping his obligations. He'd participated in carnaval many times. He noted that, every year, the locals had grown a little more courageous, a tad more daring. But he wasn't expecting the parade to be infiltrated by cloaked doves in their undergarments. Indeed, they were beauties, and Wil nearly fell over himself as they weaved in and out of the crowd. He watched curiously, as certain men were encouraged to remove the ribbons from their bodies. It seemed to be a game the women were playing, and he noticed they were targeting the gentlemen in the crowd. The men who'd gotten the ribbons were swinging them high above their heads like a prize.

"I want one of those ribbons!" Wil shouted with a slur. He nearly stumbled from his drunken lack of coordination, and he instinctively grabbed Alderic's lapels to regain his stance.

"Wil, let go of my coat or I will break your fingers," Alderic said with little heat. He eyed Wil's attire, then smirked. "You are not getting a ribbon in those shabby clothes."

Wil looked down at his torn, oversized breeches and loose-fitting linen shirt. He frowned. "Can I borrow your coat?"

Alderic laughed at Wil's ridiculous question just before he felt a hand slide along his neck. He spun around as one of the young doves in a black cloak gripped his cravat, keeping a good hold. She was a lovely lass with flawless, swarthy skin and bright eyes. He tipped one corner of his mouth into a smile, as she stood on her toes, and attempted to draw him down. He obliged the young woman, and she kissed him, wrapping her arms around his neck and clinging to him as she drove her tongue inside his mouth. She'd meant to send his senses wheeling, and it worked, if only for a moment before he broke their kiss. "Take one of my ribbons, *monsieur*," she whispered against his mouth.

"I'll take one," Wil said with much enthusiasm. Unbidden, he untied the ribbon from her wrist.

The woman glared at Wil, then quickly recovered, when she realized Wil was with Alderic. She smiled. "Your friend can come…if you do."

"Please, Cap'n," Wil begged, nudging him. "I need this!"

He looked at Wil with a blessed amount of patience,

much more than Wil deserved. Finally, he sighed and gazed back at the lovely dove. She spotted his shift immediately and smiled. She lifted her chin, exposing the ribbon tied into a delicate bow on her neck. Alderic untied the ribbon and watched it slide off her skin.

"Return it to me at the Bird House," she said, offering him one last seductive smile. Then she vanished into the crowd. Just as quickly as they'd come, the women disappeared, leaving a bunch of lusty men in their wake. Alderic played with the ribbon in his fingers as he observed the effect they'd had on the other men. And him.

"Clever," he mused.

Chapter Twelve

Half an hour had passed when the door burst open again and all the girls flooded into Delaney's room, relaying with excitement how they'd shocked everyone in the Quarter. "You should've seen it," they said, laughing and squealing. "It was amazing! They were stunned!"

"The men were speechless!" Fannie shouted.

"Oh, and some were so handsome!" Billy added with an exaggerated sigh.

Delaney wondered if her plan would work, if those invited would actually come. She wanted that scoundrel Jack Chanfray to regret the day he'd called them gutter whores.

"Delaney, what did you do to yourself?" Remi said, weaving through the gathering of ladies. Once the initial excitement died down, they all inspected her closer.

Delaney instinctively reached to touch her face, but restrained. "Does it look so terrible?"

"It's amazing!" Gertie said.

"Oh, my God, Delaney," Fannie breathed. "No one will have any idea who you are now!"

"It's beautiful!"

Delaney was able to breathe now and released a shaky near-sigh as she ran her palms down her gown. "Then it's time. Ladies, remember your manners. Remi, open the doors. Rafe, ready the parlors," she said, trying to appear calm despite the unsteadiness of her hands. "Fannie and Billy, load the trays." She paused as the women displayed their excitement by jumping and checking each other and everything on the trays. She nearly chuckled at how giddy they looked. And why not? They'd worked hard and tirelessly these last two weeks. She was so proud of their progress. Indeed, it would be a momentous time for everyone. Even her. With that, she gave a beaming smile as she said, "Then let us indulge in the intrigue…"

Minutes ticked by. After the paint dried on her face, it began to itch. She reminded herself not to scratch as she sat quietly at her desk, staring at the empty street from her window. Time passed slowly, and the only ones who showed up were the regulars—the drunkards and braggarts Remi promptly turned away. She let out a long breath and fought the stinging in the backs of her eyes. She feared she'd failed. Had the procession ended yet?

Then something in the energies shifted, catching her attention. She went to the window and witnessed a vision growing before her eyes. Outside, was a group of gentlemen strolling up the street, ribbons dangling from their fingers. Soon carriages were rolling up to the house, and guests were sauntering up the steps. She closed her eyes and swallowed the blockage forming in her throat. It had worked! Relief flooded her so quickly she nearly let a flow of tears destroy her painted face.

As the line of men stretched out the door, she listened from her office, safely tucked away for the time being. Laughter rang out, and she could hear Fannie and Billy flirting mercilessly in the main entrance.

Then there was a knock at her door, and she unlocked it. Remi stepped inside, holding a silken cloak.

"It's been long enough, Delaney," he said. "Men are beginning to ask who's hosting this party."

She felt herself grow pale, and she ran her hands nervously down her soft velvet gown. "Is there no way around this?"

"Not if you want to be successful. But I brought you this…" He held out the cloak.

She took it and stared blankly.

He motioned flippantly at her face and neck and said, "I thought it was appropriate for a theatrical entrance since…all this you have going on."

She laughed. "Do I look so ridiculous?"

His expression sobered. "Not at all. Indeed, I've never seen such a thing. You've pulled it off nicely. You're a vision."

"Thank you, Remi."

"But," he said brightly, "this is your coming out, *Madame*. And you must make it as intriguing and dramatic as everything else you've done. So put on the hooded cloak and enter with as much confidence and enigmatic air as you can muster. I'll announce you in the parlor."

"If it must be dramatic, then gather them in the hall and announce me at the bottom of the grand staircase."

He grinned. "I approve. Slip along the corridor and sneak up the back stairs. I'll announce you. First, give me a chance to create a diversion so you can get out of the office."

She fumbled for words to construct confidence, but she drew a blank. Nervously she took a deep breath. It all seemed like a dream as she snuck past the guests in the parlor and headed toward the servant stairs.

****

The parade ended, and the crew headed for the tavern. Wil pleaded for Alderic to accept the woman's invitation. "I can't go if you don't, Cap'n. Please?"

Alderic sighed and offered his farewell to the rest of the partygoers. Wil all but leapt forward. "I was told the Bird House was shut down," Wil said as they walked away from the Cabildo, "and it was reopened by someone else. But no one really knows who, for sure."

"Probably Chanfray," Alderic said as he carefully folded his coat and tossed it over his shoulder. The night was dreadfully warm.

"I heard it was Birdie's daughter."

"Birdie had a daughter?"

Wil shrugged. "I suppose so. Some people don't believe it. They say it's just a story."

He shrugged and said, "I am only going because you insist on it. I will stay long enough to make sure they do not toss you out, but then I am leaving."

"I appreciate it, Cap'n."

"Hmph," he grunted. "I'm not sure how—with all your trifling issues—you manage to be such a good quartermaster."

Wil put a hand over his heart, and chuckled. "Cap'n, you wound me."

Alderic flashed a look at his longtime chief crewmember, then continued walking in silence. Because of Wil he'd be forced to endure the superficial chatter of squawking females pretending to be interested in what he had to say so he'd pay coin to go upstairs.

The corner house was lit up, and at the sight of all the men lining out the door, Wil hooted. They were filing in when Alderic recognized Remi at the door. *When did Remi return?*

"If you don't have a ribbon," Remi announced, "then I'm sorry, but you've not been invited to our re-opening. Please return tomorrow night."

Several men groaned and growled as they stormed off. The line shrank considerably.

"A bold move," Alderic mumbled, wondering who would turn away so much business.

"Alderic!" Rafe said boisterously. He took Alderic's outstretched hand and gave it a firm shake. "I should've known the ladies would single you out."

"*Bonjour*, Rafe," Alderic said. "Remi, where have you been?"

"Traveling. Good to see you, Alderic. Where's Nye?"

"A lot has happened while you were gone," he replied. "Nye is home with his wife—and happily so."

"Really?" Remi laughed heartily. "If anyone deserves happiness, it's him. When are you going to settle down?"

Alderic chuckled. "*Ami*, you cannot ask a man such a question while he is standing outside a bordello."

"You make a good point," Remi said, his eyes shooting from Alderic to Wil. He cocked a brow at the shabby quartermaster but noticed the ribbon in his hand and shrugged, saying, "Enjoy yourselves, gentlemen."

Rafe then stopped Alderic as he passed. "You have a good eye, Beaumont. Keep watch, for the scenery may enthrall you."

Alderic didn't have time to ask Rafe to elaborate on his statement, as he was practically shoved in by the rest of the guests. When he stepped through the entrance, he was instantly taken in. He remembered the house being decked in gold trim, soaked with gilded and scroll designs on top of damask. Now there was an interesting blend of the old French court and the great civilizations of antiquity. Painted murals of romantic gardens enriched the walls and staircase. The place smelled fresh and citrusy. The Bird House was competing with Chanfray's establishment. If it wasn't Chanfray himself, then someone was treading on dangerous ground.

"Where's the beauty who invited us? Is she in the parlor?" Wil asked, his anticipation as clear in his voice as it was in his expression. In that moment, Alderic had never missed Nye more. For years, they'd entertained the streets all hours and had a grand time. But since Nye had married his own beauty, Alderic had become Wil's sitter.

"Go, and see," Alderic said, suddenly feeling like a parent. He hoped Wil would find her and disappear upstairs.

"Which lucky girl found you in the crowd?" a voice said behind him.

He turned and watched a brunette woman in a pink striped corset stroll up to him, her hips exaggerating their sway. "Would you like a drink?"

She held out her tray, and he accepted a glass of wine. He took a sip and was surprised at the smooth taste. "You offer a fine wine," he said.

"Our madam wants nothing but the best for our clients," she said as she leaned in. He could've sworn she was inhaling his scent. The look in her glimmering gaze told him she approved.

"Your madam," he said. "She is responsible for all this?" He pointed at the grand foyer, and the brunette nodded.

"*Oui*. She is an exquisite creature. My name's Fannie. Find me later, and I promise..." She brushed her lips against his ear as she whispered, "You can put it anywhere, *monsieur*."

He raised a brow and gave a lopsided grin. "I will remember you said that, *mam'selle*."

"Oh, please don't forget." She gave him an extended look, with the ghost of a smile, and sauntered away, weaving through the crowd of men gathering in the hall.

"Attention, please," Remi said, putting his hands up and gesturing for everyone to settle down. "I hope you're enjoying the fine wine, and all the lovely candy walking around—which is also *quite* delectable and... consumable."

The crowd cheered, and the ladies curtsied as they came to pose along the bottom stairs. Alderic observed the gathering. Every man had a drink in his hand. They'd all been lured in by mystery and were now waiting to claim their prizes. They seemed hypnotized by everything going on around them. He remained standing at the back of the crowd, leaning against the parlor doorway, as he observed the scene. The guests—most of whom he knew well—reminded him of excited children, hanging onto Remi's words and observing every move the women made. Silently, he commended the one who'd orchestrated this affair. The *exquisite creature*, Fannie had called her. She was a master in the art of seduction.

"Each of you was especially selected to be among the first to meet the one responsible for this unique environment graciously accommodating you this evening—and every evening from now on. The one who has complimented you with the fine wine tingling your tongues, the one responsible for all the festivities you will enjoy from here on out at the Bird House. You're invited to help us welcome our new madam...Vanessa

Cardui."

Applause erupted. Every man there was sold. Alderic smirked at how the house had just won their loyalty. Alderic's attention was drawn to the top of the grand staircase, where a cloaked woman now appeared. The hood hung low and veiled her face from his eyes.

The crowd also spotted her atop the stairs and started cheering and applauding again. Alderic pushed away from the doorway to get a closer look. He drew near and watched her gracefully descend the stairs like royalty. Her gloved hand slowly slid down the railing, and each step she took exposed the full length of her legs through her sheer petticoat.

As she grew closer, he could see her face was masked in the spirit of carnaval. He wished her face wasn't so covered. She seemed familiar, but he couldn't place her. She stopped halfway down the steps to remove her hood and cloak. He'd never been so entranced. Suddenly, he found himself just as stupefied as the men around him. Her hair was streaked with color and as lavishly decorated as her face. Much like the artwork in the foyer, her face had been delicately painted to accentuate every curve of her face, neck, and shoulders. He stared, just as the other men did, at the rather petite beauty who'd lured them in that night, ensnared them, caught them in her web.

He was determined to pull out of whatever form of bewitchment she'd cast over him, but as the new madam of the Bird House dipped into a curtsy, he was not successful. She took Remi's arm and waited for the cheers to subside before she spoke. "Lovers, please, you have been invited here tonight," she said in a thickly accented voice, "as my first guests, drinks are complimentary." Then she added with a teasing wink, "My birds, however, *are not*."

They absorbed her charm with vigor, and she gave them a dazzling smile that made Alderic catch his breath. Her smile was gracious and sweet. Oddly innocent.

"We are officially open for business," Rafe announced from the parlor doorway, and the gathering began to migrate through it, though many took the opportunity to speak with the madam. Alderic couldn't lie; he was fascinated. He watched intently, noting that each one of her moves was calculated, designed to entice. Fannie had been right. She was an exquisite creature. Alderic shook his head and tried to gather his wits. What was wrong with him?

He finished his wine and searched out Wil. He discovered his young friend in the back parlor with a redhead on his arm. Good. Wil was going to have a romp upstairs, so he'd done his job. He was ready to leave. He could appreciate beauty and intrigue, and he adored sinking himself into the sweet warmth of a gorgeous woman, but his reaction to this place was disarming. He was no stranger to the admiration of his assets. Indeed, he didn't have to search far if he needed comfort. But to find himself on the opposite side of seduction, and succumbing to it like an unseasoned boy, bothered him.

He set his wine glass on the nearest server's tray and spun on his heel. He turned around rather abruptly. That was when he nearly fell over the madam.

Heavens, she appeared so delicate. He could've truly hurt her if he'd slammed into her. But now, having her so close to him, that nagging sense that he knew her plagued him again.

"*Monsieur* Beaumont, what are you doing here?"

she asked, the faintest smile crossing her lovely mouth.

"I was invited…it is Madame Cardui, no?"

"*Oui*," she replied.

He smiled. "How do you know who I am?"

She seemed stumped for a moment and didn't answer, only solidified another flirtatious grin. "I should not be surprised that you were discovered amongst the birds."

She hadn't answered him. Perhaps he did know her? "I've heard that a couple of times tonight, madam. Tell me, is it my lavish attire, or my charm?"

"Neither, *monsieur*," she said, offhandedly waving her gloved hand and turning away. She gave him one last glance over her shoulder, and said simply, "You are quite tall. You stand above the crowd."

He couldn't help but gape at her audaciousness— like he was just another bee in her hive, and she was completely unimpressed with him. A wicked grin formed on his lips as he watched her walk away, her exposed shoulders moving seductively while she weaved through the crowded parlor.

He was honestly speechless, a condition he'd never experienced until now.

Chapter Thirteen

Delaney was startled out of her slumber, and nearly flew out of her bed. Fannie and Billy had rushed into her room and flung themselves onto her.

"It worked, Delaney!" said Fannie.

"The whole town is talking about us and our new, *enigmatic* madam!" added Billy.

Remi walked in, his nose buried in a ledger, and soon a few more people had gathered. How did her room keep becoming the unofficial meeting place? "You need to look at these numbers," Remi said. "I think you'll be pleased."

Gertie filed into the room with Jane. "There will be even more people tonight!"

Her plan was working! "How splendid!" Delaney exclaimed, then paused and looked curiously at everyone crowding her room. "But could this information not have waited until after I got out of bed?"

They didn't appear moved by her question, nor did they think it important enough to warrant a response. Instead, Fannie pointed at her and grimaced. "Delaney, you went to bed with all that paint on."

She lightly touched her face and cringed at the stiff, dried paint on her skin. "Ugh, I know. I was so tired I just collapsed and fell asleep." She sighed. "How do all of you manage to stay up so late?"

Remi closed the ledger with a snap and herded the

girls toward the door. "Cook has a meal prepared, and coffee," he said. "See you in a few minutes, Delaney." She watched everyone file out of her room as she stifled a wide yawn.

"Can Cook prepare me tea, Remi?"

Remi halted and pinched the bridge of his nose. "*Oui*, Delaney. Cook is well aware of your preferences and has prepared the awful stuff for you."

She chuckled at his disgruntled expression as he spun on his heel and left the chamber. She pushed back the covers and trudged to the water basin.

Minutes later, everyone in the house rushed back to her chamber when she released a blood-curdling scream that echoed through the halls. Rafe and Remi charged into the room, nearly colliding into one another. "Delaney, dear God, what's wrong?" Remi demanded as he was nearly toppled by everyone else storming into the room.

She continuously scrubbed her face, until tears sprung to her eyes. "My face! It won't come off!" Delaney cried. "The color won't come off! It's stuck on my face!"

Remi pulled her away from the basin to observe the situation. Gertie and Fannie rushed over, with Billy and Jane close behind, and they all took turns inspecting her dilemma.

"That's bad, Delaney," Fannie said.

"Thank you," Delaney replied dryly as she wiped away fresh tears. She turned back to the basin and recommenced her scrubbing, only faster.

"Delaney, stop," Gertie said, snatching Delaney's hand away. "You're going to remove your skin completely if you scrub any harder."

"What do I do?" she cried.

"The water's cold," Gertie observed. "We'll have Cook warm some."

"Yes, that's a good idea," Fannie said brightly. "Let's go to the kitchen."

Delaney gently blotted her sore face with a dry linen, and they all filed into the kitchen. She was enormously pleased by the change in the kitchen since the first time she had seen it, her first day at the house. Today she was welcomed by the alluring smell of fresh biscuits. The kitchen was clean and tidy, and fresh fruits and vegetables were laid out on the table as Cook prepped for the day's meals.

The cook, a plump woman with silver hair peeking out from under her cap, looked curiously at them as they filled the kitchen. Delaney felt a little uncomfortable. She'd been so busy with the opening she'd barely introduced herself to the cook. Now their first real meeting was going to be under these circumstances?

The cook wiped her hands on her striped apron and marched over to Delaney. "What's wrong wit' ye?" she said sternly. Mentally, Delaney had returned to her youth, when her nanny would demand to know what kind of mischief she'd gotten into. She covered her now-burning cheeks with her palms.

"This is Madame," Fannie said.

The woman curled her nose and let out a "hmph" before she chuckled. "She looks ridiculous."

Gertie puffed up, tossed her flaming hair, and eyed the woman.

"Boil some water," Gertie ordered.

The cook lifted her chin, unmoved by the sassy red-haired beauty. "I don't take orders from you, lass," she said. "Talk to me like that again, and I'll toss you out on your skinny arse."

Gertie let out a shocked sound and crossed her arms over her chest. She came nose to nose with the cook. "Is that so?"

"But you do take orders from your employer. Which is me," Delaney said, shaking out of her initial reaction. The plump woman braced one hand on the table and another firmly on her hip, and eyed her. Delaney gently guided Gertie to step aside, and stepped forward, saying, "Gertie, don't ever argue with the person who cooks your food. You'll regret it."

The cook grunted—almost a chuckle—then straightened as she wiped flour from her hands.

"Cook, do you have any idea how to get this off my face?" Delaney asked.

Delaney was taken back as the cook snatched her chin with her beefy fingers and tilted her face toward the light.

"Aye, I do," she said. "And me name's Barb."

Barb turned to Gertie, who was still simmering, and ordered, "Get me some water out of the pot there." Then cook waddled to a skillet and dipped a towel in it. "Warm grease should do it."

Before Delaney could protest, Barb plopped a glob of grease on Delaney's face and began scrubbing.

Delaney cringed and held her breath. She wanted to complain about the smell of it, but she feared Barb might threaten to toss her out on her arse, too. Instead, she refrained from gagging openly.

"It's gone, though it looks like ye scratched off a layer of yer skin. Take the hot water and wash off the grease. Ye'll be right as rain."

Delaney let out a sigh of relief and smiled up at Barb. "Thank you."

Barb replied with an unimpressed grunt, then returned to cooking.

Chapter Fourteen

Delaney sat at her desk, spinning her quill between her thumb and forefinger while staring at the coin in her other hand.

"Alderic Beaumont," she muttered, then dropped the quill and sat back.

Last night had been conflicting. Standing atop the staircase, she'd spotted Alderic easily in the crowd and thought she'd tumble down the stairs. The intensity in his gaze at her as he inched through the crowd captured the air from her lungs. Her first reaction was the flutter of excitement in her stomach. But then reality set in, and she was mortified. He was attending an opening at a brothel. *Her* brothel, for which she was madam. Neither of their positions appeared in a flattering light.

When he ran into her in the parlor, she feared he'd recognize her. But she couldn't shake one harsh fact…she dreaded the idea of him going upstairs with any of the girls.

"Wake up, Delaney," Remi said as he moseyed into the office. "What is Madame Cardui's plan for this evening? You caused quite a stir. I have a feeling the place will be swarming with gentlemen tonight. The whole ribbon escapade set the bar."

"Hmm," she said, her eyes dropping to the coin in her hand. "I didn't even think about using another name. You have my gratitude." More than anything, he'd protected her identity from the one she wanted most to keep it from.

He chuckled. "It was an oversight, but I figured Vanessa Cardui was appropriate. Not bad for a last-second idea, eh?"

"It was clever, I must admit. I suppose I'll have to get used to being called Madame Cardui." She closed the coin in her palm and prayed all would work out.

****

As night fell, the Bird House prepared to open.

Delaney slipped into a recently altered black dress, given to her by Gertie, and pinned back her streaked hair, arranging it to curl down the side of her face. Then she donned her butterfly mask. After mixing the colors on her board, she painted a pink rose on her cheek and petals falling down her neck and chest. She opened her mother's jewelry box and discovered a delicate set of diamond earrings and a matching necklace. She inspected her artwork in the mirror. The pink rose and falling petals weren't nearly enough to draw attention away from her features, so she mixed some green paint and painted vines and leaves on her shoulders.

Remi peeked into her chamber. "Everyone is waiting for you."

Several minutes later, she was announced. Her presence was eagerly accepted, and many rushed to greet her. She was flooded with compliments, and she needed an extra moment to adjust to all the attention. She swallowed down the unsettled turns in her stomach, and put on her best performance, reminding herself that she was not Delaney. She was Madame Cardui.

"Compliments to you!" She smiled to the surrounding crowd. "How many distinguished,

111

handsome gentlemen have come tonight?" she said, heavily accenting her words. She put her hand over her heart, her fingertips toying with her necklace, noting that the men's eyes had trailed from her face to her breasts. "We have a game we will be playing this evening just before midnight. If you are downstairs, then please, join us in the front parlor for your instructions. Until then, please help yourselves to entertainment and drinks." After searching the crowd and greeting each guest, she knew Alderic wasn't there. She told herself that was a relief, but admittedly, she was also disappointed.

"Madame Cardui, good evening." She was greeted by a man who was almost middle-aged and quite handsome. His chocolate eyes glittered as they swooped up and down her body.

"You have the advantage, *monsieur*," she said.

"Eh, *si*. I am Diego d'Raoul, a judiciary member of the local magistrate." He bowed, took her hand, and kissed it. "Would you have a drink with me?"

"Absolutely," she said with a smile.

He led her into the parlor and took two glasses from a tray, offering her one. As Delaney sipped her wine, she could feel his eyes watching her every move.

"How is it you came to be in New Orleans?" he asked.

"How do you know I haven't been here my entire life, *monsieur*?"

He gave her a winning smile. "Your accent gives you away."

"Does it?" she said sweetly.

"*Oui*, Madame, it does," came another voice, interrupting the conversation. She recognized it immediately. She turned, and there was Alderic, looking stunning in his crisp white cravat, deep red silk waistcoat, black breeches, and coat. As perfect as was every detail in his attire, his hair was carelessly tossed across his brow. She itched to brush it aside, and she wondered if it felt as silken and thick as it appeared.

He said something to her in his native tongue, but she had no idea what he'd said. He repeated it, and she panicked, as she still couldn't decipher it. She'd learned some French and spent a lot of time in Paris—but she certainly wasn't fluent in his country's language. She didn't recognize anything he was saying!

She remained cool and looked at him suspiciously. There was that playful glint in his eyes, and a satisfied smirk on his lips. He knew she didn't understand him! When she remained silent, his smirk widened into a grin, and then he turned to Diego. "Might I steal Madame away for just a moment?"

Diego looked reluctant and unhappy, but he bowed politely and excused himself.

Once they were alone, she lifted her chin, prepared to take whatever he planned on hitting her with. "Is there something you want to say to me, *Monsieur* Beaumont?" Her tone carried a slight edge because she was fuming. How dare he test her in front of her guests?

He stepped closer and leaned forward. He lowered his lips to her ear. He smelled of sandalwood and musk. His lips just brushed her neck, and her skin went into a fit of prickles. "You are not French, Madame," he whispered.

She snapped out of her trance and stepped away. "How can you insult me so, *monsieur*?" she demanded, her temper beginning to fester.

He straightened and his mouth curled as he offered

his arm, knowing too well that her refusal would cause a scene. Not desiring to draw more attention to their conversation, she took his arm, and they wandered through the parlor. A few men stopped to greet her, and she flashed them flirtatious glances. She noted he was steering her toward the parlor exit, and she glanced up at him from the corner of her eye. Though her gaze was steamy, she silently appreciated his handsome profile.

He didn't return her glare, yet offered a grin, as if he could feel her eyes and hear her thoughts.

"The Painted Lady," he mused.

"Pardon me?"

"Your name," he clarified. "Vanessa Cardui. You are named after the Painted Lady butterfly." He stopped abruptly when they entered the foyer, and then he turned to her, his grin gone. Her breath locked in her lungs as his playful expression diminished. His gaze crossed over her mask and painted face, even trailed down the length of her neck. It stopped at her low neckline and then returned to her eyes.

"Appropriately selected, but about as authentic as your accent," he said.

"You said something I did not understand and assume I am not who I say I am?" she asked, growing winded under his scrutiny.

His smile returned. "If you were French, Madame, you would have been more confident that I was not speaking the language."

She felt her face blush with embarrassment. She could deny his claim and continue to argue, but what was the point? But she wouldn't lose her fake accent. She didn't need him recognizing her true English drawl.

"Does it matter who I am, *monsieur*?" She sighed.

"If I deliver what I am selling, do you believe anyone will care?"

His gaze swept hungrily over her again. "What are you selling?"

She swallowed a lump forming in her throat, and she couldn't breathe. She was prepared for many men to assume she was for sale—she knew that was only logical—but she didn't like the idea of Alderic insinuating that he'd buy her. She certainly didn't like the excitement it stoked in her.

The clock chimed in the foyer, and the distraction helped her to find her composure. She looked at the time and calculated an hour and a half before the games in the back parlor began. She stepped back, putting more distance between them, and pasted a small smile on her face.

"There is a list of women in this house eager to accommodate you, *monsieur*," she said, silently praying he didn't take that offer. "I am *not* on the list."

His golden-green eyes swept over her, warming her instantly. "That is unfortunate, *non*? However, despite your opulent transformation, I must say the house still lacks something your competitors have."

His declaration made her ears burn and she inhaled sharply. Lifting her chin, she said with a calmness worthy of praise, "How so, *monsieur*?"

He took a step toward her and seemed comfortable stoking her temper. "Gaming tables," he replied.

She sighed inwardly. Oh, how he was correct. She wanted gaming tables...

"I did not wish to upset you. However, it is pleasing to have your undivided attention—if only for the moment," he said. "Indeed, your striking presence has captivated all the men of the Quarter, and I fear I may be struck down soon if I keep you away any longer. So let me make my point. I understand how difficult it is to obtain—and how costly it is—to offer such a luxury. I can help you."

If only he knew how he'd stolen her time and attention, since the day he kissed her on the street. She closed the last bit of space between them, looking up at him as she inquired, "How can you help me? And what would it cost me?"

He grinned, and she could see the wheels turning as he gazed down at her. She held her breath in anticipation of his response. What did Alderic Beaumont want with Madame Cardui in exchange for gaming tables and a permit? Her imagination was quickly robbing her of demeanor.

"What can you spare to make my efforts worthwhile, Madame?"

She wasn't about to be shaken by him another moment. It was clear he enjoyed the advantage too much. "Ten percent of the house winnings."

He cocked a brow and nearly scoffed. He took a step back. "I won't take less than twenty."

She nearly gasped but swiftly recovered. She placed a hand on her hip and boldly followed his backstep. "How many tables can you get me for that absurd amount?"

He thought a moment, then said, "You have not the space for more than two tables."

She chuckled. "I decide what I have space for, *monsieur*. And if you can only produce a permit and two tables, then I can't consider more than twelve percent."

He leaned in and countered, "Fifteen, madam."

She was about to jump up and down, but restrained her excitement. Alderic was giving her the one luxury she couldn't get on her own! This made her pause. She stepped back and arched her brows. "Why are you eager to assist, *monsieur*? If you think your generosity will put me on the list, then your efforts will be for naught."

Alderic released a deep laugh, and the rich rumble captured her ears. "No, Madame, I have nothing nefarious planned in exchange for my kind nature. I'm too confident in my own charm for such lowly measures."

"You're quite confident, *Monsieur* Beaumont." She smiled.

"*Absolument*," he said. "But I'll admit, I have my own reasons for wishing to see the Bird House surpass even its previous status."

"Are you at war with my competitors, *monsieur*?" she asked.

"Only one, Madame. Can you handle the heat that will come with your wild success?"

She thought a moment. "The only one I would think a worthy adversary for you would be Jack Chanfray. Is he the one from whom I will receive the most backlash?"

"*Oui*, I will not lie," he said, all humor fading from his eyes. "And it will be substantial. But I plan to protect my investment to the best of my ability. Your house is included in that promise. Are you willing to accept the challenge?"

Her gaze dropped to her wrist, where Jack Chanfray had traced the line of her glove, making an offer to deal with her if she was willing to sleep with him. The recollection of his penetrating gaze sent her skin crawling. He didn't seem like a man willing to sit back and allow her to take his business. And that was exactly what she was going to do. He'd taken away her mother's clientele, and she was determined to get them back. And then some. She looked at Alderic and was reminded of her conversation with Remi. He'd mentioned how fierce Alderic was. As was his friend, Nye Tarquin. If she was going to war with Chanfray anyway, it seemed logical to have a man like Alderic looking out for her. Although she thought it best to keep her distance from Alderic, she didn't seem to have a choice. It was her responsibility to make sure the house and those residing in it were safe. And Alderic was—according to Remi—trustworthy.

"What say you, Madame?" he asked.

"Two tables, fifteen percent," she said. "And you will offer protection against Chanfray?"

"*Oui*, you have my word," he said.

"Then he may bring all the heat he wishes, *monsieur*." She gave him another smile. "*Excusez-moi*."

She brushed past him before her legs gave out and called to the first five girls she saw. She sent them to her chamber, then signaled Remi. He acknowledged her silent gesture, and he and Rafe began tapping their wine glasses, quieting the room.

She needed to address the crowded room, but in order to do so she needed a way for everyone to see and hear her. She motioned for Rafe, and he helped her step onto a side table, carefully avoiding the array of crystalline decanters and snifters.

A hush fell over the crowd, and she avoided Alderic's gaze as he watched her from the background.

"All right, fellows," she began. "There are five birds out back just aching to be satisfied."

"Where are they? I'll satisfy them! Right now!"

Diego shouted.

She laughed, fiddling again with the diamond hanging from her neck. "Not so easily done, Diego."

He gestured his heartbreak.

"It is a game of surrender. The birds, well, they have expectations," she continued, pouting her lips slightly as she purred her following words. "They lie in bed during the day, alone and cold, just waiting to find a man to meet their expectations, to fulfill their…fantasies." Her voice had become thick, seductive, putting them under a spell as her hands strategically grazed the neckline of her gown, then barely brushed her neck. "Are there any men here who think they can fulfill them? Can you let them use your body for whatever pleases *them*?"

She saw many brows raise, as they looked at each other, and nodded.

"Splendid," she said, clapping. "The five highest bidders—minimum is listed—will be matched up with a woman begging to fulfill her secret fantasy. Who wants to play?"

Cheers erupted, and she let out a breath of relief. Remi and Rafe went around the room, collecting written bids, while she asked the nearest man to help her off the table. He was eager to lift her in his arms, but he wouldn't release her. Cheers flared again, and she was surrounded within seconds. Remi quickly broke up the gathering around her, and she slipped past the men, flashing smiles and winks. After all, it was all in good fun. Clearly, they were intrigued by her, and why not? She was hostess in a house of sex.

She made her way through the parlor and rushed to her room, where the ladies waited.

"Take off your corsets," she said and went to her

paintbox. "You have your roles, correct?"

"Yes," Billy answered. "Rafe gave them to us."

"Good. Let's hurry. We don't have a lot of time."

Within minutes, she was painting all over their bare bodies.

Fannie chuckled. "How can you blush at the mention of anything having to do with sex, but you can paint over my breasts like you're just buttering a biscuit?"

Delaney let out a laugh. "I have a lot of experience painting naked bodies on canvas," she said as she made a long brushstroke down the side of Fannie's ribs. "Why not paint on them? The human body is beautiful."

"Sex can be beautiful, too," Gertie added.

"I wouldn't know," Delaney said. "I have no experience with that."

"Well, you're doing a swell job pretending you do," Penelope said. "The men are eating up every word you say."

Delaney finished her work. "You need time to dry. Be at the staircase at midnight. When it's time to go, lace your corsets loosely, but not until just before you leave. And please try not to move too much, so you don't rub off the color."

She swiftly exited her chamber and went to her office. When she entered, Remi was there, taking payment from a gentleman for services. She recalled his name: William Bennington. He stopped in front of her and tipped his hat. "Madame Cardui," he said, bowing.

"*Monsieur*," she replied with a smile, offering her hand.

He kissed it appropriately, but he didn't release it as he said, "What a difference you have made in this place.

It's truly a pleasure."

"Will you be returning, then?" she asked.

His eyes warmed as they looked at her. "Without a doubt. Is it too presumptuous to ask Madame's price?"

She smiled. "'Tis a king's ransom, *Monsieur* Bennington."

He lifted a corner of his mouth and leaned over her hand, slowly kissing the top again. Then he lifted his head and boldly kissed her cheek.

"No doubt you are worth it." He leaned back, winked at her, and then left the office.

Once the man had gone, Remi closed the ledger. Delaney picked it up and skimmed through the list of customers so far that evening.

"Are you looking for something?" he asked.

"Eh, no. Just seeing how we're doing."

"Quite well. We have the five highest bidders."

She looked at his list of names and their bids, and then she stared at him, wide-eyed.

"I didn't think it would work," he said, chuckling, "but they're actually paying to fulfill someone else's fantasy."

She mentally calculated what they'd just made on the bids alone, and smirked. "Submission. Surrender. Sometimes allowing someone to overpower you is a fantasy in itself."

"I think you're catching onto this business too quickly, Madame Cardui."

At midnight, the bidders and many spectators gathered in the foyer. Her birds were perched along the stairs, just as she'd instructed, and she offered them a smile of pride and approval. After a small speech to the crowd, she read off the five winners of the night's bids.

After the announcement, Rafe handed out random cards with butterflies painted on them. Curiosity kept everyone there, even if they hadn't bid high enough.

She took a deep breath and paused. She glanced at Billy, who looked so lovely, and felt a pang of guilt. It struck hard. In that moment, she questioned whether she could keep up the façade as the seductress. But then, she noted Billy's wide-eyed expression. She looked panicked, and her expression urged Delaney to snap out of it. She glanced at the rest of the girls, then to Remi. They all had that same expression. Despite her own reservations, the house was depending on her, and this moment.

She thawed and found her voice. "Billy is a fierce, fiery lady who wants to rule," Delaney said with a dramatic flair of her hand as she gestured to her.

Billy stepped forward and took out two leather straps. She twisted them in her hands as she slid them up and down her inner thighs. "Who's the bidder who'll let her take control and make him beg for her to stop?"

"I'm the man!" one guy shouted out, raising his glass high.

She shook her head playfully. "You haven't a card, *monsieur*. You should have offered more."

Alderic unknowingly caught her attention, and she regretted it instantly. He didn't seem interested in the spectacle. She'd been relieved to discover he didn't even put in a bid. Instead, he was in the back corner with a couple of men, quietly discussing something over drinks. He was grinning at something someone had said, and she was struck by his comely smile. She didn't know why her gaze had sought him out. He'd done nothing to receive her attention. As she stared, his eyes caught hers for that brief second, and his laughter faded. It was replaced with something so intense, she had to drag her gaze away. "Let's find out who her bidder is—and it's not you, Diego." She chuckled.

Diego frowned and dropped his head, playfully shaming himself. His fellow men laughed and patted his shoulder in consolation.

It was Billy's moment, and Delaney noted how she embraced it. She sauntered up a couple of steps so everyone in the back could see her as she slowly unlaced her corset and opened it, revealing her breasts and an orange-and-black butterfly.

"Behold the monarch butterfly!" Delaney shouted. "Who has the monarch?"

"That's me!"

A man Delaney remembered as Walt held up his card with the monarch butterfly painted upon it. He shoved through the crowd, his paunch nearly knocking over a few younger men who were deep in their cups. He ran up to Billy and buried his face in her breasts. Billy enacted her role and started pulling him up the stairs, shouting orders at him, and cursing him for being a peasant.

"You're in for a rough night, Walt," Delaney commented, and laughter rang out.

After the crowd died down a bit, she continued. "Next is Gertie, who loves to please, and she's hungry. Very hungry." She turned to Gertie. Gertie leaned back on the railing and licked her lips. Then she untied her corset and exposed a black-and-white butterfly.

"The swallowtail," Delaney announced. All the men roared and cheered, holding up their glasses and saluting Gertie. "You can guess what she wants to do."

There was a rush of excitement, and they eagerly bowed to Gertie. Honestly, Delaney didn't understand what made them so overly roused, but she played along. Raymond, who'd gotten the swallowtail butterfly card, nearly flew over the crowd to take Gertie upstairs.

"None of you can compare!" Raymond shouted as Gertie pulled him upstairs. "I have the winning card!"

Everyone cheered.

Delaney went on to Fannie, who—after exposing her fantasy and her butterfly—was whisked up the stairs by a man named Bouchard. Then Delaney lined up both Marla and Penelope for the final reveal. A hush fell over the crowd. The last two men with cards looked at each other, shaking hands and nodding. They were both so drunk Delaney wasn't sure how they were going to accomplish anything.

She continued. "Marla's fantasy is to assist her man as he pleasures another, and Penelope's fantasy is to…well, have an audience. Are you two still willing to play?"

The men glanced at one another, sizing each other up, and then they lifted their glasses in salute to the ladies. "We're willing," they replied in unison.

Marla and Penelope opened each other's corsets and exposed colorful, spotted butterflies. The last men holding cards were Marcus and Jean. They puffed up and marched over to Penelope and Marla.

"Please, if the four of you could take that upstairs," Delaney asked, trying to avoid staring as Marla and Penelope began undressing the men.

Delaney took her leave quickly after that, without making it obvious. She called out to the birds still on the floor, and they rushed over. "Aye, madam?"

"The rest of the men will be looking for company after that arousing display," Delaney said, and the ladies stormed the parlor, ready to offer their services to the men who hadn't won the bids. Her game had been successful, and with a satisfied grin, Delaney brusquely left the foyer. She was seeking refuge in the solace of her office.

"Madame Cardui," Alderic said, halting her steps.

Delaney started at the sound of Alderic's voice but quickly recovered. She turned and slid one corner of her mouth up. "*Monsieur* Beaumont, you have my tables already?"

He laughed, and she swore she noted a slight reddening in his cheeks. She continued her pursuit, as she discovered his unease made him even more appealing. Something she hadn't thought was possible. "You did not put in a bid. Do you not like games?" she asked, then swiftly entered her office.

"No, Madame, I rarely play games," he replied, casually following her.

She raised her brows. "But your manner seems so playful, *non*?"

His smile deepened, and she had to shake off the effects of it by busying herself. She poured a snifter of brandy and held it out to him. That was when she noted he was standing directly in front of her mother's portrait. He needed only to turn around and he'd see a face resembling that of the woman he'd kissed on the street. Her heart hammered as she realized she needed to keep his attention on her and his back to her mother's portrait.

He politely took the drink, saying, "It was a clever scheme. You convinced those fools to pay extra for things the ladies would have done anyway."

"Sometimes people do not know what they want. I think they paid extra for the surprise, *monsieur*. And the attention."

She skirted around him and crossed the room.

"You are talented at selling intrigue. That is why I am confident in my investment in you," he said as he casually followed her.

"You flatter, *monsieur*," she said.

"Though you are not comfortable with it."

She nearly halted again at his statement, and mentally scrutinized all her actions that evening that would have led him to such an idea. Had anyone else noticed? To put more distance between them, she rounded the desk and relaxed in her chair. "Ah, you believe you've gone beneath the surface of who I truly am?"

He leaned his thigh on her desk and smiled down at her. "I am working on it."

"What else have you discovered, pray tell?"

"You are an artist. And educated."

Her smile faded. "*Artist* is a claim I do not believe I am qualified to receive."

He tilted his head at her. "But I am allowed to counter that. It is my opinion." He pointed to the painting on her face. "The style and use of color on your face carry the same flair as the murals on the walls. They were done by the same hand, and I think it is safe to presume it was your hand."

"You have an eye for art?" she asked.

"I have an interest," he said. "I like beautiful things. Art is amongst them. I have supported and followed many aspiring artists, known many accomplished ones, so I can feel comfortable saying you have talent. Not only a natural skill but an understanding."

"What do you mean?"

"To discover a way to brilliantly paint skin—which is uncharted territory to this degree. And you have a well-trained hand. You've been formally taught. It shows that you were an apt student."

She shifted in her plush chair, suddenly feeling stiff in it, as she remained under his gaze. "Thank you for the compliment," she said. She quickly shifted topics. "Now, why are you here?"

"Madame?"

She clarified. "This is your second night at the Bird House, and you have yet to ask for any of the ladies," she said. "Do you not seek pleasure?"

He mused over her question a moment before he asked, "Are you selling me on one of your birds...or you?"

She inhaled deeply to compose her sudden, heavy breathing. "I was trying to make a point, that you have shown no interest in hiring one of the ladies." Her discomfort increased despite his natural smile and satiny eyes. Her attention was brought back to the image of her mother behind him. Simply by turning around he could destroy all her efforts to protect her identity. She stood up and shook out the wrinkles of her gown. She left her desk and headed for the door, luring him away from the portrait with her escape. Besides, being that close to Alderic was unnerving.

Alderic swiftly reached out as she passed and grabbed her hand. He halted her stride, then he almost immediately released it. She didn't turn back to him. She remained planted in place, frozen. She felt him straighten from the desk, and take a step closer.

"My interest is not in your birds," he said, his voice low. "I think it would be obvious that my interest lies with you."

Her ears were pounding, echoing her accelerated heartbeat. She had to gain clarity. She felt her walls foundering and her cheeks scorching. Alderic wanted the illusion, he—like everyone else who attended the Bird House—was fascinated by the facade she'd created. While she considered it a triumph to have the others under her spell, deceiving Alderic wasn't so gratifying. She shook away her trailing thoughts and turned, arching her brow, to give a small smirk.

"You are not alone on that, *monsieur*," she said briskly. "But there are plenty of women who carry no mystery, simply the desire to please. I am not the one to slake your physical needs."

Her hands were shaking. She dreaded his response. Would he take one of the birds upstairs? When he straightened his coat, she held her breath. *Please don't go upstairs,* she prayed.

"Physical desires are easily satiated," he replied, cocking a confident brow. "And I am no schoolboy. I think I prefer the mystery."

She hadn't a response, but her relief and excitement knotted her insides. She was relieved that he had no interest in buying sex from her ladies. Her heart hammered when he stated he wanted her. But at the same time, she was disappointed. A part of her wanted him to walk away from the Bird House and never return. He should search for the real her. Delaney. Not Madame Vanessa Cardui. Yet she alone had made that impossible for him. When she'd had the opportunity to let him in, as Delaney, she'd run away. She'd refused him.

He lightly touched her mask. She feared he'd remove it, but she refrained from pulling away. She didn't want to. Her skin reacted to his touch as his fingers slowly slid away from her mask, and down the side of her face. Her blood was pulsing through her as he traced the rose stem painted along the column of her neck. Her body warmed at his touch, as he lowered his lips to hers. She wanted so badly to experience again what she had the first night she'd met him. His lips barely touched hers, and her lips parted slightly, invitingly.

He was about to accept the invitation when the door opened, and Remi walked in. Delaney felt her face turning every shade of red as she gaped at him.

His eyes shot from her to Alderic, then back. "Should I return later?" he asked as he crossed his arms and jutted chin. His very stance contradicted his question. He looked like he had no intention of leaving.

Alderic slowly removed his hand and her skin went cold. "I was just leaving, Remi."

"It appears as though you were," Remi snapped back.

Alderic glanced at her once more with a small smile and a gracious bow, then flashed a look at Remi. "Good evening," he said, and left the Bird House.

Once alone with Remi in the office, she cooled her burning cheeks with her hands, careful not to mess the paint. The room remained silent, and the tension thick. She avoided Remi's piercing stare.

"Oh, Delaney," he said with a sigh. "You're looking to have your heart broken, *ma chérie*."

Chapter Fifteen

The following week, Delaney immersed herself in work. The house had quickly rebuilt its reputation, and it hadn't been long before they had to start turning customers away. The ledgers were getting filled with bookings for frequent visitors. She doted on the ladies, buying them new clothes and hiring servers to distribute food and drinks. She'd even had to hire Barb and Jane more assistance in the kitchen to keep up with the influx of customers.

She'd built a reputation of her own. She was—as Alderic first called her—the Painted Lady. She was the madam no one could have. Several men had tried to remove her mask, and some tried bribing the people of the house to reveal her identity. But to reveal her identity would be foolish, and no one was lost on that. It was soon understood that anyone who reached for her mask would not only suffer dearly but never be welcomed back to the Bird House. The mystery was catapulting them into wild success.

Alderic kept to his word. Within days after he nearly kissed Madame, he had two gaming tables brought in, and his own dealers. He'd also contributed two men who remained in the house while the tables were in operation, Kit and Elijah, who kept close watch on Alderic's investment, in the guise of clients.

But Alderic hadn't returned. This was troublesome,

and it bothered her more than she cared to admit. He'd almost kissed her, and then he walked out of the house and didn't come back. The first couple of nights, she'd found herself checking the door every time guests were admitted. But it was clear he wasn't returning.

In a way, she was relieved. She pondered the idea of finding him as Delaney. He'd seen Delaney first. He'd kissed Delaney and said he wanted to do it again. Madame Cardui was only a fantasy. But then she wondered how all that would work out. Would anything ever come of it if he found out that, at night, Delaney was Madame?

When she thought too long on it, she went in circles. So she engaged in work and art to keep away her thoughts. Alderic wasn't an option for her right now, if ever. She finished painting her latest mask and observed her work. It looked like a hand of cards. She'd focused on the queen of hearts and the ace of spades. Then, inspecting the newly arrived gowns she'd ordered, she decided on a red dress with four slits starting from a black ribbon at the gown's high waist and ending at the floor. It would be worn with a sheer white petticoat that barely concealed her stockings and garters. The dress had only one sleeve, which clung to her arm all the way to the wrist, where a bit of black lace cuffed the end. Her mask matched the dress perfectly. She nodded her satisfaction, then smothered a yawn. She'd spent the day breaking up arguments between the birds over clothing and clients. She desperately wanted to paint but was low on oil, so her stock had to be reserved for Madame Cardui. Besides, her shoulders felt weighted, and she was tired. Her hand on the lid, ready to close her paintbox, she caught sight of Alderic's club coin. She picked it up and her eyes burned with longing. Longing to tell Alderic who she was. Remi broke her thoughts as he called to her about something. She refused to listen.

She grabbed her reticule and went for the door. She needed to get out of the Bird House, if only for an hour. She used a path in the courtyard out back to leave without detection, and moseyed several streets away, losing herself in thought. She'd been in New Orleans for weeks, and so much in her life had changed. Some nights, she watched the lewdness that was both captivating and frightening. Sometimes men and women engaged in acts right in front of her, and she was expected to walk by, smile, and make a light comment like it was perfectly normal. Because, for the life of a madam, it was the norm. It confused her. She'd been raised in schools that pushed morality. They'd told her there was no saving the sinful, that she'd burn in hell for desiring a man's touch, for wanting to be filled and inflamed with passion. But, night after night, she watched those at the brothel succumbing to their desires.

Of late, she'd become worldly and jaded regarding intimacy. And now she thought of Alderic Beaumont in ways that conflicted with everything she'd been taught. He'd stoked those first emotions in her, and now when she imagined her first time of being with a man, she wanted a man like him. No…she wanted *him*. She discovered her curiosity about Alderic growing by the day. And it was now that he'd abandoned her!

She wandered to the cemetery. Sighing, she sought out her mother's tomb and sat there for a long time, staring blankly at the name etched on the marker. She'd never felt so lost, so confused.

"I can't do this, Mother," she cried. She stayed a

while longer and wallowed in pity and regret. She wanted someone to tell her everything was all right. That the choices she'd made were right. That the things she wanted weren't so terrible. But everything was left unanswered. In the end, she was left staring at a name etched in cold stone. She wiped away her useless tears—they wouldn't help solve her problems at all—and stood up. She shook out the folds of her skirts, gave her mother's name one last look, and turned away.

She walked through the Quarter for most of the afternoon. She'd been there long enough to learn which streets to avoid.

"Stay away from the swamp," Remi had warned numerous times.

Delaney wasn't headed there, but she was still headed for trouble. She was going to the wharf in search of a ship, one with a very handsome captain aboard. He hadn't visited the brothel in over a week, and she wasn't sure if she'd find him on his ship, either. Perhaps he was out of town? Even if he'd chosen not to see the elusive madam, maybe he'd welcome Delaney. He'd told her he wanted her to seek him out. She'd decided to concede.

She discovered Alderic unloading goods from his ship with his crew. He wasn't as neatly attired as usual, wearing brown breeches and a simple linen shirt rolled at the elbows. He barked orders as he was tossed a series of sacks while the men beside him stacked crates. He was carrying a barrel on his shoulder when he finally noticed her. He paused, appearing almost startled. Perhaps he didn't want to see her anymore, and she grimaced at that idea. But then, as if he sensed her fears, he offered a brilliantly bright smile that stole her breath. He appeared genuinely happy to see her.

"*Mam'selle*," he called from his ship, slightly out of breath. He put down the barrel and wiped away the straying hair from his eyes. He looked like an unruly king as his hands braced the railing of his ship, and stared down at her on the dock. "I thought you had left New Orleans, or just decided it was best to stay clear of me."

"Why would I do that?" she asked.

"You must tell me. You were adamant about not letting me know how to find you."

She fixed her gaze on her wringing hands. "That was rude of me."

"Already forgiven." He smiled. "Give me one moment."

He disappeared, and as she waited, she tried to ignore all the curious eyes of his crew. It wasn't long before he was walking down the gangway. He had on fresh clothes, and his hair looked damp. She was rather impressed at how quickly he'd washed and changed.

She raised her brows as he approached her, his arms swinging rhythmically as his cane swayed from one hand. Remi had told her he'd been an aristocrat, and she didn't doubt it. He carried himself with a regal air that required no conscious effort.

"You transformed in miraculous time," she observed.

He glanced down at himself and gave a short laugh. "If such a lady seeks me out, I find making myself presentable a priority."

"Why do you assume I'm a lady, *monsieur*?"

Alderic didn't seem to be taken off guard by her question. "Do I assume incorrectly?"

She hesitated, chewing her lower lip as she considered her answer. "I don't think I meet the standard of a lady."

He cocked his head at her and grunted. "Well, then, I suppose it's a good thing I decide my standards."

She smiled at that. How she wished it were that easy! She decided not to argue the point. Instead, she held out her hand and presented the coin he'd tossed her the night of the procession. "I wanted to return this."

He made no move to take it. "It was a token, *mam'selle*. Do you wish me to believe you came out here to return my gift?"

She closed her palm, unable to reply. Her discomfort was put at ease when he released a laugh. It was rich and deep, and she supposed she was fond of his voice, too. She was glad he laughed so often. "*Mam'selle*, it is all right. You have not offended me."

His lighthearted manner was infectious, and her mood lightened—a much-needed change from the heavy emotions plaguing her.

"You've just returned from somewhere?" she asked, watching his men carry goods off the ship.

"*Oui*, I docked today. I will tell myself that you've been anxiously awaiting my return this entire time." He held out his elbow and flashed her a wink.

She chuckled and took the crook of his arm. "If that's what you wish to believe, *monsieur*."

"It is," he said as they fell into step. "Would you mind accompanying me to the coffee house?"

Somehow, she felt quite comfortable in his company. Even more so that she could be herself with him. "I think I'd enjoy that."

He turned to the men still unloading the ship. "Wil, have the last of these crates brought to the warehouse." She recognized Wil and quickly turned away.

"Aye, Cap'n."

As she and Alderic strolled down the cobblestone street, he asked, "You know more about me, *mam'selle*, than I know of you. May I ask what brought you to New Orleans?"

She conceded, for conversation's sake, as best she could. "I'm settling family business."

"Will you be leaving when you are done?"

Delaney fixed her eyes on the cobblestones in front of her. "I haven't decided."

"There is a chance you might stay then, *non*?"

"I suppose so." She met his gaze. "If I have a reason."

Alderic steered her to a small café tucked between two massive structures. A myriad of scents encompassed her, and light chatter filled the air. The small shop was so full that many customers were sitting outside.

"Afternoon, Beaumont," one man said from the far corner.

"Afternoon," Alderic replied.

She recognized the silver-haired man as Sir Gregory Madelaine, one of Fannie's regulars. Delaney had heard Fannie refer to him as "vivacious." She recalled Fannie's conversation about him and blushed. She quickly turned away, hoping her expression didn't reveal her thoughts.

They met the man behind the counter, and Alderic took the liberty of ordering. She only picked up certain words, such *as café au lait* and *beignets*. She was too distracted by the artwork hanging on the bright blue walls. "What would you prefer?" he asked her.

"Tea, please," she replied.

The man behind the counter gave her a strange look, as though almost offended. "Londoners." His tone bordered on disappointment, and he curled up his nose.

Alderic smiled. "*Non, mademoiselle*. I was asking if you wish to sit here or in the courtyard? They offer tables outside under a canopy."

"Oh," she said. "It's a little crowded in here."

He gestured toward the back door. "Then let us go into the courtyard."

Alderic guided her toward a set of wide-open glass doors, and they found a table by a small fountain. The sounds of trickling water smoothed over the sounds of the people on the street. Within moments, a young man came over with a tray that offered two cups and a small array of pastries sprinkled with sugar.

As Alderic watched her inspect the contents of her cup, he chuckled. "You have never had coffee?" he asked, raising a brow.

"I have," she said, giving him a tight smile.

"You have never had this coffee, I assure you. Sebby brews his with something quite special."

She sipped the coffee and found it savory and mild. It was sweet, not nearly as bitter as the coffee she'd had in the past. The flavor also had a nutty hint to it.

"Much better than I thought," she admitted. Then she reluctantly added, "Actually, it's quite good. What's in it?"

He shook his head. "I am not at liberty to say. Sebby would have my head on a pike if I did."

Sipping the coffee, she tried to separate the flavors in her mind, but she simply couldn't. "I believe I've found something I could enjoy more than tea," she said.

"That would be good," he ventured as he lifted his cup. "You will find asking for tea here will give you many frowns. It speaks louder than your accent."

She chuckled at that. "I'll have to remember that. Being English isn't popular here, I see."

He handed her a warm pastry doused with sugar. It was heavenly. She'd had something similar when she'd traveled to Paris, but much like the coffee, this had a unique flair. She was basking in its goodness when she noticed him grinning at her as he sat back in his chair. "*Mademoiselle*, I must ask. What brought you to my ship?"

An influx of uncertainty rushed through her, and she put her pastry down, eyes focused in front of her. "I'm not sure," she admitted.

"You are here with me, unchaperoned. Every time I have met you, you have been alone, but nothing about your manner indicates you are anything less than a woman of breeding. So I am quite confused." Delaney tapped her fingers on the fine linen tablecloth as she tried to come up with answers to his questions. She felt him assessing her another moment. "If I may be blunt, I was told you arrived at *l'hôtel* with another man, an older man. Do you belong to someone, *mam'selle*?"

"Would that matter?"

He let out a short laugh as he braced his elbow on the arm of his chair and rested his jaw on his fist. "Usually, no," he admitted, "but I believe my intentions toward you are more…sincere. I am not looking for a simple tryst. Do you understand?"

She tucked her unsteady hands on her lap. Her chest flooded with hope at his declaration. She wondered if he would look upon Madame Cardui with the same respectful intentions. "You flatter me, *monsieur*. But you don't know me."

"I have a gift with judging character." He smiled.

"But I would like to know you, Delaney. I think I would enjoy it a great deal."

Damn. Tears stung her eyes. His admission didn't make her any more inclined to tell him she ran a brothel. She endured a sinking feeling as the seconds passed. He was waiting for answers to his questions. She felt him— and any happiness she could have with him—slipping away by the second. He was looking for something genuine. Would he feel the same way if she told him the truth? What was the truth? She didn't really know. She didn't know herself anymore. Her sense of self had been destroyed the moment Remi told her about her mother.

"Delaney?"

Just the sound of her given name on his lips gave her a crushing dose of reality. She'd have to tell him and, ultimately, withstand his open rejection. He said her name again and she winced. Finally, she found the words she needed to speak. "The man I checked in with is…my lover." She was digging her grave, and her stomach twisted when she watched his expression change.

"I see," he replied after a momentary silence.

"I suppose you don't want to speak with me again," she said, miserable.

He looked away, the muscles in his jaw flexing.

"I think, a few months ago, I would not have cared," he said. "Taken or not, I would've still pursued you. My attraction to you isn't *entirely* pure, if I might be so bold."

"I don't understand."

The hand that he perched his jaw on tightened and relaxed as he spoke.

"My best friend…" He stopped to clear his throat and shifted slightly in his seat. "My best friend married about a year ago. She was and is the love of his life. Since then, I have watched the hard, hateful part of him become but a shadow."

"Isn't that what you'd want for your friend?"

"Of course. He was probably one of the most troubled souls I've ever known. Then he met her. She knew every one of his flaws…and loved him anyway. And he's a better man having let her love him—despite himself."

"And that's what you're looking for," she said, wishing he would meet her gaze. But he didn't.

"I have not much experience with being the better man, but I am trying. I suspect that whoever your lover is, he is a content man." His eyes swept over her. "I would not interfere in that."

"You're tenderhearted, *monsieur*."

He waved his hand in the air and scoffed. "I've been accused of a lot of things. Having a tender heart isn't one of them."

There was a small bout of silence, and she cursed herself fervently for lying.

"This may sound selfish, *monsieur*, but if I'm ever free to find my own happiness, I hope you've not found yours yet," she said, sadness consuming her with each word.

His gaze locked with hers, and his eyes were filled with questions—questions she didn't want to give answers to.

"Why can you not be free to find your own happiness, Delaney?"

After meeting Alderic Beaumont, she knew she'd discovered what she wanted in her life. No amount of art or education could give her what he could. Yes, they offered tenor and depth, but they didn't fill that void she felt every time she saw him. She wanted his affection, his heart.

"It's just...not possible," she said, dreading the sound of each word as it spilled from her lips.

"And still you sought me out, no?"

She didn't have an answer. What she wanted to tell him, she couldn't. Her gaze lowered to the table, and she remained silent. A long stretch of silence continued until he finally stood and held out his hand. She took it, still unable to meet his gaze. Neither spoke as they left the coffee house. The silence furthered during their walk to the end of the street.

"Farewell, *monsieur*," she said. "I'm going in the opposite direction."

He took her hand and kissed it, "*Enchantée*, Delaney."

She was making a mistake; she knew that. She regretted all the decisions she'd made since the day she arrived in New Orleans. Swallowing hard, she took her hand from his and rushed off. She could feel his gaze still on her, and she tried to keep her shoulders squared, her chin high, despite the harrowing sentiments amplifying inside.

Chapter Sixteen

Alderic reined in his horse just outside the protective stone walls surrounding the fortress. By the iron gate, he spotted Langley lounging under a shady tree. At this time two years ago, the fortress had been locked down, with men guarding every weak point of access to the manor inside. Now he could hear laughter beyond the walls, and Langley's lanky form was stretched out comfortably in the shade. Indeed, the manor was far more welcoming now.

He dropped the reins and sauntered over to Langley. Taking out his pistol, he aimed and cocked it. Upon hearing the familiar clicking sound, Langley's pale eyes shot open. His instant fearful expression was priceless. When Langley's vision cleared, and he saw it was Alderic pointing the pistol at him. Langley laughed and he jumped up from the ground. "Alderic, how are ye?"

Alderic uncocked the pistol and put it away. He took Langley's hand and swung his other arm around, slapping his friend's back in greeting.

"Some guard you are," Alderic said with a chuckle. "Where's Nye?"

"With the missus and the babe."

"Good to see you, *mon ami*."

Alderic marched past the great iron gates. Nye's property was always impressive, but he noticed a change. Where Nye had always been particular about keeping everything in order, much like the tight ship he ran, the grounds were now lush and wild. Fountains and ornamental pieces decorated the grounds, with flowers and vines draping over them.

"Alderic, it's been a while since you've come here," he heard a voice say. He turned and saw Mitch coming up, his boyish features sporting a wide grin.

Alderic stopped and shook his hand. "How are things?"

"Lazy and tranquil," Mitch said, shoving his hand through his messy locks.

"*Bien sur*, *mon ami*, the way things should be."

"Aye, but I'm ready to get into trouble," Mitch said. "We all are—'cept the cap'n. He's quite comfortable."

"But of course, you know you'd be the same if you had what he does."

"True," Mitch said. "We've been readying the ship all week. We leave in a couple of days."

"I'm sure the crew is ready to sail."

"Aye, but Nye's been a bear. Ye know the cap'n. Before he leaves, everything—"

"Has to be just right." Alderic chuckled, finishing Mitch's sentence. He remembered all too well when he'd sailed with Nye. If ever there was a man with the problem of wanting things too neat and organized, Nye was that man.

Mitch's eyes brightened suddenly. "Do ye want to come with us, Alderic? It'll be just like old times!"

"I am afraid I cannot. I have too much going on here. Where is Nye now?"

Mitch's shoulders slumped, but he pointed toward the house. "You'll find him in his office."

"*A tout à l'heure*, Mitch," Alderic said, as he headed

through the courtyard.

When he entered the manor, he immediately heard shouting coming from the office, and he looked at Annabelle, who was arranging flowers in the foyer. She tossed her hand in the air and shook her head.

"It'll be done and forgotten in two minutes," she said.

"Sarafina's temper getting the best of her?"

"She wants another fountain in the courtyard. Cap'n thinks the yard is too cluttered."

Alderic smiled. "So…they are getting another fountain."

"Of course they are," she replied with a chuckle.

Alderic shook his head and headed for the office. The door was wide open, and he leaned against the doorway, barely containing his mirth as he watched the scene playing out in front of him.

Nye sat relaxed in his chair behind the desk, a tolerant look on his face, while Sarafina was in the center of the room, her back to Alderic, with a vase in her hand. Nye glanced at Alderic, and his usual stern frown lightened slightly. But then he returned his gaze to his wife as she continued pleading her case for a new fountain.

"Don't throw that, *chérie*. You'll regret it later," Alderic said.

She spun around, and her expression instantly brightened. She put down the vase and ran to him.

"Alderic!" she shouted and wrapped her arms around him, squeezing tightly. He returned her embrace. "I wasn't going to throw it, I swear!"

"Tired of cleaning up your messes?" he asked, chuckling.

"Tired of replacing things," she corrected. "It gets expensive." She planted a kiss on his cheek. "It's good to see you, Alderic. It's been too long!"

"It has." He smiled. "However, we should stop embracing before I get a blade in my chest."

She pulled away and glanced at Nye. "Oh, Nye's been so unreasonable," she said with a scowl, though her voice held no heat. "You've not seen Mikiel in a while!" Alderic opened his mouth to speak, but she continued, and he promptly closed it. "He's grown so much—and doing so much already. He's been walking, Alderic! Let me get him. Are you staying for dinner?"

Nye came around his desk and his eyes warmed as they locked on Sarafina. "Of course he is, love. Get Mikiel while Alderic and I catch up," Nye said.

When she turned to him, she must have noted the change in his eyes and offered a small smile. "I thought you were angry with me, Captain."

The corners of his mouth lifted as he said simply, "Never."

"My fountain?" she asked.

Alderic watched his old friend wince just slightly, his warm expression somewhat strained. "We'll discuss it later?"

Sarafina didn't reply but placed a small kiss on Nye's lips before she spun on her heel and went to get Mikiel.

Alderic shook his head at the scene and chided as she reached the doorway, "I thought you were angry with him."

Sarafina snorted. "It does me no good to be angry with him. Besides, I'll get my fountain before he sails."

"You're not going?" Alderic inquired softly.

"On a ship with a baby for two weeks?" She laughed. "I think not. It's best for us to wait here."

She promptly left the office, leaving Nye and Alderic to stare after her.

Nye stood shoulder to shoulder with Alderic and asked when she was out of earshot, "You'll check in on her while I'm gone, will you not?"

"You know I will," Alderic said.

"Thank you for handling the situation with Mitch and Amadi," Nye said.

"It was not a problem," he said. "The visit to the magistrate was necessary, otherwise my warehouse would have been confiscated."

Nye's carefree nature hardened, as did his tone and the lines on his face. "Do you know who has decided to sign their own death warrant?"

"I have an idea. And I think you do, too."

"Jack has forgotten his place," Nye continued. "I'll kindly remind him."

"No need. I am taking care of it," Alderic said, giving a sly grin, as his eyes slid to Nye. "I have heard an important shipment is coming in from Barbados soon. I think it is best you are gone when he is relieved of it."

"I know the cargo in which Jack specializes." Nye inhaled and fixed the loose rolls of his linen shirt. "Jack is a self-indulging arse and his demise in long overdue."

"Justice will be visiting him soon enough." He added with a grin, "You have much going on, with your voyage and your new family, Nye. Chanfray is a small player, once the stakes are evaluated and put on the table. Allow me to take care of it."

Nye turned to face him and placed a strong hand on his shoulder. Nye's features lightened again, as did his mood. "It's good to see you, old friend."

He chuckled. "Do not think me old, Nye. I am not prepared for that."

"Have a drink." Nye marched to a side table lined with fine crystal decanters. But he didn't pour from them. Instead, he opened the cabinet door at the bottom and took out a bottle of rum. He took a slug, and then handed it to Alderic. "Let us catch up. Where've you been? It's been months since I've seen you."

Alderic took the bottle and swallowed down a good deal of it. "Your voice is growing stronger, Nye."

Nye's hand went to the scar that had long since healed across his neck. The anger Nye used to carry when his injury was mentioned was almost nonexistent now. Nye was finally healing on the inside as well as on the outside.

"Survival, Alderic. My voice has grown louder so I can talk over my wife," he said with a smirk.

Alderic laughed. "I can imagine. But you look happy." He handed the rum back to Nye.

"I am. How about you? When are you going to find a lady of your own?"

Alderic's gaze sought refuge out the window, but he couldn't suppress a throaty chuckle.

"Ah, you have?" Nye said, trying to draw Alderic's attention away from the window.

"No, *mon pote*. You and Sarafina have set a high bar."

"I don't believe your shite, Alderic. You've met someone. It's written on your face."

He shrugged. He couldn't lie to Nye. The man knew him all too well. "*Someones*, as it were," Alderic said, hardly able to believe his own words. He ran a tired hand down his face.

Nye sighed. "Then you're right. There can never be *someones*. When you meet the one, there can only be the one. You taught me that, you soppy romantic."

Alderic gave his friend a weak smile. Nye was correct that there could only be one. Why he was torn between Delaney and Madame Cardui was a mystery. He pondered it a moment and then said, "It is strange. They are alike in some ways, yet...profoundly different. I do not know either of them all that well, but they both fascinate me. However, they are both unavailable."

"Do you only target women who can't commit to you?"

He shifted his stance and tugged on his crisp cravat, curling one corner of his mouth as he imagined both women. Kissing Delaney created an instant surge within him. Barely brushing Madame's lips staggered him. "Perhaps."

"Here he is," Sarafina announced, breaking his thoughts, as she breezed into the room with Mikiel on her hip.

Alderic and Nye stood up in unison as she placed Mikiel carefully on the floor. They watched as Mikiel wobbled just a bit before he took careful steps toward his father. As he grew closer to his father, Nye knelt and held out his hands.

Slowly and unsteadily, the little boy reached him. Nye chuckled when Mikiel squealed, having been victorious in his long journey across the floor.

Alderic watched Nye take his son in his arms. He wondered if he, too, would be fortunate enough to find such happiness. Then the memory of Nye nearly losing his family struck him hard. All at the hands of Nye's own father. Because, as cruel as it sounded, they were men enacting a dangerous game of chance which had dire consequences to those around them. And Nye's father had also played that game. Their businesses had forced them to stare in the eyes of death many times. They'd fought the devil, only to trust that same devil to have their back. Nye had released Sarafina and his child to protect them from his life. But in the end, love overruled his decision.

Alderic had never known such love.

Nye was a lucky bastard.

"Want to hold him, Alderic?" Sarafina's voice caught him, finding him lost again in his own thoughts. Alderic stepped back, returning to the present. Her question struck him as he looked at the wriggling dark-haired boy. Cleverly masking his heavy thoughts, he continued in his carefree nature and light tone. "Absolutely *non*. I needn't have my silk coat soiled."

Sarafina rolled her eyes to the heavens. "I hope to witness the day you have a child of your own and your coats are ruined daily."

Alderic grinned, watching the little boy as he reached for his father's face and clasped his cheek. Nye gingerly released the boy's grip on his flesh and kissed Mikiel's hand. The little boy laughed, and Alderic noted the warm look in his best friend's eyes as he gazed at his son. It was interesting to see someone as fierce as Nye melt at the hands of a small child—much like he melted at the sight of his wife. Alderic had never envied Nye more.

"I've been handing him my dagger every day, but he hasn't lifted it yet," Nye said. "When he does, that will be the day he has his first lesson."

Sarafina gave her husband a stern look and took back Mikiel. "I think not, Captain," she scorned and marched from the room.

"Where are you going, *chérie*?" Alderic playfully called after her.

"I'm going to the kitchen to tell Ewan to prepare another plate," she said over her shoulder. "The two of you are impossible."

Alderic and Nye shared a hearty laugh and then promptly returned to their chairs and rum.

"Alderic," Nye said, his merriment sobering, "if you can figure out what it is about those two women that fascinates you so, then find those qualities in just one—who *is* available—and it'll be well worth it."

"Thank you, old friend."

Nye raised his brows. "Now I'm old, too?" He chugged down another bit of rum. "Can you do me a favor?

"What do you need?"

"Take a few of the men into the city for the night. They're driving me mad and need revelry before we sail."

"Aye, Cap'n."

Chapter Seventeen

When the sun set over New Orleans, Delaney's mood hadn't lifted in the slightest. She'd lied to Alderic so he'd give up on any intentions he had toward her. She tried to ignore her misery as she slipped on her sheer chemise, silk stockings, and garters. Then she slid on a matching sheer petticoat, its thin fabric delicately brushing over her skin. Billy made black and red streaks in Delaney's hair and then loosely pinned the curls to fall over her right shoulder and down the one sleeve on her red dress. Delaney stood in front of the mirror and secured her mask. She inspected her reflection for a bit as she assessed the deck of cards painted across her mask and envisioned how she'd match her face to the image. She dabbed one of her brushes and began painting cards on her cheek, positioning them to appear as though they were falling off the mask and down the left side of her face. She made the hearts and spades look like they were bouncing off the cards, falling onto her chest, and tumbling down her exposed arm.

When she was done, she inspected her work carefully. Then she touched up the images to make them more realistic. She'd almost mastered the technique, and puffed up proudly. Finally, she dangled diamonds from her ears.

The house was bursting at the seams. She'd spent a good amount of time booking clients and taking money.

Remi remained busy, as did Rafe. There seemed to be a different feel in the air. The crowd was rowdier. She told the servers to slow down the drinks. Remi was focusing on the gaming tables, while Rafe was making his rounds upstairs and scouring the main floor.

She stopped midstride in the foyer when Alderic came in. She'd just had coffee with him that afternoon, and there he was with three other men, laughing loudly about something indecipherable. It took Delaney about three seconds to realize they were deep in the cups. She observed Alderic, his coat flung over his shoulder, his crisp white shirt sleeves rolled up, and his face flushed. Though thoroughly intoxicated, he was still striking. "Gentlemen," she said, glancing at each of the men accompanying him, "please join us in the parlor."

Alderic's usual flirtatious and mischievous demeanor was gone. His laughter didn't reach his eyes, and she was afraid she might have something to do with his solemn mood.

One of his friends, whom he introduced as Langley, took her hand in his and kissed it. "It's a pleasure, Madame Cardui."

"You're the Painted Lady," the other man said, his boyish features brightening at the sight of her.

"How did you know, Mitch?" Langley asked, shoving his friend as he assessed the cards painted on her face.

She motioned to Fannie, who happened to be walking through the foyer.

Fannie nodded, and swayed over to them, her hand on her hip. "Follow me, fellas," she said in a low voice.

Alderic's companions followed Fannie, but he remained where he stood.

His eyes didn't meet her gaze as he straightened and slid his coat from his shoulder.

"You're not in good spirits this evening, *monsieur*," she said. She noted a distance in his eyes. A look she recognized from earlier that day. Though he maintained his casual composure, she could see past the facade. She'd hurt him. She shoved aside her guilt, knowing there was nothing she as a madam could do. She took his coat and hung it in the small room near the front door.

"I suppose I'm not," he admitted, and offered his arm.

Her fingers curled around his elbow, and he led her into the parlor. "Well, if ever a place returned men to their blithe state, it's the Bird House," she said in a light, airy tone.

They were just crossing the doorway when he stopped.

She lifted her gaze and regretted it immediately, for his stare unnerved her. "Is something the matter, *monsieur*?"

"When will you go on that list, Madame?" he asked.

She steadied her breathing as best she could, torn between being furious and being mesmerized. "I-I'll never be on the list, *monsieur*."

He was quite drunk, and she didn't need him throwing her off balance any more than he already did. As much as it bothered her to do so—even fearing he might actually choose one of the birds to go upstairs with—she motioned for Billy. She decided it was best to stay away from him tonight. She gave Billy the honor of accompanying him into the parlor.

She curtsied and strode away, making her way to the safety of the crowd. As always, she spent another hour flirting and chatting. She assisted several men in playing cards, and she made several trips to her office as others enjoyed the accommodations upstairs. The house was busy. As word spread, and trust began to grow amongst those attending the house, even women were coming to gamble and drink heartily. Many of them wore masks, and their names were never used. Delaney was adamant about discretion and made it clear that this was the rule for all who wished to play in the Bird House. And she discovered that women enjoyed the games as much as the men did.

Later that evening, a group of men and women were drinking and lounging on the sofas in the back parlor, discussing a wide range of topics. The conversation had shifted to art. "I prefer the more rational approach to art, like Canova's sculptures," Diego said.

"Ah, yes," Raymond agreed. "Like the Romans, take charge and own our destiny!"

"*Touché, monsieur,*" another man, Bouchard, chimed in. "But the light and content side of life, as in Watteau's work, is so much more elegant."

"What about you, Madame?" Diego looked at Delaney. "You obviously enjoy the arts."

She looked the part of the seductress as she lounged in an overstuffed blue brocade chair, the slit of her red dress exposing her entire leg as it hung over the armrest. She twirled her hair around her finger, not fully immersed in the discussion. Mentally, she was sitting in a café with Alderic when they called on her. She snapped out of her daydream and accepted the reality. That Alderic was in the far corner, with Marla perched on his lap, Marla giggling at something he'd said. And the gentlemen surrounding her were anxiously awaiting her opinion.

"Madame, which do you prefer?" Bouchard urged.

Luckily, she'd listened enough to form a response. "It's hardly fair to ask me to choose between a painter and a sculptor. I can appreciate both," she replied.

"Will you paint for us tonight, Madame?" Bouchard asked over the rim of his glass.

She looked at him from under lowered lids and offered him a coy smile. "I haven't any canvas, *monsieur*."

"Can you not make anything into a canvas?" Alderic asked.

Her eyes shot to him. When had he started listening in on the conversation?

"Your own skin is proof of that." He smirked, gesturing to the elaborate display on her body.

Diego quickly removed Penelope from his lap where she'd been relaxing. She squealed as he began untying her corset. Delaney eyed Remi. He was watching Diego closely, waiting for Penelope to signal that she was fine. Only then would either of them relax.

She did, just as Diego chuckled. "This lovely skin makes the perfect canvas."

Delaney barely heard him when her eyes locked with Alderic. He was in a rare mood that evening, and she didn't appreciate the smug way he was looking at her. He was challenging her—for what reason, she wasn't sure. She tilted her head, lifted her chin proudly, and said, "Rafe, would you be so kind as to get my paintbox?"

Rafe nodded and disappeared from the parlor.

"Penelope and Marla, do you wish to assist me in a game?" she asked.

They both nodded.

There was an eruption of inspired energy in the room, and soon guests from both parlors started gathering. She whispered her plan to Marla and Penelope, and they eagerly agreed to play, along with two of the other girls.

Rafe came in with her supplies, and she quickly mixed up several colors. Upon her signal, Marla untied her corset, and Delaney dipped her brush in red paint.

"The first one to guess the painting gets the girl," she announced. "And I will cover half your fee."

One of the women who'd accompanied Bouchard leaned forward. "*Anyone* who guesses the painting?"

"*Anyone*, madam," Delaney stressed.

She'd made a mere two strokes before guests started shouting out random answers. It took several guesses until someone said, "Cupid and Psyche!"

She stopped painting mid-stroke. "Diego, she's all yours."

"I'm going to be covered in paint tonight," he said as he lifted Penelope over his shoulder.

Delaney could hear Penelope's laughter as they disappeared up the stairs. Then she went down the line, painting each girl until someone guessed correctly. Finally, every girl had been whisked away upstairs, and the game was over. She curtsied, and the servers came around with drinks for those who remained downstairs. Normally, while she'd get loud applause and praise, tonight had been different. The energy in the room had become tense, heavy.

She heard several grumbles until someone shouted out, "What about you, Madame?"

"*Oui*, when will we win a night with you?"

Bouchard asked.

Delaney was grateful for all the paint on her face, because she was sure she'd just grown pale. Laughing nervously, she racked her brain for a clever reply to placate them. Tension was building in the parlor, so much so that Remi and Rafe came in from the other rooms. They watched carefully as the guests ranted over her unwillingness to be bought.

"Come now, at least a kiss?" Bouchard asked.

"A token, perhaps?" the woman with Bouchard asked.

"Something! Anything, Madame Cardui!" another shouted.

She remained cool as she said lightly, "All my girls are upstairs. I can't very well paint the front of my own body."

Her guests weren't satisfied with her response. She could see the concern growing on Remi's and Rafe's faces. She had to concede. "Very well, then. One more painting, for a token and a kiss."

The good mood returned quickly, and she released a long breath. Remi and Rafe relaxed as well.

"All right, who am I painting on?" she asked.

A hush blanketed the room. Everyone stared at one another, and she laughed. "Truly, you were so excited! Is no one willing to strip themselves and allow me to paint them?"

"I will."

Her next statement was going to be clever and amused, but the voice that had spoken up was one she knew well, and her witty words caught in her throat. Her eyes darted to the corner of the room and she watched Alderic slowly stand up. His eyes held hers and she couldn't breathe. As he casually weaved through the crowd, she remained silent.

Chapter Eighteen

"Beaumont, you braggart, I was going to volunteer!" Bouchard sneered.

Alderic didn't release his hold on her gaze as he chuckled, his fingers already releasing the buttons of his waistcoat. "You hesitated, Bouchard," he said.

Her mind raced as she tore away from the image of him undressing and mixed more paint. She needed a minute. Her hands were shaking so badly she wasn't sure she could make one decent line. And she couldn't even think of what to paint. The only thing she could think about was that he was unbuttoning his shirt. She'd be a liar if she said she hadn't imagined what he looked like underneath his clothing.

From the corner of her eye, she noted him peeling away his shirt. She wasn't prepared for her own reaction. His wide shoulders and smooth chest were sculpted. His abdomen was flat and strong, and his breeches were sitting far too low on his narrow waist. His skin was deeply tanned from years on a ship, and his arms were...

"Alderic, did you have to show us up?" one paunchy man said with a chuckle from his chair.

He was being taunted by the men around him, but he didn't seem to be paying any mind. She was thoroughly shaken, and she suspected he knew it. When she finished mixing her paint, she straightened and leveled her stare, despite the panic barreling through her.

He spread his corded arms. "Your canvas, Madame."

Laughter, teasing comments, and several whistles echoed in the parlor.

She cleared her throat. "Indeed," she said tersely. She centered on his chest and abdomen and tried to focus on her approach.

The smirk on his face told her he was enjoying her discomfort far too much, and she wanted to curse him. He'd volunteered only to shake her, and it had worked. But he wasn't without feeling. Could she not faze him, too? She most certainly could! A sense of power made one corner of her mouth tip as she closed the distance between them and steadied her gaze.

For dramatic flair, she slowly circled him and openly assessed him, subjecting him to snickers from the spectators. She took the end of the brush, dipped it in the black paint, and held it tauntingly against his chest. "This may be cold," she warned, as she made her first stroke on the right side of his chest. She noticed a terrible scar on his side that looked like a bullet wound. It was a staunch reminder of the man standing before her. A man not to be trifled with. But trifle she did! He didn't jolt outright when she brushed over his skin, but he tensed. His chest muscles flexed ever so slightly from her touch. She began painting, and the spectators again shouted out guesses after only a few strokes. She painted a woman's body with an exaggerated hip pose, a thin chiton clinging tightly to her body and the draping folds of her cloak hanging between her legs.

"It's an angel!" a woman shouted.

"A headless angel?" another person countered.

"Well, it doesn't have wings, either."

"Maybe she just hasn't gotten to them yet," the paunchy man argued.

"It doesn't matter," sighed Bouchard. "You have to know what angel it is."

As the brush stroked down the side of Alderic's waist to the line of his breeches, she noticed his body shiver and his skin prickle. She looked up and could see he was staring intently at her, all too aware of how the strokes of her brush were affecting him.

"Come on, it's a sculpture," Bouchard said, breaking their silent hold on each other's attention.

"What is the token the winner gets with your kiss?" Alderic asked. His voice was low, thick, and strangely intimate.

"Yes, what is the token, Madame?" the woman with Bouchard asked.

She thought a moment, then answered, "My garter." That earned a resounding cheer. She was almost finished painting the curvy woman on his bare body, and no one had guessed the sculpture. She chuckled, then flashed her guests a wicked grin. "I'm nearly done. Will no one win my kiss?" Several more guesses were thrown out, but she only shook her head, chuckling. She would maintain her untouchable reputation, she was certain.

"It's Aphrodite." Her brush ceased mid-stroke on Alderic's torso and she stared up at him.

"Y-You sound so sure," she said.

His voice was quiet, but it seared her ears. "There is a seashell at her feet, a dove upon her shoulder. There is no doubt she is Aphrodite, the unattainable goddess of beauty and sexual pleasure."

"What did he say?" the woman asked, leaning forward.

"Did he get it?" Bouchard asked.

The paunchy man in the chair threw up his hands and let out an annoyed sigh.

She felt her mouth go dry as she looked up at Alderic. "You're correct, *monsieur*."

There was a wash of groans and moans when they realized they'd lost the game and wouldn't get Madame's kiss. A few of them moved on to the front parlor to gamble. The rest started chanting, "Kiss, kiss, kiss!"

She could feel everyone's eyes on her, but she was captured in Alderic's gaze as he knelt on one knee. She tried not to look so startled when he clasped her ankle and propped her foot on his knee. She wasn't sure how she remained standing. The backdrop of the spectators' cheers and heckles was drowned out as his hand slipped underneath her sheer petticoat. His fingers gently trailed up the length of her leg, sending shivers all through her, until he reached her garter. Her legs were shaking, and her knees weakened as he entwined his fingers around the lace and glided the garment down her leg.

"Kiss her!" was shouted several more times.

She was no longer pale as he stood up. The exact opposite, for the blood was coursing through her and her flesh was burning as she anticipated his kiss. To her astonishment, he took her hand instead, and his lips brushed the inside of her wrist.

"That's all you have, Alderic?" Bouchard snickered. "Madame, let me do your beauty justice and give you a real kiss!" A wave of chuckles sounded throughout the room.

Her confusion must've been noted, and Alderic leaned in, his mouth brushing her ear. His words sent her skin tingling again. "If Madame agrees, I prefer to collect my winning another time."

She stared up at him, wide-eyed, until someone tossed him his shirt. "Cover yourself, Alderic. You're making the rest of us look deficient."

Alderic didn't break his stare until she nodded. When he stepped back, the space between them still scorched her chest as she watched him slip on his shirt and flash her one last, devilish grin before he left the parlor. A moment or so went by, and as it appeared the fun was over, the crowd dispersed. As everyone returned to their drinks and gambling, Delaney had time to recover. She commended herself for not collapsing, considering her mind was racing hysterically and her body was in a fit of emotions.

Remi startled her, saying over her shoulder, "Is everything all right, Madame Cardui?"

She watched Alderic disappear and she nervously chewed her lip, acknowledging Remi with a curt nod.

****

As the clock chimed the early hours of the morning, the Bird House began to quiet down. They were beginning to wrap up the night. Remi was checking in on the birds, and Rafe was escorting out many of the guests. Delaney helped the servers clean up the empty snifters and wine glasses sitting upon mantels and tables. She stepped over a few articles of clothing and headed for her chamber door. She wasn't touching those. The house had cleared out, and she wanted to remove her mask and paint before she went to the office. She pulled out a key from her bodice and unlocked her chamber door. Safely in her room, she covered a wide yawn. She'd almost removed her mask when she discovered someone stretched out on her bed, and she gasped.

Alderic was perched on her pillow, one arm resting behind his head and the other holding a piece of parchment. His shirt was open, exposing Aphrodite on his chest and abdomen.

"What are you doing in here?" she demanded, her glare shooting to the letter in his hand.

"Reading," he said. He swung his legs off her bed and stood up in one swift motion, dangling the piece of parchment in his hand.

"Th-this door was locked."

"No lock can keep me out of something I wish to explore, Madame," he replied.

"Why do you wish to explore my chamber?"

"I'm a curious individual."

He leaned against her vanity, and she realized the parchment in his hand was a letter her mother had written. Although she wasn't sure what information the letter revealed, one thing was a relief: her mother never addressed her by her name. She always called her *ma petite*.

"You are Birdie Harper's daughter," he ventured as he scanned the letter. "Who would have thought Birdie had a daughter... Where have you been all these years?"

His gaze held hers, and she lifted her chin at him. She didn't need Alderic nosing around her room. She reached for the parchment, but he swiftly moved it away. She planted her hand on her hip and drummed her fingers.

"You are out of character this evening, *monsieur*," she said. "Has something gone wrong with your personal life that you wish to unleash here?"

His eyes hardened, and he frowned as he tossed her

mother's letter onto the vanity. "The term *personal* implies that it would be private and not your business," he replied.

She raised her brows and braced her hand on the vanity. "So is my chamber."

"Hm, that is true." His golden gaze swept over her before moving to the contents on her vanity. He picked up a jar of thick white mush, sniffed it, and cringed. "Grease." He shot her a confused look.

She laughed at his twisted expression. "It removes paint quite well, though it requires a thorough washing afterward."

"Should I use this for my chest?" he asked, a smile tugging his perfectly curved lips.

"It would make the process easier," she replied. "Steal some from your cook."

He examined the intricate painting of cards down the side of her body, all the way down her arm.

"Why the shroud, Madame? Are you covering a terrible wart of some sort? Scars from the pox, perhaps?"

She grinned. "Maybe."

"Or maybe you know what an arousing enigma it makes you?"

"That is not it, *monsieur*."

He used both his hands to flank her, trapping her between his body and the vanity. He paused another moment and she swore he was listening to her heart slamming against her chest. Her blood was pumping loudly in her ears, and the room was growing warmer by the second.

"You are intelligent and shrewd," Alderic said. "I would guess you have been at school a good part of your life."

"I commend you. You are perceptive."

"Not really, Madame. It is suggested in the letter." He chuckled and cocked his head at her. "Were you aware how your mother paid for your education?"

"Why do you ask?"

"Well, she sent you away. In the letter, she made many points contrary to her lifestyle."

"Does it matter?"

"I would think it mattered to you and your mother," he ventured. "I do not have children, but I would assume that as a parent, I would not purchase an expensive education so my child could enter the life of prostitution. I would want my child to rise above that from which she came. Unless, your education was not traditional, and you were being groomed to take over this business. Tell me, when did you take your first lesson in the art of seduction?"

His assumption stung. "You are prying, *monsieur*," she said. "I do not think you would appreciate it if I became so inquisitive of your private life. I wish you to leave now."

He pushed away from the vanity and straightened to his full height. He was so close she was forced to look up at him. "I can do that, Madame," he said, the corner of his mouth upturning just a bit, "as soon as I collect my winnings."

She paused, thinking that holding her breath would keep her chest from heaving. But it only made it more difficult to appear unmoved as his hand lightly grazed the line of her jaw. His thumb fiddled with the diamond dangling from her ear.

"Why did you not collect your kiss earlier? That would have been far more appropriate," she said.

He chuckled. "You speak of propriety in a bordello?"

"More the reason for you to have taken your kiss for all to see," she said, her tone becoming heated.

"I suppose it would have been quite the spectacle. One I would have been comfortable with." He tilted his head at her when he added, "But not you."

Delaney creased her brow. "*Monsieur*?"

"You were shaking," he said. "You are frightened of me, Madame."

"You are a man, *Monsieur* Beaumont." Delaney scoffed. "I have known many men. You are no different. I have no reason to fear you."

His eyes searched hers for a long moment. "You are only playing, Madame," he said, his tone low as his eyes captured hers. "What is underneath all that color, I wonder."

She didn't respond. She couldn't. Her lips parted to finally breathe as she watched him, mesmerized, until his head sank to hers, his mouth capturing hers. She was instantly entranced with a sense of irresistible sensations. Her soft breath encouraged him to further his advance and slide his tongue past her lips. He tasted of wine, like the first time he'd kissed her on the street. But this time, their kiss wasn't rushed or playful. His head slanted and his hand laced through her hair, tipping back her head so he could more deeply and thoroughly penetrate her mouth. This kiss far surpassed the kiss he'd given Delaney, and she welcomed it. She clasped the folds of his shirt and drew him closer. With Madame Cardui, there seemed no barrier. And strangely, she didn't want him to be concerned about crossing lines but to treat her as a woman, willing and experienced.

And he did just that. He gripped her waist and held her against his hard body before sliding his hand beneath the slit of her gown. He glided over the sheer material of her petticoat and down the curve of her backside, grabbing her inner thigh, and she instantly gripped his neck and pulled herself up to smother any sliver of space between them. He groaned in her mouth and pushed her against the wall beside the vanity as his kiss became fiercer, more demanding. His body was solid, and having him pressed against her created a sense of urgency that was overpowering. She kissed him back with fervor.

He slid up her skirts, then dipped his body. Her mouth followed, unwilling to break their kiss as he sank lower to cup the back of her knees and swiftly straighten, lifting her high, and supporting her with his waist as he pressed himself hard against her. The center of her burned. She could feel him between her thighs, and she ached.

Was this what the rest of the girls in the house raved about? It was torture! She wanted so badly for him to end the torment building inside her. She was craving it, begging for it! So much that she wasn't prepared for the loud knock on her door. At first, she thought the sound was just her heart pounding in her ears.

It was Remi. "Madame? Madame, are you all right?"

They broke their kiss as Remi's sobering voice sounded through the door. Her breathing was as rapid as his. His smoky-green eyes clung to hers.

"Y-yes, I'm fine!" Did she use her accent? God, she couldn't tell; her brain was scattered.

"I need you in the office," he said.

Accent, accent, damn it! "Ah, *oui*. I-I will be there

momentarily."

She heard Remi walk away from the door. Alderic's lips found her neck, and she felt herself melting between him and the wall again.

"*Monsieur*, please," she said, pushing him away. Her body hated doing what was right just then, and consequently, she hated Remi at the moment.

Alderic took his time drawing away, and slowly set her down. She had a strong desire to yank him back. His eyes were dark and smoldering with lust, and his mouth was swollen from their kisses. He was a sight to be seen. "Whatever your price, Madame, I will pay it," he said, his tone desperate with need.

She felt her insides crumble, and reality hit her like a slap on her cheek, jarring her back to reality. She could feel the dried paint on her skin; no longer did it burn from his touch. Closing her eyes briefly, she blinked back her misery. Oh, how she wanted him without him thinking she was a madam. Oh, how she wanted to cry at that moment.

"You have collected your winnings, *monsieur*," she said, her voice unsteady. "You may leave now."

She watched his gaze harden and his frown increase as he stepped back. "I will return, Madame," he vowed.

She'd gathered only a second's strength, but it was enough to walk away from him and rush out of her room.

Chapter Nineteen

She was in the office until the first light of day came over the horizon. The clock in the foyer chimed as she put down her quill and went to her chamber. She looked at her vanity, where her mother's letter lay. Her eyes drifted to where Alderic had kissed her until she thought she'd burn from the inside out. She let out a long, unsteady breath and began pinning up all her hair so she could remove her paint. In the far corner was a tub full of water, long since grown cold. It had become routine, every night, to have her tub filled so she could wash away all the paint from her body. But after what had happened between her and Alderic, she'd remained in her office for hours instead.

Alderic had promised to return. Did he mean tonight? Tomorrow? She didn't know, but he meant it. What they'd started wasn't over. She shook off the image of him kissing her again and tore off her clothing. Perhaps a cold bath was a good idea. She washed up quickly and climbed into bed. She slept late, well past noon, and was grateful for it. When she woke, she lay in the oversized bed a long while, sorting through all her thoughts, before she finally dragged herself from it and began dressing. She slipped into a simple muslin gown and left her hair loose.

"Madame," Rafe called from the outside her door.

She opened the door. "Yes?"

"You might want to put on one of your masks. Someone is here to talk to you."

"Who is it?"

"Jack Chanfray."

"I'll be right there."

She pinned on a simple white mask that scooped low down the sides of her face and marched to her office. Jack Chanfray was seated on the settee, sipping a glass of brandy. When he saw her enter, he put down the glass and stood up.

"Madame, it's a pleasure," he greeted.

She offered a crisp reply as she came around her desk. "I doubt it. However, if you're sincere, I assure you, the pleasure is yours."

"Admittedly, I deserve that," he said as he casually found the chair opposite her desk and flashed her a brilliant smile, his smooth, languid movements ever meant to entice. The advantage of being the madam was that she was learning about people and their ways of seduction. She was growing immune to them. Well, to all except one…and that "one" was *not* Jack Chanfray. "What can I help you with, *Monsieur* Chanfray?"

"I'm impressed at how you turned this place around in such little time," he said. "Maybe I was hasty. We should've talked further about the price of this place."

"As I recall, *monsieur*, you wanted to discuss it further…in your bedchamber."

He gave a sly chuckle. "I do apologize, madam. That was callous. We're in the same business. We shouldn't be competing or scheming against one another."

"Are we competing? Oh, yes, I suppose we are. Since I've taken several of your most elite clients." She smirked. "Not bad for a house full of gutter whores, don't you think?"

His impression shifted from dashingly charming to dangerously dark.

"Your success won't last long, madam. Your enigmatic games will only be tolerated for so long. Eventually, they'll be expecting your unmasking. Then what will you have?"

"That remains to be seen, *monsieur*," she replied coolly.

"I thought on your price and find that you've done much to improve this place and increase its value. I'd like to reconsider buying it from you."

"The only problem with that, *Monsieur* Chanfray, is that I no longer wish to sell it to you."

"Why not?" he said with an edge to his voice.

"That's the benefit of being the owner of this establishment," she countered, her tone airy, yet carrying a glacial tone. "I can change my mind anytime I wish. And I don't have to explain my reasons."

He flew from his chair. "Do you really wish to compete with me, Madame? I own the entertainment in this city. You'll lose, profoundly."

She remained seated despite his threatening tone and continued calmly. "I think you'll find that I'm not in a position to lose anything. I've become exceedingly popular and intriguing. None of your scheming can account for the things you lack…and I have."

He leaned over the desk, his white-knuckled fists braced on its surface. "You're a haughty bitch, madam. I have a mind to find out who you are and expose you as nothing but a scared little mouse hiding behind a mask, teasing men's cocks for coin!"

She refused to be intimidated by the likes of

Chanfray. "I'm a whore, *monsieur*, just as you are. Are we not both teasing men's cocks for a bit of coin?" She held her breath, waiting to see if he was going to try to throttle her. He certainly looked like he wanted to.

He slammed his fist on the desktop and growled, "Who are you? Remove your mask!" His eyes pierced into hers, the growl in his voice contradicting the smooth gentleman he portrayed to the rest of the world. His bark truly was intimidating, but she kept her mouth clamped shut, her fingers laced comfortably on her desk. She was relieved when Remi and Rafe entered the office and stood behind her. He snickered as he observed them. "Do you think these two can stop the likes of a man with my connections?"

"They may not, but we can."

She then watched as Alderic's men, Elijah and Kit, strode into the room and stood on each side of Chanfray. He straightened and took a step back. It was obvious he recognized them. His rage swelled to new heights. He peered back at her. "Beaumont? That's who is backing you?"

When she remained silent still, he belted a sinister laugh. "Oh, *ma chérie*, you've no idea the contractor you've lost your soul to. And it will be a failed deal, for men like Beaumont are out for their own gains. Once had, you'll be nothing more than an expired whore living out her pathetic existence in the swamps!"

Regardless of who spewed the words, they still stung, and she inhaled sharply, though she remained quiet, her hands neatly folded.

She looked to Alderic's men and said, "Please escort *Monsieur* Chanfray out of the Bird House."

"Absolutely, Madame," they said in unison.

Chanfray's eyes were like blades, ready to slice through her. "No need for an escort," he snarled. "I can remove myself." Chanfray stormed from the office, and within moments the room was cleared. Once alone, she rushed to the window and watched him climb into his coach. It jolted forward and started down the street.

Remi promptly returned to the office and shut the door. "Are you all right, Delaney?" he asked.

"I have to find a new owner for the Bird House, Remi."

"Don't let Chanfray intimidate you. He's losing business and looking to lash out."

She chewed her lip as she watched the now-empty street outside her window. "He was right about one thing."

"What's that?"

"I am a scared mouse," she said. Then she recalled Alderic's words: "…playing madam. This will last only so long."

"What do you plan to do?"

"The show will go on," she said, arching her brows, "until it doesn't."

****

The front parlor was being completely redone, with white linen hung on the walls and all the furniture moved to one side of the room.

Gertie and Billy marched in while Delaney was painting a papered fan.

"Delaney, what's this?" Gertie asked, holding out a long, silken robe-like garment.

"It's your costume. Inspired by your own interest in the *onna-kabuki*. It's altered a little from an authentic *kabuki* costume, but it'll work. It was the best I could do."

"We've been practicing that performance all week. It's not easy, Delaney," Billy said.

"Nothing worthy of such a high price ever is." Delaney chuckled as she blew on the fan, drying the paint. Six birds would be performing, while the rest would remain on the floor for men looking to partake of their usual services. But if they wanted to purchase an *onna*, then they would have to pay a little more. "We can practice it one more time."

When evening fell, the Bird House was lit up and bustling like every other night since she'd been open. But the nights were growing louder and a little more crowded as word spread that the Painted Lady always had some sort of special performance or intrigue. She greeted her clients and guests as she always did. After a couple of hours, she and the girls snuck to her room so she could paint their faces. She started by making their faces white. Then she took a brush dipped in red and painted a curved line that extended from the inner corners of their eyes to the hairline, stopping at a point just above the temples. She tried to remember from her travels the images she'd seen in a museum where her professor had explained the history of the *kabuki* performers, which had been told by a captain who worked for the East India Company. The captain had relayed the Japanese culture in detail and brought back cherry trees that had been replanted and were growing in abundance at the museum gardens. He'd also explained about the concubines of the *kabuki* in Kyoto, but he'd said their performances had been taken over by men since the *onna* performers had been banned for instigating "poor morality." She shook her head at that. She stood back and admired her work.

"You look beautiful," she said and handed them each a fan. "Are you ready?"

She'd hired a few performers who played music similar to that performed during the *kabuki*. When she signaled, the music started, and the patrons found their seats.

The girls took the center of the room as their stage. Their painted faces hushed the crowd, as did their beautiful attire. She'd done her best to capture the spirit of the real *onna-kabuki*. Toward the end of their performance, she herself joined them in a white-and-red gown. Her mask was black, her face painted white and red.

Just as she took center stage, Alderic walked into the parlor with his quartermaster, Wil. Alderic was dressed severely in black, with only his starched cravat and crisp white shirt breaking the darkness of his suit. She couldn't allow herself to be distracted by him.

She opened her paper fan with a snap and shifted her focus to the performance. She elegantly moved her long skirt aside to reveal her stockinged leg. This caused a stir in the guests, and she moved her exposed leg seductively from back to front. She posed, stopped to flip her fan in the air, and then winked playfully at her audience when she caught it. She walked forward gracefully, slid her other foot from front to back, stopped, and posed again. The women behind her followed.

The music sped up, and the girls quickened their steps, dancing seductively, using their fans as tools to flirt with the audience. On cue, Remi walked by, and men flagged him down to purchase the performers. By the time the dance had ended, all the birds were spoken for, and the men flooded the stage to collect their ladies for the night. Delaney quietly commended herself and the birds for another successful performance. Triumphantly snapping her fan closed, she walked off the stage—and nearly ran into Alderic.

"You are not claimed yet, Madame," Alderic said, his assessing eyes caressing hers. When his warm gaze focused on her lips, she couldn't deny his effect on her. She took a deep breath, snapped her fan open, held it over the bottom half of her face, and gave him a mischievous stare. "How many times must I remind you that I'm not to be claimed, *monsieur*?"

He gave her a winning smile, and at that moment, he looked almost boyish. "If you were?"

"*None* could afford me."

"If I cannot buy you, then I will be inclined to seduce you instead," he said teasingly. But something told her it was no jest.

"You can have any other woman in this room, and something tells me they would do it at no charge." She leveled her stare at him, attempting to not be shaken by the memory of his lips on hers, his hands caressing her. It was agonizing not to succumb. "Why must you pursue me?"

"Because you are the only woman in this room I cannot have."

"*Euh*, you like a challenge," she said dryly. "Men always seek that which is not to be had."

"I think you only wish to defy that which is ultimately unchangeable," he replied, taking a glass of wine from a server walking by.

She let out a short laugh. "You are rather confident, *monsieur*."

He took a sip of the wine, his eyes stealing a glance

over the rim of his glass.

"Do not be fooled by my generosity in indulging you your winnings last night. You will be disappointed," she added.

"Your generosity," he mused. "Perhaps we remember things differently."

Wil approached them. His eyes were glossed over from too much drink, and he nearly stumbled into Alderic as his gaze diligently raked over her, lingering over her exposed leg.

"Painted Lady," he slurred. He attempted to bow but almost lost his balance again.

"Wil, I think you should find a seat," Alderic said, steadying him.

"I'm looking for Billy," Wil said.

Delaney glanced at the clock on the mantel.

"I am so sorry," Delaney said, leaning into Wil, who was unprepared for the drop in her voice and how she played with his loosely tied cravat. "She will be occupied for a while."

He let out a disappointed sigh, and she leaned in closer.

"But Marla is over there," she said, and then she whispered in his ear, "She would love to bring you upstairs. You are just the sort she desires."

"Truly?" Wil asked, his eyes wide pools of hope.

Her voice lowered another shade. "*Oui, monsieur.* Come with me, and I will give you some tips on what she just adores. What drives her simply mindless."

"*O-Oui*, aye, let's go," he said, bobbing his head.

She chuckled softly, took his elbow, and brought him to Marla, who was resting her scantily clad bum on the local magistrate's lap.

Marla was happy to have an excuse to dump the magistrate and take on young Wil. She flashed Delaney a grateful look. Nodding to Marla, Delaney turned her attention back to Alderic. He was engaged in conversation with Diego.

Diego's expression brightened upon seeing her, and he placed a kiss on her cheek in greeting.

"What are you discussing?" she asked.

"Business," Diego said. "Alderic acquires Bourgogne wine, and I simply can't seem to get in touch with him fast enough to secure an order."

Alderic sipped his wine. "It is in high demand."

"I thought French wine was banned in Nouvelle Orleans."

Alderic and Diego shared a look.

"That is accurate," Diego said evenly.

"Then you are a smuggler, *Monsieur* Beaumont," she said, cocking her brow.

Alderic only grinned, but Diego sighed and stepped forward. "That is such a derogatory term, Madame."

"What else do you acquire, *monsieur*?" she asked.

"What are you looking for?" Alderic asked.

"Oil," she replied, "particularly poppyseed."

"For your paint," he commented.

"*Oui*. It gets expensive."

Boldly sliding his gaze over her face, then down her neck and shoulders, he said, "I can imagine it does."

A series of shouts rang out over the crowd, breaking their conversation. All other conversations ceased, and everyone's attention turned to a heated confrontation building in the foyer. The argument quickly escalated into a scuffle. Within seconds, Remi and Rafe were pulling them apart, but not before Gertie was thrown back by one of the men. Suddenly, two more men joined in the fight, grabbing Remi and Rafe. Then Elijah and Kit left the tables and another few more men joined in. It was as though fighting had become something contagious. As Remi and Rafe struggled to contain all the men, Alderic mumbled a curse, handed her his wine, and he and Diego went to their aid. The disturbance was quickly turning into a brawl.

She watched Alderic block the blow from a man who'd just swung at Rafe. He grabbed the man's fist, twisted his arm, and threw him to the ground. Another man came after him, but he dodged the punch and swung his fist into the man's gut. The man crumpled to the ground.

The brawl grew within seconds, and somehow she was shoved into the center of it. She dropped Alderic's glass of wine, then lost her footing on her train and stumbled into the server. The tray of wine splashed the front of her gown.

"Blast it!" she shouted. Before she knew it, three men with handkerchiefs were dabbing the front of her gown and her chest. "I'm all right, thank you," she said tersely, brushing their hands off her bosom. She stormed out of the parlor just as Alderic, Rafe, and Remi tossed several men out of the house. As she headed for her chamber, she looked at her ruined dress and groaned. She slammed the door behind her and strode to her wardrobe to find another gown. "Such a beautiful dress," she muttered. "Completely ruined." She grabbed a fresh, dark blue silk gown and marched to her vanity. She looked in the mirror and discovered she also had wine in her hair. She unpinned it, blotted off the red wine with a linen, and quickly brushed her hair out. She'd started to pin it back up when Alderic's voice broke the silence in her room.

"By all means, Madame, leave it down."

The rest of her became just as immovable as she watched his reflection. He shut the door behind him, and her feet rooted to the floor. She didn't dare turn around. Their eyes connected in the mirror and held for a moment.

Alderic drank in her disheveled appearance with unnerving thoroughness as he pushed away from her chamber door, and slowly closed the space between them. She remained still as he braced his hands on the vanity, flanking her, her back pressed against his body.

"W-what are you doing in here?" she asked.

He kept his gaze on her in the mirror. "I thought it would be obvious, Madame."

Her breathing increased despite her attempt to control it. "*Non, monsieur.*"

"I wanted to see if you were all right."

"The tone of your voice says that is not the reason."

He released a soft chuckle. "I told you I would seduce you if I must."

His lips brushed her ear, and his tongue toyed with the diamond dangling from it. "The night you walked down that grand staircase, you cast a wicked spell upon me. I have thought of little else but you."

That stung slightly, and her words were a little less breathy. "Surely, there is not a lady of the day whom you think of?"

The muscles in his jaw tightened and his heated gaze sobered slightly. "I have made a habit of wanting that which I cannot have. A lady I wish to have I cannot pursue, the first woman to catch my interest in quite some time."

"And since you cannot have her, you will settle for seducing me in my chamber," she said dryly.

His lips trailed from her ear to the curve of her shoulder. "I want you in ways very differently. Perhaps in ways that would not be welcomed in her arms. I suppose I do not know, though I will admit her rejection of me has allowed me to pursue you freely."

"But it is she you still want?"

"It is she I cannot have."

"And you think I am so easily had?"

"No, I do not think that." He chuckled and shook his head. "But I think you want me as badly as I want you. And you are free to choose me, where she is not."

"You are still settling, *Monsieur* Beaumont," she declared, with a tone that was cutting. Although she knew he was torn between two women—and both were her—it bothered her that he was pursuing Madame instead of hunting down Delaney.

He gripped her waist, and she remained still. His touch made her lose her bearings. "I am not settling. You steal a part of me that I cannot explain. That woman I could be happily married to, grow old and have children with. But there's a part of me that craves you."

His thick, low words wielded a fog that screamed, *It doesn't matter! Both women he wants are you.* But she shook that statement away. She wasn't Madame. Madame Vanessa Cardui was a facade, an act. It wasn't her he wanted right now, it was a fantasy she'd created. She wanted him to only want *Delaney*. She wanted him to desire her true self more. It was so confusing.

Slowly he leaned in. His mouth brushed her cheek when her nagging questions spilled past her lips. "If given the opportunity, would you have both of us, then? To satisfy both worlds in which you wish to dwell?"

He paused and straightened. "Madame, I do not wish to dwell in your world. I have spent far too long in such empty existence."

"Then why are you here?"

Her thoughts didn't become any clearer when his hand slid to her breast as he replied, "You. Perhaps that is what draws me to you. I suspect you don't wish to be in this world any more than I do. I question at what value you hold yourself. Do you not believe you are deserving of a more fruitful life? If not, then you make my pursuit far more palatable. Though, admittedly—and to my own detriment—I hope you do not consider yourself in the position of prey. That you know you are worthy of being the hunter."

His thumb swept over the hard peaks of her breasts, teasing them through the thin material of her wine-drenched gown. She submerged in another series of his kisses as they started at the curve of her shoulder, then inched closer to her neck. He moved her hair aside with his other hand so his tongue could now torment the back of her neck.

"That certainly would not serve your interests right now," she said.

He smirked. Then, his words sent her skin tingling as he whispered, "My thoughts are most haunting. They put me in a moral predicament, constantly."

"Do they?"

He straightened and pulled her back against his chest, as his hand left her hair and gripped her other breast. He met her gaze in the mirror again. "Tell me to leave, and I will."

She struggled with her own morality. She parted her lips to speak, but no words were voiced. Upon her failed attempt to banish him from her chamber, he slid his hand down the front of her, and he inched up her robe-like gown until his fingers tucked underneath, gliding up her stockinged leg to graze over her skin. When his hand dipped between her thighs, she thought her knees would give and she'd collapse. But he was holding her tightly against him, watching her in the mirror, seemingly mesmerized by her reaction. He circled over the most private part of her. Never had she ever felt such erotic pleasure; never had someone touched her like this.

While one hand provoked her hot center, the other teased her breast. She closed her eyes as scorching sensations ripped through her, and she threw her head back against his chest.

"Do not come yet, Madame. I am not finished with you," he whispered in her ear.

Her thoughts had become so hazy she barely understood what he'd said in his native tongue. Suddenly he spun her around and smothered her surprised gasp with a crushing kiss, devouring her. Her lips tingled as the tip of his tongue slid along the roof of her mouth, then suckled her upper lip…then her lower lip. He slanted his head and captured her mouth again, and she couldn't cease the spin he was putting her in.

What was she doing, and why wasn't she pushing him away? He wanted her because she'd said he couldn't have Delaney. Unbeknownst to him, he was having both the women he wanted, quite easily. His hands gripped her waist, and his solid body pressed hard against her stoked that burning within her. She wanted him, was waiting for him.

Then there was solid banging outside her door. Another damned knock at the door! Truly?

There were several more knocks. It was then she realized how loud the house had gotten. Laughter and cheers echoed throughout. Alderic looked confused as well, and he drew away. He appeared just as affected as her. The door burst open, and Fannie, Gertie, and several more women charged into her room with sashes in their hands. They were tugging along blindfolded men behind them.

She sobered considerably, and stole a glance at Alderic. He seemed unmoved that he'd just been discovered in her chamber by the whole house. Instead, he seemed more amused by the scene in front of them. But she was embarrassed!

"Madame, we are taking these men upstairs," Gertie said, laughing as one of the blindfolded men nearly fell over.

"Yes, they've been bad, Madame—very bad!" Fannie shouted playfully.

Then the humor died, and everyone looked at Alderic, then back to Delaney. She felt her cheeks and ears burning from raw humiliation.

"Is this strapping man bothering you, Madame?" Gertie asked, eyeing Alderic.

Alderic straightened, his low-lidded gaze sweeping from Gertie to Delaney.

"Madame, we'll take him, if he's not wanted here," Fannie chimed in.

"Are we going or not?" one of the blindfolded men said.

Alderic stared at Delaney, and she couldn't read his expression. She didn't know what to do. A part of her wanted him to leave her chamber because she didn't have the willpower to stop his seduction. He was correct when he said she wanted him as badly as he wanted her. But she wasn't an experienced woman, and she still had a limited understanding of intimacy. To give herself to him was precarious. It wasn't just simple, carnal pleasure. She could lose her heart, and he wouldn't understand why.

When she didn't speak up quickly enough, Fannie ran behind Alderic and attempted to blindfold him. He looked mystified as he waited for her to speak up. "You wish me to leave, Madame?" he asked.

She shook her head. "I find myself worthy, after all. Of more than what you are prepared to offer."

He shifted his stance, and his stare pierced hers. "You make assumptions about what I am prepared to offer, or what I am worthy of receiving?"

Silence hovered between them as the tension built, and it sobered the gaiety surrounding them. Everyone glanced awkwardly at one another. She was all too aware of their audience. "I believe what you have to offer was made quite clear. Thus, I am uninterested."

"You did not seem uninterested," he coolly replied.

She felt her cheeks turning every shade of red. But she kept her tone calm when she spoke, despite her embarrassment. "It is difficult to see clearly through the lens of self-importance," she shot back.

Alderic glared at her, and she swallowed the blockage forming in her throat.

"I am beginning to believe you are deeply detached, Madame," he said. His tone was chilling.

He had no idea how connected she was, but his comment—whether warranted or not—made her lift her chin and square her shoulders. "Let me remind you I am not a conquest, *monsieur*. And you are correct in that I'm no one's prey."

He was silent for another moment. Finally, he said, "I understand and respect that completely. Perhaps it's time I turn my interest elsewhere."

He gave her a mocking bow, and his eyes darkened before he looked to Fannie. Her eyes widened with glee, and she squealed. Delaney winced as she watched Fannie blindfold him. The laughter, good humor, and excitement instantly returned amongst the group, and then all the men followed the birds out of her room.

Alderic didn't look back.

Chapter Twenty

Her bedroom cleared, Delaney slammed the door. Her chest heaved as she paced her room. She was vexed—and God, she wanted Alderic to fulfill whatever his hands had promised! She grabbed the brush from her vanity and flung it across the room. She stared at her reflection and envisioned Alderic standing behind her. She relived his hands gliding over her, stoking the flames in her. Fannie had taken him away. Would he touch her the same way?

He was going to fulfill Fannie now, not her. And when he did, she'd be lost to him. He'd called her unfeeling. Indifferent. Alderic was going to give Fannie everything he'd wanted to give her. And it was her own fault because she'd coldly rejected him in front of half the house! And why? Because she wanted him to pine for Delaney. Despite telling him she had a lover and wasn't free to be with him, she wanted him to fight for her anyway. To go on wishing. She didn't want him pursuing Madame Cardui. And yet both women he wanted were still her. She released a long, ragged breath and bit back the threat of tears. What was wrong with her?

She was so confused. All she could think about was him making Fannie cry out with pleasure. That image was clear, and it made her bitter, instantly jealous. She hated Fannie for taking what she'd so stupidly surrendered. Voicing her lamentation, she finally ceased her pacing. No matter what version of her he pursued, in the end, he wanted *her*. Delaney *and* Madame Cardui. No matter which identity she assumed at the moment, the fact was, Alderic was hers.

With that realization, she spun around and fled her chamber. She raced up the back stairs and down the long corridor to Fannie's chamber. She could hear various sounds through the closed doors as she passed, a compilation of moans, laughter, and shouts. Her steps faltered slightly, but she refused to be intimidated now. She steadied her shaking hands and cracked opened Fannie's door. Her eyes widened as she peeked inside and discovered both Gertie and Fannie in the room with Alderic.

Fannie saw her and rushed over. "Madame," she whispered, "what are you doing here?"

Gertie came up behind Fannie, a leather strap in her hand. Dear God, what were they all going to do? She glanced past them and saw Alderic lying blindfolded on the bed.

"Madame, is something wrong?" Fannie whispered.

Gertie chimed in, "We're going to have such a good time with him." She giggled quietly. "We've wanted him since the first night he came here."

She gaped at them. She didn't know what she was supposed to say. What was she supposed to do? Thankfully, she didn't have to say a word. It must've been written on her face, and Fannie read it. "Uh, Gertie?" Fannie took away Gertie's leather strap. "I don't think he's ours tonight."

The heat in her cheeks flared again.

Gertie blinked owlishly several times, and then

pouted. "No. Really?"

"It's about time, Madame." Fannie smiled, flashed Delaney a wink, and left.

Gertie let out a heavy sigh and followed Fannie. "Better tell us about it later," she said, and made Delaney jump as she smacked her bottom on her way out of the room.

Delaney was left alone in the chamber with Alderic, his head relaxed on his arm as he lay blindfolded on the bed. He looked like a perfect statue, naked and beautiful. His physique was more than intimidating. She fumbled with the ties of her gown until she heard him chuckle. "If you ladies do not get on with it, I may fall asleep."

Her silken garment became a heap on the floor. Clad only in her stockings, she walked to the bed and admired the figure before her.

Crawling over to him, she rested on her heels, and gazed at him as he waited for her to…do something— anything at this point, she was sure.

She scanned the lines of his body, the outline of his muscles, the thick cords that ran up his arms. He had many scars on his chest and abdomen, but nothing that deterred from his allure. In fact, they only accentuated his appeal. Using her fingers like the tips of her brushes, she lightly swept over his body, and his skin prickled at her touch. When she'd painted his body, she'd wanted to explore him. Now she could.

Her fingertips continued to graze over him, stopping over his scars, skimming along the marred skin. As her touch continued farther down his stomach, just brushing a narrow line that started at his navel, he reacted to her caresses. She'd seen enough sculptures to know what a man looked like. But to see one in the flesh, to feel the warmth of his skin, his pulse in her hand, was very different. Her fascination overtook fear.

"Though I'm really enjoying your light touch, I feel you're hesitating." He smiled. "My body can't possibly frighten either of you."

She wanted to tell him that Fannie and Gertie were no longer in the room, but she was unsure of retaliation. He'd been angry with her. Was he still?

"The two of you have grown silent," he said. "You were quite verbal about what you wanted on the way up here."

She didn't want to hear about that. Whatever they'd planned for him didn't matter. He was hers, at least for tonight. If he still wanted her. He shifted under her touch, and his expression changed. He cleared his throat before he quietly said, "While I anticipate your attention, I must apologize for wasting your time. I believe that I will not be good company tonight."

He started to sit up, holding no more interest in Gertie and Fannie. She smiled at the thought that now he wanted to leave, and she pressed her mouth gently against his. He instinctively parted his lips, and she slid her tongue past them, tasting him. Then he broke their kiss. "Perhaps it was unfair of me to accept your invitation. But I'm afraid I must leave."

Strange how she found his hesitation and sudden discomfort so charming. He truly wanted to leave, but was trying not to insult Fannie and Gertie. As he reached for his blindfold, she stopped him and kissed him again, this time with more fervor. This time, he moved his arm from underneath his head, and gently cupped her face. He started to gently push her away, again attempting to break her kiss. And that was when his thumbs grazed her mask.

His movements stilled, and she witnessed the moment of realization as it crossed his face. He tore off his blindfold and their eyes met. She waited for his reaction, but still, he said nothing. She started to question her decision to come to him. Now, she wondered if he'd tell her to leave. She wasn't sure how her heart would handle such a rejection. But rejection wasn't his response. He curled his fingers behind her neck, and drew her down, kissing her fully. There was no more hesitation, but a demand for her mouth. It was savage, full of desire and need. Her hair brushed his body, and she felt his skin react to the light touch. His hand gripped her thigh, and his thumb wrapped around her garter as he positioned her to straddle him. He sucked in his breath as the feel of her body atop his sparked a deeper sense of need for both of them. He kissed her chin, her cheek, and down the column of her neck.

Then his arm snaked around her, and he swiftly flipped her onto her back. Balancing above her, he continued kissing her, his hand sliding down the length of her body. When he shifted between her thighs and pressed against her, she gasped.

She entwined her fingers in his hair, drawing him closer as he sent kisses down her side, over her hips, and down her legs. Her body tingled everywhere, and the inside of her swirled with sensations. Alderic inched his body downward until he was kissing her inner thighs, and she moaned.

"Madame," he finally said, his voice thick.

She stared, mesmerized, as her kissed her thighs. His eyes were just as devouring as his mouth. He caressed her with his lips, his tongue, his gaze, as he lightly brushed between her thighs. The sensation he caused was instant and frighteningly intense. She jolted, and she was so stunned she shoved him away. He gave her a strange look. When he tried to kiss her again, she panicked and scooted away. "Has no man ever done this to you?" he asked, bewildered.

She wished she'd paid more attention when the girls had talked about their experiences. She didn't know what she was supposed to do, and she couldn't really tell him. He swiftly climbed over her and kissed her until she relaxed again.

"The roles have reversed, Madame, and you have pursued me," he said against her mouth. "You wish me to pleasure you still, no?"

Her skin was hot, her body heightened; she hadn't come to him to stop now. Her gaze swept his, and held it, unrelenting. Confidently. Trustingly.

Alderic's lips curled; she'd given her answer. He swiftly gripped both her wrists with one hand and secured them to the headboard with his discarded blindfold. He'd done it so quickly she only stared at him, stunned. "If no man has kissed you the way I'm going to, then those men were fools," he said.

He'd given her nothing but pleasure so far. She'd come to him because she'd wanted him to make love to her. And she still did. Her body was anxiously tremoring as she lay back and savored another trail of his kisses. He made a soft, teasing line down the center of her stomach, until his mouth again settled between her thighs. He gently moved her legs farther apart, and she closed her eyes, biting down on her lower lip, smothering a surprised cry, as his mouth covered the center of her. His tongue slid between her folds, sending her into a frenzy of sensations. Her nails dug into her palms, and her restraints tightened around her wrists as she flexed. His tongue licked over her, and he suckled much like he'd done to her mouth. Those daunting sensations he'd stoked in her surged and spread down her thighs until she was arching her back, pushing against his mouth, writhing against him.

He moaned and gripped her thighs, as he kissed her longer, deeper, harder. She cried out as her body started to shake and her stomach clenched. Waves of heat rippled through her. Her only instinct was to rock into him, to take in each lap of his tongue and savor it until she trembled and thrust uncontrollably.

"You torment me, Madame." His voice was broken; he sounded strained, almost pained. His eyes were glossed and dark. "The first time you walked down those stairs, I wanted to hear you whimpering beneath me, begging me to come inside you."

She watched him with fascination as his words seeped into her brain, arousing her more than she'd ever thought possible. Caught in his heated gaze, she was unprepared for how quickly he climbed above her, settled between her burning thighs, and released her hands from their bonds. He snaked his hand beneath her, lifted her bottom, and thrust past her sheath, hard and deep. He instantly broke through her barrier, and she gasped, biting back a cry at the sharp pain.

He halted and stared down at her. His body was shaking, and yet he held still.

"*Qu'est-ce*... It can't be. Madame, are you..."

He searched her face, and his voice sounded lost, his brow furrowed with marked worry.

She hadn't thought about what would happen at that

point; she'd heard that men could tell when they'd deflowered a woman. And Alderic looked stunned, troubled. Maybe it was naïve, but she'd hoped he wouldn't notice.

But it no longer mattered. It was done. She strained to receive him, and what he'd done to her had heightened her senses and sent the blood rushing to her loins. His body was inside hers, painfully stretching her, and it was driving her to madness. She reached up and kissed him boldly, tasting herself on his tongue.

"Why have you stopped," she breathed against his mouth.

"But, euh… You are a—"

"I don't think kindly of your hesitations, *monsieur*," she breathed on his lips. "You have made promises. And if you do not deliver, longing will spark my temper."

He stared another moment as she noted the worried lines of his face soften, his lids lower. She kissed his neck, inhaling the fresh scent of him, and her hands slid up his back as she rested her thigh around his waist and pushed against him. His dithering foundered and he melded with her again. He moved in and out of her slowly, lifting her bottom higher as he began to drive deeper into her, and each thrust made her writhe as his forceful contact rippled waves of ecstasy through her. She latched naturally onto his rhythm and met each thrust with equal fervor while he pumped himself into her harder and faster. She was beginning to shake with his intensified motion. He was building her up again, just as he had when his tongue lapped between her thighs.

For a moment, he rested his brow against hers, and his eyes locked with hers.

Hot, shattering sensations tore through her, and she

cried out, throwing her head back as she shuddered, her body writhing wildly with his. He groaned as he continued to drive into her. Each time their bodies clashed, it jolted both of them. A disjointed sound escaped her as his deep thrusts forced out her very breath—and then they both released.

Her thoughts were blurred as her body flooded with warm quivers. Their rapid breaths broke the silence in the room. He kissed her, catching her soft moan in his mouth, and placed small kisses down the curve of her jaw before lifting his gaze once more.

"Madame…" The question was in his voice, but his words trailed. She could see emotion crossing his face as he battled with his thoughts.

Whatever he wanted to say, he'd thought better of it, and she found his stammer becoming. He looked almost boyish. She suspected he wanted to ask her if she was a virgin, but he had to know the notion was ridiculous. After all, she was a madam, was she not? She brought him down to her again and kissed him passionately.

"Is something wrong?" she asked, breaking their kiss.

"No, I had a rather ridiculous thought, is all." He chuckled softly, then kissed her again. "But I do not think I'm done with you yet," he said against her mouth, and there was a glint in his eyes that sparked a fascination within her. Curiosity. She wanted to know more. She wanted him to show her more. A part of her feared that if she confirmed what he'd suspected, then he'd hold back his knowledge. She was tired of feeling deficient. Less than. Innocent. The way the women of the house hushed their tone around her, trying not to sully her ears with details about their encounters with men.

"'Tis hours before sunup." She smiled.

He no longer appeared apprehensive but returned her wicked smile.

****

Hours later, just after sunrise, Alderic dressed, then leaned over the bed where she lay. Delaney smiled lazily up at him. He returned the smile before taking her hand and kissing it. Her cheeks felt as warm as his gaze when he finally said farewell and left the Bird House.

Once alone in Fannie's chamber, Delaney slowly sat up. Her thighs were sore, but oh, how he'd slaked that need he'd stoked inside her since the day he'd kissed her on the street.

She was sure there was some elated smile still lingering on her lips, but she couldn't stop it. She removed her mask, got out of the bed, and slowly dressed. She carefully made her way to her own chamber, her body thoroughly aware of what she and Alderic had done. When she opened the door, she found her bed occupied. All the Bird House's women were sprawled on her bed!

When she walked in, they jumped up, and there was a resounding cheer. She covered her face, knowing all too well she was turning every shade of red.

"Oh, you better tell us everything!" Fannie shouted.

"Come on, spill it, Delaney," Marla urged.

"You must be sore. Sit down," Billy said, jumping up and pulling Delaney onto the bed.

Suddenly she was surrounded. They looked like children anxiously awaiting story time.

"How did he feel about deflowering you?" Gertie asked.

"I didn't tell him," Delaney replied meekly.

There was a hush around her, and their faces fell.

"Is he daft? Couldn't he tell?" Gertie asked.

"He did, but I might've led him to think he was mistaken."

"You what?" Fannie asked.

Delaney gave her a defensive look. "It wasn't so difficult when he believes I'm madam to a brothel."

There was a small bout of silence as they looked at one another.

"Uh, wait," Fannie said, standing up on Delaney's mattress. "So, you slept with a man like Alderic Beaumont, and you didn't tell him you were a virgin?"

"Oh, my," Billy said, covering her mouth.

Delaney's embarrassment engulfed her face in flames. She couldn't believe everyone was sitting on her bed, talking about her night with Alderic like they were chatting over what Barb was serving for supper.

"Come now, how did you do?" Gertie asked.

Delaney cocked her brow. "I don't know, but he didn't complain about anything."

Laughter broke out around her.

"Quiet down. Look at the poor girl. She's mortified," Billy said. "What they're saying, Delaney, is that you should've told him, and he would've gone easy on you. A man like that could keep a girl up all night. When you're inexperienced, men will treat you more delicately."

"Oh," she muttered. "But I didn't want that. And I liked all of it."

They squealed and clapped for her.

Fannie sat back down. "Well, we want details!"

"Yes, tell us everything he did to you," Billy said.

"Aye, we'll probably never have him now," Fannie

said.

"We can make recommendations," Billy added. "You don't want him having all the power."

What were they talking about? She shook her head, but for the next hour or so, they all lounged in her bed, frequently sighing as she recounted her night and answered their questions.

"Ah, I'm going to need a few minutes alone in my room after this," Gertie sighed.

There were a few chuckles, and Delaney looked at her blankly.

"You know, Delaney," Billy said, "you can make him as mindless as he made you."

Delaney tilted her head, deep in thought. Alderic hadn't seemed disappointed in any way, but the idea of making him as carelessly wanton as he made her was appealing. "What do I do?"

Billy leaned in. "You're smart, and you have a knack for the essence of this world. Use your mouth and your imagination. You can do the same things he did to you."

Delaney's eyes opened so wide she feared they'd fall out of their sockets. "What?"

Laughter broke out at her stunned expression.

"Your mouth feels just as good on him as his feels on you," Fannie said, and the rest of the women echoed agreement.

"Just be ready if you bring him to release that way," Billy chimed in.

She paused and tried to imagine what they were saying. She blinked. "Why?"

Fannie shoved Billy and scoffed. "Don't worry about it. You'll figure all that out," she said, patting

Delaney's hand.

"Do you think…from what I told you," she stammered to ask, "d-do you think he…"

Gertie put up her hand and smiled. "Honey, it sounds like he was enjoying himself immensely."

Fannie leaned forward. "He's had his eyes on only you since the moment you came out as madam. You were enchanting. Sounds like he couldn't get enough of you! Prepare yourself. He'll be back."

Chapter Twenty-One

Later that afternoon, Delaney washed and dressed in a simple gray gown and tied her hair in a careless chignon, ignoring the tendrils that escaped the pins. Her mind kept drifting to last night. She caught herself every time, realizing with a sigh that she still had that ridiculous grin on her face. She went to her office to sort through numbers and discovered a letter on her ledger. She broke the seal and read the contents. It was an invitation. She called to Remi.

"I've been invited to bring some girls to a ball at the *La Salle Condé Théâtre*," she said as he entered the room and they both found their seats. "What is this about?"

Remi took the invitation and looked it over. "The event is mostly for visitors wanting to find company for the night," he explained. "Or New Orleans men looking for mistresses."

"Mistresses?"

"Women explicitly kept for them, for a monthly fee. It's understood that the man can come at any time and she'll be available."

"Do you know if any of the girls here wish to be mistresses?"

"You'll have to ask them," he replied. "Some women like having one man. Many times, men come to care very deeply for their mistresses, sometimes more than their own wives. They keep them under their protection and sometimes purchase their own cottages for privacy."

"That would be ideal, would it not?"

Remi scratched his jaw. "Some women like the freedom to choose who and when."

"Please ask who wishes to attend," she announced as she stood up from her chair and headed for the door. She picked up her bonnet, considered how warm the weather was, and tossed the hat aside. She wanted the sun on her face. "Tell them that if they wish to go, they can. We'll be leaving at nine."

"*Oui*, Madame."

She was ready to leave, but then Remi's words stopped her: "I heard you had an eventful evening."

Delaney stopped and spun around. "I beg your pardon?"

"Please be careful, Delaney. I think this place may be confusing you," he replied solemnly. "Beaumont is a good man, but he doesn't know your position. And I don't think you do, either."

Clasping her hands primly in front of her, she leaned back. "Pray tell, what is my position that I'm so ignorant of?"

"Your mindset isn't equipped for the heartbreaking truth about the standard set for a madam."

"You think I don't know that I'm not the sort of woman a man brings home to meet his family?"

Remi released a heavy sigh and momentarily anchored his eyes to his boot, before he mumbled, "You've spent your life as a lady worthy of marriage and respectability." Then he lifted his gaze and said with an ounce of reprimand, "Your decision last night shut the door on that dream. I don't think you're prepared to experience that reality. Knowing, and being treated as such, are two very different things."

"What I understand about my decisions are my business, Remi," she said firmly.

"I just wanted to give you fair warning before you get hurt," he said. "I'm starting to conclude that bringing you here was a monumental fault on my part."

She inhaled sharply and then grabbed her sketchbook. She didn't take kindly to the judgement in Remi's tone. "I didn't ask to be here, if you recall. I also didn't ask for your advice or opinion."

She breezed past him and left the house. She walked several blocks to the market and found a seat. There, she watched the swarms of people browsing the lines of vendors. Many others just stood along the street, chatting with one another, some speaking in languages she'd never heard. She took out her book and began sketching the lively setting, trying to capture some of the most interesting people she witnessed. "That's a good likeness."

She shielded her eyes from the sun as she looked up at a young man standing above her. He was dressed in a simple shirt and breeches, with a hat low over his eyes.

"Excuse me, but I thought I recognized you," he said with a wide grin. She immediately tensed at that statement. He came around the bench and held out his hand. "Remember, from the store?"

She took another moment and then recognition flooded in. She returned his warm expression. "Yes, I remember you. You're also an artist," she commented.

He followed her eyes to his stained hands and chuckled. "Yes, I am." He wiped them down his breeches, as if the gesture would remove the years of color that had stained his hands and nails. "My name is Fernand."

"Afternoon, Fernand. I'm...D-Delaney."

"A pleasure."

"I'm painting a mural in a church a few streets away. I came to the market for a late lunch. I was headed back when I saw you, and I'll admit I snuck up so I could steal a glance at your sketch. It's impressive."

"What are you painting in the church?"

"A depiction of St. Catherine."

"To be given that privilege, you must be quite good."

He shrugged. "I'm adequate enough," he said, his high cheekbones blushing. "I studied under a Parisian artist for several years."

She closed her sketchbook and sat back with a small smile.

"So did I," she said, her voice and spirit lifting. "I wanted to attend the academy, but being a woman disqualified me."

He shook his head. "That's disappointing, is it not? I think art can be successfully captured by a woman just as it can by a man."

"I agree."

He took the liberty of sitting next to her, his eyes glimmering. "I wonder sometimes how art would change if a woman's perspective were given as much professional recognition and respect as that of the rest of us. How would it impact the world around us?"

"Our views on painting have interesting differences, I believe."

"Yes, I agree," he said, his voice rising with excitement. "It's unfortunate you couldn't pursue art in the academy."

She had been wholeheartedly upset at their rejection, and the reminder still stung, but she shrugged. Instead, she focused on the alternative. "I studied with a group of students, and we went on an expedition, traveling to different countries to see and experience art in the flesh."

"How fascinating. I'd like your perspective on my mural. Will you accompany me to the church?"

She smiled. "I'd enjoy that."

As they walked, she admired the Spanish-inspired stucco, iron balconies, and galleries decorating the buildings. She came upon the modest church and stood in awe of the center steeple. A good part of the structure was under construction.

"Most of the church was destroyed by fire last year," he explained as they approached the entrance. "A team of us were hired to paint the inside. We've been doing this for a month now, but it's nearly done."

She stepped into the vestibule and inhaled the scent of frankincense and beeswax. As she made her way inside, she could see, in the far back, his unfinished depiction of St. Catherine.

"What do you think?" he asked as they neared the mural. His fingers retraced his earlier strokes. "I combined these lines, using the blue with a sun setting I thought would be interesting."

"It's worthy of praise, Fernand. The colors heighten dramatic tension. Did you choose St. Catherine?" she asked.

"Yes, I was given the freedom by Lucien," he said. "I chose Catherine because of her sympathy for the ill. This city has suffered from yellow fever so often I thought it would give hope to those who come here. Remind the faithful that God is looking over us, sending his saints to watch out for us."

She noted the serene expression on the saint's face and smiled. "She signifies hope."

"Yes," he agreed.

"Where will you put the lily?"

He creased his brow and looked at the mural. "Is it necessary?"

"It's a prime example of symbolism to help identify her."

He removed his hat and scratched his brown curls, seemingly lost in thought. "I'm not sure. My flowers are not, well…"

She eyed his paint board and brushes. He had whites, greens, and yellows mixed. She mixed in the egg wash to moisten the paints and dipped the brush in green.

"I'm skilled with flowers. May I?"

"Your sketch was amazing. I think I can trust that you can make a lily," he said.

"If not, it can easily be covered," she said.

She painted the flower, paying close attention to the delicate petals. Then she made a long stem, taking into account the light emanating from Catherine's halo. She completed the lily and stepped back, proud that her lighting was correct, but then she realized that his had been off.

Now hers looked awkward. It was an easy fix, though, since he'd only missed a few places. She made a few more strokes, dabbing the rounded lines of the saint's shoulders, which seemed to readjust the lighting.

"What do you think?" She turned around to get his approval and found him chewing nervously on his nails.

He looked troubled, and she ruefully turned back to the mural. "Fernand? You don't like it?"

"Eh, no, it looks amazing," he said. "I'm not sure how you fixed the problem I was having with the rays of light over her shoulders. I've been working on it for days, and I didn't want to bother Lucien."

"Oh." She sighed, glad he wasn't angry with her for taking over his mural. "Here was the problem, and you also had to take into account the sun you have in the corner."

He held his stomach, rested his head in his other hand, and let out a moan. "How did I not catch that?" he grumbled.

"It seems one can look at something so long the brain trains itself to overlook the flaw."

His thin lips slid into a wide smile. "I'm indebted to you. Please, speak with my mentor?"

She put his brush and board down and stepped away from the mural. "No, I have to go."

He held out his hands, pleading. "No, please. You see, we still have much to do. We could use your skills. Please, talk to Lucien?"

Her eyes lit up for a second before reality hit. Her current situation was far too demanding.

It appeared that he could foresee her rejection, and he took her hand in his. "Just think on it," he insisted. "Give yourself until tomorrow morning. If you don't come back to speak with Lucien, then I'll acknowledge your rejection. But I simply can't accept it so quickly."

She swallowed down her refusal, and with a nod, she smiled.

He let out an exaggerated sigh of relief and rested his hand over his heart.

"Fernand, charming the ladies, are we?"

Slowly, she turned as Alderic strolled up to them. Her eyes instantly went to his curved mouth and was reminded of the way he'd kissed her… everywhere. Just last night.

She dropped her hand from Fernand's and tried to avoid Alderic's gaze. The silly part of her wondered if there was any telltale sign that she was the madam he'd made love to last night. Would he know who she was now because he'd explored every part of her body?

"Are you well, Delaney?" Fernand asked, resting a concerned hand on her shoulder.

She cleared her throat and pasted a small smile on her lips.

"*Mam'selle*," Alderic said, and he took her hand and kissed it. "Given the status you expressed the last time we spoke, I find it…interesting that you are here."

She raised a brow. *Why such a tone?* she wondered. Was he passing judgment about her being in a church because she was unmarried and told him she had a lover? The audacity of him! She knew what he had been doing until the early hours of morning. And it hadn't been praying!

"You as well," she said coolly. "Tell me, do you hold your breath when you step through the holy threshold?"

Alderic nearly choked, holding back his laughter, and Fernand looked confused. "You know each other?" he asked.

"We're acquaintances," she supplied, "as it seems *Monsieur* Beaumont knows everyone in the city."

"Not everyone," Alderic replied. Then his eyes settled on Fernand's paint board. "Some people shroud themselves rather well."

His brow creased as he continued to stare at the paints. Then he lifted his eyes. "Does art interest you, *mam'selle*?"

"Not at all," she fibbed with a convincingly flippant air. "I'm here to admire fantastic Spanish architecture. You, *monsieur*?"

Fernand shot her an odd look, but he didn't expose the lie.

"I'm on business," Alderic said, then turned to Fernand. "I've come across a great deal of poppyseed oil and thought Lucien might be interested."

Fernand lit up. So did Delaney, but she caught herself before jumping at the opportunity of purchasing some.

"Let me take you to him," Fernand said excitedly. "He's in the choir loft."

"*Merci*," Alderic said. "*Euh, mam'selle*, would you wait for my return? I would like to show you something."

She clasped her hands and twisted, hoping to steady them. "I'm afraid I can't."

Alderic said smoothly, "I beg of you, *mam'selle*. Will you wait just one moment?"

Taking her hesitation as agreement, he acknowledged his gratitude for her patience—even if she hadn't consented to wait—and then briskly turned and strode off with Fernand, promising a quick return.

Delaney considered fleeing. She really couldn't spend too much time with Alderic as Delaney. She imagined it wouldn't take him long to grow suspicious of her likeness to the woman he'd just spent the night with. But she didn't leave. When he returned, he stood in the aisle, genuflected, mumbled something in Latin, and made the sign of the cross. When he stood again, he offered her his elbow. "Accompany me?"

She accepted his arm. "I didn't take you for a spiritual man," she said.

"I've been at death's door many times," he said as he opened the church's tall oak door. "When you've seen as much evil as I have, you have to believe in something good."

"Are you well versed in your faith?"

He winked at her. "My family insisted on it."

They left the church and began strolling down the sidewalk.

"Where's your family?" she asked.

"My parents died several years ago," he said. "Since the revolt, my brother and his family moved to England."

"I heard you…weren't of humble origins, *monsieur*," she ventured.

"Ah, I'm flattered you've taken such interest as to inquire about me."

She felt the tips of her ears burning. "I was asking about your coin," she quickly clarified, but he didn't look convinced. "They said you were an aristocrat who almost hung as a pirate."

"*Corsair* rolls off the tongue a little sweeter, I think," he said.

She laughed. "Call it what you like. How does someone born to nobility become a corsair?"

"I was an heir. But I didn't enjoy nobility."

She glanced at him. "What a ludicrous declaration. Who doesn't want to hold such status?"

He chuckled. "I went through years and years of school. Every moment was scheduled, and my whole life was planned for me, belaboring this obsession of *la gloire* and *la grandeur*. I did not enjoy these things."

His laughter was thin, his smile strained. He wasn't being authentic; the humor in his tone didn't meet his eyes.

"You left your country and your responsibility as an heir," she said. "There must be more to it than that."

"I suppose," he replied after several moments of silence. "There was that whole ordeal with a woman I would not marry." Her eyes widened. He turned to her and grinned at her obvious shock. "I really didn't enjoy my position as the titled heir. Since I was a child, I defied my family in every way I could." He looked up as if recalling certain memories. "I suspect I always had a problem with authority. However, the end of the line came when they told me I had to marry this insipid countess. I truly would have gone mad if I had been forced to listen to her boring chatter for the rest of my life."

"Could you not ask your father to reconsider the match?"

The merriment in his demeanor began to dwindle. "I did. My pleas fell on deaf ears." The laughter in his voice had completely died. "So I refused outright, and my father was furious with me. We quarreled, and the day before my nuptials, I boarded a ship bound for America."

She watched him carefully, observing the conflicting emotions crossing his face as his mind left her and New Orleans altogether. His eyes told her he was in another place, another time. "Is that when you became a corsair?"

Her question seemed to jounce him back to the present, and he shook his head as he plucked at the cuff of his coat. "No, that was when I was enslaved."

Her brows snapped together. "Enslaved?"

"*Oui*," he replied with a shrug as he fidgeted with his cuff. "My ship was intercepted by barbary pirates. A captain by the name of Basil Ward, who—despite his English heritage—flew an Ottoman flag. I was brought to Algiers, where I was sold with countless others."

As the details of his story sank in, she noted how the fidgeting on his cuff increased. "But you must've escaped?"

"I had given my identity, in hopes of being ransomed. Secretly, I had imagined my family receiving the ransom demand and conducting a grand rescue, but…there was no ransom and no rescue. After a couple of years, I surrendered to my slave status, having my spirit broken as well as my pride and my flesh. A part of me believed that I had deserved such treatment for being so uncompromising with my father." His chuckle seemed out of place, considering the tragic events he described. But she remained quiet, encouraging him to continue his story. To her surprise, he did, and spoke rather nonchalantly. "That is how I met Nye Tarquin. I was sent to unload goods delivered to my slave holder, and Nye was the supplier. I saw a captain who wasn't much older than I, and he had his own ship, and had already built a reputation as an impressive businessman."

"Impressive?"

"He was trustworthy," he clarified. "Some highly placed men would buy only from him. He guaranteed timely and safe deliveries with extreme discretion. He and I talked briefly—as you can imagine, I wasn't allowed to speak much. He asked me only a couple of questions, and I cannot even remember what they were.

Before I left, Nye slipped me the smallest of blades and told me where to locate his ship. He said if I could get there before dawn, I would be welcome aboard."

"So you embarked on the life of a pirate," she commented.

He finally moved from fidgeting with his coat to looking off into the distance. "Euh, not exactly. I managed an escape, but once aboard, I told him I wished to go home."

She leaned back in disbelief. "I'm truly surprised that you wanted to go back."

He shrugged. "Adversity can make one grow and reflect. I realized I had made a muck of my life and handled the situation with my family badly. I wanted to make amends with my father and mother. Nye had some…business to attend in Marseille, so I agreed to assist so I could pay my way home."

"Did your parents receive you? I would think they'd be relieved to find you well."

Alderic's expression looked pained. "My parents were killed in a carriage accident the year prior to my return. I discovered from my brother that, before they died, they'd refused to pay the ransom. To further their message, they erased me from the family, stripping me of any title or acknowledgment."

She covered her mouth, hoping to smooth over her initial reaction. "They disowned you."

He glanced at her, then chuckled. "They did," he said, perking up his tone. "So I said farewell to my brother and returned to Nye's ship. I asked him if his offer to join his crew was still open. It was, and I did not look back."

He'd started plucking at his cuff again, and she

gently placed her hand over his. He stopped his fidgeting and lifted his gaze. She felt the caress in his eyes, and she boldly held his stare. "You weave a heartbreaking tale, Alderic."

"No tale, *mam'selle*. Merely life."

"I don't believe it so simple," she replied softly. She couldn't have imagined what he'd endured during his enslavement, but the marks she'd seen on his body offered a small insight. She imagined herself in his arms just last night, and her stomach began to grow warm with the urge to be so again.

He leaned in and flashed another brilliant smile. His mood and demeanor changed instantly as he said, "I wish you would be more generous with information about yourself. I don't know much more than I did the night I stole a kiss."

She joined him in lightening the mood and scoffed, waving her hand absently. "You would grow bored, believe me. I'm not an interesting person."

He didn't appear convinced, but he didn't press the matter. They fell back into step.

"Where is your family?" he asked. "In London?"

"Why do you assume that?"

"Your accent."

"Oh, of course." She chuckled. "No, I grew up in England—hence the accent. But it isn't where I'm from."

"Then where's your family?"

"H-here, in…Louisiana." He offered a look that reflected her vague answer, and now she had a sudden desire to change the subject. "You insisted I wait for you, *monsieur*," she said, looking pointedly at the path they were strolling down. "What did you want to show me?"

"Do you like New Orleans?" he asked, leaving her

question unanswered.

She offered him a patient look as he ignored her question completely. "Parts of it," she admitted.

"Fair enough. Have you left your lover yet?"

Her eyes widened. Had he not been in Madame Cardui's arms, last night? "Why do you ask? Do you wish to be my next lover?" she asked, an icy edge to her voice.

He cast her a sideways glance and smiled. "Only curious. I accept that you are unavailable, and I am making an effort to move forward."

She fixed her gaze ahead, wondering if that effort was Madame. "I apologize. That was rude."

"My ears aren't sensitive," he said with a wink. "However, your lover is a fool, Delaney."

"What do you mean? He might be disarmingly enchanting."

He flashed her a side glance that screamed doubt. "I think whoever is selfish enough to keep you as just a lover isn't worthy. He may be content, but he clearly doesn't know what he has, which makes him daft."

She briefly imagined what it would be like to spend every night with him—like she had last night—for the rest of her life. "How can you be so certain you know something he doesn't? I might not be as valuable as you believe me to be."

"Then he is a fool and you are blind. Maybe you are a good match, after all." He laughed.

She halted and gave him a steamy glare. He held up his hand in surrender and stopped laughing. His expression sobered, as did his tone. "Some things I can see despite your efforts to conceal them."

"Such as?"

He searched her face for a moment. "You seem rather…lost, and 'tis lonely, I suspect."

Her eyes widened, and she raised her brows. "Is that a compliment meant to reiterate my claimed high value?"

"Not at all," he said, carelessly waving his hand as he went on. "I'm beginning to think you have no family, and no friends, either."

"You're trying to jest with me," she said, her tone carrying a slight edge.

"I'm most serious. But, underneath all that dysfunction, you're a romantic. This tells me you very much want those things; you just don't know how to get them."

She released his elbow and stepped back, glaring at him. "Explain how you can compliment me with the notion that you're sincere, and then spend the next several moments insulting me?"

"The truth isn't insulting," he said matter-of-factly. "You are searching, *mam'selle*, and I am still not sure what brought you to New Orleans, but I am grateful. I would not have met you otherwise. Perhaps I can help you find what you are looking for."

"Do you see yourself as a savior, *monsieur*?" she asked tersely.

Her voice was rising, and yet he stood there, seemingly unfazed, as though what he was saying shouldn't be considered offensive at all.

Alderic closed the distance she'd made between them. "I don't wish to upset you, Delaney," he said, his tone low. "What I am trying to express is my interest in you despite these things. I believe the journey to finding yourself would be an interesting quest. I think the result would be something spectacular."

"What if it isn't?"

The corners of his lips turned up. "That is an impossible outcome."

A cloud overhead moved past the sun, and the light was nearly blinding. In that second, she saw a change in his expression. He was looking curiously at the lines of her face, and she panicked. She could see that his curiosity had been sparked, and she looked away. If he recognized her as Madame, she might as well just confess he'd taken her innocence, too. Shaking away the remembrance of his lips on the most sacred parts of her body, she quickly stepped away from him. Her tone was crisp as she said, "I think you are the romantic, *monsieur*."

He dropped his hand, which, at some point, had reached up to touch her face, and his mischievous manner returned. "I have heard that before," he said, then continued with a flippant air. "We will move on, *non*? You said you like architecture, and I thought it would be splendid to explore the cathedral with you. I would love to hear your thoughts."

"Oh, that would be a far more uplifting venture than exploring the path that is me." She smiled. "What cathedral?"

He stopped briefly, and his jaw slackened slightly. "You have been to St. Louis's, *non*?"

"I haven't had the pleasure, no," she replied.

His eyes softened. "Well, then, I am honored to be the first one to show it to you." Then he flashed her a wink.

He held out his elbow once again, and she took it without hesitation. Refusing Alderic was becoming as increasingly difficult as remaining upset with him. They rounded the corner, entering a well-manicured street, and he guided her past the Cabildo. She looked in awe at the building and wished to take out her sketchbook so she might capture it in a sketch. Not far from the council building was the cathedral. She took in every detail and memorized the lines so she could replicate them on paper when she returned to the Bird House.

"I haven't seen any of this."

He gave her an odd look. "Then you have not seen much of the nicer side of New Orleans. *Oui*, this city is growing nicely. The structures are not as extravagant as Paris, but this place is young. I see its potential, do you not?"

"It's pleasant. I've heard it's suffered several fires," she commented.

"Yes, unfortunately. The Spanish have done much to rebuild it, and they have used creative methods to protect the city from future damage. The cathedral itself was just reconstructed because of a devastating fire."

She admired every detail of the structure. But it was the pride in Alderic's eyes as he observed—not just the church—but the surrounding structures and people bustling about their lives around them, that opened her eyes to the magnificence of it all. She watched his fine profile with curiosity. He was born with privilege, raised with extravagance. Yet he walked away from his birthright and endured hardship. He was a man who'd been stripped of all comfort and had built his fortune within the meager walls of a city struck by misfortune time and time again. He looked past the desolation and fear that haunted the streets and focused on hope. Hope for what, exactly? She wasn't sure. A part of her wondered what Alderic Beaumont truly was looking for, and why had he decided to look for it in this most unique city with its uncertain future?

She conceded that he offered her hope in her situation. Perhaps she wasn't so lost after all. Maybe she could succeed in her dreams. But what were they? What did *she* truly want?

"Let us go inside," Alderic said as he took a step toward the church. "I believe you'll be surprised by the remarkable…" His words trailed off, when she didn't step alongside him, and he turned to her.

She had looked at her small timepiece and realized how long she'd been gone. She still had so much to do before the Bird House opened. She abruptly pulled away from his arm, as crushing as it felt. As crushing as his expression when he looked upon her sudden change. But she couldn't be distracted. She had an objective, and she had to succeed in that, first and foremost. "I have to go," she said.

"Is something wrong?"

"Yes." She smiled, gave him a quick curtsy, and scanned her surroundings for a hackney. "I lost track of time. Thank you for the tour, *monsieur*." She spotted a hackney and flagged it over.

He held her fast. His fingers encircling her arm stoked a warmth on her flesh that she recognized. A flickering memory of last night flashed in her mind. "Delaney, tell me how I can contact you."

She squeezed her eyes shut for a second, cursing herself for her fairytale belief she could walk around town with him in the light of day like a true lady. She couldn't even tell him where she lived.

"I'll find you," she suggested.

Her response was unimpressive, to say the least, and

the hardness in his golden-green gaze reflected as much. "I might not always be at liberty to accommodate you, Delaney."

She felt guilty for deceiving him. One part of her wanted him to wait for Delaney, but a big part of her wanted him to return to the madam. At least, as Madame, she could have him now. "*Monsieur*, please don't forget that I told you I hope you will be available when I'm in a position to find happiness. But I don't know how long that will be. If ever. 'Tis best you mind that, so not to miss out on your own opportunity to seek joy."

She'd just told him to not waste his time on her, and it was as painful to say as it was to see reflected in his eyes. Slowly, he straightened his shoulders, and the line of his jaw flexed. He looked grave and made his displeasure known in his expression. "I understand, *mam'selle*."

Chapter Twenty-Two

Billy, Penelope, and Delaney were getting dressed for the ball in Fannie's room.

"You don't want to come, Gertie?" Billy asked.

"No, I have a client coming. He's booked me for the whole night."

Gertie was lying on Fannie's bed, her toe tapping the headboard as she watched them streaking Delaney's hair.

Delaney had decided she wanted a lot more extravagance that evening. She chose a high-waisted gown with an exceptional design. The dark green silk skirt was wrapped and tied underneath her left breast, and the top fold was cut dramatically in front to reveal a golden silk petticoat embellished with embroidery. The bodice was green and gold and had small straps draping from the shoulders instead of sleeves. It was her favorite costume. Billy streaked Delaney's hair with purple and small lines of green, and then Fannie helped Delaney pin on her golden mask. Long purple and green feathers swooped high up the right side of the mask. Ribbons draped down and entwined with her streaked curls. She painted romantic lines of purple and green on the lower half of her face and down her neck. She dotted jewels in her hair.

Billy and Penelope put on their masks and gloves while Gertie inspected their costumes. Billy looked dazzling in her blue-and-green gown, with elaborate peacock feathers draping each side of her white mask. Penelope wore a provocative bright-orange-and-deep-blue gown with matching mask, and her dark hair was piled high, with curls tumbling down her back.

"Breathtaking," Gertie sighed, and all three playfully curtsied.

Remi knocked on the door and announced their coach was waiting.

"I've never been to anything like this," Billy said excitedly as they headed down the long corridor.

"Neither have I," Delaney said. She'd attended a few balls in London, but they were nothing compared to what she was doing now. Her costume was the most lavish thing she'd worn yet. When they reached the main staircase, Delaney sighed. "I forgot my gloves. Go ahead. I'll be along."

She raced back to Fannie's room and slid on her long black gloves. Then she retraced her steps to the stairs. Billy and Penelope were waiting in the foyer, chatting with several other patrons coming for refreshments and entertainment. She was halfway down the staircase when Alderic entered the foyer. Her last words to him rang in her ears and she held her breath, remembering all too well how he was affected by them. But as Madame Cardui, she felt more confident in receiving him. In fact, she relished her position, for she could flirt with him and touch him. They could enjoy each other's company without expectations beyond passion and pleasure. The pedestal he put Madame on was far different from the standards he put on Delaney.

He stepped into the entrance and was greeting Remi when he sighted her from the corner of his eye. Suddenly he seemed to have forgotten about Remi and whatever they were discussing. He watched her descend the staircase, his ever-present smile lingering as he sauntered to the bottom of the staircase. When she reached the last step, he was waiting, holding out his hand.

"Good evening, *monsieur*," she said with a smile.

As he kissed her hand, the intensity of his gaze made her warm.

"Madame," he said.

"Doesn't she look lovely, Alderic?" Billy said, breezing over to them.

Penelope also joined them, swinging her arm around Billy's shoulders. "We plan to steal all the attention tonight."

"Ladies, you are stunning," Alderic said. Then his eyes rested again on Delaney. "*Tu es belle.*"

"*Merci, monsieur.*"

"I came to see you this evening, but it seems you are leaving."

"We're going to a ball," said Penelope.

"At *La Salle*," added Billy.

"You do not attend such festivities, *monsieur*?" Delaney asked. "I heard it is a popular event."

"It is for travelers and men looking to heighten their New Orleans experience," he said. "I am already schooled in New Orleans' ways."

"Would you escort us anyway?" Penelope asked.

"Rafe and Remi have to stay here and manage the house," Billy filled in.

Penelope and Billy leaned closer to him and slid their fingers along the lapels of his coat. "We'd appreciate it so much, Alderic."

He observed the women hanging off his lapels, and then Delaney, who was stifling a grin. He cleared his throat. "It will be an honor to attend a ball with such lovely women on my arms."

Delaney grimaced when Penelope and Billy squealed. He held out his hand. "Allow me, Madame?"

She took his hand, and they strolled to the door. "I was not prepared to go to a ball," he said. "I would have dressed more appropriately."

She eyed his long tailcoat, dark blue waistcoat, and crisp white cravat—perfectly tied. "I think you are dressed rather finely," she said.

"Thank you, Madame, but anything less than exceptional is unacceptable," he said with a slanted smile. Then he lifted his chin so high that he was glancing down at her from over his nose. In an exaggerated, haughty tone, he said with a drawl, "But I s'pose 'twill have to do."

Penelope rushed up to him with a simple black mask in her hand, and she tied it on Alderic.

The coach was a tight fit with all of them. Delaney was squeezed against Alderic, though she didn't mind it in the least. She leaned in. He smelled of sandalwood and something like pine, and a slight hint of tobacco.

They rolled up St. Phillip's Street and stopped next to the opera house and *La Salle*. The whole block was lit up, and people were flooding inside. Everyone was dressed lavishly in bright costumes and masks. She could hear the music as soon as the coach door opened.

Alderic helped them out of the carriage, and she frowned at the long line to get in.

"Perhaps we should've come earlier," she muttered.

Alderic tipped his head and chuckled. "Nonsense. You are right on time." He took her hand, folded it into the crook of his elbow, then guided her and the birds past the lines of people. Alderic knew the man at the door admitting the guests, and they were swiftly ushered inside.

"I am glad you came with us," she said.

His easy smile returned as he replied, "I do not wait in lines, Madame. And neither should you."

"Why is everyone staring at us?" she asked.

"They are staring at me." He gave her a wink and added, "They covet my situation."

She gave a breathy laugh as she was swept into the ballroom, where she gazed about with admiration. She was glowing with excitement.

"We'll find you later," Penelope said. "I appreciate the escort, *monsieur.*"

Billy said similar thanks.

"The pleasure was mine, *mademoiselles,*" Alderic replied.

Delaney watched them flutter away in pursuit of a few fine gentlemen. Alderic didn't hesitate in guiding her straight to the dance floor. He whirled her into the crowd of dancers, and they both fell into the steps of a quadrille.

"You're a brilliant dancer, *monsieur,*" she said with a smile.

Grinning wolfishly as he turned her, he said, "I am only trying charm you, Madame. I have my own motives." The intensity in his eyes as they raked over her gave her a good indication of his motives, and she felt her cheeks burning. He added playfully, "If this does not work, I plan to overwhelm you with wine."

She laughed. "Is that so?"

Alderic pulled her close for a moment, and his smile faded. "Though it would be flattering if you told me my tactics are not necessary. That you need no persuasion."

His words made her legs grow weak, and she tried not to stumble. The music ended, and he bowed as she dipped down in a deep curtsy.

A long-legged man with wide shoulders and chocolate hair came up behind her and bowed. "Madame Cardui, may I have this dance?" His American accent appeared familiar, though she couldn't place him. A good part of his face was concealed behind a mask. Alderic kissed Delaney's hand and gracefully excused himself from the dance floor.

"You look amazing this evening, Madame Cardui," the man said as he led her into the steps of a reel.

"Thank you," she replied, "but you have the advantage of knowing my name, *monsieur*."

He didn't offer his name. Instead, he said, "I am very much interested in Billy."

"You must be more specific about your interests, *monsieur*."

He briskly ended the dance and motioned her away from the dance floor. They walked casually toward the large open doors leading to the balcony.

"My work is stressful, Madame," he explained. "My hours are rather odd since my business demands a lot of my time. I've acquired Billy's services before. Yet I've struggled to find her available again, as she is in high demand."

Delaney wasn't sure she'd get used to talking about the birds like property, their bodies a business on demand.

"I'm seeking to make her my mistress," he said.

"May I ask who you are and what you do, *monsieur*?" she asked. "Before any consideration is granted, I must know that you can afford such an obligation."

"Understandable. My name is Alexander Wilton. I'm an American and a local politician. I own a small cottage here in the Quarter and would like her to stay there."

Delaney lifted her chin as she considered Billy staying in his cottage instead of at the house. It was disheartening to imagine not seeing her every day. "Come by tomorrow evening," she said. "I will speak with her, and we can discuss the matter further."

He bowed. "Yes, Madame."

"Good evening, *Monsieur* Wilton."

Hours passed, and she was approached by a lot of gentlemen with the same intentions as Alexander Wilton. She discovered that going to the ball would be profitable indeed. Tomorrow, several prospects were coming to the Bird House to discuss the details.

As the night continued, Alderic sought her out with two glasses of champagne. "You have been busy, Madame," Alderic said, handing her a flute.

"I suppose," she replied, sipping her champagne.

He considered her tepid tone and cocked a brow. "Your expectations were not met?"

"No, they have been," Delaney said, pasting on a smile. "The girls will be excited to hear how many men wish to retain their services. Some on a more permanent basis."

He eyed her. "But it does not please you."

She caught herself staring at the floor, so she lifted her eyes and feigned a smile. "Of course I'm pleased," she said. "My profits grow by the day."

He lowered his lids suspiciously. "You need not

pretend with me. I am well aware that you have not the stomach for the business you are in."

"You make a bold claim, *monsieur*," she replied, her gaze icing over.

"Your interest is in the arts," he said, "not selling women to the highest bidder. I have seen your expression change when you have to conduct a transaction. You find the whole business distasteful, and no layer of paint can conceal that."

She gaped at him as he continued to nonchalantly drink his champagne. "I did not realize I was under surveillance."

Alderic chuckled. "I think it is obvious. Perhaps others do not pick up on it at all."

"I confess, I don't find my position appealing."

"Then why are you continuing this farce?" he asked. "Let someone else assume the responsibility."

"It is not that simple," she mumbled.

"It can be," he said. Then he added, as more of an afterthought, "But if you let the Bird House go, then it would be like letting your mother go—there is that plightful matter."

He had a point she hadn't considered. His insight made her own reaction slightly uncomfortable. She tilted her head at him. "And then what?"

"A good question indeed, Madame." He flashed her a wink and then took her empty glass and walked over to a nearby server with a tray. Upon his return to her, he was stopped by an acquaintance.

She was left standing alone for a moment, pondering Alderic's words.

A man approached her wearing an elaborate mask, and he blocked the distance between her and Alderic.

"Do you wish to dance, Madame Cardui?" His dark, piercing eyes were haunting and unnerving. And telling. Jack Chanfray.

She lifted her chin and straightened her shoulders. "I think *non, monsieur*."

His usual sly grin splayed across his face. "Has tonight been profitable?"

"That is not your concern."

"You needn't use that false accent with me." He took a step closer and peered down at her, saying suggestively, "I had the pleasure of meeting you before your elaborate disguise. I saw Alexander Wilton approach you. Is he interested in securing one of your girls?"

"I don't believe that is your business, either," she replied.

"He is a well-connected client of mine, Madame. If I were you, I'd tell him she's unavailable."

She eyed him a moment. "Do not threaten me, *monsieur*."

"I don't make threats." His voice was menacing. "I do not bluff."

She arched her brows and said lightly, though her tone carried an edge, "I do not even play. If you are losing customers, perhaps you need to consider why."

She curled up the corners of her mouth, though she didn't give the impression she was at all amused. She turned to leave. "Have a wonderful evening, *mon*—"

He gripped her upper arm, nearly encircling it completely in his hand and gripping so hard she winced. "You'll regret crossing me. I have designs on this city, and you, Madame Cardui, are fucking with them!"

"Jack, how are you this evening?" Alderic said in

that familiar, vibrant tone. He held out his hand in greeting, and Chanfray readily released Delaney.

"Beaumont." He smiled thinly as he shook Alderic's hand. "I thought my order would be delivered yesterday. Your supply of wine is rare, and heavily sought out by my patrons."

Alderic's easy smile never faltered, nor did his light tone as he said, "I am afraid, due to my latest warehouse complications, shipments have been delayed a bit."

"But everyone else received theirs," Jack replied, and he stepped a little closer. His voice dropped dangerously as he continued. "I've been a dependable client and should've gotten my goods *before* others."

"You prioritize yourself far higher than I do. Since our latest kerfuffle with the authorities, we've had to shorten our client list. My partner and I agree that we cannot guarantee your goods any longer. You would do best to find another supplier."

She watched Jack's piercing eyes and felt a chill run through her. Yet Alderic seemed unfazed. Actually, he looked like he enjoyed delivering the news.

"You're telling me this now," he growled. "You and Tarquin are making a grave mistake. There are consequences for cutting me off."

"There are consequences for sending the authorities to my warehouses," Alderic replied.

Jack sniffed loudly and retook his step back. "I don't appreciate false accusations, Beaumont."

"Lest you forget, I know everyone in this city," Alderic said, straightening the cuff of his coat. "Do you still dare lie to me?"

After another second, Jack recovered his disgruntled look and gave a sly grin. "We are businessmen. Men of profit. Perhaps there's been a misunderstanding and things have been taken a bit far. I'm one of your best customers, Alderic."

"You are that no longer," Alderic said with a rather dismissive wave, he looked away from Jack and turned to her. "Shall we get some air?"

The tension was stifling, and she was more than ready to leave its vicinity.

She nodded, and that was when Jack spat. "This whore?" His words were delivered with a slice, and she inhaled deeply to recover from their sting. Her eyes burned into his. He peered back at her and scoffed. "They said Madame was untouchable, but apparently you do have a price. You'll spread your legs to the highest bidder, after all."

Jack twisted her stomach and made her skin flush with instant rage. She was about to lash out at him when Alderic held her fast.

"This display of desperation will not serve you, Jack," Alderic said. For the first time, she witnessed a change in Alderic that shut the door completely on his carefree nature. His easy smile was nonexistent and his brilliant gaze darkened. His voice became dangerously low, and his manner reeked of a warning that was unmistakable—even to Jack.

Jack leaned in, and his expression became as dire as his tone. "You're trying ruin me, aren't you?"

"It would be wise for you to remain within the scope of business you were granted when you came to this city."

Jack raised his chin and chewed the inside of his cheek a moment before he said, "You and Tarquin believe you're the dominant forces here. Allow me to remind you that you are not. I have contacts up the river that will not think kindly of your threats."

Delaney watched an icy smile slide across Alderic's face that could strike fear to one's soul. "If you wish to continue down this path, I will be forced to commence a commination such as you've never seen, one that will rain destruction down upon you and all your investments."

"You exaggerate your capabilities," Chanfray said.

Alderic chuckled, and nothing within his tone or expression offered humor. In fact, the sound of it made her cold. Indeed, she'd never witnessed this side of Alderic. Then, just as swiftly, his mood changed, and his languid nature returned. His features softened, and his golden-green eyes regained their dazzling hue. "Enjoy the remainder of your evening, Jack."

Jack retreated another step, then flashed her a look that alerted every inch of her spine. "An ensnaring gift a woman can have. So that she may launch a war, and reap the spoils from both sides as they burn to the ground. I assure you, your deceptions will return tenfold, my unfledged bird. And such a retaliation will be unfathomable to you."

Alderic had been right, Jack Chanfray reeked of desperation, and his temper bordered on flaring madness. "You're a snake, Chanfray," she said. "Therefore, you cannot think more than as a reptile." With that, she turned her back so she could end her encounter with him and allow Alderic to lead her away. That was when Jack curled his long fingers around her arm again and dug into her flesh. She barely had a moment to feel their sting before a blade was pressed against his throat. She watched, wide-eyed, as Alderic pressed a dagger against

Jack's flesh. Suddenly, surrounding conversations halted. Everyone within eyesight of the scene gaped.

Chapter Twenty-Three

Delaney had not seen Alderic move, let alone when and from whence he retrieved the weapon. The hard lines of his face matched that of the steel threatening Jack's throat.

Jack instantly released her arm and inched from the dagger. "I hope the chit is worth it, Beaumont," he seethed.

Alderic's frown deepened. "You look for a scapegoat because you think me fool enough to lose sight of your own deception? I hope not, for that is almost as insulting as you taking liberties upon that which I have already claimed as mine," Aderic replied coolly.

Jack's nostrils flared, his lips making a tight line that curled. He said nothing—only gave a terse nod—then whirled away, and shoved through the crowd.

Alderic didn't miss a beat as he turned away from Jack's retreating back and asked her, "Are you all right, Madame?" He spoke casually as he slid the dagger within his sleeve. She needed another moment to adjust to yet another swift change in his behavior. She shook her head, nearly rubbing her temples at the new display of Alderic. He'd just revealed a dangerously dark side. "How is it that you laugh constantly, and everyone considers you a friend…yet, at the same time, you can make anyone fear you?"

His easy smile faded, and he shifted his stance as he

glanced at the spectators slowly returning to their previous chatter. He looked almost uncomfortable, and his gaze seemed dire, as did his words. "Did I make you fear me, Madame? I assure you, it would never be my intention to do so."

"Of course you frightened me, Alderic," she stressed. "You boldly announced a claim on me, and threatened to kill a man in the middle of a crowd for touching me!"

His easy smile returned. "I had no intention of killing him and ruining our evening. However, it was necessary to remind him that one must evaluate one's own behavior."

In normal circumstances, she would've laughed at the exaggerated innocence pasted on his face and laced within his voice. But her sense of humor couldn't be dredged up. "I do not belong to you, Alderic. Or to anyone."

He offered no response, only held out his hand and took her back to the dance floor. He led her into the steps of another dance, and soon the tension between them dissipated. He kept his body close, holding her longer than was considered appropriate for the dance. All was done subtly, smoothly. Just as he did everything else. Soon the incident with Jack was forgotten as he weaved his spell of charismatic movements. The intoxicating scent of him and the intensity of his touch enmeshed her in his presence. The mere brush of her skin, a gentle breath upon her neck, sent her into a series of trembles and desire. When the dance ended, she lingered in a haze as he escorted her off the dance floor.

"I'm growing weary of this ball," he said with a wicked smile. "I would love to escort you back to the

Bird House."

She understood from the tone of his voice and the keen interest in his eyes just why he wanted to leave. Her reply to his comment would determine the rest of her evening. And she had to admit that spending it with Alderic was tempting.

However, he was confident enough. She didn't need to further nourish his already healthy sense of confidence. "*Monsieur*, why should I leave this wonderful masquerade so early?"

"There is far better entertainment I can expose you to," he suggested.

"Such as?" She was flirting with him, taunting him in hopes he wouldn't continue staring at her with his cocky smile. But she wasn't expecting it when he halted his steps, turned to her, and snaked his arm around her waist. He kissed her fully in front of everyone. Again he'd stunned her with his ability to make her forget everything around them as he delved into her mouth. She momentarily felt as though she'd been whisked back into the steps of a whirlwind dance, but with a pulsating heat that seared through her. When he pulled a mere breath away, he held her gaze, and she was entranced.

"Beaumont, the inn is next door," someone from the crowd chortled.

"We are leaving," he said, and steered her through the crowd to where Penelope and Billy were waiting for them.

"I suppose it is time to go?" Penelope said, winking at them.

"Ladies, this party has dulled," Alderic said, and he held out his other arm. Billy and Penelope both grabbed it, and he escorted them all to the door.

They had their wraps and were walking across the street toward the coach several yards away. Delaney glanced at the people dallying outside. The night air was cool, a blessing after the heat during the day. She looked overhead and saw the clear sky parading its infinite sparkles, and she took time to appreciate its beauty. It was the perfect backdrop to a magical evening. In the moment, she could forget she'd attended a ball intended to connect gentlemen with available women. She could imagine that she and Alderic were within the throes of a true courtship. Yes, it was a dream, and she was being delusional. But it was her imagination, and she was relishing the idea. If only for a moment.

Her momentary serenity was broken, however, when Alderic's mood shifted. His arm flexed beneath her gloved hand and she noted how his manner had stiffened. She looked at his strong profile and followed his stare to a group of men gathering across the way. They weren't dressed as if part of the event going on at the theater. In fact, they looked rather scrappy. And their chatter amongst each other seemed to be directed at Alderic.

Alderic stopped in the middle of the street as they continued to stare at him. They shielded their hands at their sides as they closed the distance, and she suspected they were concealing weapons. Delaney watched Alderic carefully. She felt his earlier tension relax beneath her touch. His flexed jaw slackened and his casual stance returned. It was confusing, to say the least. Clearly, danger was imminent.

Their carriage approached and halted. She felt a whoosh of relief. Maybe that was why Alderic had relaxed. Whoever those men were, glaring at him, they weren't crossing the street, so she and the others could leave without any trouble.

"Alderic, let us hurry and go?" she asked nervously. The girls stepped into the carriage and, once he'd helped her into the carriage, Delaney waited for him to climb in also. But he didn't. Her eyes widened. "Alderic? Please get in the carriage so we can depart."

Alderic took her hand and kissed it. "I'm afraid I must leave you in the driver's capable hands."

Her eyes shot from the men to Alderic. "No, Alderic, you are my escort."

He handed the driver a generous amount of coins and muttered something to him in French. "I will be along later, as I have important business to attend."

"Alone?" she asked. "Can you not just come back with me?"

"Nothing would please me more, Madame," he replied with a smoky gaze. "But I think it necessary that you leave immediately."

"Alderic, we are not leaving without you," she insisted, as she noted the men finally starting to cross the street. He noticed, as well.

He ignored her words and signaled to the driver. The carriage quickly rolled forward. She called to him, but he only remained silent as the space between them stretched.

****

Alderic watched the carriage pulling away, and a small smile tugged at his lips. No mask could disguise the concern in her eyes as they departed. The plea in her voice and the fear for his welfare within the depths of her amazing eyes were indisputable. And the idea warmed him. The Painted Lady *was* his, whether she wanted to admit that or not.

He let out a long, heavy breath as his attention was forced away from the beauty anticipating his return to the Bird House. His ears piqued as a number of booted heels echoed across the cobblestones toward him. He knew Chanfray was overcome with defeat, but he had thought him smart enough to exhibit restraint. Having his buffoons rough him up—or end his life completely—on the street was a sad display, equivalent to a child's tantrum. He shook his head and turned around. He lit some of his finely rolled tobacco, and inhaled. He slowly blew out a cloud of smoke and calmly watched the men close in. He glanced around, holding onto hope that he'd see someone who might assist him. But the streets were bare. Everyone was inside, enjoying the evening's entertainment. Any shouts of anguish would be drowned out by the music and gaiety of the ball. Mentally, he took inventory of his weapons. He certainly hadn't armed himself well. His intention had been to spend the evening with Madame. He had only a dagger in his sleeve. That was it. He looked at the men and started forming a plan. The image of Nye, a few years ago, flashed in his mind. When he came upon his friend, so long ago, he'd been drowning in a pool of his blood. Nye had survived only because he'd been discovered in time to stop the attack. But something told him the same fortune wouldn't be bestowed upon him. He looked toward the safely lit ballroom across the street and the men spread out to block that path. He took another drag of tobacco and released a cloud.

"And what are your orders? To kill me? To maim me—send a message?" Alderic asked with a smirk.

Of the four men slowly surrounding him, the tallest one spoke up. "You're about to find out."

"You realize the consequences will be grave, and—if you're not dead by sun-up—you will certainly be unemployed."

A series of soft chuckles bounced around him. "I think it's time you realize that you and Nye Tarquin have occupied this city far too long. It's time for the lot of you to bow out. Your death will pack a punch with that message."

"My death?" Alderic laughed, shaking his head. "Death is final and the stench of it lingers only a short time for men like us, before we're seeking retribution. You do recall what Tarquin did when he was attacked and left for dead? You cannot fathom the hell that will come upon you when he discovers his friend and business associate was murdered." He shook his head and curled his nose. "Chanfray doesn't understand the art of—"

"Jack told us you talk too much." The man said as he aimed his pistol at Alderic's chest.

Alderic growled inwardly. His options were far too limited. He'd spent those few seconds assessing each man surrounding him, their weapons, and devising a course of attack. No part of his healthy imagination envisioned him making it out unscathed, or even alive. He cursed and held up his hands. "Can you grant me a final request?"

"We've already been generous. We allowed those whores to leave first, so they wouldn't witness your demise."

It was true. When he saw the men waiting for him, he knew if he got into the carriage, they would halt it and all the women would suffer the same fate as that planned for him. He couldn't bear the idea of them suffering because of him. Especially Madame.

Alderic cocked a brow and scoffed. "They were only tonight's entertainment. I spared you a lot of screaming and crying—and not even the thrilling kind, but the annoying shrills of a fearful woman. So grant me a request, I insist."

The man cocked his pistol. "If it'll shut you up. What do ye want, Beaumont?"

"This is one of my favorite pieces," Alderic said and started unbuttoning his coat. "I do not want it damaged."

The men glanced at one another and raised their brows. "We'll make sure you're buried in it," the man said with curl of his thin lips.

Alderic chuckled softly, and slowly removed his coat, his eyes darting around him. Still, no one was within sight on the darkened side of the street. He carefully folded his coat and held it out to the man on his left, a young, pox-scarred lad. He concentrated on his breath just as the young man reached for it, and he deliberately dropped his coat. Simultaneously—and unexpectedly—a shot rang out. He didn't feel a bullet puncture him, but he saw the man with the pistol aimed at his chest buckle over. Alderic didn't have time to assess what had happened, but he took the moment as a blessing. He dropped to the ground and grabbed his coat as the other men readied their pistols. Some were aiming behind him toward the one who'd fired at their lead man. Some were ready to fire at him. He swung his coat at the man on his left, causing the young man's pistol to fire randomly in the air. Alderic unsheathed his dagger, and the following seconds passed in a blur as he easily took down the young man, then another. All pistols had been fired and the last man, of a rather stocky nature, had only a knife. He lunged at Alderic, who took a step back, maneuvering so he could trap the stocky man's hand with both of his and pin the blade at his side.

The maneuver worked, but the assailant grabbed the back of Alderic's neck and used his body to fling them to the ground. During their tumble, Alderic snatched the knife from the man's grip. He slammed his fist into his opponent's jaw, but it wasn't enough to get the man off him. The man went for the blade but couldn't stop Alderic from sinking it into his fleshy gut. The man howled, but then a loud thud sent the man limp, and he collapsed into a heap on top of him. When he looked up, he saw Madame staring down at him, gripping a pistol tightly in her hands. Her eyes wide, she was shaking uncontrollably.

He swiftly rolled the body off him and stood up. Her eyes were fixed on the man lying in the street. "D-Did I kill him?"

Alderic reached for the pistol in her trembling hands. "No, Madame, you showed him mercy by knocking him unconscious with the butt of that pistol. I'm certain the blade I put in his gut will be his death."

She spun around and looked at the lead man she'd shot. The man wasn't dead, but badly wounded. He was scrambling to get on his knees and crawl away, his hand protecting his injury. "I-I've never fired a pistol before," she stammered.

Alderic registered her words and cocked his brows. He considered her admission, recalling just how close his assailant had been to him… She could very well have shot him instead!

He was grateful when she finally released the pistol, and he tossed it aside. His hand slid to her jaw and gently shifted her gaze from the bloody heaps at their feet to himself. He held her stare. "You shouldn't have come back here. You could've been on the losing end of a nasty scene."

She seemed to shake out of her fog as she replied, "And if I didn't, you certainly would've been. You are welcome, *monsieur*."

He was relieved to see the return of that spark in her eyes. He grinned. "*Touché*, Madame. You saved my life, and I thank you."

Activity across the street caught his attention, and he cleared his throat. "We need to leave." He picked up his coat and shook it out. That was when he felt the pain shooting in his chest.

"You're hurt," Madame said.

He grunted as he inspected the wound. "It's no more than a scratch. Sadly, you would have thought they could have done better, with such an advantage."

She shot him a steamy glare. "Are you ever serious?"

He responded with a lopsided grin as he straightened his cravat and folded his coat over one arm before offering her his other.

Chapter Twenty-Four

They walked silently down the street, and she could see Alderic was biting back the pain from his injury. She noted the increase of blood staining his clothing and a bead of sweat forming on his brow.

"I had Penelope and Billy tell Remi to send help, so I'm sure a carriage will be arriving soon," she said.

"*Merci*, Madame," he chimed, and flashed her a wink. "Your concern for me is warming. I do believe I have harnessed your sentiments."

She gave him a side glance and shook away his mischievousness. Alderic had no idea how the simplest look or just his mere presence could affect her. In truth, he could crush her, thoroughly. She was becoming completely taken by him.

After she'd climbed into the carriage earlier, she watched him shrink in the distance as they pulled away, and she felt as though someone was gripping her heart, pulling it out of her chest. She demanded that the driver stop, and she took his pistol. Before he could argue, she jumped out of the carriage and rushed back to *La Salle*. As she watched Alderic's assailant aim a pistol at his chest, she feared she might not be able to help—she'd never fired a pistol, and she could only guess how well her aim would be. With an admission she'd take to her grave, she was certain she closed her eyes when she fired.

"Were those Chanfray's men?" she asked, breaking the silence.

"*Oui.*"

She waited for him to expound, but heard only the sounds of their steps on the cobblestones. "You are going to retaliate, aren't you?"

"*Oui,*" he replied. "Promptly."

"You and Nye Tarquin, whom I have heard much about?"

"Nye need not be informed of this incident," he said.

"Should he not know that he has an enemy targeting him and his associates?"

Alderic glanced at her with a smirk she was growing to expect and anticipate. Somehow, his playful nature put her at ease and told her that even the direst of circumstances weren't quite as grim. "Nye is well aware he has enemies. And Jack's recklessness tonight surprises none. I prefer to handle this on my own, while Nye has more important matters to attend."

"But you were almost killed!"

"I'm often nearly killed, Madame," he said. "It comes with my position."

"Then why do you choose such a profession? Surely, there are safer ways to make your living."

He stopped briefly and turned to her. "I was raised amongst the most elite, and yet I still looked over my shoulder each day." He started walking again, and she listened as the tone in his voice changed in a way that piqued her interest. "My entitlements were threatened profoundly, and by those whom I'd even considered my friends. This put me in a constant state of paranoia that eventually seeped into my soul, and which I could not shake. On the streets, I discovered a candid expression of the same threat. However, it is a situation I can relax in, slightly, so I can still enjoy my existence. Reckless brutality is easier to spot in the weeds than a calculated stalker cleverly camouflaged amongst the trees."

"You accepted your fate as a target, and thus chose the path where you could outsmart those targeting you. Did it ever occur to you that you can have a peaceful existence, a living that carries no threat, in an environment that does not wish you ill will?"

He stopped again, and brushed his thumb over the fine layer of paint swirling over her skin. He looked almost sad, as his voice sounded distant. Lost. "No such place exists."

"I do not believe that," she commented.

He raised a brow. "Really? And what do you believe?" he asked.

"I believe we create our reality, based on the fundamental beliefs of who we are. How has your own perception created your world?"

He paused a moment and searched her eyes. She wasn't sure what he was looking for, what thoughts were crossing his mind. But she wondered…had she'd revealed too much of herself to him?

"Can I ask how one's perception has led an artist to a house of lust, forced to conceal her identity behind a gift that is simply washed away every evening, never to be seen twice?"

She didn't appreciate his inquiry in the slightest. She shifted her stance and straightened her spine. She couldn't explain to Alderic the events that had sent her hiding behind a mask. She couldn't have him prying into the dark depths of her mind, in which she herself hadn't yet discovered the answers. Madame Cardui needed to remain aloof to the depths of soul and understanding. To understand the foundation of why and how she was— that was a path too winding to tread, too uncomfortable to explore.

"Perhaps our friendship should remain within the everyday," she suggested. "Our escape of such uncomfortable truths."

He chuckled. "Superficial? Simple?"

She smiled. "A light. Relieving us from the darkness that plagues our dreams at night and wakes us from our deep slumbers."

He removed her fingers from his sleeve and folded them within his. He brought them to his lips and kissed her hand. "I would enjoy having you as my light."

The thickness in his voice sent her heart racing, and she struggled to remain seemingly calm. "It is settled. Now let us get you mended."

Almost as if he'd forgotten he was bleeding, he glanced at his bloodied attire and nodded. He returned her hand to the crook of his elbow, and they continued walking until they met a carriage racing toward them. When it stopped abruptly in front of them, she saw Remi in the driver's seat.

"Penelope and Billy told me there was trouble and to hurry. What happened to you, Alderic?" Remi asked, his gaze running over the seeping blood.

Alderic helped Delaney into the carriage, barely glancing at his injury. "We will discuss it along the way. I believe we must get out of here before my assailants are discovered and a search is conducted."

Remi's frown deepened as he eyed Alderic climbing in. With a terse nod, he snapped the reins, and the horses instantly lurched forward.

When they returned to the Bird House, it was filled with people, and she noted Alderic was struggling. He slowly slid on his coat to cover his bloody attire, and she noticed he was losing color in his face. His weak attempt to conceal his condition was with a small, tight smile.

"We need to send for a physician," she said.

"I'd prefer your services, Madame."

She turned a wide-eyed gaze at him. "I am not a doctor."

"It is nothing too serious. I would rather not wait to fetch someone."

"Alderic—"

"And I think discretion is necessary," he insisted.

She picked up the underlying tone in his words, the hard look in his eyes. It was then she realized that the consequences of that evening were the beginning of something much larger than she thought. With a brisk nod, she leaned in and shared some of his weight. They met Rafe at the door, and he led them through a mass of people just to get to her chamber.

"Rafe, can you have someone bring me linens, water, needle and thread?" she asked.

She shut the door to block out all the noise in the foyer. Turning, she saw Alderic at her side table, pouring a drink. He offered her one, but she waved it away.

"Take off your jacket," she said.

He rested on the edge of the bed and raised a brow. "Cannot wait to take off my clothes, Madame?" he teased.

She rolled her eyes heavenward. "You are not as amusing as you think you are."

He grunted and took a sip of brandy. "I am mildly amusing, I think," he muttered, and she noticed how he swayed. She gave a heavy sigh and took his snifter after he gulped down the last of its contents.

"You'll have to help undress me, Madame," he whined, exaggerating his helplessness.

She didn't have to state the obvious: that he wasn't concerned about any pain. As usual, he was teasing her. She decided she could either argue with him or instead play along to hurry things so she could see how badly he'd been hurt. She began untying his cravat, and all the while, he held her with a steady, wicked gaze as his hands encircled her waist.

"You acquired my gambling tables to compete with Jack," she began. "You wanted me to hurt his business. What is the situation between the two of you?"

"He was a loyal client of mine," he replied. "I supplied him with quality luxuries... But Chanfray's business extends far beyond gaming houses and bordellos. Almost two years ago, my own personal affairs sent a bullet through the skull of one of his business associates, halting Jack's safe transports of undocumented human cargo to surrounding cities."

She tossed aside his cravat, then paused. "Human cargo?"

"*Oui*," he said, and she detected the hint of steel in his voice. "It was something I'd suspected for some time but couldn't say for sure. It was confirmed recently when he offered to pay me handsomely as his new transporter."

His admission sickened her, and made her despise Jack Chanfray even more. She didn't think that was possible! "You refused, of course," she said as she started unbuttoning his shirt.

"I did. I do not associate myself with even the legal side of that market. However, when I refused, he tried different tactics to express his displeasure and sway me to his way. Including sending authorities to my door."

She helped him remove his jacket, eliciting his first genuine display of pain. She gently peeled the stained linen off his shoulder and inspected the injury. She folded up a small piece of linen and held it over the bleeding wound. "That is no scratch," she said.

"Women like to fuss," he scoffed. "I've had much worse; you needn't stitch it. Luckily, my clothing softened the blade's edge."

She put her hand on her hip and glared at him, unable to contain her annoyance. "Well, you're losing quite a bit of blood. If not stitching, then what do you suggest, Doctor Beaumont?"

His eyes strayed from hers and lingered over the elaborate designs painted on her face and neck. Then his attention strayed over her shoulders and settled on the low neckline of her gown. She was aware how his heated stare made her chest heave. He watched her breathing intensify, straining her breasts against the bodice. He pulled her closer, so his thighs trapped her as he cupped her face and captured her mouth with his. She felt her anticipation grow as images of last night flashed in her head.

He pushed from the edge of the bed to stand, and his kisses became more demanding. She held her breath, relishing the sensations his lips created as they moved to her ear and down her neck. He cupped one breast, and she felt that familiar ache building deep in her stomach. His hand slid down to grip her bottom, and he pulled her against him.

And then there was the blasted knock at the door.

"Why is there always someone knocking on your

door?" he growled.

She stepped away from his embrace. "It's your bandages."

Alderic let out a guttural sound. "I do not need bandages." He captured her mouth with his again.

The knocking resumed, annoyingly so. She broke their kiss and ducked away, his frustrated growl sounding in her ears as she rushed to the door. It was Barb with a basin of water, bandages, and a small sewing kit.

"Thank you," Delaney said.

She could barely express her appreciation before Alderic shut the door and locked it. He took the basin and other things from her hands and set them carelessly on the floor. Then he crushed her with more kisses, and she felt her head spinning.

He held her against the door as his kisses ventured down her neck. He pulled up her skirts, and tugged on his breeches. As they inched their way back toward the bed, he started untying the laces of her gown.

"I have thought of little else today," she said between kisses.

"I echo your claim," he said, his voice low.

"But don't you think we should wrap your wound first?" she asked, eying fresh blood seeping through the simple linen she'd covered it with.

His hand slid between her thighs. "You are mine, Madame," he breathed. He found her ready for him and started stroking her hot center. "I want you now." He sat on the bed and swiftly pulled her onto him. She straddled him, and he lay back, adjusting so he could quickly thrust inside her. She sucked in her breath and gripped the bedding above his head, her body adapting to the strain of him intensely stretching her. She rested her brow on his cheek, and his heavy breathing sounded in her ear. His pounding heart vibrated against her as his body connected with hers in every way, sending hot sensations from her stomach, down her thighs, and all through her.

He cupped her face and kissed her. She met his ardent kiss with fervor.

"If you weren't so ready for me, I'm not sure I could even fit inside you," he said with a shaky breath. He gripped her hips, and they savored the feel of their bodies tightly against one another. Waves of desire tore through her, and she happily embraced them. She brushed away the sun-kissed locks that had fallen over his brow so she could hold his fiery gaze.

Alderic swept away the long tresses that had fallen from her pins, tucking them behind her ears. Then his hand slid to her mask. His fingertips lightly touched the ribbons, the question was in his eyes, showing his desire to untie them and remove her mask. Part of her wanted to allow him to take it off, to finally show him that she was the one he'd kissed on the street. She was the one he'd said he wanted to get to know, the one he'd expressed his honorable intentions to. But honor wasn't anything he ever declared when with Madame Cardui. That last thought made her pull away. She thought he'd be angry that she was denying him. In truth, all he had to do was pull the ribbons and the deception would be over.

He didn't. He looked disappointed, but not angry. His fingers dropped from her mask and instead untied the last ribbons securing her skirt. Freeing her of her gown completely, he pulled down her chemise and captured her breast in his mouth. Her body tingled as his tongue teased a taut peak and his hands slid down to grip her hips. He slowly guided her movements, and as her slick body sheathed him, he released a moan that vibrated from deep in his throat. She held her breath as he penetrated deeper inside and steered her rhythm with more force. Delaney leaned forward again and gripped the bedding as their desire built on the very movements that threatened to set her ablaze. She moved to a feverish pace that communicated to her what seemed like an insatiable need. He groaned, clutching her bottom as he ground deep inside her. His lucent gaze held hers for a long moment, and his breath caught incrementally as they sped up their rhythm to match their growing passion. The heat inside her scorched her skin, and she arched her back, tipping her head back as those heated sensations began to ripple through her.

His hand slid to her neck and then slowly down her body, trailing down her stomach and sinking between her thighs. She jolted forward as he again stroked between the folds of her wet center. With his body filling her and his fingers taunting her, she moved wildly over him and drove him toward those same sensations. He tensed, and he gripped her bottom tightly with his other hand so he could guide them both to climax. She cried out, and he pumped into her with unbridled hunger until he, too, released and spilled inside her.

She collapsed on top of him, resting her face in the crook of his shoulder.

Their uneven, heavy breaths filled the silence for several moments while their bodies absorbed the gratifying effects of pleasure. Alderic took her face in his hands once more and kissed her slowly, tenderly. She braced her hand on his other shoulder, and he winced. She instantly remembered his injury, and she quickly moved her hand. How could she have possibly forgotten? Now blood was running down his chest.

"Your shoulder," she said worriedly.

"What have you done, Madame?" He looked at his shoulder and frowned. "How do you plan to make this up to me?"

"Really, Alderic…" She sighed, rolled off the bed, and quickly adjusted her clothing.

Carefully, with weak legs, she stood up and trod unsteadily to the door. Her body was still coming down from the high he'd brought her to. She rather clumsily grabbed the basin and bandages.

Alderic straightened his breeches and sat up. He was wiping the stream of blood from his chest when she brought over the basin and bandages and inspected the wound.

"The cut is rather deep, *monsieur*," she said, as she dipped the rag in the basin. She brushed away his hand and began washing the blood off his shoulder and chest.

The closer she got to his wound, the more he grimaced. "We have moved past the *monsieur* stage, Madame."

She stopped wiping down his chest. "And yet you call me 'Madame.' "

"I do not know what else to call you. Vanessa?" She stole a glance at him before further inspecting the cut on his shoulder, and he shook his head, saying, "That is not your name."

She didn't respond. He took her hand from his shoulder and held it in a loose grip. "Maybe one day you'll tell me what it is," he said.

She focused on her task. "I am not sure why that matters, Alderic. I'm just a madam. If I were to leave this place, I would soon be forgotten."

"Is that why you keep your identity secret? You plan on leaving this life, one day?"

She didn't want to answer that. If she left, she wanted to search him out as her true self. Would it be right to deceive him so? Would he figure it out, and hate her for lying to him? She also thought of Billy, Penelope, Gertie, and all the birds she'd come to care so much for. A part of her was starting to fear that the longer she stayed, the harder it would be to leave.

"I am not much for plans these days." She sighed. "I am taking things day by day. What about you? Does Alderic Beaumont have plans for the future?"

His gaze dropped. "I am planning on legitimizing my business."

She raised her brows. "How do you plan on doing that?"

"It will happen naturally, and I am preparing for it. Smuggling is a necessary evil because of laws set in place that restrict trade. But that will pass because, ultimately, the governments want their cut."

"Eliminating the threats to your business and succumbing so easily to legitimization," she commented as she finished tying the bandage around his shoulder. "It seems like you desire safety and stability. Do you also fancy a more settled presence? A family, perhaps?"

He raised a brow and smirked. "I am a retired corsair, Madame. For a woman worthy of marriage, to get involved with someone like me is not desirable, *non*?"

She observed his disheveled appearance. "You believe you are not good enough for marriage? Worthy of a family?" she asked. Even in his current state, his features were captivating. His noble brow was unmistakable. And his charm melted her, as it did every other woman with whom she'd witnessed him interact. She'd also seen his capability to be kind and gentle. He was comely, wealthy, and refined. Despite his past, she couldn't imagine a woman rejecting his heart.

Alderic slid his arms carefully into his shirt. "I was nearly hung for piracy, and I have many enemies. What you saw tonight was a common threat, one that will not disappear with the legalization of my trade. What woman wants to share my reputation, or the threats associated with me?"

She opened her mouth to respond, then closed it. They were silent as he buttoned his shirt.

"Alderic, you should not make such assumptions. Do not underestimate the capacity of a woman's love."

Something had changed in his demeanor, and he was distracted all of a sudden.

"I must leave, Madame," he announced. "And you have a house to run. No doubt Remi is waiting in the foyer for you."

The conversation was clearly over. The idea of Alderic leaving gave her a sudden sense of melancholy.

"Y-yes, of course. Good evening, Alderic," she said quietly.

The house was still bustling with clients, and she had a few more hours of revelry before the doors closed. The night before, she had been able to spend most of the early morning hours with Alderic. Tonight, that wasn't an option.

He kept his bloodied cravat in his hand after he tenderly slipped on his waistcoat and jacket.

She smoothed out the wrinkles of her gown, since

she couldn't quite meet his gaze. She didn't know what was expected. Last night, when she'd given herself to him, it had been so private. An entire night of passion. Now, they'd shared a quick romp in her chamber, and he was dressing and leaving. She was a fallen woman, and the fact that Alderic was quickly leaving should be perfectly normal. But still, she didn't feel…right. She wanted him to stay. She imagined being with him like she had the night before, in her chamber until morning, but that wasn't their type of relationship, was it? That realization was a cruel reality that made her feel terrible.

"I am sure that, in the next few minutes, someone will be knocking on the door, wondering where Madame is hiding," he said.

She gave him a quick glance before diverting her gaze again. All thoughts running through her mind just then made looking at him difficult. Perhaps he sensed it. He closed the distance between them and gave her a long, tantalizing kiss. When he pulled away, his thumb traced the line of her jaw, and his eyes searched the many painted lines on her face and then her mask.

"When I'm in the city, I do not stay on my ship," he said. "I stay at Le Grand Inn, if you ever wish to see me. But Madame, please, don't come to me in a mask."

Her head shot up and she gave him a clouded look, so he clarified: "I have come to you, and this is your house. I respect your decision to separate yourself from a position that, for whatever reason, you feel compelled to keep. But if you choose to come to me, Madame, I ask that you leave your mask here."

With one last, brief kiss, he quietly left her chamber.

****

Delaney had spent most of the night and the early

hours of the morning analyzing her life in its entirety. She'd never known her mother, and her mother had never mentioned her father during all their years of correspondence. She'd spent her whole life doing what was expected of her without argument or question. She'd done what her teachers, nannies, and professors had wanted. Now, she was doing what the brothel required of her, taking care of the birds, Remi, and Rafe. Now Alderic wanted her to drop her pretenses and come to him. What did that mean? Would she not see him again unless she went to him? Without her mask? Reveal that she'd been deceiving him this whole time? It was all so overwhelming, so suffocating. What did she want for herself, for her life? Beyond her duties, responsibilities, and everyone else's expectations, that is.

She wasn't sure. But she decided it was easier to focus on the Bird House, with the birds and all their problems, rather than look at herself and make decisions about her own life. So she clung to her obligations. They were her greatest distraction. But she couldn't put it off much longer. She loved art and had been offered a job doing what she was passionate about. She wanted Alderic, and he desired her. If she made the wrong choices or waited too long, she could lose both him and the opportunity to pursue her dream.

She washed and dressed, then put her hair up in a loose chignon after donning a comfortable pale pink gown with embroidered silver flowers down the skirt. She put on a simple bonnet, wrote out a brief missive to Remi, grabbed her gloves and wrap, and marched out of the Bird House. With determined strides, she walked several blocks to the small church where she'd been offered the job. She discovered Fernand working on his impressive mural of Saint Catherine.

"Good morning," she said brightly.

Fernand spun, and nearly dropped his paint board.

"Delaney! You came! Does this mean you're ready to talk to Lucien?"

"I am," she said confidently.

He quickly set aside his paint and rushed her up a narrow staircase to the choir loft. There she met Lucien, a short, thinly framed, balding man with kind blue eyes. He gave her a wide grin as he set down his paints and took her hand, kissing it.

"How lovely it is to meet you," he said warmly. "I saw how you improved Fernand's mural. I'm excited you returned today."

He showed her what he was working on.

"Sir, that is impressive," Delaney said. The mural looked almost like a window depicting the resurrection. The lines were beautifully executed, and he'd used lots of color to brighten the dimly lit section of the church. "You use a lot of symbolism, and your subject looks like a force of energy to be reckoned with."

"Yes, is he not?" Lucien puffed up with pride. "I wanted something with a lot of light so it'll brighten this grim loft."

Delaney nodded as she observed the mural. "He's practically erupting from the tomb, yet with all his grace, as well."

Lucien eyed her curiously. "What are your thoughts on it? What would be your approach?"

She creased her brow and wrung her hands on the delicate fabric of her day dress. "I-I…"

Lucien raised his brows. "Well, I want to hear how you'd do something like this. I'm evaluating your creativity and vision."

"Oh." Delaney scanned the unfinished mural again and imagined what she'd do if she had free rein of the piece. "I'd make his surroundings more shattered by his presence. Like breaking the tomb behind him and the ground beneath him to make him appear even more powerful and dramatic."

He began assessing the mural with her.

"He's on a hill with the angels surrounding him," she continued, "but I'd make it as if all life has come to see him rise."

"Yes, maybe more nature would be brighter and offset the stone," he said.

"I agree. The perspective gives me the notion I'm looking out a window. Perhaps you can border it with flowers, nature, and symbolism?"

He clapped, and the cracking sound echoed throughout the loft. "That will be amazing, yes," he said. "Fernand was right! You have vision. I saw your lily downstairs. You're good with flowers?"

"I have experience," she admitted. "I favor nature."

"Well, pick up a brush." He pointed to a cup full of various brushes. "Mix your colors. You'll be bordering the resurrection."

Delaney lifted her brows as a surge of excitement rushed through her. "I'm hired?"

"Yes, of course. I need all the good artists I can get. We'll discuss payment as we paint."

Fernand flashed her a nod of approval and a wide, toothy grin. "Glad you returned, Delaney."

She gave a sigh of relief. "Thank you for inviting me, Fernand."

He bowed respectfully and then promptly left the

loft.

She considered all Lucien's colors, decided which shades she would use to border his painting, and set to work. She found him to be a pleasant fellow, though they didn't talk much while they painted. She was also introduced to a couple of other artists.

By the end of the day, she'd done a fair amount for a good portion of the border. She'd used ivy leaves, draping willows, and even dogwood to border the scene, but she was nowhere near finished. It had been a long day, and she was hungry and covered in paint. But not tired. Quite the opposite.

"We're losing the light, Miss Delaney," Lucien said. "We'll start again in the morning, bright and early. Don't be late. We have another church to start, so we must conclude our work here soon."

Delaney cleaned up the tools Lucien had been kind enough to share with her, and she promised she'd return with her own paintbox. Saying farewell to the others, she stepped outside to the welcome sound of music and the smell of food drifting through the air. Her stomach grumbled.

Carnaval season was wrapping up in about a week, and she had been told the city would calm down a bit. Every night since she'd come to the city, though, she'd heard parties and parades, music and laughter. She couldn't imagine it quiet.

Chapter Twenty-Five

Delaney took a hackney back to the Bird House.

"Where have you been?" Remi demanded.

"I wrote you a message telling you I'd be gone for the day," she said as she breezed past him and went to the kitchen.

"Where were you? Wilton and Bennington are coming this evening, and we haven't even discussed their terms."

"I will speak to Billy and Penelope after I get something to eat," she said over her shoulder. She was mildly annoyed by Remi, and by the Bird House in general. She'd spent the day quietly painting within the serenity of a church. Everything the artists discussed in the church had been in hushed tones. Now her ears were ringing as the girls rushed through the house, arguing. She ate and then spoke with Billy. Billy favored Alexander Wilton, and Penelope had decided Bennington was acceptable. Delaney felt a flood of relief as she realized two girls were now taken care of.

Later that day, Marla discovered that she was with child, and one of her regulars wanted to marry her despite the child's questionable parentage. He was a kind man with a paunch and bushy brows, but a warm smile. He'd paid extra to make sure Marla was available when he came, and now he wanted to buy a small cottage and make a life with her.

Inwardly Delaney sighed, imagining how romantic it was for him to love Marla like that. She recalled Alderic's story of his friend Nye. He'd said Nye Tarquin was a tormented man who'd found a love so strong that none of his faults could drive it away.

She slowly chewed on a honeyed biscuit as she stared blankly at the ledgers. Alderic had given her more than one reason to tell him the truth, but something kept holding her back. Right now, he had a lady he wished to court and another lady he lusted after. She was both. But she couldn't guarantee he'd accept both Delaney and the Painted Lady. She acknowledged that the longer she kept the secret from him, the deeper would be his sense of betrayal. She also had no solution to the predicament she found herself in. That evening, Alderic didn't come to the Bird House, and she convinced herself it was a relief. She had to sort out everything that had happened since she'd come to New Orleans.

The next day, he didn't come again, and she reminded herself she needed to figure out her next moves and assess her possible destination. Without Alderic there, she wouldn't be distracted. So she conducted business as usual. But business was becoming routinely—and mildly—irksome. The birds weren't just workers but her friends. Each of them was unique and had so much potential. Taking payment from men for the use of their bodies only continued to riddle Delaney with guilt.

****

Night had fallen, and the air was thick and sticky. Alderic swatted at something on his arm and cursed the mark left on his skin. He eyed Wil, who was also brushing away the pesky bugs as they waited silently within the brush along the river. It was a miserable night to be sitting along the water's edge...and there were better ways to spend his time. But the ache in his shoulder reminded him why he and several of his men were pushing through the wretched conditions. Whether or not Jack Chanfray had acted impulsively out of fear or desperation—or both—didn't matter. The bastard would pay dearly for sending his thugs after him. The moon wasn't as bright as he'd hoped, and the clouds spreading across the sky limited his vision. He pulled out his timepiece and checked the hour before he looked up at the sky again. A batch of clouds lazily moved passed the moon, and the light momentarily illuminated the river below. That was when he spotted the small barge slowly easing along. He leaned forward and keenly observed the rather unsophisticated contraption making its way up the river under the protection of darkness. To anyone not looking for it, it certainly wasn't noticeable. And of course that was the intention. But Alderic was well aware of the shipment. He'd made it a priority to find out who was working for Jack. And by seizing that shipment, Chanfray would rue the day he'd crossed him.

He looked at Wil and the rest of his crew hidden along the river. He gave the signal. It was time to remind Jack Chanfray of his place...but he couldn't have prepared himself for all that would unfold within those next few minutes...

****

The foyer clock chimed half past midnight as Delaney weaved through the bustling house. She greeted new guests and conducted conversations about local politics and art while drinks were served. Everyone seemed content and happy. Except her. She was growing weary, emotionally, and she wasn't sure if the sudden influx of turmoil within her was because of her position as madam of a brothel or the fact that she hadn't heard from Alderic. The thought of him sent her heart sinking, and she sucked in a deep breath and released it. She squared her shoulders and focused on her surroundings. From the corner of her eye, she saw Fannie heading for the parlor. She'd been upstairs with Diego and now looked troubled. Delaney politely excused herself from the group who'd approached her for conversation, and met up with Fannie.

"Is everything all right?" Delaney asked, taking note of the girl's deep frown.

"Diego's terribly drunk, Madame."

Delaney searched for Remi and Rafe. Usually, when a customer was drunk enough that the girls complained, one of the men dealt with them. But she didn't see either around. Fortunately, she knew Diego well and felt comfortable approaching him—even in his inebriated state. She met him in the foyer and pasted on a smile. He was holding the banister, taking slow steps, and concentrating on his coordination as he descended the stairs.

"Diego," she said, "it appears you have indulged in more than the company."

He looked at her as he reached the ground floor, and his frown lifted slightly. He held out his elbow, and she linked her arm with his. "It appears so," he slurred with a smirk. "You treat us men well, Madame."

"I try to." She felt him leaning on her a bit as they made their way into the office. When they reached her desk, she asked him if he wanted to take a seat in the nearest chair, but he declined. She made sure he was steady before she released him, but Diego's arm tightened around hers.

"Why won't you tell me your price, Madame?" he asked, leaning so close to her she couldn't miss the reeking scent of brandy on his breath.

She feigned another nonchalant smile. "Diego, we cannot have this conversation again," she chided playfully. "I am not—"

She tried to slide away again, but he reiterated his question by gripping her arm with his other hand. Her smile disappeared. "You treat us well, Madame," he said, his tone turning icy. "But if you want to please us, perhaps it's time you stop playing with us. Give us what we're all really here for."

She pulled away again, but despite his intoxication, he was still far stronger. Another attempt to free herself from his grip was futile. "Diego, think about what you are doing," she warned calmly. "You are a favored customer—"

"Correction. I'm the law," he said firmly.

Her spine straightened instantly. "That almost sounded like a threat. I do not wish for you to be thrown out of this establishment, so please respect my words. I am not for sale."

He didn't appear to be listening. His eyes trailed to the low cut of her gown and her partially exposed charms. "Jack's right," he said with a sluggish drawl. "You're a siren meant to lure men into the water and then leave them to drown."

Her eyes hardened. "Jack Chanfray?"

"*Si*, Madame. You'll make money off us, but none of us are good enough for you!"

"Do not listen to Chanfray," she calmly insisted.

He grabbed her around the waist and pulled her against him. "What's behind that mask?" he demanded as he reached for her face covering.

She quickly managed enough space between them to strike him with her free hand. The clash with his cheek didn't get the stunned reaction she'd expected. She'd hoped that he'd come to his senses, or at least release her. Instead, he yanked her toward the settee. She struggled, the searing sound as her gown tore reverberated, and she was shoved onto the cushions.

"I'll not play your games any longer," he said through gritted teeth and started pulling up her skirts. Despite her shouts and flailing arms, he wasn't deterred.

"Diego, stop it!" she shouted.

He was reaching for the buttons of his breeches when he was suddenly thrown off her and tumbled to the floor. The blood pumped wildly in her ears as she witnessed Alderic lift Diego and throw him again. Diego flew across the room, knocking over a small table. Its delicate contents crashed to the floor along with him. Diego dragged himself upright. He stumbled a moment as he tried to gather his wits as well as his footing. Then he charged Alderic, his face twisted with rage as he took a swing at him. Alderic stepped aside, and Diego missed him and stumbled again before spinning around and shouting, "Stay out of this, Beaumont!"

Alderic's jaw clenched and glared as the man regained his balance. "I think not, Diego."

Diego marched up to Alderic, his fists at his sides, his face flushed with fury as he fired his accusation at him: "Is it you she takes her mask off for?"

Alderic squared his shoulders, and she could see every muscle in him tighten as he refrained from striking

Diego.

When Diego didn't rile a response, he spit on Alderic.

In that instant, she realized Alderic wasn't going to back down. He grabbed the drunkard by the lapels of his coat, looking as though he might very well kill Diego.

Diego's earlier reminder that he was the law suddenly rang in her ears, and she rushed to them. "Alderic," she said, "he's inebriated. That is all."

Drilling her with his glare, Alderic demanded, "Would you say that if had I not come in here and stopped him from raping you?"

His blatant words struck her, and it took her a moment to recover from them. He was correct, but what Diego had said was also correct. He was the law, and Alderic was a criminal. "I appreciate your assistance, but I will have Remi take care of this."

Diego shoved at Alderic. "Get off me, Beaumont," he snarled.

Alderic released him, stepped back, and wiped his face with his handkerchief.

"Diego, please leave," she ordered.

Humiliated and flushed with anger, Diego ignored her. Instead of leaving, he swung at Alderic again. This time, he connected with Alderic's jaw.

There was no stopping Alderic now. He grabbed Diego by his cravat and slammed his fist into his face. Diego would have crumpled to the floor, but Alderic was holding him up so he could hit him again. And again.

Delaney ran into the foyer, shouting for Remi and Rafe. *Where the hell were they?*

Finally, Remi appeared and bolted toward the office. His jaw slackened when he discovered Alderic continuously punching Diego. "Alderic, release him!" Remi shouted. He slung his arms around Alderic's shoulders and pulled him back.

With Alderic somewhat detained, Diego charged him and started swinging wildly. Alderic got another fist in the jaw. Alderic immediately broke from Remi and roared, "Do not touch me, Remi!"

Alderic charged Diego, and the scuffle somehow extended into the foyer. Rafe was descending the staircase when he saw the confrontation and rushed over. He and Remi had almost separated them, but then Alderic swung at Diego so fast and hard that Diego fell into a groaning heap.

That should have ended it, but then Remi shoved Alderic aside and barked, "Get out, Beaumont!"

Not even when he was fighting Jack's thugs had she'd seen Alderic so enraged. He shoved Remi back. "Where the hell were you when your Madame was being assaulted in her office?" Alderic shouted. "Too busy diddling Gertie behind the screen, perhaps?"

Remi's temper flared, and he swung at Alderic. Alderic ducked and then punched Remi in the face. Blood exploded from Remi's nose and splattered onto the floor. Remi instantly sank to his knees. His handkerchief did nothing to slow the blood gushing between his fingers. By then, Diego was slowly standing back up, nursing a swollen cheek.

Delaney watched, wide-eyed, at the bloody scene. "Rafe, escort Diego out!" she ordered. "Alderic, such violence is not necessary! What are you doing?"

"Protecting what is mine," he said through gritted teeth.

She looked at him incredulously. "This is my

house," she spat angrily. "The only thing here that is yours are the tables. And they are not in danger!"

His voice lowered and his eyes bore into hers. "I don't give a damn about the tables."

He'd staked a claim on her during the masquerade, and it hadn't set well then. Even more so, now that she watched the consequences of his desire unfold. There could be dire repercussions for attacking Diego in her establishment. It would be detrimental to all her hard work, all her money spent, and all the plans for her future. And it could very well put Alderic in prison.

She sighed. "Diego was drunk and went too far, but..." Remi groaned, and she sank to her knees, inspecting Remi's face. He rested his head on her knee, and she tilted his head back. She pressed her own handkerchief against Remi's nose, and he howled in agony.

Alderic's gaze hardened. "You think he was going to come to his senses, Madame, before he finished with you?" His brow creased as he looked at her incredulously.

"You overreacted, Alderic," she said firmly. "And hitting Remi was crossing a line."

"Maybe he should've been doing his job—which I thought was protecting you!"

Alderic glared down at her. She averted her gaze to avoid a sudden, shrinking feeling. A friend was bleeding on her lap, and a valued client had just been tossed out. And now Alderic was looking at her with an expectation of gratitude. And she was grateful to him. She knew what would have happened had he not come in. But she also knew the possibility of retribution from Diego.

"I appreciate your assistance, Alderic. I truly do,"

Delaney said softly. She didn't know what she was supposed to do. It was like her whole world was starting to crumble down around her. Remi groaned in pain, breaking her thoughts. She sighed, and when she spoke, she couldn't meet his stare. "Please leave."

Seconds stretched, and she finally lifted her eyes. She regretted it. Alderic's eyes had iced over, and that was the only sign of emotion in him. The rest of his face had turned expressionless as he dabbed away the blood seeping from the corner of his mouth.

"You do not belong here, Madame," Alderic declared, his tone harsh. "You have no idea what you have gotten yourself into. Your naïveté has put everyone in this predicament. I can help remedy your problem by eliminating one constituent." He abruptly turned and strode for the door.

"Alderic," she called to him, but the door slammed.

She wanted to run after him, to stop him and explain. Unfortunately, she couldn't decode what was happening herself, or why. Remi groaned a curse, and stole her attention from the door. By now, the guests had gathered in the foyer. She had a mess to mend, a story to smooth over. In the end, she had a duty to the house and her birds. Rectifying with Alderic would have to wait.

She and Rafe helped Remi stand up. "My nose hurts like hell!" Remi howled.

"Stop sobbing like a child," Rafe drawled.

"Let us get you cleaned up," Delaney said quietly, a step behind them. Then she turned to the foyer full of guests, watching intently. She put on her best smile, shouted, "A round of drinks, on me!"

Chapter Twenty-Six

Alderic lowered his head and gave his charger the lead. His mood was grim and his temper violent. He was a man of discipline…for the most part. A man who had a code and acted accordingly. He rarely lost sight of that. He'd proven his self-control by keeping a cool head in the direst of situations, even in the face of death. But seeing Diego attacking Madame had sent him into a rage he could barely contain. It took all his restraint not to crush his throat with his bare hands. Even so, he'd beaten the hell out of the man. And Diego was a man he'd considered both an acquaintance and a client.

He imagined Madame's lips upon his own skin, slightly parted, as she released the sounds of pleasure he'd invoked within her. After the terrible evening he'd had, that image kept his sanity intact as duty called him to the river. When the night's plans went sour and the reality of his world sent him reeling, it was the soft sound of her voice in his ears, her touch, that kept him grounded. No matter how awfully his evening had started, it would end within the comfort of Madame's body. That idea was soothing, motivating. For his troubled mind, it was distressingly desired.

When he entered the Bird House, his mood had lifted, and for a moment, he'd found peace. He nearly shook his head at that thought—finding peace within the walls of a bordello? But it was a cage containing a woman he'd found increasingly fascinating, a place he dared to tread only because duty kept her locked and hidden there. A woman he was more and more desperate to discover and release. Expeditiously so.

When he walked into her office and discovered Diego tearing at her clothes, her cries for help ringing in his ears, instant rage overcame him. The earlier events of that evening crashed onto his shoulders, and the hopes he'd had when he went to the house were dashed. There was no reasoning—he saw only her anguish, and it instantly maddened him. Perhaps, that was why he found her rejection of his help so wounding. Her naïveté in the situation was frustrating, angering... It also opened his eyes to suspicions he wasn't ready to accept.

He shook away his troubling thoughts as he charged out of the Quarter and headed to Tarquin Manor. Only the earliest signs of morning were witness as he rode up the stretch to the iron gates. The men perched by the stone wall opened the gates when they saw him, and he gave them a swift nod as they waved him by. The home was still brightly lit, and a small sense of guilt overcame him as he dismounted and marched up the steps. The door was already opening, and Sarafina greeted him. She looked tired. He couldn't dismiss the faint smudges beneath her eyes, not that it took away from her beauty. Even after a sleepless and stressful evening, her eyes sparkled like the afternoon sun shining upon the Mediterranean. *Oui*, Nye was a man blessed.

She smiled and held out her hand. "Alderic, you returned so soon."

Alderic took her hand and planted a small kiss on her cheek. "I apologize. I feel like I burdened you, and then abandoned you."

Sarafina stepped aside, and he entered the foyer. "Nonsense," she scoffed as she took his jacket, gloves, and hat. "If you needed a moment after what you witnessed tonight, it's more than warranted."

He gave her a warm look and shook his head. "Inexcusable," he said.

She offered a stern correction. "Necessary."

He took her correction with regard. Had he not left the manor and gone to see Madame, God only knew how far things would've gone. He nodded, and pasted a smile over that returned sense of rage he'd experienced upon seeing Diego with Madame. "Perhaps, you are right."

"Of course I am," she said. "Never doubt it."

He couldn't suppress his chuckle at that. "I will not." Their light humor was brief before the severity of the night's events were no longer avoidable. "How are they?"

Sarafina's expression sobered. "Ahmet is with them now."

Ahmet. A saddened smile graced his face as he recalled the old root doctor he'd come to rely on during the past few years. Another sense of guilt overwhelmed him. He'd not seen the woman since she'd saved his own life. Indeed, he owed her much. He followed Sarafina upstairs to a spare chamber now set up with several cots, each one filled with bodies. Ahmet was sitting beside one near the window. She stood and walked over.

He glanced at the room and counted the cots. Not as many as there should've been, which meant…

As if she'd read his thoughts, Ahmet crossed her hands in front of her and said, "No, Alderic, not all of dem could be saved."

He felt a stab in his chest. When he'd seized Jack's

shipment earlier that evening, he took into his custody Jack's silks and tobacco. But it was the number of young women on board, and the conditions in which they were contained, that sickened him. When he and his crew appeared and it seemed like the illegal shipment would be lost—Jack's crew on the barge had tied together the young women, weighted them, and kicked them overboard.

His anguish must've been apparent, since Sarafina placed her hand on his arm and said quietly, "It's not your fault, Alderic. You did what you could."

He wanted to say he'd intercepted the barge tonight simply to rescue the young women being smuggled up the river. But that wasn't the case, however noble. It was business. No, it was revenge. He'd wanted to make Jack Chanfray pay for sending his lackies to kill him.

Just then Nye walked into the chamber, and the surprise on his face was no match for the glee in Sarafina's. "You're back!" She lifted her skirts and rushed to him before he could take another step into the room.

He watched Sarafina and Nye embrace. Plagued with admiration, Alderic swiftly downcast his eyes to the tip of his fine boot, until his attention was caught by the young lady lying in the cot not two steps away. She wasn't sleeping but staring up at him with round eyes. She had a charming splash of freckles across her nose and cheeks. Alderic guessed she wasn't much more than a child.

"Ye fished me out of the water," she whispered with a small smile.

Her accent was unmistakable, for she carried the lilting brogue of a country he'd visited often. He saw something tangled in her hair, and he gingerly removed it from her flaming red curls. He held it up to her and smiled. "I also fished a stick from your hair."

She chuckled. "Yer a master fisher, sir."

Her smile was infectious. "*Oui, mam'selle*. And now you are safe."

"Thank ye, those men were awful."

"You do not have to worry about them anymore," he said. "What part of Ireland are you from?"

"Cork," she replied.

"I know that place well enough," he said. "Perhaps we can reunite you with your family."

Her fingers twisted in her thin blanket and she avoided his eyes. "Aye, maybe."

"Do you know where your family is?"

When she looked back up at him, he couldn't ignore the tears welling in them. "I don't think they want to see me, since they were the ones who took me to the ship that brought me here."

His heart ached at the torment and sorrow he witnessed in the girl's face. He wondered how someone could do such a thing to a child. And not just any child, their own blood. He didn't want to believe it. "They must've not known what fate awaited you on that ship," he said softly.

The girl swiped away a bout of tears that streamed from the far corners of her eyes. "They're very poor, sir. When my parents died, my aunt and uncle couldn't afford another mouth to feed, having six children of their own. They were very put out by the situation and kept apologizing."

"What did they tell you?"

She shrugged. "Not much. They said I was going to

America to work, and earn my way. I assumed it was because I'm talented with the needle."

"You thought you were coming here to sew?"

"Aye, I'm a damned good seamstress," she said, then instantly covered her mouth. Muffled behind her hand, she said, "Sorry, sir, I have a vocabulary. It gets me into trouble."

The mention of her talent had brightened her gaze, and he found a bit of hope within her that shot through him, lifting him slightly. "It will be our secret," he said.

She propped on her elbow and in a whisper louder with excitement said, "It's my dream to have a shop of my own. I want to make gowns for the whole of society."

Alderic frowned at the innocence of the girl. She'd been betrayed by her own blood. "I will see to it that you do someday."

She cocked a brow at him. "Do ye mean that, sir?"

"Absolutely," he replied. "What is your name?"

"Fiadh. And ye?"

"Alderic."

"Pleasure to meet ye, Alderic. Will ye shake on yer promise?" She spit on her palm and held it out for a shake. He suppressed a chuckle as he gingerly took her hand and gave it a quick kiss on top instead.

"The pleasure is mine, *mam'selle*. And you have my word," he said. "Now, get some rest."

She gave a wide, bright smile, and nodded. She swiftly nestled back into her cot.

He turned to leave, and met Nye at the door.

"How goes it, Alderic?" Nye asked, then glanced around the chamber. "We have things to discuss."

Alderic worked a knot out of his neck and winced at the shooting pain through his head. "We do." He headed for the parlor behind Nye.

Nye poured them a couple of brandies and silently waited for him to speak first. He swallowed the contents of his glass and began pacing before Nye. "I acted impulsively when I got the information about his shipment. I should have known this would happen."

Nye sat down on the nearest chair and took a hearty gulp of his brandy before saying, "These women are brought into the market because they're so disposable."

That admission made Alderic wince, and he growled, "Perhaps I should have waited for the barge to reach its destination."

"That also would've been folly," Nye said. "We don't know the men Jack works with, nor their connections. That could've gotten you, the crew, and all those women killed."

"Innocent people died tonight, and it's my fault!" Alderic questioned every decision he'd made for the past several weeks.

Nye slowly shook his head. "Ahmet told me those who died tonight died from injuries unrelated to what happened. They were most likely knocking on death's door when—"

"Unacceptable, and it doesn't excuse my rash decision!"

Nye didn't respond, and his silence was agonizing.

Alderic wanted Nye to reiterate his claim, to tell him how stupid he was for doing what he did. But he didn't, frustrating him even more.

"Tonight, I started a war," he said. "And now it's imperative that I find out exactly what we are dealing with. I will set this right."

"I've no doubt." Nye remained in his seat, relaxed,

and calmly watching him pace the floor. "I'll admit you were unusually hasty, Alderic. Be truthful with me. What has turned the smooth, charismatic Alderic Beaumont into the nervous wreck I see before me?"

Alderic's steps halted and glared at Nye, who was blatantly disregarding any attempt to conceal his humor. He knew he couldn't lie as he searched the plastered ceiling of Nye's fine parlor. The pain in his head didn't cease, nor could the image of Madame. With eyes squeezed shut, he still couldn't block her out, nor the idea that she was…

His lack of answer caused Nye to smother a laugh with the last gulp of his brandy. He set down the glass and laced his fingers over his abdomen. "A man so distraught must've fallen quite thoroughly. Tell me, old friend, did you finally find a woman who is both captivating *and* available?"

Alderic gave in to his frustrations and collapsed on the sofa. He cradled his brow in his palms, cursing the blasted pain that wouldn't stop pounding in his head. "Captivating, yes. *Available*…is questionable."

"Elaborate."

"I suspect her heart may be untouchable," he said, resting his back on the sofa. "And I haven't a notion as to why, exactly."

"A woman immune to Alderic Beaumont's charm? Fascinating."

"Maddening," Alderic clarified. "She is intelligent and complicated…" Alderic momentarily forgot Nye was in the room as words spilled from his mouth. "I took her innocence. I cannot deny that any longer."

Nye leaned forward. "You were unsure?"

Alderic snapped out of his thoughts and looked at

his longtime friend. "It is a knotty affair I have involved myself in, Nye."

"Who is this woman? I want to commend her efforts to put my best friend through the very misery he heckled me for, once upon a time."

"I do not find you amusing. The misery she has caused has been with little to no effort. But I have put her in danger with my actions tonight, and thus she must be protected. However, I must keep her at a distance. I have acted shamelessly and selfishly."

Nye returned to the sideboard and pulled out a bottle of rum. He took a slug, then handed the bottle to Alderic before he said, "You sound like me a year or so ago. Back then, you were adamant that I open myself to love. That I deserved happiness."

Alderic was silent a long time as he pondered Nye's words. "I wanted to see you and Sarafina happy, because then…it gave me a glimmer of hope that I can have happiness, too."

"And perhaps you've already found it," Nye suggested as he took the bottle from Nye and sat back.

"But it is not so simple."

"Nothing worth having is." Nye chuckled. "It means taking a risk to reach much farther than anything we've experienced before, that's certain."

Alderic smirked and shook his head. "What is more reaching than the multiple possibilities of death we have faced over the years?"

"We risk being exposed, Alderic," Nye said. "Being vulnerable, and then, possibly, being rejected. Confirmation of our own fear that we're not worthy of having the one thing in life everyone longs to experience."

Alderic grunted as he reached over and snatched the bottle back from Nye. "Romantic fool. Let us change the subject."

Laughter rumbled from Nye's chest. "All right." He straightened, and his mood changed. "We're caring for Jack Chanfray's victims, but you're correct, we must find out what—exactly—we're dealing with."

"It is my top priority," Alderic said, relieved to change the subject from his personal life. "How was your first trip back to sea?"

"It was profitable. Once all of this is cleared up with Jack, we'll work on disbursing my cargo. Then we can discuss why the hell there's another fountain in my courtyard."

Chapter Twenty-Seven

Delaney glanced at the clock every chance she got, hoping Alderic would return. She wanted to explain things to him, tell him she was grateful that he'd stopped Diego's attack.

The Bird House had suffered many fights since she'd been there, but they'd little affected the business. Apparently, it was to be expected in a room full of men, spirits, and half-dressed women for sale. However, witnessing Remi and Diego fighting Alderic Beaumont—with little information revealed as to the cause of the bloody skirmish—was quite the scandal. It sent people flooding her with questions. Word spread that she was involved with Alderic, and now she had another problem brewing. Men thought she was available. And with Alderic nowhere around, they were becoming increasingly aggressive in their pursuit of her.

The only bit of light in her situation seemed to be painting in the church. It was something she desperately needed. It made sense to her. Painting was an escape from her problems…and her thoughts of Alderic.

"What an interesting likeness," Lucien said, shaking her from the imaginary world meant for her escape. She followed Lucien's gaze to her painted dove. She was nearly finished with its mate in the far corner, perched on an olive branch. The one he was looking at was in flight.

"Thank you," she said.

"You swirled gray and white with a bit of yellow, making a realistic color scheme."

"Well, the light emanating from the resurrection has to reflect off everything, does it not?"

Lucien inspected the painting more closely before he stood back, deep in thought. Finally, he nodded with approval. "You're talented."

"Coming from you, that's quite a compliment."

"Well, it's late, and we need to start cleaning up. Get on home, Miss Delaney." He smiled, then added warmly, "Wherever that may be."

****

Alderic rode into town and headed straight to St. Thomas Aquinas Church. The memory of Delaney enveloped him. The last time he was at that church had been the last time he'd seen her. Delaney. Who seemed more like a dream now. She was untouchable and didn't wish to be found or pursued by him. He'd never know what could've been with the shy, withdrawn woman he'd stolen a kiss from on the street.

But there was Madame. Madame had stolen his waking thoughts, and his loins ached every time he imagined her. She'd quickly become a sweet morsel he couldn't get enough of. Since the night she'd come down the main staircase with that blasted mask on her face and her silken skin basking in rich colors, she'd slowly weaved him into a spell that clouded his senses. At first, he'd thought she was coy, that her subtle innocence was a ploy to increase her desirability and develop intrigue. It took claiming her body to know she wasn't acting a part.

And this only made her more alluring. When he

pleased her, she was lost in it. On his first night with her, she had been stunned several times, and had had no idea what to do. He'd thought then she was still acting the part, giving him the reins to show her *how things were done*. The more time he spent with her, the clearer it was that she wasn't being crafty. There was no attempt to stroke his ego or clock a quick finish. Those were common practices for a professional seductress. She was genuine, authentic.

Truly innocent. Since his first night with her, he'd struggled with the idea that, despite her position as madam to a whorehouse, she'd remained a maiden. The idea that he'd carelessly taken her innocence was too disturbing to delve into. He'd wanted her for so long that, when she finally came to him, he could hardly hold himself back. Her sweet reaction to him had been blinding, endearing, and extremely unexpected.

And he was instantly addicted. So he'd convinced himself that he'd been mistaken when he deflowered her.

He'd started out a young aristocrat who'd gone rogue and nearly swung from a noose. But no longer did he want to work within the shrouds of darkness. He wanted to know true peace. To know what it felt like to have the same woman beside him every night. Now, he was battling between two women who taunted him with undeniable similarities. He'd nearly called one the other on several occasions. The reason, he suspected, was a narrative he wasn't prepared to challenge. In fact, the anger it invoked was too much, and it put him in a position he wasn't ready to take on just yet.

Alderic neared the church and shook away the troubles associated with Delaney and Madame. He focused on his task. He halted his charger, promptly dismounted, and proceeded up the steps as he checked his timepiece. He wasn't sure if he'd catch Father Charles, the hour was growing so late. He quietly entered the vestibule. Glancing around, he didn't see anyone, and took the flight of stairs to the choir loft, where he found Father talking quietly with Lucien.

Upon seeing Alderic, Father Charles' thinly skinned face lined with a wide grin. He and Lucien greeted him with warmth and much familiarity.

Alderic responded in kind, then said, "Father, I was hoping not to find you too busy, so I may speak with you."

"What can I do for you, *monsieur*?"

"Might I have a word in private?"

"Of course, son." Father Charles glanced at Lucien, then nodded to Alderic. "Let us talk downstairs." Father Charles proceeded to leave the choir loft, and Alderic almost followed when he noted Lucien preparing to leave. He was closing his paintbox and slipping on his modest jacket when Alderic said, "I have your oil, Lucien. You should come by the café tomorrow."

Lucien perked up. "Perfect timing, as usual, Beaumont. I've nearly run out. I have so many projects going on, I can barely keep up."

Alderic stepped closer to observe the mural Lucien had been painting. Lucien had great talent, and Alderic always took the time to appreciate his work. His eyes widened as he inspected the depiction of the resurrection.

"Sublime, Lucien," he said as he leaned in, looking at the intricate details of the mural.

"You're too kind." Lucien grinned. "Soon, I'll be finished here. We'll be painting in the cathedral when I'm done."

"Your group is talented, *non*? They will do a magnificent job," he said confidently. "When I have my own home, I will be calling on you."

"I'm not sure that's good for me." Lucien chuckled. "Your attention to art is almost as keen as mine. If something is unsatisfactory, you'll call me on it."

Alderic laughed. "You'd want me to."

Lucien nodded and laughed. "Yes, I would."

Alderic stepped back to admire the entire scene and became increasingly interested in the border. The setting surrounding the resurrection carried a more fabled aspect, giving attention to the spiritual atmosphere. It was familiar, but not recognized as Lucien's work.

"This here isn't your style."

"Perceptive as always," Lucien said, planting his feet apart and taking a stance next to Alderic. "My newest artist created this border."

"Newest artist?" Alderic leaned in. He'd seen those flowers before, that use of color, those curved strokes. His eyes rested on the doves, and they instantly sparked something in him. He knew very well where he'd seen those birds. The corners of his mouth lifted, though he was sure the color had drained from his face. Many of them were painted throughout the Bird House. His words were a little disjointed when he asked, "Is your newest artist a woman?"

Lucien gave another short laugh. "Is it obvious? I suppose it is quite flowery…feminine. But it's so magical, is it not? Infectiously dreamy, I'd say."

Alderic shook his head as he recalled who he'd run into in this very church. His suspicions had been correct all along. Suspicions he had not dared entertain before, to avoid addressing all the implications and responsibilities associated with the truth. That blissful ignorance he could no longer sustain as the truth manifested before his eyes on a paint-covered wall. The same artwork on her body, on her house, and now in a church. She'd even made her mark on him. "I would say…"

"She's talented," Lucien said. "She was the protégé of a Parisian professor from the art academy. I'll admit, she brings a certain flair, doesn't she?"

Alderic's smile faded as everything slowly sank in, and all his questions were slowly answered. Then more came to the surface. Several times, she'd stood before him, unmasked. And he'd refused to accept what his eyes and mind had told him.

"*Oui*. She does."

"Her name is Miss—"

"Delaney."

"Yes, you know her?"

Alderic's brows knitted into a frown as he continued staring at the mural. His silence lingered until he finally dragged his hawkish gaze away from the painting. "If you will excuse me, Lucien, I have matters to attend."

Lucien looked surprised by Alderic's abrupt change in mood and hasty departure. "Farewell, Alderic," he called, though Alderic was already down the stairs. He'd completely forgotten why he'd come to the church until he nearly flew into Father Charles.

Father Charles stammered as he, too, observed the change in Alderic. "A-Are you still needing to speak with me?"

Alderic was burning, the blood in his veins was starting to boil, as the revelation of Madame's betrayal—and even his own common sense—pumped through his body. He paused and took a moment to breathe. His fists tightened repeatedly to refrain from marching to the Bird House and lashing out. Momentarily, he calmed his reaction to the confirmation of his underlying suspicions.

He cleared his throat and said, "*Oui*, Father, but I'll be brief. I have several young women needing sanctuary. Can you help?"

"This house is open to all in need, *Monsieur* Beaumont. But I must ask—"

"Please, any questions must be directed to Sarafina Tarquin. She insists upon working closely with the church and the girls to help them decide their next course of action. A carriage will be arriving here in the morning, along with a handsome donation and provisions."

The father's jaw slackened momentarily, questions multiplied in his eyes and across his face. But he didn't voice any of them. Instead, he nodded. "I'll have Sister Mary here to help them settle in."

"*Merci*," he said. "If you'll excuse me, Father, I don't wish to be rude, but something has come up and I'm afraid I must go."

He gave a swift farewell, turned on his heel, and marched out of St. Thomas Aquinas Church.

Chapter Twenty-Eight

Delaney laid out her dress and mask. Ivy and butterflies would be the artwork painted on her body that evening.

"If you keep painting yourself and coloring your hair, eventually, it's going to stop coming off," Billy said as she laid out on Delaney's bed. She picked up another one of Delaney's masks and began toying with it.

Delaney looked at herself in the mirror, and she could see the faint purple still in her hair from last night.

"I know," she mumbled. "But I won't be doing this much longer."

Billy quickly sat up on her knees and her face lit up. "What are you going to do, have a grand unmasking?"

Delaney turned and looked at Billy's excited expression, and a pang shot through her. She frowned as she considered how her next words would sting Billy. "No, I think I'm going to slip out of the city as quietly as I slipped in."

Billy's jaw went slack and she tossed aside the mask. She inched closer to the end of the bed, and her voice shook. "You're going to leave us, Delaney?"

"I-I'm starting to make a muck of everything, Billy," she said sadly.

Billy jumped off the bed, and her voice raised considerably. "Delaney, you've made the Bird House the talk of the Quarter. The house needs you!" She stomped her foot to emphasize her words as she said, "You can't just leave!"

Delaney started to speak, but Billy stormed out of the room, leaving her reply to die in her throat. She sighed as she went to her mother's jewelry box and searched out earrings to match her dress. Her frustration was growing as she rummaged through the box. She felt terrible about leaving everyone. They'd all become so close. Friends...or like family. As close to family as she'd ever had. She was searching the jewelry box, none too gently, when the bottom tipped up. She inspected it further and realized the bottom was false. She removed all the jewelry and then the false bottom. Underneath, she discovered a stack of letters. They were hers! She smiled as she thumbed through the letters she'd written to her mother over the years.

As she reached the bottom of the stack, she found letters from Remi. It seemed reasonable that Remi would've written her mother, he was her guardian, after all, while touring Europe. She took them out and decided she should give them to him. He might appreciate having them back. Her finger tapped over Remi's lettering, curiosity weaving its pesky web. She itched to open them. She shook her head and thought better of it. They were to her mother...but probably about her. She teetered on whether it was right or wrong to snoop into their correspondence.

In the end, her curiosity got the best of her. Going by the dates, she opened Remi's earliest dated letter. Within seconds, her knees weakened, and she had to sit on her bed.

Mon amour,

I met our daughter today. You should see her. What

a beautiful and intelligent lady she has become...

The parchment shook in Delaney's hand so badly she could barely continue reading. Her stomach grew sick, and her mind raced as the first line kept repeating in her head. Remi...

Questions erupted, hitting her like a tempest. Often, growing up within the cold, brick walls of boarding schools, she'd wondered about her father. When she asked her nannies and professors—even her mother—it was simply relayed that she didn't have one. She was told until it was understood and she eventually stopped asking. Other children had fathers. She did not. Now, at nearly twenty-and-one, she had discovered she had a father—and he'd been alongside her for the last few years. He'd lied to her! And he'd brought her to New Orleans despite what her mother would have wished.

Moments ticked by as a numbness seeped into her blood and infected her bones. She remained silent, replaying everything from the last few years. Then she focused on the events since her arrival in New Orleans. Why hadn't he told her? Did anyone else know? If so, why hadn't someone said something? Was he ever going to tell her?

Numbness was quickly festering to fury, returned the strength to her body. She stood up and paced the floor as one question after another developed in her mind. Her eyes stung, but no tears welled. Nearly an hour went by before she made her way to the office and stared out the window. Her father had lured her to New Orleans and urged her to save her mother's brothel. A brothel her mother had never wanted her to see. Her mother had paid an exorbitant amount to make sure Delaney didn't end up like her. And Remi had dismantled everything. Her dreams, her perception of life and love had been shattered when she was forced into saving the establishment that had provided the very clothes on her back. He'd stripped her of everything she'd known life to be. He'd shown her the darker side of the world, the world she'd truly come from. Her life—until the moment she'd stepped into New Orleans—had been a lie. Outside her office, she heard the house slowly coming to life. Opening time was approaching, but Delaney remained like a statue at the window. She had no desire to return to her room and dress for the evening. Several people came in to ask questions about this or that, but she wasn't paying attention. She just nodded or said, "Mm-hm," to heaven only knew what. She was reliving every conversation, every moment she'd ever had with Remi.

Finally, when Remi entered the office, she couldn't look at him. She confined herself to the sanctuary of the window, finding peace in the gardens she'd designed for the guests. Her guests. Madame Vanessa Cardui's clients. She heard him close the door behind him. She felt him inch into the room.

"Delaney, is everything all right?"

Silence.

His voice and presence generated a strange reaction now. She didn't know if she was outraged or disappointed. So many emotions had rushed through her, and she didn't know how to handle them, how to sort them out.

"Delaney? You should be getting ready, shouldn't you?"

She could feel him watching her, and his words were received like a slither in her ears, luring her attention away from the window. His tone changed, and for the moment, he almost sounded like the friend she once knew, once thought he was. "I-I know that things went terribly the other night with Alderic. He means something to you, and that had to be difficult. Would you like to talk about you and Beau—"

"No." She didn't want Remi even speaking his name, for he was unworthy of it. Alderic was protecting her, she knew that. Despite all the confusion, all the facades, Alderic had treated both Madame and Delaney with esteem. His intentions toward her—no matter which identity she wore—were spoken honestly. It was she who'd deceived him. Confused him.

She found her voice, though her words spilled out flatly. "Did you love my mother, Remi?"

Silence.

She turned away from the window and observed how he'd paled. The shock and horror she witnessed in his eyes gave her some sort of satisfaction. "I found a stack of letters in my mother's jewelry box. Letters you sent her while you were traveling with me."

He remained silent, still. She noted his eyes for the first time. She thought how strange it was she'd never noticed their similarity to hers until then. He ran a shaky hand down his face and let out a long, heavy breath.

"Nothing to say, Remi?" She couldn't disguise the bitterness in her tone. The accusation in her words.

He dropped his gaze and took a seat on the opposite side of her desk. His discomfort was fitting and apparent, as his eyes shot from one direction to another. Anywhere but at her. He cleared his throat, but it didn't smooth away the unsteadiness of his voice. "I-I looked for those letters when I returned. I couldn't find them."

"Were you ever going to tell me you were my

father?"

She watched his eyes glisten as tears filled their depths before he covered his face with both hands. "No one knows the truth, Delaney. Please be careful what you say."

She marched away from the window and glared at him. "Why didn't you tell me?"

"Forgive me, Delaney, for not telling you." His words were muffled as he continued behind the wall he'd made with his hands. "Much like your mother, I thought you'd be ashamed."

That fear triggered her own anger, and she squared her shoulders. "Look at me, Remi!"

Several sobs escaped him, and it was a long time before he removed the safe barrier and wiped his tearstained cheeks. After taking a deep breath, he straightened in his chair and met her eyes as he said, "When I first saw you in London, all grown and beautiful...so smart, I was so proud. Then, when your mother died, I didn't want to ruin all that you'd worked so hard to achieve."

"But you did anyway!"

"I ruined the illusion of your origins—"

"You ruined everything, Remi! I've lost everything!"

"You're still the amazing woman I met in London. That hasn't changed. You've lost nothing but the fairytale your mother created for you. With that collapse of your false identity, you've rebuilt yourself even stronger. Even more spectacular!"

"I've no need of your flattery, Remi. She was protecting me! You destroyed me and betrayed her."

He shot up from the chair, and took a step closer, the

remnants of his defeat almost nonexistent. "She wanted to mend the pain within her by giving you everything she'd lost. Commendable, but hardly fair! I discussed with her many times the dangers of her secrets. To let you believe yourself a lady of status was cruel. But your modest origin doesn't define you, Delaney. What you have is yours. Whatever else you've lost, you've given up freely."

"It was my duty to restore the house that gave me my education and luxuries. I had no choice!"

He crossed his arms over his chest and leaned back. "You always have a choice, Delaney. Coming here—seeing where you truly come from—probably reiterated a narrative playing in the back of your mind your entire life, growing up alone in those damned schools."

She matched his stance and stared him down. "And what narrative is that?"

The hard lines in his face softened, as did his tone. "That you were deficient. Not good enough. After all, if your own mother didn't want to raise you, then you must be something unworthy."

More silence. She wanted to bark back at him, give him a tart reply. But the stinging in her eyes returned as his words sliced through her. "Why did you remain in the shadows? Maybe it would've helped to know I had a father."

He winced and shifted his stance. "I was no prouder to look my daughter in the face and tell her what I am, any more than Birdie was. You deserved the best. On that, I was in complete agreement with Birdie. But I didn't agree with her methods. In the end, my silence was cowardice, and it has had grave consequences. For that, I am truly sorry, Delaney."

The tension built between them, and the silence continued to thicken.

"Why would you put this burden on me?"

Another fresh bout of tears swelled in his eyes and ran down his cheeks as he sat back down. "When she died, I'd never been so lost. I didn't know what to do. Her creation had fallen to ruin." He released a heavy sigh and wiped a tired hand down his face. "A part of me just wanted you to sell it and be rid of it. But the women working here needed their madam. I knew that when I returned. And the way you took it over? You changed this place and built a friendship and respect with them… You were so much like your mother when she was young. She was vivacious and…brilliant. For a while, I saw her again. Somehow, you brought her back."

"Indeed, you are selfish, Remi," she finally said. "While drowning in your own sorrows, you put me in a horrifyingly confused state! And I almost sold this house and all the girls to who? Chanfray! He would've just thrown them on the street!"

"What do you want from me, Delaney? What can I do to make this right?"

She grimaced at his words. She was furious and didn't want him to make things right. She wanted to remain angry with him. It all made no sense, and she didn't know how to respond. She just knew she had to get away. "You've been with my mother all these years. Did anyone suspect the two of you?"

He shook his head. "She hid everything so well."

"Why are you not taking over this house?" she asked.

He was quiet a long time before he finally cleared his throat and regained a bit of composure in his tone.

"It's not the same here without her."

"I can't stay here, Remi," she insisted. "And I don't think my mother would've approved, either."

"I know," he muttered so quietly she almost missed it. "God knows, I've tormented myself over it."

"You must take it over," she said firmly. "And something tells me my mother expected it of you all along."

He grew silent again.

"I want to be gone by the time carnaval comes to a close," she declared. "We must have everything settled by then."

His eyes fixed on the floor as his thumb tapped the armrest. "Agreed."

For a long time, they just stared silently in different directions. The clock chimed nine times. The doors would be opening soon. She wasn't ready, and she still had no desire to be. What she desired left several days ago.

"You can start tonight," she said and promptly left the office. She donned her cloak, pulled the hood over her head, and slipped out of the house without detection.

Remi was rushing after her, and she quickened her steps. "Where are you going?"

She stopped and spun around. "That isn't your concern."

Remi let out a long, heavy breath. "He can't solve the problems dwelling within the core of you, Delaney."

She lifted her chin and offered no response. She spotted a hackney and signaled. It rolled to a stop, and she readily climbed inside. "Le Grand Inn," she told the driver.

Chapter Twenty-Nine

Delaney stood at the front of the inn. She wasn't sure if Alderic was there. If he was, he might not wish to see her. The last time she saw him as Delaney, she'd told him not to waste his time on her. To move on. And now she was showing up at his door. She had no idea how he'd receive her.

With small, tottering steps, she went inside and approached a man at the front desk. "May I help you, *mam'selle?*"

"A-Alderic Beaumont's room," she said. He searched the ledger, gave her a side glance, then sighed. "*Mam'selle*, I can't give out that kind of information."

She laid out a few coins, and he smiled. "Up the stairs, last door on the right."

"*Merci beaucoup.*"

She slowly climbed the stairs. Her knees were growing so weak, she hoped she wouldn't trip and tumble down the steps. She'd almost lost her nerve completely by the time she reached his door. Alderic had every right to turn her away, but the idea still sent tears to her eyes.

She forced herself to knock.

There was no answer.

She knocked again.

The door opened, just as she prepared to leave. Alderic was standing there clad only his breeches.

"Delaney?"

She didn't know what to say. Where to start? Her feet were rooted to the corridor floor. She noted the stern set of his jaw and the hardened look in his eyes as he waited for her to speak. His disposition spoke volumes. She felt her heart sink into her stomach, and this caused a whole spectrum of emotions to fire off within her.

"Y-You said if I ever wanted to find you…" Her voice trailed off a moment, then she rushed out, "I'm accepting your invitation. I hoped my last words hadn't sealed our fate."

He leaned slightly. "Your last words…" His voice trailed off, his eyes looking at her expectantly.

"Outside the cathedral," she filled in.

He straightened and his jaw clenched. "That was the last time we spoke?"

"Do you not remember?" She'd told him not to wait for her, but she'd come back. She was there, and that didn't seem to appease him at all. Could it be that he was finished with Delaney? She stared wide-eyed as he stepped away and disappeared into his room, spouting something in his native tongue that was too fast and unclear to decipher. Something told her she didn't want to know what he'd said.

But he didn't shut the door on her. She entered the room and discovered him at a side table, shoving away a decanter and gulping down a drink. She watched him carefully as he poured himself another glass. His silence was torturous.

"I've played with your sentiments, Alderic. I know this," she began. "I'm deceitful and shrewd."

His back still to her, he chuckled. It was the most unpleasant laugh she'd ever heard. "Aren't we all?" he asked.

She shook her head. "I don't want to believe so. I want to believe the world can be bright and good."

"You want a fairytale, Delaney," he snapped. Then he released a long, slow breath. "I haven't the patience for your games, this evening. I think it wise you leave. I'm in a foul mood."

If she were wise, she would've taken his advice. But she felt responsible for the tumultuous display she was witnessing. Instead of retreating, she took another step forward. "You're angry with me—"

His tone was rather crisp when he asked, "Why are you here, Delaney?"

Honestly, she wasn't sure anymore. She stammered for a reply as he finished his snifter and finally turned around. She didn't recognize him just then. She'd never seen such fury twisting his handsome features, nor the darkness lacing his tone when he harshly added, "Are you here to tell me the truth about all that is you, or to fuck?"

The lamentation laced in his words was jarring. She squared her shoulders, adjusting to the change from his usually carefree, charming nature. "Alderic, you're not yourself—"

He slammed down his snifter with a near shattering clash upon the side table. "Which is it?" he demanded.

Her voice caught in her throat. She struggled—frustratingly so—as she considered telling him everything. She was determined to do just that on the carriage ride over. She wasn't certain when she'd changed her mind. Right now, all her words were stuck. Her voice abandoned her until the notion of telling him the truth bailed completely. "I want to spend this night with you, free from all that haunts me."

In the briefest of moments, he looked taken back. Then the coolness in his gaze returned. "If you recall—outside of the cathedral—I said I won't always be at liberty to accommodate you," he said.

"I recall." Her stare dipped from his and anchored to the floor.

"You're asking me to forget everything, so you can hold on to a fairytale a little while longer?" He shook his head, scoffing. "You ask a lot of me, Delaney."

Seconds ticked by like days as she watched the chill emanating from his eyes. She couldn't stand their scrutinization another second, and she nervously glanced around the chamber. As Delaney, she'd told him he needed to move on. And perhaps he did. Maybe he'd chosen Madame Cardui. Was he unable to accommodate Delaney because he cared more for Madame Cardui? Could that be where all his anger was stemming from? But Madame Cardui had also hurt him. He'd saved her from the most deplorable violation she could've experienced, and she'd told him to leave.

He leaned against the side table, with his arms lightly crossed over his bare chest. His tousled hair brushed his brow, and the low light danced across the lines of his body. She wanted nothing more than to forget all the terrible decisions she'd made since she'd come to New Orleans. She wanted to forget the Bird House, Remi, and her responsibilities. She wanted to explain everything to Alderic, and hope he'd forgive her. She wanted to set things right, to move on with her life… with him. But now, he looked untouchable. Unrelenting.

A tangled web she had weaved.

She shifted her stance and dreaded asking her next

question. "You are taken then?"

He made no motion to respond. One corner of his mouth tilted and looked away. She couldn't guess what he was thinking at all, what he was feeling.

"Are you in love with her?"

His eyes snapped back to her. The ferocity her question provoked was undeniable. And telling. He pushed away from the table and closed the space between them so quickly, she inhaled sharply, and stepped back. "Does it matter if I'm unworthy of trust?"

"You are trustworthy, Alderic—"

"I am a fool!"

"You are not that!" He brushed past her, marched to the door, and slammed it shut. He spun back around and started pacing. He drove his hand through his hair. She'd angered him to an unanticipated degree, and guilt overwhelmed her. He wanted Madame's trust, and no longer had an interest in her as Delaney. That realization sent a pang shooting through her. It was frustrating! He wanted a façade. Madame was intriguing, and mysterious. She was wickedly playful and exuded the very essence of carnal pleasure. Delaney could never live up to the seductress she'd created. Could he ever accept her for who she truly was—if he could even forgive her?

"Anyone unable to give you their trust is the fool," she said. She felt a knot in her stomach, a sickening admission that she was that fool. She was furious with herself for sending him into Madame Cardui's arms in the first place. All because she was too cowardly to tell him the truth. She gathered the remaining pieces of her pride and went for the door. "You've found someone, and I shouldn't be here… as I'm not that person."

She reached for the door when he snatched her wrist.

His fervent grip startled her.

"Aren't you?"

"Clearly not! You've made me aware that my invitation has expired." She attempted to pull away, but he didn't release her.

"You assume I want another woman, and that your own lack of honesty hasn't expired my invite?"

"I'm certain that's the reason!"

"Because that belief suits you better!"

"Wanting what another woman can give you, and I cannot, doesn't suit me! It devastates me!"

"You think you cannot give me what she has?"

"I know I can't!"

"Why not?" His voice had risen to an intimidating level, but she was too crushed to shrink away.

She stomped her foot, hoping the jolt would release the frustration his taunting words were conjuring within her. More tears were welling and threatening to spill down her cheeks. "Because I am Delaney! I am only... Delaney!"

He leaned down, their glares matching and mere inches from the other. His deep voice was cutting. "Who? Is? Delaney!"

She shoved at him, his body was too close, his eyes too piercing, too searching. But he barely budged. She attempted to make more space—at least enough to skirt around him and leave. "It was a mistake to come here!"

Alderic caught her again, halting her escape out the door. She lashed out but he halted her flailing arms. Her wrists felt like they were going to splinter in his fists when he yanked her closer, holding her tightly until her thrashing ceased. She glared at him, her nostrils flaring as her exertion demanded deeper, quicker breaths. He'd easily overpowered her and held her still. She opened her mouth to demand that he release her, but his mouth crushed hers and smothered her words, stole her breath. His kiss offered no more tenderness than his hold on her, and he didn't stop until she was gasping for air. Only then, did he release her. He held her gaze until she finally calmed the heaving in her chest. The tension between them became increasingly uncomfortable.

He finally broke the silence. "*Adieu*, Delaney," he said.

The finality she felt in his farewell was sobering. Somber. She wondered if walking out that door would seal her chances of ever seeing him again. Would Madame Cardui? She couldn't work out the conflicting thoughts and questions cramming her brain.

"You have every right to be angry with me, probably more than you realize," she said. "But I don't want you to desire another, Alderic. I don't want to go if it means that I lose you to her."

His eyes hadn't lessened their glare, and the lines forming the stern expression on his face, hadn't softened as he stepped forward. "You came here for a reason. You may have abandoned your nerve—your convictions—but I do not care right now." His tone carried a stark warning. "I will not be kind."

She sucked in a deep breath and couldn't steady the shaking in her hands. "I know."

When she failed to take a step toward the door, he straightened. "If you stay, you will give me all that she has. And more, Delaney. I'll make certain of it."

"Do you seek to punish me for something I've done, Alderic?" she asked. "Or something she has?"

"No, I don't wish to punish you," he said, in tone

she couldn't quite read. Was he still angry, or just… hurt? "But I gave more than I was prepared to admit, until just now. And I've nothing in return."

"What do you want?"

His lips made a thin line, and she watched the muscles in his face tighten. "I want everything from you tonight, Delaney. No more of your games, no childish insecurities, or fairytales."

She remained silent, registering everything he'd just declared. It was a dire warning, and she considered it carefully. She didn't voice a response. There was no rejection, nor an agreement. But she stood her ground… and she didn't leave.

When his mouth crushed her again, she felt a jolt within her. An instant reaction to him that couldn't be turned off, couldn't be ignored. He swiftly unpinned her hair and curled his fingers in her thick locks, gripping so tightly she was motionless as his tongue invaded her mouth. Her blood pumped wildly and the flames he so easily stoked consumed her. Her skin was burning, and she started untying the laces of her gown. He brushed aside her hands and tore them off her.

She spared his clothing no gentleness either, barely regarding the sounds of fallen buttons from his breeches tumbling onto the floor as she carelessly discarded the fabric shielding her touch. He removed his breeches, and she stepped back. He stood motionless, his frown as deep as the shadow within the depths of his eyes. Her gaze lingered on his statuesque figure, the soft light dancing on each angle of his finely sculpted body. But it was the darkness in his expression that truly fascinated her, for it was a revelation of the man she hadn't yet experienced. Alderic frequently wore an easy smile and made light of most situations. But there wasn't an ounce of that façade now. It was slightly frightening, but vastly invigorating. "You and I aren't so different, Alderic. Your carefree nature is merely a shield."

"Perhaps we all wear masks, Delaney," he replied.

"For whatever reasons you have abandoned yours tonight, I crave experiencing you without it," she said as she laced her fingers behind his neck and kissed him soundly. Her lips desperately sought out his and her tongue dove into his mouth, any hesitation he may have harbored subsided. She kissed him hungrily, and he returned that passion. She released her hold on his neck and slid her hands wantonly over his body. She followed the line of his abdomen, until she was boldly clasping him, and stroking him until a groan reverberated from his throat. His hands slid down her arms and the length of her back until he was gripping her bottom, squeezing her generous flesh. He pulled her against him. This made the inside of her thighs rage, and she ached for him to slake that need. But she refrained. She broke from their kiss, pushing at his chest, and caused Alderic to lean into the side table, upsetting the crystalline decanters and snifters. His eyes were glistening, his mouth swollen. There was no question in his eyes, only demands.

She'd been a fool. Since the first time he'd seen her, he'd pursued her. He'd told her he wanted her, and she'd only kept him at bay. She knew, the first night she saw him, there couldn't be another. She could've lost him. She might still. But she was there now.

Her body was trembling, begging for release, as she began kissing the trail leading below his navel. She recalled Billy's words about giving him the same pleasure he'd given her, and she'd never wanted so badly to drive him as mindless as he'd driven her. She kneeled, listening to his breath quicken. It was strangely satisfying when she glanced up and recognized the want burning in his eyes.

"Delaney..."

The deep, breathy sound of her name drove her desire even more. Her lips closed over him, taking him into her mouth, as much she could. She discovered that his breath catching was even more elating than the sound of her name on his lips. He closed his eyes, and his head tipped back as he struggled for breath. He gripped the side table, bracing himself as she continued enjoying him. She was captured by him, of how shaken his demeanor had become. Suddenly it seemed natural to her. She began massaging him with her mouth, her tongue, seizing him with her hands and stroking him. Savagely. Until every muscle in him tensed and throbbed. She could feel his rapid pulse in her mouth, and it instinctively made her efforts more rewarding. When he leaned down, he groaned her name. It was the most erotic sound she'd ever heard.

Until he moaned for her to stop. She didn't want to. But there was no debating. He tightened his hold on her hair and made a safe distance.

"You are not leading this, Delaney." His strained voice still carried a hint of steel, as solid as his fiery stare. "The only submission we're having tonight is yours." There was a moment when she locked eyes with him and noted a shift. No longer was there anger in his expression, but a level of passion in his gaze that was devouring. In one swift motion, he lifted her off her knees and veered her against the side table. He entered her with a force that drove the air from her lungs. She gasped as he did so again. The storm his thrusts generated made her thighs burn, her knees weaken. There was no gentleness, as he sent scorching waves tearing through her, diverting her from any thought other than reaching that shattering high. She gripped the table, bracing her other hand on the wall, and met his strength with a fierce appetite of her own, meeting his unbridled passion. A sound escaped him just then, and he unleashed himself completely, gripping the plump flesh of her bottom, and pursued her harder, and deeper. She felt every part of her body heighten and shake, causing her gasps and cries to escape from deep within her chest. Their bodies clashed, never faltering, never relenting, not even when her legs lost their strength to stand, or even when the glasses and decanters had been thrust off the table, broken and scattered across the floor. Moments were a blur, and she vaguely recalled when she'd ended up in his bed, wracking from a climax so intense, her skin was tingling and sheen from the heat of it. But Alderic wasn't finished with her, nor was she ready for him to be.

They'd begun a long night of an inescapable demand to have the other, to give and take everything the other had. Tonight, neither had found their resolve, a mindfulness that usually came with their series of shields and facades. Alderic had soundly and thoroughly ravished her in every way she thought possible... and in many ways she thought not. But she succumbed to it and was instantly addicted to that ungoverned desire. He'd taken her to a breathtaking and almost frightening degree of ecstasy, and now, it was something she didn't want any other way.

Chapter Thirty

The sun had just barely come over the horizon when Alderic opened his eyes and looked down at Delaney curled up against him, sleeping soundly. He played with a strand of hair that still held color in it, then moved it away from her face. She still had small traces of paint by her ear and neck. When his thumb brushed over the remnants of color, she snuggled closer to him. He wrapped his arm around her, pulling her naked body closer. What had happened since the last time he'd seen her? What had brought her to his room without her mask? Whatever it had been, it had made her careless enough to forget the obvious evidence of Madame Cardui.

Madame... He shook his head. All those nights running a house built on pleasure and sex, surrounded by lust, and she'd remained untouched, untried. Why give her innocence to him? The notion that he'd pursued her mercilessly wracked him with guilt. He'd treated Madame Cardui like the experienced woman he assumed she was. He'd lusted after her more than any other woman in his life. So much that he sought her out with callousness, blind to the signs that could've been in front of him. He cursed himself for succumbing to his temper last night. The discovery of her deceit had been too fresh. He was too upset, having just learned what she'd done...and all he'd failed to see. When he saw Delaney standing at his door, he should've turned her away. He curiously searched the soft lines of her face as she slept. How did a virgin become a bordello's madam? An overwhelming sense of protectiveness swelled within him.

She shifted in her sleep, and he watched her eyes moving beneath her lids as she slipped between sleep and wakefulness.

"*Je t'aime*," he whispered, and she moved slightly as she began to steer toward wakefulness.

"Hmm?" she barely whispered, and he grinned.

He lightly and tenderly kissed her lips, and she started to rise from her slumber. She smiled and began kissing him back. Opening her eyes, she pulled him over her as she wrapped her legs around his narrow waist. He met her heavy-lidded gaze as he touched her face. His finger ran along the lines of her jaw and lips. "What happened that you came knocking on my door?" he whispered.

He could feel her tense beneath him, and he wondered if she'd finally tell him the truth. She lowered her lids and shook her head, tightening her thighs around him. "I don't want to talk about it," she mumbled.

He rested his brow against hers as she began to shift underneath him. His desire to talk quickly dwindled. He swiftly immersed himself in her, and she moaned. He suspected she'd had no intention of telling him she was Madame Cardui.

He was conflicted, that was certain. But then she began to move beneath him, and his mind became muddled. His need swelled, and his thoughts started to drift away. In moments, his resolve had evaporated, and he was melding with her.

They delved into the depths of yearning until they were both crying out from the intensity of it.

****

The sun was spilling through the room when Alderic and Delaney woke again. Their bodies were entangled when their eyes settled on one another.

Alderic stretched and reached for his timepiece.

"It's well past noon," he said as he disentangled himself and climbed out of bed.

Delaney took advantage of the full light and watched him lazily walk about the chamber, searching for his breeches and shirt. He was an impressive man, with wide shoulders and well-defined torso. His back was equally powerful. She supposed years of manning a ship was taxing on the body. His body was scarred and rugged, but his face bore a more youthful aspect, even now, with a shadow on his strong jaw.

He flashed her a smile as his gaze raked over her. "If you continue to lie so enticingly in my bed, staring at me with those soft green eyes, I won't make it to my appointment."

"Oh, you have an appointment," she said. "I'll be leaving as soon as I'm dressed," She quickly removed the covers and began searching for her clothing. Alderic halted her search when he took her wrist and closed the space between them. He lifted her chin, and she met him with round eyes. He looked at her with such warmth that she held her breath, and her stomach fluttered.

"You should come with me," he suggested.

"You would like me to accompany you to your appointment? Where are you going?"

"I have a few errands to run today," he admitted. "Since you expressed to me you like architecture, you might enjoy spending the day with me. I am traveling to the outskirts of town in search of a house."

She stared blankly for a moment, blinking owlishly. "Y-you want me to accompany you while you hunt for a house?"

He chuckled. "Don't pale so, or I will feel guilty for having asked. I've been searching for a while and have been unsuccessful. I have considered having my own built to my specifications, but *Monsieur* Dupuis insists I will be satisfied by one of the homes today. He has arranged to have them ready for me."

"I don't b-believe that would be appropriate for me to show up with you, Alderic. He may ask questions, a-and I—"

He held up his hand, and her stammering words died in her throat. "*Monsieur* has arranged the showings, but he won't be there. Indeed, I have been difficult and quite particular. We have reduced to correspondences. He makes the appointments with the owners, and I have time to look around without interference."

She raised her brows and tilted her head. "You're a difficult customer?"

"I suppose I have been." He gave her a sheepish grin. "Would you do me the honor of picking apart these homes?"

She shook her head, laughing. "I'd be honored to help you find reasons not to buy them."

He brightened and gave her a winning smile. "Splendid."

He quickly took her chemise out of her hand and tossed it to the floor. She looked at him, as he removed the shirt he'd just slipped on.

"What are you doing? I thought we had to leave,"

she said.

He swiftly removed his breeches, and she could see he had no intention of leaving just yet.

"We have about ten minutes," he said huskily as he lifted her in his arms and laid her back on the bed. Her laughter belted out as the weight of him crushed her.

****

A carriage brought them into the heart of the Quarter, and Delaney regarded the pleasant property and its luscious Spanish flair. The white stucco was fresh, and the archway ornately designed. Greenery and bright, colorful flowers dotted the stone-walled entrance to the door. Alderic helped her out of the carriage and curled her hand in the crook of his arm as he guided her up the pathway to the house.

Delaney's eyes fixed on the amazing surroundings. The archway was breathtaking. "It's absolutely beautiful, Alderic."

He opened the door, and set up in the foyer was a table with pastries and a fresh pitcher of lemonade.

"Would you care for something?" he asked, eyeing the table.

"Thank you," she said before she went into the parlor. "You could appreciate owning a home like this." She turned to him and noted that he didn't appear as impressed as she did. "You don't like it?"

Alderic walked farther in the parlor and inspected the tilework and window dressings. "It is impressive."

"But…" She cocked a brow. He motioned her to the next room across the hall.

"I told Dupuis I did not want to be so close to town," he said, "and the windows are small. They offer little light into the rooms."

"Yes, but the walls are thick," she said, trying to give him a positive point since he didn't seem convinced this would be his future home. "It'll make the evenings cooler and more comfortable."

Alderic didn't respond; he drank his lemonade and continued guiding her through the house. The courtyard was small but stately. When they left the house, it was clear Alderic hadn't found his home. They ventured outside the city to a rococo house more in line with his Parisian tastes. While the outside was rather plain, the inside had gilded molding and elaborate décor on the windows, walls, and ceilings. The home was beautiful and impressive, but it reminded her of a more expensive version of the brothel before she'd gotten there. She chewed her lip, wondering what Alderic was thinking. He seemed very interested in the *trompe l'oeil* frescoes.

"Do you like it?" she asked, holding her breath.

He clasped his hands behind his back and made lazy strides back to her. "It brings me back to my youth." He smiled, glancing around. "Not exactly my idea of moving forward."

Being an aristocrat, she could imagine he'd spent his younger years within the salons of Paris. "So what are you looking for, Alderic?"

He chuckled. "I have seen just about everything. I liked elements from everything I have witnessed. I suspect I won't be satisfied unless I have it all, Delaney."

She raised her brows and looked around, suppressing a bout of laughter. "Very specific. Perhaps this is why *Monsieur* Dupuis has started only making appointments for you."

"That is likely."

"Do you know how to get everything you want in

one?"

"Pray tell, *mam'selle*."

"Create it from scratch. Mold something to match the very uniqueness of you and your life. The houses you're looking at are someone else's experiences and have probably been limited to one style. You're a traveled man; maybe you should build what you like."

Alderic assessed her for a moment and relaxed his crossed arms over his chest. "To build would take a momentous amount of time. I am tired of living in a rented room, and I have long since outgrown the quarters on my ship."

"Then take that which is closest to the structure you prefer and modify it. Simple as that."

He flashed her a grin and then took her hand and kissed it. "A wonderful idea. But do you know what this means?"

"What?"

"Now I have to revisit every home I have already seen," he said, unable to conceal the merriment in his dazzling golden-green gaze.

She shook her head. "I think *Monsieur* Dupuis may quit on you."

"That is possible." He thought for another moment. "But I think I have a place in mind. Would you come with me tomorrow morning if I can set up a showing?"

"I must ask why you want me to accompany you tomorrow, as well."

That mischievous glint flashed in his eyes again as he pulled her closer. "I would think it would be obvious. I told you I wanted you. Not for a night, Delaney."

His words seeped into her heart, and she couldn't fight back the mist welling behind her eyes.

He lifted her chin. "Delaney, what is wrong?"

"I'm not who you think I am," she said.

"Who are you, then?"

She chewed the inside of her cheek. She wanted to spill it out. She was a deceiver. She'd tricked him, played games with him. She'd lied to him. Repeatedly. She squeezed her eyes closed, shutting away the tears stinging them, and stepped back.

Alderic stubbornly reclaimed some of the space. "Tell me, Delaney. Trust me."

She shook her head. "Alderic, please. Stop your interrogation. Just trust that you'll be disappointed in me."

He stared at her quietly for a long moment, and she shifted uncomfortably under his scrutiny. Then his easy smile returned, and he said lightly, "All right, *mam'selle*. Have it your way for now. I will not press you. But I still could use your assistance in examining the house I wish to see. You seem to understand architecture. I need a good eye if I am going to modify something."

Delaney didn't believe him. And he knew she didn't, but he'd lightened their mood, and in truth, she didn't want to think about anything other than spending more time with him. Just staring at him now, she wanted to return to the inn.

Something in her gaze indicated exactly what she was thinking, and he picked up on it immediately. His humor faded, and heat penetrated his eyes. "We need to leave, *mam'selle*."

She cast him a sly grin. "You know my thoughts too well."

"Because they are also mine."

They quickly exited the house and climbed into the

coach, and he ordered the driver to take them back to the inn. They rushed up the stairs and were barely inside the room before Delaney was unbuttoning his breeches and he was hiking up her skirts. Time passed in a whirlwind of passion as they slaked each other's desires. Rocking the erotic waves of need, they brought one another through the heat-driven throes of longing, crying out their climax. It felt as though time had stood still as their sheened bodies lay entwined, watching the sun set outside the window.

"I just realized we haven't eaten today," Alderic said, checking his timepiece before climbing over and resting himself between her welcoming thighs. He placed small kisses on her mouth, her chin, and her cheek, and made a tantalizing trail down her neck. "What boring food do Londoners eat?"

"You're so amusing," she said dryly.

He lifted his head. "What do you want to eat?"

Her time had thawed and expired. That realization forced her to avoid his gaze. "I have to go, Alderic."

"I want to escort you so you may arrive safely."

"I don't need an escort."

He inhaled and searched her face. "You said you were free, Delaney. We have long since passed the lines of propriety, so a formal courtship would be a farce. Why do you not want me to escort you home?"

She nervously chewed the inside of her lip while she considered her answer. When she stalled and had no reply, he asked, "Are you not free, after all?"

"No, Alderic, I'm not. Not yet, at least," she said with a sigh. But she wanted to be, and why couldn't she be? She held his gaze squarely. "But I will be, and I'll tell you everything when I am. I swear it."

He stared at her silently for a long time. She couldn't read his expression, the dull look in his brilliant eyes. The tension in his body, the pulsing against his skin, his very breath, had her complete attention as she anticipated his response.

"So be it, Delaney," he finally said, his tone rather terse.

Chapter Thirty-One

Delaney was sublimely happy, her body languid and relaxed. And a little sore. But when she rolled up to the Bird House, her happiness faded. The hackney stopped, and she pulled up her hood before she climbed out. She didn't want to face Remi. A part of her was grateful that he'd brought her to New Orleans. She never would have met Alderic otherwise. But she was still very angry with him, and she couldn't shake that feeling of betrayal. Remi had been her friend, but he'd deceived her.

Sorrow magnified with each step taken toward the front door. She'd never had a family while growing up, but she'd built one there at the Bird House—Fannie, Gertie, Billy, Penelope, Marla, Rafe, and all the others had become good friends. She'd never had friends. Growing up, she'd always been isolated.

She wanted to be with Alderic, though she wondered if he'd feel the same if he knew how she'd deceived him. How was she different from her father? She shook off the troubling thoughts. It would be a sad day when she said farewell to everyone at the house, however necessary that farewell was.

The house wasn't open yet, and it wouldn't be for a few more hours. She quickly entered the office and found Remi sitting behind the desk. When she spotted him, she turned on her heel and attempted to leave.

"Delaney, please wait," he called.

She stopped, turned back, and waited with her arms crossed over her chest. He was clean-shaven, and his hair was smoothed down. She noted his finely cut coat and tan breeches when he came around the desk and motioned for her to sit down. "I'd like to speak with you."

She took a deep breath and removed her cloak. She sat, and Remi sat across from her.

"Delaney, I can't express how ashamed I am for putting you in this predicament. I can't even ask for your forgiveness because I don't deserve it. Your mother and I, we weren't perfect by any means, but we loved you very much. You were the only thing we ever got right. And I ruined it. I ruined your innocence and made you take on responsibilities you never should've felt obligated to fulfill. For that, I'm wholeheartedly sorry." Delaney couldn't meet his gaze, and she couldn't identify what feeling his words evoked. Everything was too fresh to evaluate. He took her hand in his and gave it a squeeze. "The Bird House was my responsibility, and it's time for me to be held accountable. I think Birdie wanted me to take it over. You're free from the house, and I want you to know that everyone here will be taken care of. It's time for you to get on with your life."

A weight lifted from her shoulders, but she wasn't ready to admit that to Remi. It conflicted with a sense of loss. Relief from this burden had been what she was striving for ever since she discovered she owned a brothel. She glanced around the office, then settled on the magnificent portrait of her mother. Somehow, her mother didn't seem so intimidating now, staring back at her. She straightened her spine and released a long breath. She finally met Remi's gaze. "The house is yours,

Remi."

An awkward hush lingered between them for several moments, as he shifted the position of his hands several times before him. He wiped a hand down his face and cleared his throat. "Do you know what you want to do, Delaney?" he finally asked.

She numbly stared at the carpet beneath her feet. "I have to think on it further. I was offered a position with a group of artists. They want to bring New Orleans to a new level of beauty."

He lifted his brows. "That's wonderful, Delaney. You're a grown woman with plenty of money now to do whatever you want."

"I've been helping them paint murals at St. Thomas Aquinas church," she confessed.

"Is that so?" He laughed. "Is that where you keep running off to? I know I probably don't have a right to say this, but I was very worried about you last night. I didn't know where you'd gone. Though...I suspected you went to see Beaumont."

Her lips made a tight line.

"Ah." He sighed as he sat back and scratched his jaw. "I see. Does your future also lie with him?"

"He knows me as two separate people. I'm not sure how he'll feel when he finds I've deceived him."

Remi looked at her curiously, and when he spoke, his tone sounded skeptical. "He's spent time with you as yourself and as the madam, and he has no idea you are one and the same?"

She lifted her eyes from the floor. "No, he doesn't."

Remi laced his fingers over his stomach and tapped his thumbs together. "Why haven't you told him, Delaney?"

She avoided his stare again. "I'm afraid he may turn me away. Or be angry that I tricked him."

He propped his elbow on the chair's armrest and perched his chin on his palm. After a moment, he said, "Alderic is a seasoned man with years of life experience, Delaney. While he's a force to be reckoned with, he's an honorable man."

"I suppose that's true," she mumbled, twisting her gown in her fingers.

"The longer you wait to tell him the truth, the thicker the foggy layer of deception will be to see through."

Delaney wiped away the sudden stream of tears that spilled out and nodded, saying meekly, "I know. I'm going to straighten everything out. Once that's done, I'll decide accordingly."

"When will your last night as Madame be?"

"Tonight."

He shifted in his seat, and after another moment, he nodded. "We'll make an announcement that you're leaving."

"There might be a riot if they never get to see my face."

"You're right, and we must capitalize on the drama." He chuckled, then thought another moment. "Maybe we'll announce your unmasking at midnight. Just make sure you slip out before then."

She arched a delicate brow. "You'll have an angry crowd to manage."

Remi waved his hand. "Don't worry about me, Delaney. I've been in this town my entire life. I know these people. They love a good intrigue and mystery. The one woman they never had? Never knew? You'll become a legend, a ghost. Trust me, all will be well in the end."

Delaney realized that everything was fleshing out in reality. It really was time for her to begin her life. She'd completed her schooling, her training, and fulfilled all her obligations. Now she needed to start the next chapter in her book.

"For the sake of precaution, I'll bring in a few strongarms to help tonight. Alderic's men are here, as well. They're rather intimidating," he added with a chuckle.

Delaney felt a surge of excitement swelling. She wanted to tell Alderic everything. That moment! She was supposed to meet him in the morning, and she could see him without a mask haunting her. She could tell him the truth, and hopefully, he'd forgive her. Something told her he would. She was so overjoyed that she flew from her chair and charged out of the room.

Remi called to her, and she stopped at the doorway and spun back. Remi stood, and when he walked to her, he looked as though he wanted to reach for her but refrained. Instead, he said, "I hope you know how proud I am of the woman you've become. I've wanted so long to tell you that."

She didn't have a reply. Strangely, a part of her wanted to hug him. The grumpy grouse who'd followed her around Europe was her father. She shook her head and shifted her stance as he clasped his hands behind his back and cleared his throat. "I'll have your bags slipped out the back, and we'll bring them to Le Grand Inn. A coach will be waiting for you shortly after your announcement, so you will be long on your way before the clientele realizes they will never see the Painted Lady's face."

All reservations collapsed the moment that reality

hit. It was over. She was free! Suddenly, she knew everything was going to be all right. The house and everyone within its walls, and her and Alderic. She beamed with bliss. "I'll start packing now."

Chapter Thirty-Two

Alderic slowly sipped his coffee and puffed on finely rolled tobacco as he sat silently in *Le Café de Deux*. The hour was late, and the shop had closed hours ago. Yet he sat there, quietly reading the pages of the local gazette. He heard horses gather outside, and his gaze shot to the far corners of the shop, where Wil and several of his men stood, cautiously waiting, their hands lightly resting on their weapons. He took another sip of the hot brew just as the door burst open. Jack Chanfray and four of his strongarms stormed inside, their weapons drawn and aimed at his chest. Alderic watched his own men exit the shadows and surround Jack. The sounds of cocking pistols echoed, and Alderic sat back in his chair as the tension in the room heightened in the mere second before chaos.

"You look perplexed, Jack, not quite with your usually tailored presence," Alderic said. "I suggest you lower your weapons and sit with me."

Jack's eyes darkened and pierced Alderic as he sipped his coffee. Jack threw down his weapon and marched to the table. "Are you looking for a war, Beaumont?"

He smirked as he flicked the end of his tobacco and released a cloud of smoke. "A scuffle, perhaps. War would suggest a worthy opponent of equal measure. You are not that."

"You rescued my shipment from the river."

"*Oui*."

"The transporters were fools and have been sufficicently dealt with." His eyes bore into Alderic's. "I want my cargo back!"

"No. They were discarded and now they belong to me."

Jack flipped the chair that had been set out for him. "It was your fault they were disposed of, in the first place. The least you can do, is give what's left of the shipment back to me!"

Just then, not only Alderic's men were surrounding Jack and his mere four thugs, but Nye's crew came out of the shadows and raised weapons at them. Alderic watched the color drain from Jack's face. Suddenly, his aggressiveness lessened considerably, and Alderic smiled. Jack took a step back, and Alderic snuffed out the burning end of his tobacco.

"I understand that, at times, men can become confused about their place in this world. They may overvalue or overestimate their level of importance, but it does not take a lot to rein that back in. Thus, the loss of your shipment. It is a small price to pay for such a lesson."

"You cannot make me suffer such a loss! I have obligations—a reputation to uphold! By not delivering, I look the fool and—more so—untrustworthy!"

Alderic's smile faded, and his light mood sobered considerably as he spoke. "Perhaps you should have taken a moment to consider the repercussions before telling your men to kill me. Indeed, you are lucky to be standing here. You have been a nuisance of late, Jack, and I don't take kindly to threats upon my person."

Moments ticked by as Jack glared at Alderic calmly sipping his coffee. Through gritted teeth, Jack finally muttered, "Are you going to kill me?"

Alderic grinned as he set down his cup. "That is up to you."

"What do you want?"

"It's time to embrace your new place. And that place is anywhere other than New Orleans."

Jack exploded. "I'm not leaving New Orleans! I'm the entertainment in this city. I own the night life here."

"I believe you might have lost some of that status, Jack," Alderic remarked calmly.

Jack relaxed somewhat, a light chuckle bubbling from his throat. "If you're referring to the harlot at the Bird House, she reached a small peak and will phase out soon enough. If I were you, I'd cut my losses on that investment soon, Beaumont."

Alderic carefully observed the warning in Jack's words, the desperation in his expression, and questions rose within him. How desperate was Jack at the moment? Desperate enough to go after Madame? After Delaney... He glanced at Wil, who promptly nodded and left the coffee house.

"You will walk out of here on one condition, Jack. That you are gone come sunup."

"Where am I to go?"

"I care not," Alderic scoffed. "Go upriver with the fellow scum awaiting their cargo."

"They'll kill me for losing their investment!"

Alderic paused. "Ah, then you have a situation."

Jack released a long, heavy breath, and one of Alderic's men returned the thrown chair to the table. Jack sat down. "What can I do?"

"Let us negotiate." Alderic grinned.

****

Delaney donned a deep red dress of soft velvet, then pinned on a black silk mask. It would be the last time she put on a mask. She didn't paint her face.

Remi and Rafe quietly removed her trunks and had them sent to Le Grand Inn. There were teary moments for all of them as they said their early goodbyes. They wouldn't have a chance after they opened.

"You never belonged here, Delaney," Gertie cried. She squeezed Delaney tightly, and they sobbed. "We'll miss you, honey."

"I hope to still come visit."

Penelope took her turn hugging Delaney. "We'll have to be discreet. And wait until the commotion dies down. There will be some disgruntled customers."

Delaney nodded, and then she hugged Marla. She didn't have the chance to say farewell to Billy, who had already moved into Alexander's cottage, but she'd visit her soon. Some of the girls were leaving the Bird House, but they'd all made a pact to stay in touch.

She looked around her mother's room. Her fingertips lightly ran across her wardrobe of elaborate costumes. Each one had at least one distinct memory now. She brushed the vanity, and when her eye caught her reflection, she could almost see Alderic standing behind her, caressing her. She glanced one last time at the chamber she'd occupied these past weeks. A strange and enthralling story she'd weaved within the walls of the Bird House, within the walls of that chamber.

Finally, she doused the lamp and shut the door. She walked down the hall, peeking into the parlor where all the girls lounged, waiting to open. Delaney glanced at her paintings on the walls, the birds dotting various corners throughout the house.

Rafe was waiting by the entrance door, ready to unlock it for the night, and she nodded to him. He gave her a deep bow and a small grin.

"I'll miss you, Rafe," she said.

"And I you, Madame."

She smiled and went into the office. Her eyes lingered over the portrait of her mother. If nothing else, Delaney had saved that which her mother had created and all whom she had cared for. Everything was taken care of, and Delaney could walk away. Hopefully, with the man she'd fallen in love with. That last thought brought a new surge of life shooting through her. She was in love with Alderic. It was staggeringly undeniable. She grinned at knowing she didn't have to wait until tomorrow to see him. To tell him.

So lost in her thoughts, she barely paid attention to the sound of horses outside. It wasn't until a commotion ensued that something caught her attention. She ran to the window just as three men astride chargers darted down the street. Within seconds, she heard Rafe shouting, and the door slamming. Delaney rushed out of her office and witnessed Billy in Rafe's arms. She smothered a cry at the sight of blood running freely down Billy's face and body. Remi ran from the parlor, and seconds later, everyone else followed him.

"Oh, my God, Billy!" Delaney choked out.

Rafe dropped to his knees and carefully adjusted Billy's limp body in his arms. "Billy," he cooed. "Come on, darling. Open your eyes."

The foyer was awash in sighs and cries. Remi motioned the girls back when they tried to touch Billy.

"Back up, ladies," he ordered, and then he, too, sank to his knees beside Delaney.

Fannie handed Delaney her shawl. Delaney quickly rolled it up and dabbed away some of the blood from Billy's cheek, revealing a long gash down the side of her face. Her mouth and eyes were swollen badly.

"Billy," Delaney called repeatedly, but Billy remained unresponsive. She turned to Remi and demanded frantically, "Tell me she's alive!"

Billy finally moved her head, the first sign of life they'd witnessed. "She's alive," Remi sighed with relief.

Billy's eyes were so swollen they were no more than narrow slits, but they were open. She rested them on Delaney. Delaney let out a ragged breath, took Billy's hand, and gave it a gentle squeeze. "Billy, you're safe now. We're going to take care of you." Billy winced and lightly squeezed Delaney's hand.

Remi couldn't contain the contempt in his voice when he demanded, "Who did this to you?"

Billy's voice was so weak, barely a whisper, that Delaney had to lean in to hear it. "Ja…" Billy winced as pain shot through her, and Delaney echoed that pain.

"Jack?" Delaney asked, her tone hardening. "Jack Chanfray?"

Billy nodded, and her eyes closed as the pain and exhaustion overcame her. She drifted into unconsciousness.

"Come on, take her upstairs," Remi ordered. Then he turned to Alderic's men, Kit and Elijah. "Turn away those showing up at the door. Tell them we're closed. And someone, get the damned doctor!"

Rafe carefully lifted her back into his arms and quickly ascended the stairs. Everyone rushed after him.

Everyone except Delaney. She stood momentarily numbed. Shocked. Fire swirled inside her as she imagined all that Billy had just endured—and would continue to endure through her recovery. The pain, the scars—both emotional and physical—that would never heal. She gritted her teeth, and her rage burned until she thought she'd explode from it. Her mind clouded with images of Billy and what she must've experienced. She was so livid she could think of only one thing: atonement.

She went the the coat room and grabbed Remi's cane, a fine piece with a rounded silver grip and a sturdy rosewood shaft. She slid down the sheath, and a steel blade glinted in the lamplight. Snapping it closed, she held onto it tightly as she marched out of the Bird House.

Chapter Thirty-Three

Delaney marched all the way to Basin Street. The walk did nothing to cool her wrath. The sounds of the gathering inside Jack's establishment strayed onto the street as she approached the building. It was brightly lit and alive with entertainment. She barged in, skirting around the brawny man at the door. When he attempted to stop her, she unsheathed the blade within Remi's cane and pointed it at his chest.

Suddenly all socializing in the main hall ceased, and everyone gaped at the masked woman. "Where's Jack," she demanded from the doorman.

His dark gaze cut through her and then dropped to the blade's point, which was dangerously close to his chest. "He's not here, Madame." Discounting his claim, she marched into the parlor. There was an instant blanket of silence, the laughter and chatter dying immediately. Everyone stared at her as she scanned the room. Jack was nowhere to be seen. She spun on her heel and went back to the foyer. "I told you he wasn't here. Now leave!"

She took a deep breath and the shaking in her hands finally subsided. She hadn't been thinking clearly until that moment. She'd been so blinded by wrath that she'd marched right into the lion's den. Alone. Perhaps it was divine foresight that he wasn't there. When the strongarm steered her to the door, she didn't fight. She was coming to her senses. She'd been foolish and needed to leave. Now.

As she approached, both entry doors opened, and she froze as she witnessed Jack fill the doorway. His presence pervaded the air like a warning whisp of wind as he crossed the threshold into the foyer with his men, and his murderous eyes locked with hers.

"The masked mouse has climbed out of the gutter." He smirked viciously. He looked ready to pounce and tear her to shreds. "Wanted to see how those above you live, did you, Madame Cardui?"

Delaney's earlier rage resurfaced in a second. She lifted her chin and stared defiantly at him. She wasn't about to fall prey to his taunts. She refused to back down now. "Assaulting a young woman because she took your client hardly speaks to being *above* anything. It only uncloaked the mere dreg that you are—sheer worthlessness obscured by a finely tailored suit!" Whispers wafted throughout the room. "Maybe you're frightened of this gutter mouse, after all."

Several chuckles echoed in the parlor, and Jack's face flushed. His eyes pierced through her. "I care not about you or your little house of whores." He strode toward her and reached for her mask. She sliced the blade through the air, and he snatched back his hand, but not quickly enough. His eyes rounded and his nostrils flared as he covered the cut on his wrist. He looked to his men, and they started to close in.

"There will be justice for Billy," she seethed. She raised her blade once more and demanded they let her pass. Something changed in the room. A chill swept down her spine, and she cursed her temper. Her irrational act of barging into Jack's establishment had swiftly sobered. "Good evening, *monsieur*."

When she went for the door, Jack halted her with a tight grip on her arm and squeezed until she gasped. His strongarm grabbed her other arm and twisted until she dropped the cane sword. She looked over her shoulder and realized that none of his guests remained in the foyer. They'd been escorted back into the parlor and the door was closed. No one was in earshot of her. Except Jack and his men. Dread crept up on her despite her effort to remain composed.

"No need of a premature departure, Madame," Jack said.

"It is not, *monsieur*," she replied briskly. "I've said what I've come to say."

His grip on her arm tightened again, and he leaned in, seething. "And you drove your message home by cutting my flesh."

"Alderic will not be pleased to discover his investments have been compromised. I suggest you release me."

Jack snickered. "I just left a meeting with Beaumont. He's not looking for his *investment*, at the moment. Perhaps later, when he needs to nestle between your warm thighs." He glanced her up and down, a sly smile lingering on his thin lips as he added, "Until then, he's attending other matters, like planning my demise!" She squared her shoulders and lifted her chin. She wasn't about to cower to the likes of Jack Chanfray. But secretly, she prayed someone at the house would notice her gone. His next words chilled her. "What say he, if he discovered you tainted and maimed...much like your whore, Billy, was?"

The implications of his words sent her shaking. The cruel truth of his intentions had already been proven with

Billy. He was capable and willing to do the same to her. And he'd was right. No one was looking for her. Exteriorly, she remained calm as she said, "Alderic's men are at my establishment. I'm certain they're already on their way. It would be wise of you to mind Alderic's reaction when he discovers you held me against my will."

"Do you suggest I fear your lover?" He slithered out another bout of laughter. Then startled her by yanking her even closer. She bit back the pain of his steely grip. "No, the arrogance of that man infuriates me! It's time someone put *him* in *his* place...and it'll start with destroying his property—just as he destroyed mine!"

Using every ounce of strength, she pulled from his grasp and raced for the door. Her freedom was short-lived as he snatched her back up and tossed her into one of his men's arms as if she were no more than an annoying pebble in his shoe. He called to one of his other men. "Kindly announce to my guests that this establishment is closing early tonight. Line the doors and arm yourselves well. We'll have company soon enough." He took a moment to watch his men promptly disperse. He stopped one man he called Boaz and told him to follow him, but before he went anywhere he turned back on her. "Your lover thinks I'm leaving town. He believes he showed me who runs this city. No, I merely placated him. War commences come morning. But for you, Madame, hell begins tonight!"

Delaney couldn't breathe. Every inch of her skin was crawling as they dragged her toward the stairs. She tried standing her ground, but it was to no avail. Jack and his man Boaz merely pulled her along like she weighed nothing. She started to scream, but he wasn't swayed.

She fought him but then felt a barrel shoved into her side. She turned wide eyes to his man. "Please…"

"What do ye think happens when you enter the lion's den?" Boaz chuckled, shaking his head. "You won't like it, madam, I can promise you that." He added with a snicker, "I sure will!" Her heart hammered inside her chest, and her color drained. His daunting words continued, making her sink more by the second. "This will be a treat to witness. Jack rarely does his own dirty work. You should thank Beaumont for angering him so. That is…if you're still breathing when he's done with you."

Her stomach twisted as they reached the top of the long staircase. Jack pulled her toward a door at the far end of the corridor, and she couldn't hold back the tears stinging her eyes. She struggled again, kicking and screaming, but Jack changed his hold on her, grasping her wrists as Boaz opened the chamber door, and threw her inside. The room was dark, and all she could make out was a bed near the window. She tripped over something solid, a piece of furniture or something of the sort. She nursed her injured ankle, while the lamps were lit. The dim glow showed a smirk on Jack's face that sickened her. She screamed for help, but he only laughed as he cleared the space.

He snatched her off the floor and yanked her against him. He grabbed her mask and tore it from her face. She froze, her heart clamping as Jack leaned back and observed her unveiled face. Tears flowed down her cheeks, unabated. It was over. Jack had her, and no one was coming to rescue her. His long fingers traced the lines of her face, and he grinned. The satisfaction in his eyes slithered down her spine and twisted in her stomach.

"You do not disappoint, Madame." The sound of his words reiterated the malice in his expression. "How selfish of Beaumont to believe he should be the only one to taste your charms. If that is what he wished, he should not have let you out of his sight." She twisted away, and he released her, his smirk never faltering as he undid the buttons of his waistcoat. "Boaz," he called, "get the hell out of here. I have time yet to truly enjoy this."

Boaz grumbled something as he slowly slumped to the door. The lock clicking on the door deafened her. She was alone with Jack. She screamed again, and his laughter chilled her skin. "No one will hear you, Madame."

She could feel her stomach rejecting everything in it as the reality of her situation seeped into her brain. She swiftly swallowed down her sudden illness and tried to put as much distance between them as she could. She retreated until her back hit the wall farthest from the bed. Her eyes flashed to every corner of the room and lingered longingly at the window. The freedom it offered. She knew, in that moment, she was lost. And she'd rather die upon the street, than be touched by Jack Chanfray.

Chapter Thirty-Four

Alderic rode up the street at neck-breaking speed, his men close behind. He wasn't ignorant. Jack had tried to placate him, thinking it would buy him time to plan his next move. Alderic played along, as he usually did, remaining apathetic to allow his enemies to think they were faring well in their objectives. But when he'd sent Wil to warn the Bird House that trouble was brewing, only to discover him bleeding to near death on the street, there was a shift in him…and his good graces. Alderic had to leave Wil with his men and race to the Bird House, for they had no idea of the new turn of events. Wil's fate was unknown, but his fear for Delaney's safety was certain. He pulled on the reins outside of the Bird House, and something seemed different. People were usually shuffling in and out of the place, but all was silent. He quickly dismounted and flew up the front steps. The door opened before he reached the top step, and Rafe blocked the doorway.

"We're closed, Beaumont," he said, his voice grim.

"Move, Rafe." When Rafe failed to move immediately, Alderic pushed his way through the door, throwing Rafe along with it.

As Alderic forced himself inside, he immediately noted smudges of blood on the floor. He knew a simple scuffle inside the house wouldn't have shut the house down for the evening. Elijah and Kit marched over to him.

He looked expectantly at his two men, then to Rafe again. "What happened?"

"Jack," Elijah said, "roughed up one of Madame's girls."

Just then, a heavyset woman came into the foyer with a rag and started wiping up the blood. He could imagine Delaney was beside herself.

"We've been watching the front and back entrances," Kit chimed. "We're keeping the women inside and no one's being allowed in. What do you want us to do?"

Alderic glanced in Delaney's office, and it was empty. "Where's Madame?" Alderic asked.

Rafe said, "I think she's upstairs."

Alderic looked around at the house that was always booming with activity. Now it was as silent as a graveyard. He spotted Fannie at the top of the stairs, and he climbed the steps, two at a time. "Fannie, where's Madame?"

She looked puzzled and glanced nervously down the corridor. "I-I don't know. She's not in the office?"

He was losing patience quickly. "She's not."

Her eyes filled with tears, and she began sobbing. "But Billy," she cried. "Billy's badly hurt—"

He didn't give Fannie time to finish speaking before he charged down the corridor to where Gertie and Penelope were standing just outside an open doorway. Alderic peered inside and discovered Delaney wasn't amongst those surrounding the bed. He entered the chamber as the doctor began sewing up a wound on Billy's face. He flinched as the needle pierced her flesh and she cried out. Anger boiled as he observed the bloody swelling around her eyes and mouth. No doubt Delaney was just as furious…and would seek retribution. He silently prayed Delaney hadn't been so foolish. He approached Remi as he was wiping away the fresh blood seeping from Billy's wound.

Remi glanced up at Alderic and frowned. The bruising from their last encounter was still apparent on face. "Alderic, what are you doing here?" Remi demanded crisply.

"I am looking for Madame."

Remi's open disdain for him lifted, and he glanced back at Alderic. "She's not downstairs?" Remi's question was enough to flood him with anger. Alderic shook his head, spun around and headed for the door, barely overhearing Remi say, "Gertie, come over here and hold Billy. Billy, sweetheart, I'll be back momentarily," before rushing after him. They both marched into the hall and down the corridor, descended the steps, and knocked on her chamber door. She wasn't there, either. "Dear God," Remi breathed.

He turned ashen, and Alderic gave him a grave look. "Remi, was she aware that Jack Chanfray did that to Billy?" Remi stood there, his hands shaking, Alderic grew impatient.

"You don't think she'd—"

Alderic broke from the conversation and promptly headed out of the house. Remi was close at his heels, as was Rafe and his men. He was so blinded by rage that the ride to Basin Street was a blur. How long had Delaney been at Jack's?

He cleared the front entrance to Jack's establishment, causing the front doors to nearly fly off their hinges as they crashed into the walls. Alderic and his men fired before Jack's men could aim their weapons. The men left standing fired back at them. Alderic barely dodged the pistols firing at him. He felt the sting of one bullet burn into his flesh, sending his blood pumping wildly to block out the pain in his arm as his rage coursed his next actions. The men left standing clashed and a brawl instantly broke out.

Alderic recognized one of Jack's strongarms, Boaz. Boaz charged him and Alderic grabbed him by the throat and slammed him up against the wall.

Within moments, he and Boaz were on the ground, Alderic holding him so tightly by the scruff that the strongarm couldn't breathe. "I am tired of asking this question," Alderic seethed. "Where? Is! Madame!"

Boaz gave him a twisted grin, exposing his bloodstained teeth. "I suspect Jack's enjoying her upstairs, right now."

As a level of rage Alderic had never known overran his better judgment. He squeezed Boaz's scruff even more until the strongarm became useless on the floor.

Alderic barreled through the foyer, pushing aside anyone stupid enough to stand in his way. He scaled the stairs in long strides and tried each door in the corridor. When he discovered a locked door, he leaned in and vaguely heard Jack's voice. He quickly kicked open the door, sending pieces of the door splintering and soaring as he stormed in. He discovered Jack pinning Delaney down on the bed.

Alderic stole a glimpse of Delaney—her tearstained face carried no mask.

Jack gruffly released Delaney and glowered at Alderic. "We agreed I had till morning to leave, Beaumont!"

"My good-natured offer expired the moment you touched Madame Cardui."

"Ah, but she came to me," Jack sneered. Then he gave Alderic a smirk. "Ardent sentiments for a common whore, Beaumont?" Jack pulled out a pistol and fired.

Alderic had only a second to dodge out of the way, and he felt the hot sting of another ball cut his arm. In the next instant, Alderic charged him. Jack unsuccessfully reached for another weapon. Alderic threw him against the wall, nearly hitting the window. He stumbled into a side table and the lamp on it was knocked over. It instantly caught fire to the rug and spread to the bedcovers. Jack regained his balance and slammed his fist into Alderic again. Alderic lost his balance, but he grabbed Jack on his way down, and they began wrestling on the floor. Alderic took a hit to the ribs, and he readily returned a pummeling blow to Jack. His final blow to Jack's face rendered his opponent momentarily senseless. By then, the room had erupted in flames, and he leapt to his feet. He ran to Delaney as she tried to put out the fire.

"It's too late. Leave it," he ordered.

The drapes had already caught fire, and the room was quickly encompassed in smoke. He was guiding her toward the door when something slammed into his face. He didn't know what the hell Jack had just hit him with, but it dropped him to his knees, and he grabbed his head as a pain shot through it.

He couldn't open his eyes, but he felt Delaney's hands on his shoulders. "Alderic!" she cried. Smoke filled his nostrils, choking his lungs, and the heat was becoming unbearable. "Alderic, get up!"

She screamed as Jack snatched her up.

Alderic found and used every ounce of strength he had left to stand up again. When he regained his sight, he grabbed Jack and they fought again. Their chance to escape the burning chamber was closing fast. He grabbed Jack by the scruff and shoved him into the flames. Jack bellowed an agonizing, piercing scream as he was caught within the burning drapes. In his desperate attempt to free himself from the fire eating his flesh, he tripped, and the crack of shattering glass echoed over the destruction of the fire as he fell out the window.

With smoke filling Alderic's lungs and the splitting pain in his head exhausting him fast, he dropped to his knees. Delaney quickly wrapped her arms around him and pulled. "Come on, Alderic. We need to get out of here!" Delaney helped him regain his feet, and they rushed out of the chamber. Just as they exited the room, Remi and Rafe ran up the stairs. Behind him was Nye, with a line of people carrying water—most being his crew.

"Nye," Alderic sighed with relief. "How'd you know I'd need you, *mon ami*?" Nye looked past Alderic to the flames consuming Jack's chamber. His men rushed around them and charged the burning room. "Wil was brought to the manor. I knew trouble would ensue."

They prepared to enter the room with the rest of the men when Alderic witnessed Remi grabbing Delaney. "You're all right!" Remi said with a sigh.

"Remi," she said as he wrapped his arms around her.

Alderic couldn't fight that sudden pang of jealousy as he clung to Delaney.

"We have to put out those flames!" someone shouted. "The whole street will burn down!"

More men came running with water. Soon, the

house was flooded with people as they tried to stop the fire from consuming the entire house and spreading farther. Alderic watched Remi guide Delaney downstairs. After a long moment, he numbly turned away and entered the burning chamber. The fire was quickly eating up everything, consuming the walls and hall.

Nye stopped him, "Whoa, Alderic, you need to get out of here!"

Alderic shook his head. "I started this fire, I need to put it out."

Chapter Thirty-Five

Delaney was swept up into a carriage. "Where's Alderic?" she asked, searching the street frantically. "He was right behind me."

Remi shouted for the driver to bring them to the Bird House. "He's fine," Remi said. "We need to get you out of here."

"But there's a fire! And he was hurt, Remi," she insisted, looking out worriedly. "He needs to come with us!"

"Alderic stayed to help put out the fire before the whole street burns down." Remi placed a hand on Delaney's and gave her a warm smile. "Don't fret, Delaney. Alderic is there with Nye and all their men. They'll be spending the next several hours trying to put out the flames. Then he'll come for you. I'm sure of it."

She searched out the window. "I want to be certain he's safe, Remi. Please, stop the carriage!"

"Delaney, they picked up Jack's body off the sidewalk. The magistrate will be investigating, and you don't want to be there. You've lost your mask. You didn't fight so hard to conceal your identity just to have the whole town find you out now."

Delaney didn't feel right about leaving Alderic. She wanted to thank him, to tell him she loved him. She'd done a reckless thing going to Jack's and causing a scene. If it weren't for Alderic, Jack would have violated her and probably killed her.

She covered her face with hands and sighed. "This all my fault. The street could burn down because of me."

"Delaney, you had no way of knowing what would happen."

She shook her head. She didn't want Remi excusing her impulsive behavior. "How is Billy?"

"She's faring."

They reached the house, and Delaney raced up the stairs to see Billy. She was fast asleep, and most of the girls were sound asleep with her, sprawled out beside her or curled up in the chairs. Delaney's heart ached when she looked upon Billy's face. She was permanently scarred, but she would live.

Delaney wondered if Billy would have been spared had she not baited Chanfray. Riddled with guilt, she quietly left the chamber and went back downstairs. She went to the office and watched out the window, waiting for Alderic to come. The first rays of light streaked across the dark sky, but he still hadn't come. She lay on the settee and waited until she eventually fell asleep.

****

The hours it took to put out the flames seemed interminable. The faint light of the early morning hours laid the scene bare. Nearly half of Jack's brothel and gambling house was destroyed, but they had been able to stop the fire from spreading to the neighboring buildings. Alderic was covered in soot. Blood had dried on his face and mingled with sweat and filth. He looked at the two bullet grazes on his arm and cursed. Several people were sweeping up the debris and broken glass as he sluggishly weaved his way around the destruction. He paused where Jack's body had fallen and been removed long since. The

346

events that had led to yet another threatening fire in the city replayed in his mind... The feud between himsef and Jack Chanfray... Madame Vanessa Cardui... Delaney Harper. Slowly he continued on his path, nursing his aching body, until Nye stopped him. Alderic chuckled at Nye, who'd equally fought the fire with the resultant covering of filth. "A pair we make."

Nye looked at his blackened hands and cocked a brow at Alderic. "I'm unsure who ensnares more tribulations, you or me?"

Alderic was readying a response when a carriage racing toward them halted his reply. It was Nye's carriage, and before it reached a complete standstill, Sarafina jumped out. Alderic had to step back as she rushed to Nye and wrapped her arms around him. She whispered something to him, and while Alderic couldn't hear her, the small upturn of Nye's lips before he planted a kiss on her mouth, told him all he needed to know. He looked around, standing awkwardly alone, awaiting the end of their kiss. Once they did, Sarafina turned to Alderic. "I'm so relieved! The two of you and all your catastrophes will stop my heart, one day."

Alderic scoffed, "This was no catastrophe, merely another day of mischief in the lives of us and our crew."

Nye chuckled, but Sarafina didn't find Alderic amusing in the least. "Your mischief could've burned down the city."

"*Touché.*" Alderic's humor sobered. "But Jack is gone, and the smuggling of young women up the river has been interrupted, for the time being."

"Indeed," Nye chimed in. "Louis is looking into the matter. We spoke about an hour ago."

"The governor was here?" Sarafina asked.

"Aye," Nye replied.

"How is Wil?" Alderic asked.

"He will mend," Sarafina assured him. She let out a sigh and rested her head on Nye's chest. "Then you two are deserving of a decent meal and a long rest. Annabelle and I have been putting together a feast at the coffee shop for everyone working all night to put out the fire. Let us go." She took Nye's hand and pulled him toward the carriage.

Alderic watched the couple and his grin was involuntary. His admiration for his best friend couldn't be helped, nor the mood enveloping his own forlorn heart.

Nye and Sarafina were about to climb in when they stopped and turned to him. "Come, my friend," Nye called. "You don't want to walk there."

Alderic waved him off. "Go on, *mon ami*. I will be along."

Nye assisted Sarafina into the carriage, then lifted a brow at him. "Alderic—"

He recognized the concern in Nye's expression immediately, and it wasn't something he needed at the moment. He took out his handkerchief with a snap and started wiping the soot from his hands. "Go, *mon ami*. Do not keep your lady waiting after all her hard work to prepare food for the Quarter's good Samaritans."

Nye flashed him a knowing look. A look Alderic didn't want to address. He was thankful when Nye didn't press the matter. Instead, he nodded and climbed into the carriage with his wife, and the carriage jolted forward.

Alderic sat down and rested his back against a small shop door across the street. He observed the smoky remnants of Jack's gambling house. His head hurt like hell, but it was his heart that gnawed at him. He glanced around again, and Delaney was nowhere. She'd left with Remi. Remi had been gone for years, and it was obvious now that those years had been spent with her. Piecing together the story only cut him deeper. He'd already been with Delaney when her mother passed—why, he wasn't sure. But it was Birdie's death that had brought her to New Orleans. The nature of her and Remi's relationship during that time wasn't clear. But, when he and Delaney had fought the night Diego attacked her, it was Remi she defended. Now she'd returned to the Bird House with him. From the beginning, she had told him she wasn't available. Eventually, she'd confessed to already having a lover. It seemed plausible that Remi was more to her than the house's strongarm. Whatever their relationship was, it seemed more important than any other. She wouldn't even tell him the truth about her identity. She toyed with him, deceived him, then returned to Remi. Why was it so impossible to guess? It made no sense. He'd been certain she was innocent... Had he been so wrong about everything?

He shook his head and grudgingly admitted he'd been a fool. After several more minutes of reflecting on every moment he'd spent with her—as Delaney and as Madame Cardui—he slowly stood and walked away from the smoldering bordello, and away from the Bird House.

Chapter Thirty-Six

The ink lifted and ran down the parchment as Delaney's tears soaked the script of her ledgers. She was no help to Remi right now. She was a wreck. It had been two days since the fire, and still Alderic hadn't come to see her. She collapsed onto the settee and cried until her eyes were dry and her lungs ached.

Alderic was never coming to see her. The night of the fire, he'd seen her without her mask. He knew she'd deceived him. He deserved an explanation. She wanted him to understand. She wanted him to know how thoroughly she had fallen. Since the night he'd stolen a kiss from her, she'd been captivated by him.

She picked herself up off the settee, cleaned herself up, and marched out of the house. She took a hackney to the docks—and heartbreakingly discovered that his ship had left. The hours of pain and sorrow stretched to silence and melancholy. She stayed by Billy and didn't take part in anything as Madame.

She continued with administrative work while Remi had successfully assumed the role of host, claiming that Madame was taking a well-deserved break. But the time was nearing for her to go. The transitioning time had reached its end, as had her hope that Alderic would return.

On her last morning there, a calling card was delivered from Alexander Wilton, and Remi was nowhere to be found. She pulled herself together and donned a mask one last time to meet with him. She watched the strapping politician stroll in and rest in the chair opposite her.

"I hear that Wilhelmina is recovering," he said.

Delaney creased her brow. "You mean Billy?"

Alexander smiled politely. "I call her by her given name, Madame."

"I understand. Given the circumstances, Billy is unable to meet the requirements as your mistress, as stated in our agreement. Are you here to renegotiate her contract?"

"Not at all," he said, to her shock. "I simply would like to see her. If she's well enough."

Delaney leaned forward and folded her hands on the desk. "*Monsieur*, you have heard that she's—"

"I'm aware what Jack and his men did to her, and you can rest assured that although it's too late for Jack, I fully intend to hold his man Boaz accountable for that which he bestowed upon her. Justice will be served to the best of my abilities."

She grinned, looking at the young politician with newfound respect. "You're honorable, *Monsieur* Wilton."

"I hope you understand how truly sorry I am for what she endured. I've had Doctor Philman send me all the fees associated with her recovery." He briskly stood and held out his hand. "If someone could show me to her, I'd appreciate it very much. When she's well enough, she'll be returning with me."

Delaney was stunned by the man, and she stood up and took his hand. "O-of course, *monsieur*. I'll have Rafe take you upstairs."

"I appreciate your cooperation in this, Madame. And I apologize for not contacting you immediately. But I had much to attend to after what happened on Basin Street. I thought it an opportunity to give Wilhelmina time to recover."

"That was very thoughtful. And thank you, *Monsieur* Wilton, for honoring your contract," she said, coming around the desk. "I'm afraid, however, you'll not be dealing with me after today."

Alexander fell into step with her as they headed for the door. "I suspected that your 'break' is actually a retirement."

"That's correct."

"The whole town is talking about your unmasking."

Delaney cleared her throat, suddenly averting her gaze from his scrutiny. "Yes, there are many rumors of an unmasking event."

He held open the door and waited for her to enter the foyer. She saw Fannie, motioned her over, and informed her that Billy had a visitor. Fannie's eyes lit up, and she flashed a look at Alexander before she ran up the stairs. There was no doubt she'd make Billy presentable.

Alexander stopped just short of the bottom step. Leaning on the railing, he gave Delaney a wicked smile. "They shouldn't count on that event, though, should they, Madame?"

"Life has many mysteries."

"And one shall be the lady beneath the mask," he added, seemingly intrigued.

"You sound so sure no one will ever know."

"Of course I am. You went to great lengths to hide your identity."

She didn't reply, but the smile that crossed her lips

said much, and it was duly noted.

Nodding respectfully, he said, "Good luck to you, Madame."

She held out her hand, and he took it. "To you, as well, *monsieur*. I wish you the best. Rafe? Please take *Monsieur* Wilton to see Billy."

Rafe bowed and headed up the stairs, with Wilton close behind.

Chapter Thirty-Seven

It was Tuesday, the end of the carnaval season. Delaney quietly slipped out of the Bird House during the evening's festivities and never revealed her face. She would always be known as the Painted Lady, whose identity could only be speculated about and would remain shrouded in mystery. Everyone at the Bird House would take her identity to their graves. Of that, she was promised.

She accepted Lucien's offer to join the group permanently. She made a decent living, though not enough to afford to live at Le Grand Inn, so she quickly settled into a small cottage in town. She traveled all over New Orleans and even the outside parishes, painting with Lucien's group of artists...her group. Her new friends.

After nearly three months, she'd built a reputation. The citizens prided themselves on being unique and became fascinated with the idea of having a woman artist in their city. Lucien proudly told her he could barely keep up with the demand. They met every morning at a local café and, over coffee, discussed their plans for the day.

On this particular morning, Delaney smoothed the folds of her pale-blue-striped gown before tossing aside her bonnet. She left her modest cottage with only her parasol to shade her from the bright summer sun. She met her fellow painters at the café.

"Am I going to Saint Louis's Cathedral?" she asked Fernand.

Fernand said, "Yes, you can accompany me. I'm headed there."

"No, Delaney." Lucien shook his head as he put down his cup and handed Delaney a card. "You have an appointment outside of the city."

Delaney read the address. "What is the job?"

"A couple's new house. They want a fresco in the foyer," he said, continuing to sip his coffee. "You need to assess the space. I'll work up the figures when you return with your evaluation of supplies, based on the customer's order."

Delaney sipped her coffee and nibbled a small pastry. "How far out of town?"

"Not too far, but it'll be faster to access by boat. I already paid for your passage."

Delaney finished her breakfast, loaded herself and her paintbox onto a boat, manned by a young man with a toothy grin and dark locks. He helped her onto the small boat, and they quietly made their way outside the city lines. Delaney had found, during the past three months or so, small talk was not something she engaged in much. She'd grown quiet and was certain it had something to with the slow mending of her heart.

As the lines of businesses and townhouses began to fade, she saw an overabundance of greenery and great, draping trees and flowers. The season was blooming, and so was her new home city. The smell of magnolias and sage drifted in the air. A few minutes later, they came upon a clearing and a massive, three-story home with galleries supported by piers. French doors were thrown open on the second story, and flowers hung from pots along the entablature. The young man brought his simple boat to the dock and tied it before he held out his hand to assist her ashore.

"Mister Lucien said I am to wait here for you," he said boisterously as she climbed onto the dock, her bulky paintbox in hand. "You'll be about an hour or so, miss?"

"If that," she said. "Thank you…?"

He tipped his hat. "Jesse, miss."

She returned his warm smile. "Yes, Jesse. I won't dally."

"You can take your time, miss."

Jesse tilted his hat over his eyes and lay back in his boat as she climbed the stone steps leading to the white stucco home with its black shutters. She recognized various nut trees dotting the river's edge, but it was the tall magnolias blooming, emanating sweet fragrance, that was so intoxicating. She spotted cypress trees and took a moment to admire the beautiful landscaping.

Waiting by the front door was an older gentleman. "Are you Miss Delaney Harper?" he asked.

"Yes," she said, smiling.

"Right this way."

As she grew closer, she noted the impressive row of dentils lining the entablature and the bed-mold of the cornice. She stepped inside and was brought into a grand entrance with tall ceilings that kept the air cool inside. The rooms went from one to the other with no true doorways, merely an open concept, with all the doors and windows thrown open.

By the staircase was a large, empty wall. The wall alongside the stairs was just as plain. She assumed the owners wanted that painted as well. At least, that's what she'd do. She took in the light, the airy feel of the place, the bright colors, and the grand furnishings.

"There are refreshments in the parlor, *mam'selle*," the man announced, and he stepped toward an archway. "Right this way."

She followed him into the parlor where he presented her with refreshments before he bowed and swiftly left the room. She smiled at the lemonade and pastries, remembering exploring houses with Alderic. She shook her head, trying not to recall memories that made her sad. She lifted her chin and tried to think of something else. Anything else. It was a method she was getting good at since she found her thoughts straying to him often. She reminded herself of all that she had now. She was passionate about her work. She'd started a life of her own. She set down her paintbox and browsed the main floor, observing the paintings and furnishings. She took note of all that remained consistent within the styles the owners had picked to decorate their home. Then she ventured to the empty wall she assumed was where her project would be. Perhaps a beautiful garden scene, reflecting the landscaping outside? She considered the idea for a moment, then decided that she'd bring it up with the owners and see if it was something they'd consider. She smiled as she recalled Lucien's statement. A new couple. With their new house. It was a romantic notion.

"What were you thinking, Delaney?"

That familiar voice assimilated with her soul. She feared she'd lost all bearings and was now hearing his voice out of thin air. Alderic's voice had to be an illusion. She spun, and in that second, she was sure she'd been mistaken. But she wasn't. He stood in the middle of the entrance, his hair tossed carelessly by the breeze, brushing his brow. Dressed finely in a natural-colored coat, creamy silk waistcoat, and dark breeches, he fiddled with his hat and riding gloves. As he stepped farther inside, his boots clicked on the polished floors. She held her breath, trying to ignore the fact that he looked amazing. It was like the images in her dreams had just manifested before her eyes.

He glanced at the blank wall behind her and said, "I was thinking something of nature, perhaps incorporating the trees lining the river. I am partial to the magnolias."

The pain she'd buried when she went to the docks and was told he was gone now came back with a vengeance. She could barely contain the wretched feeling that had seized her then and gripped her now. Lucien said she was painting for a new couple. A husband's gift for his bride. The fact that she was there taking his order was an agonizing factor.

"W-why did you summon me here?" she asked.

Alderic glanced down at his hat, and the muscles in his face tightened, but he said nothing. Delaney couldn't bear it. She didn't need an answer. She didn't need an explanation. She wanted to leave. Many times, she'd gone to the docks and seen his ship. She had waited so long to get word from Remi that Alderic wanted to find her. But he didn't. He could have. But he didn't.

She skirted around him and hastened for the door, but he caught her arm and held her fast. His touch scorched her skin, and she closed her eyes briefly. She wouldn't fall apart.

"Please, Delaney, wait."

She pulled away from his grasp and peered at him. The tears were threatening to spill down her cheeks, but she was growing angrier by the second as she relived the misery he'd put her through.

"Why? Why would you leave, and then have me show up at your house months later? To brag? You want me to paint your foyer as a wedding gift for your new wife?"

He finally met her gaze, and his golden-green eyes were soft. "Yes, that is exactly what I want."

She felt like he'd just reached inside her chest and crushed her heart. "Do you wish to get even with me for lying to you about who I was? Is your wife here so you can flaunt her in front of me? I am wholeheartedly sorry for what I did, but is it necessary to be so cruel?"

"Not at all," he said. He released a long, shaky breath and tossed his hat and gloves onto a nearby table. "I did not want to get even with you for deceiving me. I understand why you did not tell me who you were. I knew who you were before you went to Jack's that night."

"What? When? How?"

Alderic drove his hand through his hair and shifted his stance. "I think I knew long before I was prepared to admit it. But when I saw your part of Lucien's mural at St. Thomas, I couldn't deny it any longer." He dared to take a step closer to her and reached out to cup her face. "I wanted you to tell me. To trust me."

She tried not to lean into his hand. "You didn't give me the chance. I waited for you the night of the fire."

He dropped his hand, his eyes turned cold, and he looked away. She watched curiously as his jaw flexed. "No, you did not. You returned to the Bird House with Remi, *non*?"

Her brow creased, and her mouth fell open. "Remi?

Remi took me out of there because he said I'd be discovered and everything I did to hide my identity would be for naught. I could've been blamed for what happened there!"

"Did you not think I would protect you?" he snapped. "I saved your life, but you put all your trust in Remi."

She couldn't ignore the rage she witnessed in his eyes and heard laced in his words when he said Remi's name. "Did you doubt my feelings for you because of Remi?"

Alderic straightened, and she saw that his anger had subsided, and a cool indifference had taken over his demeanor. "I knew you were lost and searching, Delaney. And I thought perhaps I could be alongside you while you discovered yourself. But that night, it became clear to me that you needed time to figure out what it was you wanted, and who you thought was worthy of your trust. I did not want to be another distraction."

Delaney saw the pain he was trying hard to conceal, and it made her heart ache. "Did what we share count for anything? You tore out my heart when I waited for you and you never came!"

He avoided her searching gaze. "I did not want to hurt you. I was doing what I thought was best for you."

"You were right, Alderic. I was very lost and using every excuse not to start my life. But...*best for me*? You were hurt over a misunderstanding, and in turn, you crushed me. I fell in love with you, and I'd gotten everything ready so I could come to you with no mask. And you left without so much as a letter, an explanation! Nothing! If that wasn't terrible enough, you wanted to settle a score by bringing me here to tell me your future wife wants a fresco!"

Tears were streaming down her cheeks, and she angrily brushed them away and sought escape from the man who'd just destroyed her. But he halted her again. His brow creased, and he didn't let her go this time when she pulled away. "What misunderstanding?"

She wiped another bout of tears away. "Remi is my father, Alderic. My adoration was with you. It has always been you…since the night you stole that kiss."

He looked at her, his eyes frantically searching the emotions crossing her face, and he dropped his hand. He let out a long, heavy breath and closed his eyes.

Delaney sniffed back another bout of tears that threatened to spill over, and she straightened her shoulders. "Tell your fiancée I won't be painting anything!"

She remembered her paintbox in the parlor and rushed to it. She needed to leave.

Again, Alderic stopped her. She shoved him away this time, but he held her fast and pressed his lips over hers. Delaney could never forget how it felt to be kissed by him. And as much as she wanted to yell at him, to pound on his chest for what he'd done, she softened in his hold. He released her, and gently cupped her face, deepening his kiss. She opened her mouth, and he slid past her lips, slaking a hunger they both knew well. The very pit of her stomach gripped her with need, and she wrapped her arms around his neck. He pulled her closer, tilting his head, and tormented her mouth again.

"Despite any misunderstanding, *mon amour*, I did not bring you here to hurt you. The wife I was hoping to please…is you."

She blinked, and her gaze clouded. "What do you

mean?"

"I could not stay away, Delaney," he said with a sigh. "I brought you here, hoping to find that you'd missed me as much as I had missed you. I thought I could convince you to stay… to paint this house for *us*."

She glanced at the beautiful home around her and then back at Alderic

"Us?"

"*Oui, mam'selle*. Would you help me fix this home?" His mischievous smile, which she knew so well, had returned, but it carried something even more. Hope. "I am very particular, and *Monsieur* Dupuis will no longer speak to me."

He'd barely finished speaking before she planted a solid kiss on him. Then another. Soon their kisses became heated and uncontrollable. He lifted her easily and scaled the stairs.

A word about the author...

Avery Sterling's love for the romance genre began in her teen years when she picked up her first novel. She was captivated by the sweeping scale of emotions brought about by the words. The experience catapulted her toward learning the art of wielding a breathtaking adventure, with a love that felt authentic.

Wanting to inspire people with her own thoughts and words, she finished her first novel at sixteen. It was a step toward understanding the essence of what she wished to create. Most of her youth was spent traveling, searching out the romance and beauty in her everchanging world. From the waves that crashed against the rocky shores of Downeast Maine, to the warm breezes of the Caribbean, she discovered that love was universal, apparent in its grandest and simplest of forms.

Her goal is to write novels an audience can relate to, that convey the truth and nature of love...with all that steamy romance.